Toxic

ALSO BY ELLEN TOMASZEWSKI

Rose Colored Glasses

ETCETERA PRESS LLC
Richland, WA
2013

Toxic

— A NOVEL —

Ellen Tomaszewski

etcetera press ʟʟᴄ

Published by Etcetera Press LLC
Richland, WA
www.etcpress.net

Copyright © 2013 by Etcetera Press LLC.

ISBN: 978-1-936824-42-7
Library of Congress Control Number: 2013955087

Printed in the United States of America
10 9 8 7 6 5 4 3 2

For my friend, Leslie
Thanks

PROLOGUE

March 7, 1972

Seven-fourteen. I'm late for work. I throw off my covers and jump out of bed. Brr. It's chilly for August, and ... this isn't my room. Am I visiting someone? I find sweatpants and sweatshirt draped over the back of a chair. Shivering, I pull them on.

The bedroom door opens and my four-year-old son, David, races in, wearing pajamas. A cowlick spikes his uncombed black hair; his smile brings that adorable dimple to one cheek. He wraps his arms around my legs and says, "Morning, Mom. How ya feelin' today?"

I squat to hug him. "Hi, David. I'm all right, I guess. My head hurts a little though. Where are we?"

"We're home. Time for breakfast; I'm hungry."

He takes my hand and leads me down the hallway. In the kitchen, I slide the curtains aside and peer out the window. The sky is a deep pink—too dark for morning. A wide brown lawn is sprinkled with ... "It snowed?"

"Yesterday, but most melted already, before we could make a snowman."

"Snow in August. Now I've seen everything," I mumble. "Shouldn't I be getting ready for work?"

David shakes his head. "After you hit your head, you don't go anymore."

"When did I hit my head?" The calendar hanging next to the stove catches my attention. March, 1972. March? 1972!? Where did 1971 disappear to?

I peer out the window again. Up a small hill to the left, a path winds up to an old barn. Some sheep graze in the pasture beyond it. To the right, down the muddy, slush-covered driveway, a narrow country road winds away through rolling hills. "Where are we?"

David purses his lips and wags his head, like he's a teacher, repeating a lesson for a child who hasn't been paying attention. He enunciates each word, as if I've lost my hearing and must read his lips. "The farm. Remember?"

I drop my head and press a palm to my forehead. I'm so confused.

"We moved here after you got married."

Apparently losing interest in the topic, he says, "Let's eat." David grabs my hands and leads me to the table. He pulls bowls from the cabinet and spoons from the drawer, then grabs the cereal box.

Marriage? But who? Patrick left for Washington and hasn't returned ... at least, I don't think he has. Even so, I don't know him well enough to have married him. And it can't be Gordon. He found someone new long ago.

David points to the refrigerator. "Time to eat," he repeats. "You get the milk, okay?"

I nod, pull the jug from the refrigerator, and set it on the table next to the cereal. "Who did I marry?"

"Leonard. He went shopping, but he'll be back for lunch. He already did our barn chores so we don't have to." David hands out his answers like he's dealing cards for Go Fish. But each affects me like bad news on a Tarot card.

I lift the cereal box and try to pour it, but my hands are too shaky. I don't know anyone named Leonard. I give up on the cereal and collapse into the chair. "Tell me about him."

David sighs and rolls his eyes, as if he's answered this question a million times before. He shakes the cereal and pours for both of us. He lifts his bowl and tilts the milk jug until his Cheerios are swimming. His big brown eyes open wider and he says, "You married him right after Christmas. Then we moved here. Can you pour your own milk?"

Accident. Christmas. Farm. Marriage. I don't recall anything after August. Have I slipped into the Twilight Zone?

"Can you pour the milk?" David asks again.

"Oh, sure. Of course I can," I say. But I'm surprised at how much effort this simple task takes. When I cap the jug and pick up my spoon, the smell of oats wafts to my nostrils. Acid rises in my esophagus and my gut clenches with nausea.

I arrive in the bathroom an instant before I throw up. After several heaves, my stomach empties. Feeling jittery, I crumple to the floor, prop my elbows on my knees and cradle my head in my hands. That's when I notice my swollen ankles. And tender breasts. I've felt this way before, I remember. Back when I was … *am I pregnant?*

I force myself to stand, splash water on my face, and stare into the mirror. My black hair frizzes in every direction, as if it's been shocked by a bolt of lightning. My face, drawn and hollow, reveals half-moon eye sockets so dark my lids look bruised. I recoil from the image and trudge back to the living room. There, I collapse onto the stiff wicker couch.

David nestles next to me, so I wrap my arms around him and rock. He lets my tears soak his hair.

That's when I notice a photo album on the coffee table. The front reads, "Emma Lee and Leonard—December 30, 1971."

"You can go play now, David. I want to look at the pictures."

He shimmies off my lap and squats on the floor with his Legos. With pounding heart I grab the book and open it. A photograph shows me wearing a low-cut short red dress and heels. I'm carrying a single rose. On my right stands a tall, thin man with grey hair, dressed in a dark suit. He's relatively handsome—for an old man—but the sight of him leaves a tight feeling in my throat. I have no idea why I married him, but there's no way I'll stay that way. I vow to get a divorce as soon as possible.

I set the album down, locate a pencil, a sheet of paper, and the phone book. The book's title, *Pittsburgh and Allegheny County* confirms that at least I am still living somewhere near Pittsburgh. Today I'll make a list of people to call; tomorrow I'll make the appointments. I scan the yellow pages for attorneys.

"Mom!" David yells. "Mom, look what I made!" He thrusts a Lego structure in my face and grins. Coherent a moment ago, at his outburst my thoughts uncoil like frayed rope. Pain shoots down my spine and I feel nauseous again. Suddenly nothing makes any sense. I rub my temples. "Davie, please don't yell. That makes my head hurt." I give the Lego creation an obligatory peek and then clamp my eyes shut again. "I love the car, but I need a nap. You can play or watch cartoons, but keep it quiet."

"Yippee!" David whispers.

I feel my way to the bedroom. I close the door and ease myself onto the bed. As I lie there breathing deeply, bits of memory tumble and reflect like glass shards in a kaleidoscope. I see myself lying on the floor. A man wearing a mask and protective suit hovers over me, looking worried and afraid. He turns my face mask so he can look into my eyes and begs, "Emma Lee. Are you okay?" Then I'm naked, in a shower with another man. The one in the album. He's running his hands over me. I try to escape but my feet won't move. My head hurts like crazy. He scans my naked body with lecherous eyes, and he keeps saying, "You're so beautiful." I recall excruciating pain. Sirens. IV tubes. Men in white asking too many questions: Then, a dark terrible void squeezes my breath and I gasp for air. What happened to me?

As I drift to slumber, I know I won't be able to make that attorney list today. I'm way too tired and confused to do anything but sleep.

I HEAR SOMEONE open the door and slide onto the edge of the bed. Then, a hand strokes my cheek.

"Hi."

It's a man's voice. The quilt is peeled from my shoulders. "You're beautiful in this light," the voice says.

I feel drugged, lost in fog someplace deep in my brain. I turn and groan. Only with effort can I force myself to wake.

A hand slides up my shirt to my breasts, and my eyelids shoot open. I push him away, grab the quilt, and yank it up to my chin again.

"All morning I've been imagining this moment, when I could caress you again. Touching your skin relaxes me. And I'm sure it does you good, too. You should thank me, not pull away," he scolds. "Relax."

"Please, don't touch me."

In the dim light, I see his scowl and his voice grows hard. "Oh come on. You know you love this."

I tuck my knees up and wrap my arms around them. Fear pokes my gut like a giant thistle, sharp and painful. "Stay. Away. From. Me."

His lips smile; his eyes don't. "You're confused. I'll go start lunch and throw in a load of laundry. You'll change your mind later."

I can't speak; I shake my head and cry.

When the man closes the door behind him, I crawl out of bed. My hands tremble as I smooth the quilt. It's true, then. I married him—that man who tried to maul me.

I slide my feet into my slippers, crack open the bedroom door, and peek down the hallway. Can't see him. The sound of a washing machine door slamming echoes up the basement stairwell. He must be down there, now. I tiptoe to the living room.

David turns off the television cartoons. "Hi Mom, we're having grilled cheese for lunch. Daddy Leonard said we should butter the bread."

I stand motionless, feeling blank, so I follow David into the kitchen. He opens the refrigerator and hands me ingredients. The bread is buttered when I hear footfalls on the stairs. With pounding heart, my feet propel me to the living room. On the sofa, I bury my face in my knees to armor myself against the man. What will I say? What *can* I say?

The man dumps the basket of clean clothes on the couch, fresh and warm. He drops into a chair and grabs a T-shirt. "We can work while we talk. Like always," he says, folding the shirt into precise fourths before placing it into the basket. "Why did you shy away from me in the bedroom? You always love my attention."

I shake my head several times. That can't be right.

The man hands me a towel. "Here, help me."

I stare. "I don't think I can do this."

His algae-colored eyes glare at me. "Your occupational therapist showed you how to fold yesterday. Think!"

"Not the folding. I mean I can't live here; I can't be married to you."

He drops his head sideways and leans over me until his face is so close I feel his breath on my face. His voice takes on a sing-song quality, like he's talking to a kitten. "You had a setback, that's all. Eventually things will settle down again and we'll all get back to normal."

Normal? I don't know what normal looks like. Somehow the yolk of my life is broken and scrambled and there was no way I can reconstruct it. "Humpty Dumpty," I mumble. "That's who I am."

The man adds another towel to the basket and picks up a pair of David's jeans. "What'd you say?"

When I shake my head, he says, "Your next appointment with Yamada is Tuesday morning. We'll get answers about what's happening to you—this sporadic return of memory, the shying away from me." He sets David's folded jeans into the basket and his eyes bore into me. "Face it; you're too hurt to care for yourself, Emma

Lee. But I know what you need and I'll make sure you get it. You can count on that."

I know he's right on one count. I *am* too wounded to care for myself. At the thought, I shove my face onto my knees and sob.

When the thin man whose name I can't recall moves closer and slips his arm over my shoulder, a shudder rattles down my spine. But I don't pull away. I relax and let him hug me.

"Don't worry," he says. "After lunch, you'll take a long nap. When you wake up you won't remember any of this. You can start all over and it will be fine."

1.

August 18, 1971

I'm called to the boss's office again—my third time in three days.

As I enter, I see the back of Dr. Baxter's grey-haired head. Oblivious to my entry, he stands facing the window, phone cord stretched to its limit. He seems to be studying the gigantic holding tanks and murky pools of stagnant chemical waste outside his window as he talks.

Baxter spreads his legs wide and props his left hand on his hip with a nonchalant arrogance that I attribute to an attitude of entitlement.

I've often seen men in power stand in this manner. My father did it when he lectured me about conserving electricity, or not wasting food or time. And when he talked to the black men who worked for him. Did men learn that stance by watching other men in power? Maybe it's like captaining a rocking, swaying ship. To survive the pettiness that threatens the ship of a man's stability, he trains his body to stand firm yet flexible. That way, he can oscillate with the constant pitch and yaw of humanity's storms.

I clear my throat but he doesn't turn. He must be twice my age; perhaps he's hard of hearing. Feeling invisible, I back up to leave when his words catch my attention.

"Trust me. Stan knows exactly when and where to dump to avoid any repercussions." He pauses several seconds and continues, "Up front, as usual."

I inch backwards.

Crash!

I miss the door and smash my elbow on the wall. My heart pounds and I wish I could float under the door and disappear like mist.

He turns, mouth open, and finds me rubbing my arm. The wrinkles in his face deepen and he winces, like he's eaten a bug. "Gotta go," he mumbles, and jams the receiver down.

"Ah, here you are, Miss Dubois."

(He pronounces it Dew Boysie.) My father never missed an opportunity to remind me that, although we lived in the south, we were still descendents of important New York Huguenots, and should defend our honor whenever necessary. If he were here, he'd protest the desecration of the pronunciation with eloquence. I try to stay calm, keep the peace, keep my job.

"Have a seat," Baxter says. His long, slender index finger points to a chair, which I slide into. No other office in the building has leather wing back chairs, or oriental carpeting, or brocade drapes like this one. As a matter of fact, no one else has drapes at all. The posh decor could be his way of making up for the odor, but nothing can do that; the chemical stink permeates everything on the island.

The wing back threatens to engulf me, so I shrug forward onto the seat edge.

"I don't recommend eavesdropping," he says. "That could be more hazardous to your health than entering the lab without your protective suit." He pretends to laugh. His eyes, the color of algae, never leave my legs. I wrap my lab coat around my mini skirt and curse my clothing choice.

"But I didn't call you in here for that, Emma Lee." His eyes squint. "I hope you don't mind me calling you that, do you?"

I paste on my Sunday School smile. "I prefer Miss Dubois."

As Baxter slurps coffee, I watch his nostrils flare like tiny bellows. He runs his fingers through his grey, thinning hair several times, then bites his lips until they disappear. With eyes shut, he says, "These are the new guidelines from the EPA on laboratory management. You'll need to train your people on this by next month."

"Okay," I mumble, forcing myself not to bite my hangnail.

I took Patrick's job when he left three days ago, and ever since, I've been a nervous wreck. I know little about the laboratory or how it functions. I had never been in a closed work environment before, and there wasn't much time for training before Patrick left. So I've been reading the procedures and trying to understand the processes, but it isn't easy. My heart slows down to normal, and I gulp slugs of air.

"Is that what you wanted to see me about?"

He stands and paces to the window, then turns to stare at me again. After thirty seconds of silence, he pinches the bridge of his nose. "No. Actually … How about you and I get together and see the sights this weekend? The ballet is at Heinz Hall, and I have box seats for Pirates baseball on Saturday. Which will it be?"

I couldn't be more shocked if I stuck my finger in a live electrical outlet. "Well … ."

To gain a few seconds to think, and wield any possible advantage over this bastion of power, I stand, stretch to my tallest five-foot-three inches, and stutter, "I … really … can't …"

Leaving the window, he positions himself in his swivel chair like Buddha, fingers tented on his lips, and waits for me to finish sputtering. "I assumed that when I gave you this promotion, you'd be grateful. People get ahead by making contacts. You scratch my back, I'll scratch yours." He winks. "Know what I mean?"

I may be young, inexperienced, and fresh from a Dixieland plantation, but I'm not that much of a hick. I know exactly what he means. And I don't like it one bit.

His face softens and he pretends to smile again. "Look, Emma Lee." He clears his throat.

"That's Miss Dubois," I reiterate.

"Yes, of course. Due-Bwah. Got it. So consider it a business meeting. We could discuss work, the way things are around here at River's Edge Chemical. You know, the corporate culture, what's expected of you. I guarantee it's in your best interest." He stands and assumes his ship captain pose again, and I'm the one feeling seasick.

I shake my head and turn to the door. Got to get out of here before I suffocate.

"Neither one of us wants to see you—a single woman with a child to support—out on the streets, now do we?"

I stand dumbfounded for several seconds. *Out on the streets—as in unemployed?* Once I regain my ability to speak, I manage, "I don't date people from work. It's my policy."

He raises an eyebrow. "That isn't what I heard. What about Patrick?"

He winks again and I want to scream.

"My personal life is none of your business," I spit the words like seeds, and race from the room.

"Time will tell," he calls after me.

2.

Patrick Kilkenny paid for the book and slipped it under his arm. The 960 pages of Michener's *Hawaii* should ensure he had plenty to read during his trip. Twelve years prior in 1959, the country assigned statehood to the small, volcanic island archipelago. Although Patrick was fourteen at the time, his wanderlust had burst into maturity then, and he had made sure his life included regular travel to faraway places ever since. Two months ago, he had expected that his next trip would be to Hawaii. But that was then. This was now.

Instead of beaches and babes, he was flying to Washington State for time undetermined, for caregiving and chores. He knew it would be years before he could again save up enough money for a tropical getaway; maybe it would never happen. So for now he'd settle for reading about Hawaii.

Stepping out of the bookstore into the Pittsburgh Airport hallway, Patrick thought, *Funny how things change.*

He strode to his gate and opened the book, but instead of reading he stared out the window. When he visited Washington State last time, four years ago, he had hiked with his sister and nephew on trails near Mt. Rainier and camped in the Cascade Mountains. This time he'd stay in town while his sister healed. But once her health improved, he hoped for a boat trip up Lake Chelan to that little town of Stehekin he'd heard about.

When they called his flight, he sighed and walked down the chute, feeling like a steer heading for slaughter.

Seventeen hours later, after haunting the Chicago, Denver, and Seattle airports during layovers, ingesting three indefinable pasta meals, reading 272 pages of *Hawaii*, and using every other moment to contemplate Emma Lee, Patrick arrived in Pasco, Washington.

He hadn't shared his reasons for leaving with most of his coworkers. So before his corporate world participation ended three days prior, some well-meaning coworkers had warned him that leaving his job would ruin his career. They labeled him zappy, whacked, or crazy for taking such a long leave of absence. But Emma Lee knew. And she had said several times that it was the most selfless thing she'd seen anyone do.

Ah, Emma Lee. Smart, energetic, and downright nice is what she was. God, she had looked great that morning seeing him off, even without makeup and that wild black curly hair of hers all disheveled. Though she worked in the stressful environment of chemical pesticide testing, she seemed separate from it, as if her spirit were encased in Plexiglas peace. Recalling her face made his heart feel lighter, as if counteracting gravity. The memory helped him forget, at least momentarily, the ache he'd been carrying.

"Hmph!" he grunted. *I find a woman I actually care about and have to move 3000 miles away. The timing really stinks.*

At the baggage carousel, Patrick retrieved his luggage and dragged it through the sliding door where several other people stood waiting for rides. Hot dusty wind stung his face and arms like biting fleas, reminding him that he was on the eastern side of the "Evergreen" State, the dry side. Shrub steppe, his sister called it. Whenever he described this terrain to people—the sage brush, scrub grass, jack rabbits, and a mere eight inches of rain a year—most were surprised, or even shocked. He liked telling them about it to see their reaction. Here he felt a lifetime away from Pittsburgh's cloudy skies and shady deciduous forests.

To a man standing near him, Patrick said, "Just as I remembered it, hot and dry."

"Hot? You must not be from around here. Eighty-nine is cool for August," the grinning man replied.

Patrick shrugged one shoulder, wondering how heat could be a point of pride.

At the curb, he handed his bags to the taxi driver and hopped in.

Looking at Patrick through the rear view mirror, the taxi driver said, "You coming home or visiting?"

"Visiting. My sister's sick so I'm here to help out." He was quiet a moment, then said, "Actually, her doctor says it's terminal."

"Oh, man, I'm sorry to hear that," the driver said.

Patrick was too; he couldn't describe how sorry. He sat silent for a few moments, noticing how the wind hit the cab in bursts, causing it to rock and sway. Along with a blizzard of dust, the wind propelled tumbleweeds that crashed into, rolled over, and scurried under the cab. Finally Patrick said, "Yeah, well, doctors can be wrong. I'm going to take her to Seattle next week to see a specialist. Have it all arranged."

"That's nice. So how long will you be here?"

"As long as it takes—till she doesn't need me anymore."

"She's lucky."

No, he was the lucky one. His sister was a saint, a woman of great strength, the person who could do anything. She couldn't die. He wouldn't let it happen. "I guess so. But she's been good to me. Raised me when our mother died."

Fifteen minutes later the driver drove down a lane lined with a barbed-wire fence on one side and a corn field on the other, pulling up to a small house. When Patrick opened the taxi door, the smell of dust and sage filled his nostrils and grit sandblasted him. Through squinted eyes, he saw the barefoot boy with a shock of dark red, unruly hair, the same color as his own, in the yard.

"Uncle Patrick, hi!" The boy waved and bounded across the yard. "I'm so glad you're here. Mom and I *need* you. I've been waiting for you for hours and hours. Now Cousin Carol and the neighbor, Mrs. Macintyre, won't have to help so much."

"Hey, Joshua, great to see you, kiddo! Look how tall you are! You've grown since I saw you last."

The boy clicked his tongue. "Geeze, Uncle Patrick, I was a baby then. Of *course* I've grown." He grabbed Patrick's hand and dragged him to the house. "Come on, Mom's waiting."

Patrick laughed. "Let me get my stuff."

He paid the driver and yanked his suitcase and duffle out of the taxi trunk. As he walked to the front door, he scanned Peggy's house. Faded, water-streaked grey paint peeled from the siding. A few shingles stood up from the roof; some were missing. A wide strip of strapping tape ran the length of one bedroom window, apparently to hold the cracked pane together. But a section of it had torn loose and was flapping in the wind.

In the past few years, Patrick had asked God many times to help Peggy. The trouble started early. After she married and moved to Washington, her husband, Richard, started drinking. Then he left her and Joshua. She scrounged a living as a waitress for a few years, but now cancer threatened her life. Based on the results of his many requests, he could only conclude that the communication channel between him and God was jammed or broken.

The dry lawn crunched as Patrick walked across it. A tree branch flew from the roof and landed at his feet. Wind threatened to rip his case out of his hand, so Patrick gripped the handle tighter. He used his other arm to hug Joshua.

When he stepped inside the living room, he gasped. The place had fallen apart since he was here, and it reminded him of how difficult life must have become for his clean-freak sister. A dirty, nap-flattened carpet track led from the front door to the bedrooms; the blinds hung catawampus. But it was the stench that got him: dust, rubbing alcohol, and bleach mixed with a touch of sewage. Patrick had to force himself to stay in the room. How could he have let his family, the people he loved most in the world, live like this while he carried on a normal, even comfortable life back in Pittsburgh? Clearly, there was much to do here, so much so he might never finish reading *Hawaii*.

His sister leaned against the kitchen doorway. "Oh, Patrick, it's so awesome that you're here." Peggy's voice sounded translucent, the ghost of its prior heartiness. Her T-shirt, her cut-off shorts, even her skin hung loose.

He wished he had known what it was like here. He wished he had come sooner. When he opened his mouth to speak, though, sadness dammed up the air and all he could manage was, "Aw, Peggy."

She pointed her mixing spoon at him. "I know that look, little brother. You can't hide from me. Yeah, I'm a mess, so let's not pretend. I'm going to die, and I'm glad you'll be here with me when it happens."

As Patrick enclosed his sister in his arms, her body felt skeletal. Secret thoughts that he had harbored—of mistaken diagnoses, of trips to specialists who would cure her, of miraculous healing, and especially thoughts of boat trips to touristy villages—blew away with the wind. There was no avoiding the truth: soon he'd be putting her affairs in order, solidifying the guardianship for Joshua ... and purchasing a coffin.

He said, "I wouldn't miss being here with you for anything." Then remembering Emma Lee and David, he added, "Or anyone."

3.

I sit in the darkened auditorium watching a slide show presented by Nancy from H.R. She drones on about procedures, forms, and routines, and I'm nodding off when I hear, "...constitute sexual harassment." My eyes pop open and I sit up straighter. She continues, "If someone's conduct interferes with your work performance, or creates an intimidating, hostile, or offensive environment at work, Title VII gives you recourse. Report the offense to H.R. or the Equal Employment Opportunity Commission office."

When the slides end and the lights come up, the middle-aged woman asks, "Any questions?"

Seventy-two employees sit blinking in the brightness. No one raises a hand. Someone coughs; feet shuffle. Eventually, Dr. Baxter stands and gives us all permission to leave early. The crowd whoops and applauds, and within minutes the auditorium disgorges itself of people.

Except my boss. He positions himself at the doorway, arms crossed; his gaze engulfs me like the octopus digesting a clam.

I smile at Katrina Kowalski, the Cover-Girl-model-gorgeous receptionist who usually sits at the front desk to get her attention. She reminds me of my mother—a woman who has refined superficial to an art form. When I lived in the south, I was convinced that females with great bodies and empty minds were consequences of the antebellum culture. But I've met women here in the north who are like that, too, which debunks my theory. I guess vapid females exist everywhere. But to her credit, Katrina is friendly, she's got a down-home charm, and she's one of the few people on the planet able to wear that popular pale pink lipstick without looking embalmed.

"Hey, Katrina, nice to see you," I say. "Got a moment?"

"Sure," she says. Placing fingers of one hand on her cheek she asks, "Like this nurkin' cool color? It's called Nude Opal." Her fingernails gleam like sharks' teeth.

Baffled as to why anyone would wear nail polish and designer outfits to this stinky chemical plant I say, "Pretty on you. Not my color, though."

Today this mini-skirted, silver-belted fashion plate will be my protection against Baxter, so I slip my arm through hers. Light versus dark, tall versus short; we're like salt and pepper together. "Hey, walk with me," I say.

"When Patrick left, you got promoted to his position, didn't you?" Katrina asks. "How's that going?"

When we exit the auditorium, I focus on Katrina's question and try to ignore the octopus in the doorway.

"Well, in the convoluted and peculiar reasoning of corporate America, I'm in charge, all right. Before, I kept track of my own work only; my little part of the project. Now, because the company can buy my master's degree cheap (since I'm a woman), I've got a whole lab to coordinate. To top it off, thanks to President Nixon's wage freeze, I get no salary increase for my added duress. Wish I could change my mind."

"You make it sound so bad," she says.

On the way down the hallway, I check over my shoulder. Dr. Baxter now follows us and my heart picks up speed like I've run a mile. "All those poisonous chemicals freak me out." The subject energizes me and I poke the air with a finger. "Am I really protected by that suit? I have no way of knowing. And get this. They *still* haven't finished the woman's dressing room yet, so I have to take turns with the men."

Katrina takes out her barrette and flips her long chestnut hair over her shoulder. "Sounds icky, all right." She looks at her watch. "Hey, look. We have forty-five minutes before the busses get here. You up for coffee? Maybe it will calm you."

I look over my shoulder. Seeing Dr. Baxter still following, I say, "Yeah, let's get out of here."

There are no sidewalks on the four-lane asphalt street outside, only weeds growing through hard packed earth, the occasional puddle, and chain-linked fences. Huge dump trucks carrying slag, rocks, and myriad other materials, grind through low gears to or from the processing plants farther down the island. It's impossible for two people to walk abreast without risking life and limb, so we trudge single file. I'm in front, she's in back.

I hear Katrina pull air into her lungs like an opera singer preparing for a concert. Then she says, "Wait until you hear about yesterday; my boyfriend, Sloan? He asks me to dinner, and I'm thinking he wants to apologize for Saturday, but first thing he says isn't even hello, it's, 'We have to talk.'"

Her words gush so fast I miss the periods, but her story distracts from the weeds and thick, acrid fumes—and Dr. Baxter—so I listen.

"His face looks all pinched, the way he gets when he's vexed, so I open the menu. 'Can it wait until we order?' I ask. I tell him I've had a hard day, but he interrupts, and yells, 'No! We talk first;' then the bastard grabs my arm and hisses, 'You slut! How dare you flirt with Michael? I'd like to smack you.'"

"Wow. That's intense. Who's Michael?" I ask.

"He and Sloan were teammates for darts last Saturday night—a sweet guy—real polite. I think he's part Chinese or something because he's got these deep, brown Oriental-looking eyes with a gaze like an x-ray. He's built, too. Slim and muscular."

The farther we walk from the plant, the less putrid the rotten-egg smell grows. I turn to look at her and check behind us; no Dr. Baxter. Thank goodness. My heart slows. "Really?" I say, getting interested. "No wonder Sloan was jealous. Michael sounds great. Want to introduce me?"

She waves her hand like my request is ridiculous and continues, "I especially like his skin color. It looks like he's been on the beach all summer." She's quiet for a few steps and I figure her imagination has floated to some tropical paradise with this Michael guy.

I continue navigating the weeds and constant truck traffic, and say over my shoulder, "Sloan was right, wasn't he? You *were* flirting with Michael."

"Who wouldn't with such a gorgeous guy?"

We enter Gino's, the tiny two-story yellow brick restaurant. Although old and dingy like the factory, Gino's feels comfortable. Several other workers are already here: suited office employees, casually dressed locals, and construction workers in jeans and blue work shirts. We slide into a booth and order coffee. Katrina continues her story.

A short '*huh*' bursts from her lungs. She flips her long, chestnut locks again and smacks the table with the flat of her hand. "Then he breaks up with me and stomps off. Can you imagine? *He* breaks up with *me*! It's surreal."

The waitress appears and pours us two cups of coffee.

I ask, "So what did you do?"

Katrina stirs cream into her cup. "I ordered dinner."

I laugh aloud.

Katrina takes a sip of coffee. "So what about you? What's your love life like, now that Patrick is gone?"

"I have a problem, but it's nothing like yours." I lean forward and say, "Dr. Baxter keeps asking me out, and he scares me. I've turned him down several times now, but he keeps hounding me. I don't know what to do."

Katrina shrugs. "You're cute, petite. My guess is some men want to protect a woman like you. It makes them feel strong. Besides, he's lecherous."

"Great," I grumble, rolling my eyes. "But there's more." I'm ready to tell her what happened in Baxter's office when she interrupts.

"Oh, shoot, I forgot," she sputters. "I was supposed to lock up tonight!" She grabs her purse and stands. "I'm sorry, but I've gotta run. See ya tomorrow."

It doesn't seem fair that she told her story but I can't finish mine. I brood for a few minutes after she goes.

Next time the restaurant door opens I'm shocked to see Dr. Baxter enter. He hesitates for a few moments, then saunters to my table. "Ah, Emma Lee. Here you are." He stares at my chest. His thin lips curve upwards and he clears his throat. "Ahem, can I join you?"

I want to say, 'No. Leave me alone, and go away.' Unfortunately, I'm an amalgam of my mother's Southern Belle hospitality and my father's business sense, so my thoughts war like my parents did before their divorce. Then my hospitality gene hijacks my brain, snaring me in a trap laid for me before I was born by my family, society, and the great palmetto state of South Carolina. I mumble, "I'm not prepared to talk about work right now."

Without permission, he slips into the seat across the table from me. "Um, well. It's not about work," he begins.

The waitress shows up, holding a coffee carafe and another cup, but I wave her away.

"Have you thought any more about going out with me? The Tamberitzins are in town—the ethnic dancers from Duquesne University? I hear they're great. Bet you'd like them." I frown as he continues, "You and I could have a great time together, you know … at the show … and … after … at my place. I've got a hot tub. Swimming suits are optional." He winks.

Almost gagging, I shake my head. "I told you, I won't go out with you."

"Work with me and the sky's the limit, Emma Lee." He winks again. "I can give you so much."

Before he died, Dad often told me: *To advance, you have to grab life by the balls.* I sigh. Not this time.

To stop Dr. Baxter's advances, I know I have to act with determination. Nancy's words from sexual harassment training come back to me. *The victim should inform the harasser directly that the conduct is unwelcome and must stop.*

He smiles but I can't read its intent. I take a deep breath, pray for strength to overcome my politeness inertia, and say, "Your conduct is unwelcome and I consider it ... harassment." His eyes grow hard as I continue, "If it doesn't stop, I *will* report you."

My heart thumps so loud I worry that the whole restaurant can hear it. I flip a nickel tip on the table, then staggering like I've ridden a merry-go-round too many times, I arrive at the cash register, pay, and bolt out the door.

When I reach the bus stop, thunderhead clouds churn overhead like dirty dishwater as Katrina arrives, grinning. "Well, I got the doors locked. Hey, I noticed Dr. Baxter going into Gino's when I was coming out." She winks. "He does seem to like you. Play your cards right and you might get a raise." Her words turn sing-song, making the word 'raise' sounded like it has two syllables.

Scrunching my nose, I grimace. "The guy gives me the willies. I think I'll call the Equal Employment Opportunity Office about him."

Katrina grins. "Go for it." She digs in her purse and pulls out a card. "Here, I forgot to give this to you earlier. It's the invitation to my Tupperware party. I've got lots of games lined up; it should be fun."

I stick the invitation in my pocket as the rain begins pelting us. My bus pulls up and I climb on. As the vehicle lumbers across the

McKees Rocks Bridge, the ad above my head reads, "Better Living through Chemistry." In my case it's "bitter living."

I'm reminded of the nursery rhyme that goes, *If wishes were horses, beggars would ride.* For me it would say, *If wishes were bosses, I'd be my own.* Out the window ahead, shiny wet maple leaves shimmer like emerald lace. Behind me, smoke belches into the drizzling, murky sky.

4.

As Patrick dragged a pack of shingles from the truck, Peggy's re-tired neighbor sauntered over. "Looks like you got a job going, so let me give you some advice." Before Patrick could respond, the wiry man pointed to the roof and continued, "Start work at dawn; otherwise, you'll fry up there."

The next morning, Patrick climbed onto the roof at five-thirty. The early hour reminded him of his uncle, a Pittsburgh cop, who rose at 4:30 a.m. every day of his life. Uncle Liam often quoted Benjamin Franklin's adage, "Early to bed and early to rise makes a man healthy, wealthy, and wise." That practice worked for his uncle, at least; he retired with both health and wealth.

Wisdom was a different matter. Patrick never thought about it until college. He and a buddy were going to the promenade deck on the 38th floor of the Gulf Building to see the city from high up. Patrick ran back to the car for the camera so he was alone on the elevator when it stopped unexpectedly between the eighteenth and nineteenth floors. After his initial panic had subsided, he had plenty of time to think. He considered who would care if he plummeted to his death at the age of twenty. Two hours later, when the maintenance crew released him back into the world, he emerged from the Gulf Building with a radically altered view of his life, his spirituality, God, the future, and a determination to grow wise. That was nine years ago. Since then, Patrick had focused on Wisdom. He took three philosophy classes in college and read profusely. He learned how to contemplate, found a spiritual director, and tried to practice kindness.

On Peggy's roof, Patrick ripped off two broken shingles and replaced them with new ones. Here in Washington he was losing wealth, not gaining it. But good things would come from it, he knew. His strength would probably improve from all the hard work. If helping Peggy didn't expand his wisdom, at least it might make him a better person. He whacked another nail into the roof as a mourning dove cooed. The clouds slid open, permitting the sun to strut its hot, proud self onto the day. "I'm here!" it seemed to shout.

A waft of cool desert air blew up from the river. It scrambled an aroma omelet of sage and ripe grapes and he inhaled it with relish. The breeze liberated his thoughts, allowing them to graze in the meadow of ideas. When the sky blushed all pink and orange, forming a glowing halo of color and cloud, he set down his hammer, lay on the roof, and slid his hands behind his head. For several minutes he stared at the sky. He heard the neighbor's dog bark; then a quail called its alarm. It was lovely and peaceful, but the sunlight reminded Patrick that searing heat would soon follow. He went back to work.

Around nine, he was sweating when he slid his hammer into the tool belt and climbed down the ladder. He wiped his forehead with his handkerchief, then gathered the debris from his job and pitched it into the garbage. When Patrick entered the house Peggy was on the couch; Joshua was spreading jam on toast in the kitchen.

Patrick said, "Roof's fixed. Now if it ever rains, we'll stay dry."

"Thank you," Peggy said. "It will be a long time until rain, but you've earned your keep already. Wish I could have helped."

Joshua handed a piece of jellied toast to his mother. "Hey, Mom, do I *have* to play with Ricky and Bobby when they get here?"

Patrick checked his watch. "I thought you liked Carol's boys. And hey, if you could work on those dishes now, that'd be great. I'll start a load of laundry."

They heard tires crunching on rocks as a maroon 1967 Ford Fairlane pulled up. Ricky, Carol's ten-year-old, and his brother Bobby, age eight, jumped out of the back door. To Patrick they looked like different-height clones with skinny limbs and shaggy, dark hair. They even dressed alike, both in madras shorts and white T-shirts.

When Cousin Carol emerged from the Ford's front door, her long legs stuck out from faded cutoff jeans and her tie-died T-shirt sleeves bulged around muscular biceps. He could tell she worked hard for a living. Before cancer ravaged Peggy's body, the women so resembled each other that people mistook them for sisters. When he thought of his emaciated sister, sorrow threatened to usurp his thoughts, but he refused to allow that now. They had company.

"You got lucky, Joshua," Patrick said. "You get to play instead of wash."

Joshua frowned. "I'd rather do dishes."

Peggy rested her head on the back of the couch and closed her eyes. "You're seven years old. Time to learn some manners. Be polite, honey. They're the only cousins you've got."

Joshua rolled his eyes again and took a huge bite of toast. "*Second* cousins," he mumbled.

Carol didn't knock. "Hi Peggy, we're here. The boys are outside waiting for you, Josh."

Joshua grabbed a ball and sauntered out, as if playing was another chore.

"Carol, welcome. Look who's here!"

They shook hands. "Nice to see you again, Patrick. You'll be a great help."

"Thanks. I appreciate all you've been doing for her, too. I'm glad you could come today, because she could use a bath, and I'm not ..." he blushed. "Well, I'm not ready to do that yet. Hey, I was about to make some coffee. Would you like some?"

"Yes, please. Black."

While Patrick worked in the kitchen he overheard the women talking.

"Before we get to the bath, while Joshua is outside, I'd like to discuss arrangements," Peggy began. "You know I'm not going to last much longer. What have you decided?" Her voice faded at the end of the sentence, as if the conversation tired her.

Patrick returned from the kitchen with three mugs of coffee. He kept one and settled into the recliner. "We'd like to get this settled soon, Carol," he said.

Staring into her mug, Carol wrapped her hands around it as if they were cold. "I understand. I'm pretty sure we can take him."

"Pretty sure isn't good enough," Patrick said.

Touching her brother's knee, Peggy said, "Let me take care of this, Patrick." To Carol she said, "I know it's hard to decide, but I want to be the one to tell Joshua where he'll be living—before I go."

Carol worried her lip with her teeth and massaged her forehead with two fingers. "Yeah, I know. Zane's nervous about getting laid off, is all. You know how it is with laborers at the Hanford Site—always in flux."

They heard a scream; Carol raced to the window. "Uh-oh, looks like Joshua's hurt." A few seconds later she said, "Must not be too bad. He's coming this way."

She sat down again and took one of Peggy's hands in hers. "I know you need an answer, honey. I'll go out on a limb here and say yes."

Patrick placed a hand on his chest. "Great. You've lifted a huge load. I'll get the adoption papers drawn up so you can sign them next time you come over. We certainly appreciate it, Carol."

"You're welcome. I hope Zane sees it my way." A quick, sharp laugh escaped her throat. "Don't worry. I'll talk him into it."

The door opened and Joshua limped in. "Mom, I hurt my ankle!"

Peggy patted the couch next to her. "Come and tell me what happened," she said.

"We were playing Dodge Ball. Ricky kept going past the line, and throwing the ball really hard at my head. I told him to quit it, but he didn't listen. He said, 'I'm oldest, so I make up the rules.' Then he pushed me and I fell and twisted my ankle."

At that moment Ricky burst in the door. "Joshua punched me, Mom. See?" Ricky pointed to his forearm, revealing a large welt of red skin.

"You shouldn't hit," Peggy said to Joshua.

"He made me," Joshua said.

Bobby appeared right behind Ricky, the screen door slamming behind him. "Joshua's a big baby," he said.

Joshua pointed at Ricky and snarled, "Am not! You jumped on me. See the bruise?" He pointed to his leg. "You did that to me."

"Tattle-tale," Bobby yelled, fist in the air. He raced for Joshua, ready to smack him, but Carol grabbed his arm.

Up to now, Patrick had limited experiences with children, and this fight seemed so, well, childish. He wished he were still on the roof, pounding nails. Even the heat would be better than this. He shut his eyes trying to escape the fray.

"You baby. Crying from a little punch!" Ricky snarled.

Carol clicked her tongue. "Stop! Both of you."

Bobby pointed an accusing finger at Joshua, "I don't care what you say, Mom. I'm never going to share my room with him."

Carol's mouth fell open, making a wide circle, but no words came out.

Joshua took his mother's arm and draped it over his shoulder, wove his arms around her waist, and clasped his fingers together. Burying his face in her shoulder, he sobbed, "Please don't die."

Patrick felt so hot he examined his chair to ensure it hadn't caught on fire. He was tempted to demand that Carol punish her boys. Then, he considered taking discipline into his own hands and spanking Bobby and Ricky. But he knew that would solve nothing but his own frustration. From his vantage point, his family looked broken, like a puzzle with missing pieces, and he had no idea how they'd all fit together. Some quiet reflection on what to do next would be great, but not likely.

"My bad luck," he mumbled. "There's no building in town with an elevator."

5.

Chocolate taffy shadows stretch across Center Avenue as I step off the bus. The world takes on the glow of campfire coals. But the soft light doesn't stop my flaws from reflecting back to me from the drugstore window. I comb my messy black curls with my fingers, tuck my escaping blouse back into my waistband, and grimace. Why did I even let Dr. Baxter talk to me? More like proposition me.

By the time I reach the baby-sitter's home, my stomach is churning, my toes long for freedom from my tight shoes. My body feels hollow, as if someone pulled plugs from the soles of my feet and drained my energy. I ring the bell. When the door opens, a savory aroma wafts out. I breathe it in hoping that smelling homemade chicken soup works on the spirit the same way eating it heals the body.

"Come on in, Emma Lee," Maria, says. As usual, David's sitter is dressed in sweat pants, T-shirt, and pearls. Her thick, brown hair is pulled into a ponytail and a dish towel hangs over her shoulder. As she leads me to the family room, she says, "David enjoyed himself today. He and Tony played outside all morning. After lunch they built and colored." She grabs papers with crayoned stick people drawn on them from the table and shoves them into my hands. "Here are his masterpieces."

Only one other person has called my son's drawings "masterpieces." That was Patrick, last Saturday.

David and I had gone to his apartment to help pack. David brought a bag full of toys, and his first question to Patrick was, "Do you want to play?"

Patrick's laugh had sounded carefree, and his answer was genuine. "I'd love to." Then his face grew somber in pretend seriousness. "But first I have to put your mother to work."

He led us into his bedroom where boxes lined the walls and piles of clothing, shoes, and toiletries covered the bed. Heaps of other items littered the floor.

"You can pack this box," he told me, "while we boys play." Then, plunking himself on the floor, Patrick said, "Let's get to the important stuff."

I remember the glee on my son's face as he dumped the bag's contents. A ball; bright red, blue, and yellow Legos; one Hot Wheels car; and a box of crayons fell onto the carpet. Patrick sat cross-legged next to him. "So what are we making?"

Three hours later, the "boys" had built and destroyed several Lego structures, played one short game of catch (which ended when the ball hit me on the head), and drew nine pictures, the so called "masterpieces." Patrick taped them to his refrigerator and promised he'd keep them there until he left, and assured us he'd even take them with him to Washington. "So I won't forget you," he said.

On Saturday, my heart was emptied. Now my lungs empty in a long sigh. I close my eyes; *I* won't forget *him*, for sure.

David sits cross-legged on the floor in the same way he had with Patrick on Saturday. Tony stands near a two-foot high tower of toddler Duplo Legos. "My turn to break it," Tony yells. He smacks the tower; blocks fly everywhere. Both boys howl in laughter.

Maria says, "Time to pick up, boys. David's going home now."

My son falls onto the carpet and splays his arms and legs, as if he's drawn and ready for quartering. Like leaving is torture. "No, I wanna stay," he yells.

I often wish I were a stay-at-home mom, the kind I see on television. I would gladly cook dinner, run errands, and plant flowers instead of going to work. In this fantasy, my handsome, (and rich) spouse adores me. He goes to work and pays the bills. I volunteer at the school and the library, and join protests against the Vietnam War. Afternoons I bake bread and hold Tupperware parties. But that's all a pipe dream. I have no prospects for marriage, so I'm stuck working. Why doesn't my child understand that and give me appreciation, respect?

I sigh. Of course he's not protesting against me. I force myself to see it his way: he's trying to say he doesn't want to stop playing. So I set aside my jealousy and wishful thinking and say, "I'm tired and hungry, Davie. You can build with Tony again tomorrow."

He groans. "Aw, Mom."

Maria brings shoes from the hallway and sits to help David put them on, but the boy pushes her away. "I can do it."

Maria shrugs and raises her eyebrows to me. "He sure is independent."

I smile. "Yes, like his father: *very* determined."

I watch my son jam his feet into the wrong shoes. Then, as his tongue slips out of his mouth in concentration, he makes a loop with one string and tries to wrap the other string around it. His fingers seem too short and clumsy. As the bow falls apart again and again, I resist the temptation to take over.

Finally, in frustration, David thrusts both feet toward me, closes his eyes and yells, "Can't do it!"

"It's okay. Let me help you." I squat behind him, reposition his shoes onto the correct feet, and place my fingers around his. Guiding his hands so that he makes the loop, I help him pull the other string around it and through the hole. "See? All done."

At least I was able to *some* motherly thing today.

David stands and beams. As we plod homeward at last, he holds my hand and skips along the sidewalk, the shoe crisis forgotten. "Mommy, why's the road yellow? Where does the sun go at night? Can we have pizza for dinner? I'm starving."

"Let's see. I think I've got pizza in the freezer, so yes, we can eat that tonight." I giggle. "And maybe this is the Yellow Brick Road that leads to Oz. Maybe we'll see Dorothy, the scarecrow, and the lion any minute. What do you think?"

David holds his hand up to block the setting sun and looks down the yellow brick-paved boulevard. Then his eyes catch mine. Maybe he notices my mischievous grin, or he remembers that Oz was only a movie. He shakes his head. "We're in Pittsburgh, not Oz."

I reach over and muss his wild black hair. "Right you are!"

"Mommy, you told Maria I'm like my daddy. Where is he? Will he come home someday?"

My shoulders slump. I have avoided this subject for four years, and I'm not keen on addressing it now. Five years ago, in 1966, Gordon and I were headed for marriage. But a college lecture changed everything.

"You'll never guess what I did at lunch," Gordon announced one afternoon after work. "I signed us up for the Peace Corps!"

My shock must have tempered his enthusiastic outburst because his voice dropped an octave and his tsunami of words slowed. "One of the professors came back from Zambia last week, and he wants to bring others to that village to dig a well. When he asked for volunteers, I signed us both up." He grabbed my hands in his and danced around the room. "Oh, Emma Lee, this is big; it's exciting. We can both use our skills for something great. This project will bring clean water to a community that drinks polluted, muddy river water. We'd learn a new language, help people, travel. I knew you'd want to go with me. What do you say?"

Up to that day, I had spent my whole life in South Carolina. School, then work, watching steeple chases, or purchasing peaches and boiled peanuts at the corner fruit stand made up my life. The shock of that announcement still stings.

"I can't believe you did that without discussing it with me, Gordon," I sputtered. "I can't drop everything and go."

"Why not?" he countered.

We argued that night, and the next, and the next. We argued for a month. The night before he left, we made up. And we made love.

I had cried and clung to him at the airport; and I cried every night after that for weeks. When I discovered the pregnancy, I couldn't tell him. I didn't want to ruin his experience or guilt him into returning. Then Gordon's training was over and he went to another country. The mail was sketchy; some of my letters were returned. A few months later I got the fateful note. I read it so often I think it will be stuck in my memory forever.

"I'm sorry to have to tell you this long distance, but I've met another woman. We share everything—values and ideals, commitment to the poor and downtrodden. It's what I had always hoped for, finding someone as wonderful as you, who also shares the work I do. I trust you'll understand. I wish you well in all you do. You are a bright, capable woman. I know you'll be all right without me."

It felt like I'd been kicked in the head by a horse.

After that, the rare letter I received from Gordon was like a Peace Corps news bulletin: the bridge has been repaired, all the village children were finally vaccinated, Corps volunteers and villagers joined together to construct a tin-roofed reed house for a family whose home burned down.

I wandered through life like a drifter, then, losing focus and friends. David's birth forced me to drag myself from that dark, lonely place, back to the biosphere, and face my responsibilities. If it weren't for my son, I may never have returned from that hell.

By the time I got the job offer in Pittsburgh, I heard that Gordon had signed up for another tour. I wasn't sure what country he was in or what he was doing. I wasn't even sure if he married the woman of his dreams. Maybe I didn't want to know. I told people David's father died because for me, he had. I know I can't keep the truth from David forever. Perhaps this is the time to tell him.

"Your daddy is far away in a different country."

"But I wanna see him. What's his name?"

"His name is Gordon. He's helping poor children who don't have clean water."

David hangs his head. "He likes other kids more than me. He doesn't love me."

"That's not it." Now I feel guilty for *not* telling him about his father. And for keeping Gordon in the dark about David.

"Maybe we should write to him, tell him to come visit," I say, wondering if I have the nerve to follow through. I don't have his address any longer.

David hops and claps his hands together. "Yeah, let's write him."

"Okay, maybe later. But right now, we have to get dinner."

When we arrive at the apartment, I'm tired and it's too late to call the Equal Opportunity people. That will have to be tomorrow.

6.

Joshua stormed to his bedroom for his requisite time out while Carol and Peggy headed to the bathroom for Peggy's bath. Patrick took his own alone time. At 100 degrees plus, it felt sauna-like, but at least he was away from the hubbub and drama. Perspiration puddled under his arms and trickled down his back so he yanked his T-shirt over his head, opened the window, and turned on the fan and the radio. The clanking fan didn't do much beyond waft the hot air from one place to another, but that was better than nothing. Meanwhile, tinny speakers cranked out, "… Wonder this time where's she's gone. Wonder if she's gone to stay. Ain't no sunshine when she's gone, and this house just ain't no home, anytime she goes away …"

Amazing how easily things we love can slip from their foundations where we think they've been fastened so firm, he thought. He closed his eyes and prayed for his sister. Perhaps God could fortify the family he saw crumbling.

On the day Peggy called to tell him about her illness, her words came in measured bursts, like it took too much energy for whole sentences. "The doctor said my tests are conclusive. I've got… stomach cancer." She stopped speaking for several seconds, and he could hear the tears in her voice when she continued, "Oh, Patrick," she wailed, "I don't want to die."

As soon as he had heard Peggy's diagnosis, Patrick knew he'd help. Okay, he had to admit he had grown excited thinking about taking the leave of absence and flying cross country. He'd erroneously chalked that up to altruism. His helper-savior ego had inflated him like hydrogen lifting a zeppelin. At least it buoyed his spirits long enough to prompt his packing everything up, saying goodbye to the woman of his dreams, and taking on this herculean task with some enthusiasm. But now the difficulties of leaving Pittsburgh pricked holes in his psyche and he could feel his optimism leaking, threatening to deflate him. He missed work, his friends, his privacy, the rain—he even missed the humidity. But especially, he missed Emma Lee.

From the top drawer of the bureau Patrick extracted a manila envelope and removed the contents. He taped a photo of Emma Lee and David to the wall above the bed, along with four of the crayon "masterpieces" that David had made for him last Saturday. Then he slid his lean, muscular, blue-jeaned body into the small chair; his long legs barely fit under the desk. He pulled out a pad of paper and a pen and began writing.

Dear Emma Lee, Washington State is hot and dusty right now and I've been busy trying to get my sister's house repaired.

He wrote for several more minutes, then stopped. There was so much to tell her. His plane trip, the countryside, Peggy's condition, his sadness for his sister, finding a home for Joshua: it was way too much for one letter.

The last time he talked about his sister to Emma Lee they were on the bus, riding home from work together. "My sister is sick, so I'm going to go help her," he had said. That afternoon, Emma Lee had been kind and compassionate; she had called him a good man. A good man! His throat constricted, as if someone yanked a chain around it. He wished he could be *her* good man. He wished he could kiss her right now.

"Stop it!" he scolded. "It's useless to go there."

The radio announcer began the news. "Yesterday Alaska Airlines Flight 1866 crashed into the side of a mountain near Juneau, Alaska, killing all 111 people on board."

He felt sorry for those killed and their families, but at least their demise was quick. Somehow that sounded good to him. He considered how easy it was for a person's life to crash into the side of a mountain, both literally and figuratively. As a matter of fact, his seemed to be headed straight for a mountain of sorrow, himself.

He suddenly realized how achy his whole body felt from the past three days' work and the morning's roofing job. He folded the letter, slid it into an envelope, and placed it in the desk drawer. He'd finish it later. Patrick sprawled onto the bed and felt his energy dissipate, as if the sheets were sucking vitality from his pores.

As he let his eyes fall shut, Patrick tried to forget Pittsburgh. He was trying to pump himself up to the task of caregiver, uncle, and handyman again, when Carole King's voice belted out a song and he was reminded of Emma Lee again. "It definately is too late to turn back," he grumbled to himself. "I *have* fallen in love." He would have called Emma Lee right then, but Peggy had no phone service.

"Get over yourself," he whispered. "Peggy and Joshua are the only people that matter right now. That's where I gotta focus."

Turning the radio off, Patrick let his eyes close again. It felt too hot to sleep, but fatigue tousled his thoughts and tripped his reason until sleep trounced consciousness and he tumbled into slumber. In his dream he was back in Pittsburgh riding on the bus. It was hot and stuffy and very dark. Out the window he could see the moon skittering through the clouds, serene and calm. For a minute, no one else was inside the bus, but suddenly, a man wearing doctor's scrubs stood before him. "Give me your money," the man demanded, brandishing a knife. As the man drew closer, Patrick tried to knock the knife away, but his arms felt paralyzed. He moaned and woke with his head pounding, sheets sticking to his sweaty skin.

A knock prompted him to sit up. "Come in," he croaked.

The bedroom door squeaked open and Joshua poked his head in. "Can we talk?" he asked.

Patrick said, "Yeah, sure." He patted the edge of the bed.

"Don't want to live with Ricky and Bobby. Why can't I live with you?"

Patrick liked kids, but he didn't see himself as parenting material. He loved his privacy, his carefree lifestyle, the ability to stay late at work or stop at the bar on his way home from work. Still, he knew what losing a parent felt like and he was sorry for his nephew. He wrapped his arm around the boy and sat in silence, perplexed as to what to say or do. Finally he said, "I … know this is tough, Joshua. But Carol knows how to be a mother, and Bobby and Ricky will get used to you. Someday you'll think of them like brothers and you'll be glad to know them. Trust me. City life is a whole different world. Please *try* to get along with them—for your mother. For me."

Joshua shook his head several times, while tears slipped down his face.

Patrick let his gaze wander out the window to the yard. Three black and white magpies cackled and squawked and scolded as they fought for bits of food from the mulch pile. The birds' long, shiny blue-black tail feathers glistened in the sun like oil on water. One bird grabbed a chunk of stale bread and bounded away. The others chased, but in the end returned to the mulch for their own morsels.

Turning back to Joshua, Patrick pointed to the birds. "That's how life is, Joshua. We have to learn to do things we don't want to do. Hard stuff. Sometimes things get taken from us. Sometimes we can change that, but sometimes we can't. And when we can't, we have to buck up and learn to live with it."

Joshua scrunched his nose. He wiped his face with the back of his hand and pursed his lips into a pout. "But that's not fair," he wailed.

"You got that right," Patrick mumbled. "Life sure isn't fair." He pulled on his shirt and stood. "But we still have to live it." He took one of Joshua's hands. "Come on. Break's done and we have company."

7.

Three River's Chemical performs pesticide testing on animals, plants, and insects in laboratories scattered throughout this huge complex. The one I am assigned to—Botany—had been carved from a storage room back in 1947, at the mandate of the newly-passed Federal Insecticide, Fungicide, and Rodenticide Act. That was twenty-five years ago; I was one year old. To the chagrin of all us employees who work here, few changes have been made since.

Hiram Eisenbaum, my laboratory assistant, shuffles out of the locker room and plops onto the bench. His grey hair sticks out from the side of his mostly-bald head. Horn-rimmed glasses perch low on his nose. Mostly, I notice his fat belly drooping over his white paper shorts and hairy legs below them. No one looks good in paper underwear I decide, but Hiram looks especially dreadful—like a naked Tweedle Dum.

I try not to look at him and instead stare at the overalls. "Hi, Hiram. How's it going?"

He mumbles, "Uh, fine."

The first time I entered this lab was two weeks ago for my orientation. Patrick had changed his clothes first and instructed me how to do it, referring to the paper underwear as "modesty clothing." When I stepped out of the locker room wearing that paper, though, I felt far from modest. Arms crossed in front of my breasts for as much coverage as I could get, I said, "Nice duds. Kind of chilly, though, even in summer. And what's the deal with sharing the shower? It's nuts."

"Yeah, I've been pressuring the company to remodel this place for months, but as you can tell, it hasn't happened yet." He pointed to the shelf labels. "The overalls are stored by size. I'm guessing you're a small."

I shrugged on my overalls, and we laughed about how huge even the small size was on me. After getting instructions about taping, tanks, masks, and air locks, I thought Patrick was one of the nicest men I ever worked with.

Since then, that feeling of vulnerability, of being naked, hasn't gone away, but I've learned to live with it, and sometimes, I can ignore my embarrassment—almost.

As I drag on my overalls, Hiram and I talk a few moments about the weather and the Pittsburgh Pirates. Then I get down to business. "I've got an appointment with someone from the EPA next Thursday, and the lack of private dressing rooms for women is high on my list of complaints. But something else is going on here, something bigger, maybe even something illegal, and I think it involves Dr. Baxter. You've been here twenty years, right? Got any information you'd like the folks down at the EPA to know about him or anything else?"

Hiram's eyes widen and he places a finger against his lips. His nostrils flair as he turns the dial of the intercom until it clicks. Then he scans the room as if he's expecting someone to jump out from behind the bench with a hatchet.

"What are you thinking, speaking so plain with that intercom on? Downright foolish. There's a lot I could tell you, but we could both ..." He scans the tiny changing area again. "Look, I've got a family to feed, so leave me out of this." He motions with his head. "Time to get to work."

I'm disappointed he's not talking, but his refusal to help won't stop me.

We enter the air lock, wait for it to seal and open into the lab, and step into the deadly air. The lab is crowded, so I have to duck to avoid the pipes that zigzag across the ceiling, some so low that I could hit my head on them if I'm not careful. Shelving, bags of potting soil, and tall stacks of clay pots block my path as I weave my way to my work bench. Another thing I'll mention to the EPA—clogged workspace.

Though the company says I'm protected inside the lab by the gear I wear, outside in the "fresh" air, no one can avoid the pesticide odors. Rachel Carson's book, *Silent Spring,* has opened my eyes to the dangers that these chemicals pose to my health. If every worker here read it, I'm convinced we'd all quit our jobs. My resolve hardens: EPA and a new job, in that order.

Hiram shuffles to the potting bench where he's filling pots with soil, and planting seeds for our next project. I go the opposite direction, to shelves lined with deadly chemicals. The hiss of my air tank reminds me again how dependent I am here on the tank and the integrity of my protective clothing; I feel my soul grow sour and clot like milk left on a counter too long.

Today I'll perform two different tasks. First, I'll construct a new sample trial. When I arrive at my station, I remove the 2,4-Dichlorophenoxyacetic acid, (commonly called 2, 4-D) from the cabinet. I secure the pesticide container on the work table, open it, and extract one milliliter of 2, 4-D with an automatic pipette. Then, sliding the tip of the pipette into the top of a jug of water, I let the pesticide slip into it. This makes a dilution of one in 1,000. From that I make greater and greater dilutions up to one in five million. I distribute five milliliters of each dilution into pots containing one plant each, and place them under the grow light.

For the second task, I inspect the plants that were treated several days ago with permethrin. I'll measure the height and width of each leaf, note which plants still thrive and which are wilted, and record the results.

As I pick up the second pot, I hear what sounds like the air lock opening. If only that were Patrick coming in. But most likely, Hiram's leaving for some reason. A stack of pots obstruct my view so I look to the air lock. I can't see that, either, so I shrug and go back to work.

As I reach across the table to replace the measured plant back under the grow lights, I remember how Patrick called me the Pillsbury Dough Girl every time I complained about my suit. I smile. Oh, how I miss his him. For a brief moment, instead of being in the tight quarters of a laboratory, I'm in Patrick's apartment, letting him kiss me. I shut my eyes and smile at the thought, wishing I could talk to him right now, wishing he'd call me.

I grab the tray of pots and straighten.

Whack!

I OPEN MY eyes and rub the back of my head.

"Ow. My head ... ow!" I look around. "How'd I get ...?" Like bobbing balloons, faces of two people come into view: Hiram Eisenbaum ... and Dr. Baxter.

"Oh, thank God you're all right."

"W-what happened?" I ask.

Hiram says, "You hit your head and blacked out. I was so worried. You've been out thirty minutes already. Dr. Baxter and I—we dragged you out. And he ... ." He blushes. "Someone had to clean you up. I went to get the EMTs and show them how to get down here. Don't think you got any chemical contamination though. The ambulance crew is right outside, waiting for you."

I push up on my elbows and notice that my hair's wet and I'm wearing my regular underwear, blouse and skirt, but no stockings, shoes, or slip. I don't recall removing my protective clothing, taking a shower, or getting dressed. Beyond the sound of the air lock opening and closing, my only memory is wishing Patrick had come in.

"Good thing I came in to check on you, or who knows how long you'd have lain there. They'll be putting you in the ambulance from here," Dr. Baxter says.

"I d-don't need an ambulance. I'm f-fine. Just a headache, that's all."

I cram my feet into my shoes and try to rise. I make it only half-way up before crumbling back to the floor. "Guess I'm dizzier than I thought."

Dr. Baxter squats next to me and drapes my arm over his shoulder. His lips tighten into a thin smile as he wraps one hand around my waist and rises, lifting me to my feet. I feel dizzier now that I'm upright. But with Dr. Baxter's help, I stumble out of the changing area and into the hallway. There, the paramedic wheels the stretcher up next to me and says, "Let me help you onto the gurney, ma'am."

I wave him away. My southern accent grows stronger as I hear myself say, "Fuh heaven's sake, I'm all right. Ah need a little r-rest, that's all."

"We're required to take anyone who's been unconscious to the ER. Standard procedure."

I take a small step to the wheeled bed. I grab Hiram's arm. "Please. Ask Katrina Kowalski ... to pick up my son from day-care after work. David knows her ..."

I rock unsteadily and close my eyes. "And ... .he'll ... be ..."

Leonard Baxter and the EMT catch me as my knees collapse.

8.

David bounced slowly on Flicker, Maria's plastic palomino horse, waiting for his mother to arrive. All day he'd been planning his surprise. Yesterday he still couldn't tie his shoes even after days of practice. But today, like magic, his fingers could do it! Wait till he showed her. His tummy felt all tingly every time he thought of it.

When the doorbell rang, David jumped off the horse and grabbed his shoes. Grinning, he squeezed his eyes shut and listened to the footsteps come down the hallway. When they entered the room, his grin widened so much that his back teeth showed. Mom would be hugging him any moment.

"Time to go home, David," Maria said.

He opened his eyes. Instead of Mommy, that long-haired lady—the one who watched him one day when Mom had to work—entered the room. She had a smile pasted on her face, but she didn't look happy.

Disappointed, he put his shoes down. Maybe Mom was behind them and he hadn't noticed.

The woman said, "I'm Katrina. Remember me?"

"Uh huh." He peered around her and when he didn't see his mom, he raced down the hallway. After checking the kitchen and living room, he returned to the playroom. "Where is she?"

"She got hurt at work. They might keep her in the hospital overnight, but don't worry, your mom will be fine. She asked me to take you to my house for dinner. Maybe even a sleep-over. Doesn't that sound like fun?"

David stared at the wall. His enthusiasm for bow-tying disappeared like his toy soldier that Maria vacuumed into her big loud Hoover. Then he remembered last time he stayed with this lady. She had let him sit on her couch and watch cartoons all morning. He wasn't usually allowed to do that, so that had been okay—for a while. After lunch, his legs had felt jumpy and his body wouldn't sit still anymore, so he had asked to go outside to play. "No," she had said. "My apartment doesn't have a playground."

"Then let's go find one," he replied.

Climbing back on the rocking horse, David rocked back and forth, faster and faster, until the frame jumped off the floor with each bounce. Mommy always put on her tennis shoes and took him outside whenever he wanted to go. But not Katrina. The day he was with her, she had mumbled something like 'they won't catch me dead,' whatever that meant. Then she took him to the *mall*. She tried on clothes; he had crawled under the racks and got scolded for it the whole time. No, he wasn't up for *that* again.

He stopped rocking abruptly. "I want to go home with Mommy, not you."

Maria said, "I know this is hard for you, but it won't be for long. Don't worry; your mom will be fine."

They kept saying that: "*Your mom will be fine.*" He knew that meant something was terribly wrong.

His heart beat so hard it felt like it might jump right out through is ribs. He placed one hand over it to make it stop, but it kept pounding.

"Can't I stay with you, Maria?" he begged. "Please." David grabbed the horse handles and started bouncing again, slower now. The springs emitted a comforting squeak, squeak, squeak, squeak.

Maria shook her head. "No honey. I'm sorry but it has to be this way."

David breathed air deep into his lungs and scrunched his mouth. He stared at Katrina, then finally said, "We don't have to go shopping again, do we?"

Katrina's smile looked like Mommy's when she wanted to take him to the dentist. "Not this time. Do you like hot dogs?"

He wished he could put on the play boxing gloves and sock somebody, or jump into the space shoes and bounce all the way to the hospital and find Mom. But he knew there was no escape; he'd have to go with this lady.

9.

Leonard Baxter's breathing grew shallow and labored; coming here wasn't easy. As he stepped into the elevator, his mind returned to the night his wife died five years ago. He had brought her in to the emergency room because she couldn't breathe, thinking the medical profession could help her. What a joke. He had spent over thirty hours in the emergency room with her, waiting and hoping.

"Listen to me," he had demanded to the nurse. "I know what she needs."

The nurse hadn't listened. She pushed him aside and barked, "Doctor Mandela will be here shortly. In the meantime, please Let. Us. Do. Our. Job."

Irene's eyes had looked as if she was gazing through him and into eternity. Recalling that look had frightened him for years after. When she died, he blamed that nurse mostly, but the hospital was at fault, too. And the doctor. He blamed everyone involved. Like a pelican scooping two fish from the ocean at once, this hospital had consumed one person's life and another person's purpose (his) in one swoop. Leonard clenched both fists as he recalled how disrespectfully he had been treated. And how alone he felt ever since. He would never have returned to this place if it wasn't for a good reason. And Emma Lee's internment here was the best reason.

When he got to her room, Leonard was disappointed to see that her head no longer carried those beautiful black curls. And those once-shapely cheeks looked thin and gaunt. Was the hospital ignoring her the way they ignored Irene? Most likely. Good thing he was here.

When she moaned and opened her eyes, he took her hand in his. Obviously she awakened for him. Perhaps it was a sign. Leonard moved closer.

I LINGER IN that velvety space between sleep and wakefulness, wondering if I'm dreaming, refusing to give in to consciousness. But it's as relentless as a door-to-door salesman. Sounds start to register: a steady fluorescent buzz from overhead; a regular bleep-bleep to my left; the rumble of wheels disappearing in the distance. Then smells—creamed corn mixed with alcohol, cherry Jell-O, adhesive tape, iodine. Suddenly, my brain feels dissected, like road kill shredded by buzzards.

This is no dream.

A moan escapes and I try to open my eyes, but they refuse to obey.

Someone touches my shoulder.

Disconnected snippets flake through my consciousness like parade ticker tape. The Lab. Pain! David. Masked men hovering, staring. David.

My eyes flutter open. Next to my bed, a cart holds a pitcher and a glass of ice. A large needle is held prisoner inside a vein on the back of my left hand with tape.

Must be in a hospital, but have no memory of an injury, of coming here, of surgery. I concentrate; quiz myself. My name? After a few seconds it comes to me. Emma Lee Dubois. At least I remember that.

Where am I? I don't know. Did I ever know? I struggle to make my brain work, but it's as if the grey matter has developed holes like a mine field where thoughts fall into deep pits and can't climb back out.

I remember that I have an apartment. An apartment with olive green shag carpet. And a floral sofa. A bedroom window that looks out to the boulevard. I know that much.

Anything else?

I think I live in Pittsburgh; not the South anymore.

Do I work at a chemical factory? I think so. Yes.

I breathe in deeply. Perhaps my memory needs priming, like a pump.

Where am I? No idea. I knew a moment ago, I'm sure. At least, I think I'm sure. My optimism sags.

I force my eyelids open for a moment again. In that scrap of time, I catch a snapshot glimpse of a man on my right, staring at me.

"Ah, you're awake," the man says. "It's me, Leonard."

"Who ...?"

"Leonard."

"Don't ... re-remember."

"That's okay. I'll help you. I'm your boss from work ... And ...

He's quiet for a few moments. "We're dating."

Now I'm really confused. I didn't think I was dating anyone. But that doesn't matter. I want to know how David is, what happened to me. Where I am. Words congeal and start sliding to my mouth, but the lips refuse to obey. All that ekes out is, "Daa ...

The man pats my un-needled hand. "No need to talk, my love. You hit your head at work this morning and I saved you. Got you out of the deadly chemicals and called the paramedics, who brought you here. Now you're in Suburban General Hospital and I'm going to ensure they take good care of you. When you get out, I'll be here for you." He pats my hand again. "Relax and don't worry. You can count on me."

I want to understand what he said but it makes no sense; I drift back to sleep.

As Emma Lee's breathing deepened back into drugged sleep, Leonard continued to hold her hand. He loved staring into her beautiful face, bruises and all. He could do so much for this lovely woman: provide for her, give her medicines, take her to doctor's appointments, whatever she needed. It would be grand. He hoped she was wounded enough to let him.

Touching her sent chills down his spine as he recalled how his soapy hands had caressed her shapely legs, flat tummy, and those wonderfully round, young breasts that very morning. It had been so long since he felt a body like that. And he had had her all to himself for a few minutes. If he played his cards right, it might be possible for him to enjoy that more often. Taking a chance she wouldn't know any better, he had added, "And we're dating." And she bought it!

As her breathing deepened back into drugged sleep, a fit-looking young Oriental man carrying a clipboard stepped into the room. His dark, straight hair hung in his eyes. A white lab coat covered his shirt and checkered bell-bottomed pants. Doctors got younger every day, it seemed. Leonard didn't like him or his haircut.

"How's she doing, doctor?" Leonard asked.

The man didn't look up. He said, "I'm not a doctor. You her relative?"

"Her boss and ... ah, and ... boyfriend, Dr. Leonard Baxter. When will she be released?"

The man brushed his hair from his forehead and raised his brows. He ran his eyes up and down Leonard. "Boyfriend, huh?" His attention returned to the chart where he added a few notes. Then he said, "Her doctor decides when she goes home. I'm Michael Yamada, her occupational therapist."

"What's her prognosis?"

When the man hesitated, Leonard continued, "Look, she hasn't got any family, so I'm probably the one who will bring her to see you. As her boyfriend and care giver, I have a right to know."

"I suppose so. Apparently, her injury caused brain trauma. We aren't sure to what extent, yet. But when she gets out, she'll probably need nursing care and therapy for an extended time. It won't be easy on her ... or you."

From the year he spent caring for his ill wife, Leonard had grown familiar with care of all sorts, and he loved it. Having the life of another person in his hands gave him a sense of purpose and power found nowhere else. He said, "I understand. And I'm willing to help in any way I can."

"Then we'll probably be seeing a lot of one another. I'll keep you in the loop."

After Michael Yamada finished his work and left the room, Leonard allowed himself another smile. Emma Lee's injury was good two times over for him. First, in spite of her prior protests, he might get to date her after all. Second, Emma Lee couldn't report him or the company to the EPA like she had threatened. As far as he was concerned, it was a win-win situation.

Leonard felt invigorated, as if he'd reversed fifteen years of aging. Perhaps hospitals weren't so bad after all.

Grinning, he left with an extra bounce in his stride.

10.

Katrina awoke feeling touchy and irritated, like her psyche had been scrubbed with steel wool. She slapped on lipstick and wrapped an elastic band around her long brown locks. It wasn't her best look, but it was quick. Then she dressed David and delivered him to day-care.

In the last two days, between making dinner for the boy and herself, reading a story before bedtime, and giving the child a bath, Katrina had felt exhausted. Now she noticed a run in her stocking; she rolled her eyes and groaned. This could be a bad day.

Shortly after Katrina sat at her desk, the Human Resources manager entered the building and an idea struck. She'd make H.R. deal with this.

Tap, tap! She opened Nancy Daugherty's office door and said, "I've got a *huge* problem that you've got to fix."

"What's up?"

Katrina tented her fingers together in front of her chin and said, "When Emma Lee left in the ambulance I promised I'd take care of her son. I thought that would be a few hours, overnight, tops. It's not that I don't want to help. But three hours would have been enough and it's been three days." She pressed a hand against her chest.

Nancy nodded and tapped her pencil on the desk. "Yeah, I know what you mean. I've got three kids of my own."

"I need you to find someone else to take over."

"Makes sense. I think we can find some relative who could keep him."

"That's what I was hoping."

Nancy opened a file drawer and pulled out a folder labeled "Dubois, Emma Lee." She set it on the edge of her desk and tapped it with an un-lacquered, ragged nail. "I'll get on this right away. Hopefully you'll know something before you leave tonight."

Katrina smiled. "Thanks. You're a peach."

At two p.m. Nancy appeared at Katrina's office.

"You're early. What'd you find out?" Katrina said.

Nancy slid into the orange plastic chair next to her desk. "Emma Lee designated Patrick Kilkenny as her emergency contact, but when he left town, she asked H.R. to remove his name. Here's the bad news: she had the paperwork, but didn't get around to listing anyone else yet."

Katrina's mouth dropped open and she shrieked, "What? You mean Emma Lee doesn't have a mother or father or ex-husband somewhere?" Her voice grew even louder and strident. "There's no one who can take that kid?"

"Geeze, Katrina. Calm down. I don't know. I tried to call Emma Lee at the hospital, but got no answer. Then I talked with David's baby-sitter, Maria. She said she had overnight guests for the next two weeks, and didn't have a place for the boy to sleep. I even tried contacting Patrick, but couldn't find any number or address where he could be reached. Don't worry. I'll stop by the hospital tonight and talk to Emma Lee personally. She'll know someone, I'm sure."

Katrina scowled and crossed one long leg over the other, careful to hide her stocking run. "And what if she's unconscious; what if she dies?"

"If Emma Lee can't designate another guardian, Dr. Baxter said he'd figure something out. You won't have to keep him much longer." Nancy raised her shoulders and turned her palms upward. "Do you think you could keep him one more evening? At least until I talk to Emma Lee?"

Katrina's gaze darted around the room. She pushed her desk chair backwards, stood, and stared out the window. When she finally dropped back into her seat, she shrugged, her earlier enthusiasm had vanished. "Guess I'm stuck. But after work I'm going with you to the hospital. So I can get it settled once and for all."

AT FIVE-FIFTEEN, Katrina followed Nancy into Emma Lee's hospital room. Odors of disinfectant, bodily fluids, and bad food wafted through the air. When they reached Emma Lee's bed, Katrina cringed at the sight of her co-worker. The skin beneath the wounded woman's closed eyes was bruised deep purple and green, and the rest of her face looked grey. Only her determination to get rid of David kept Katrina in the room.

The women sat silent for a few moments listening to the blip of the heart monitor and the hum of the fluorescent lighting.

Nancy finally whispered, "I hate to disturb her."

"We have to," Katrina said.

Nancy pulled a chair close to the bed, patted Emma Lee's hand, and whispered, "Emma Lee? Can you hear me?"

Emma Lee moaned, "Hmm?"

"Sorry to wake you, but I need help. It's about David."

Emma Lee turned her head and mumbled, "David …?" Her eyes opened for a second. "Is he … here?"

Katrina moved closer to the bed. "No, he's not allowed in the hospital. But ..."

Nancy interrupted. "David is fine, Emma Lee, and staying with Katrina in the evenings." She rolled her ring around her finger. "We need another place for him, though. Do you have a friend or a neighbor or relative—anyone who could take David until you get out of the hospital?"

"David?" Emma Lee said again. "H-how's my boy? Where ... is he?"

Nancy took Emma Lee's hand in hers. "He's fine, staying with Katrina," she said again. "But we need someone to help care for him. Is there anyone you can think of?" she asked again.

"Who's Katrina?" Emma Lee said.

The door to Emma Lee's room swung open and a tall woman wearing a crucifix on a chain around her neck stepped in. Focused on her clipboard, she turned the page and said, "Hey, Emma Lee."

When she looked up she said, "Oops, I'm sorry. I didn't notice you ladies were here. I'll come back later."

Nancy rose to her feet. "No, please, come in."

The woman set her Bible on the side table and extended her hand. "I'm Sister Martha Lenzner, the hospital chaplain. Been checking in on Emma Lee each day since she arrived." She winked and smiled. "Making sure that the nurses and doctors are doing their jobs right."

Nancy took Sister Martha's hand, glanced at Emma Lee, then back at the nun. "I am *so* glad to meet you. Listen, we're in a huge bind and maybe you can help. I'm Nancy Daugherty, the Human Resources rep from Emma Lee's company, and this is Katrina Kowalski. She's been watching Emma Lee's son, David, after work."

"Temporarily," Katrina added.

Sister Martha said, "Nice to meet you both. So what seems to be the problem?"

"Katrina can't keep the boy any longer, and Emma Lee has no emergency contact. We need someone to take David for a few days until she gets released from the hospital." Nancy dropped her voice to a whisper, "We thought Emma Lee would be able to give us some ideas, but I can tell that isn't going to happen. Any chance you know her family members, friends, anyone who could take David for a few days?"

Sister Martha pursed her lips. After a few moments she said, "You two are the first visitors she's had, as far as I know. So I don't think she's got family nearby. But as the Bible says, for those who love God, all things work together for good. And us meeting might fit that description. I have to ask Mother Superior first, but I'm fairly sure the boy can stay with us until Miss Dubois is released."

"Us? You mean with ... Sisters?"

Sr. Martha chuckled. "Yes. Although we have given our lives to God, we still know how to care for children. I'm sure we'd be able to keep him a few days."

"That would be great," Katrina said, clapping her hands together.

Sister Martha wrote something on a piece of notebook paper and handed it to Katrina. "Here's the convent phone number. Call me tonight after seven; I should have an answer by then."

Stunned, yet pleased, Katrina felt her shoulders relax and her breathing slow down. "You're a life saver, Sister."

A grinning Nancy gushed, "Oh, yes, thank you! You don't know how much this helps." To Emma Lee she asked, "Is it all right with you if David goes to stay with the sisters?"

But Emma Lee had drifted back into sleep.

11.

Down the hallway, a window air conditioner kept the living room tolerably cool. But in his bedroom, a single pane of plate glass, old venetian blinds, and thin drapes provided meager protection from the relentless sun and obstinate dusty winds. This morning it was early enough that the open window provided a slight breeze. From the desk drawer, Patrick extracted the letter he had started the day before, and began to write.

September 6, 1971 – Was too busy yesterday to finish this, but it will be in the mail to you today. Peggy seems to grow weaker moment by moment. This morning she ate a few bites and didn't even have the energy to get dressed. I want to force her to dress, to eat, so I don't have to admit how sick she is. But I know it's futile.

Patrick set his pen down for a minute and stared out the window. He was reminded of a day back when he was ten, when his sister had made beef barley soup for dinner. Those little white lumps seemed unfriendly, like tiny eyes staring at him. She had said, "You have to eat ten bites, same as your age." Both he and the untouched soup sat at the table until bedtime. Now, eating wasn't a chore, it was a luxury, one he wished he could give his sister.

He picked up his pen again.

She's losing more muscle use every day; I know she won't last much longer. It makes me so sad. What will her son do without her? What will I do when she's gone? I don't know.

Last year, before he knew his sister was ill, Patrick had seen the hit movie, *Love Story*. Although it was heart-wrenching and (he hated to admit) brought him to tears, he had liked the fact that the film was true to life; the heroine didn't receive any miraculous cure, she died. But now that he was living a story much like that, he wished he could rewrite the script.

So much of himself was tied to his relationship with her. She had been his anchor, his surrogate parent, the person who helped him balance his life. Who would he be without his sister? He didn't know. He thought about the grief, settling the estate, planning and attending the wake, saying goodbye to Joshua, and flying home alone. All of that sounded impossible. Simply impossible.

Patrick returned to the letter a third time.

It breaks my heart to watch her fade away. I feel so helpless.

His stomach clenched as a tear slipped down his cheek and left a wet stain on the page.

I miss riding the bus to work with you; I even miss working in that crazy lab with you. Mostly I miss you, that great accent of yours, and your optimistic outlook on life. I could use some of that right now. If you get a moment, write me a postcard. Or let me know when it's best to contact you. Without a phone, it's as if we're disconnected from the whole world. But today I'm going to call you from town when I get there.

His sadness grew sumo-wrestler sized, threw what hope he had to the ground, and threatened to choke him, so he stuffed the letter into the envelope, added a stamp, then went to his sister's room.

"Hey, Sis, rise and shine." Patrick said. He pulled the drapes apart to admit dazzling morning sunshine. Although it was September, the sun promised another scorcher.

As Peggy opened her eyes, Patrick noticed that her skin looked as thin as rice paper, and her scrawny arms confirmed to him that she had no fat left on her body.

"I'll stay in my PJs," she said. "No energy to get dressed."

He helped her walk to the living room and settle on the couch. As he lifted the afghan to place over her, she said, "I'm okay for now. This heat turns out to be good for something."

"So what do you want for breakfast? The usual?"

"I'm not hungry," she said.

"You have to eat. I'll make something."

A few minutes later he returned from the kitchen carrying a cup of tea and a plate with one scrambled egg and a piece of toast.

She turned her face to the wall and grimaced. "I can't. Eggs smell nasty today." .

He speared a chunk of the egg onto the fork and held it near her mouth. "Please. One bite for me. You need protein."

She rolled her eyes. "Okay," she said. "Because you're my baby brother, and you asked *so* nicely." She opened her mouth and let him place the morsel in. After swallowing she grimaceed and shut her eyes for a moment. "Eating is torture and I'll be gone soon; why prolong the misery? Why bother?"

"Joshua needs you for a while longer, that's why. So he can get used to this adoption thing before you go. Now be good and swallow."

She flashed a mischievous grin. "Man, you've gotten pushy in your old age. 'Eat this! Do that!'"

Grateful for the mood change, he smiled back. "Darn right," he said. "Someone has to take charge. You've done it to me for years. Turnabout is fair play."

Peggy's laugh was thin-walled and short-lived, a bubble of energy that survived just long enough to float into the room and burst. She rested her head on the couch arm. "I never realized how much energy it takes to laugh," she said.

When the dishes were done, Patrick settled in the recliner with a cup of coffee. "I'm worried about you, Sis."

"I'm going to get tired, that's a given." She sat for several minutes in silence sipping her tea. She clasped her bony hands together and her gaze dropped to the floor. "I'm sorry to mess with your life like this, Patrick. Wish it was different."

He sat on the coffee table and took her hand in his. "Hey, I wouldn't have it any other way," he said. "I love you and want to be here."

"I have something I'd like to talk to you about, Patrick. Something serious. I've been thinking …"

At that moment, Joshua raced in the front door holding the fuzziest bird Patrick had ever seen.

"What the heck is that?" Patrick said. He walked to Joshua.

The boy held the animal out for them to see. Wild, white feathers adorned every part of it. "Mr. Macintyre next door said I could have Fluffy, if you say it's okay. He's called a Silky Bantam rooster."

Patrick's face took on a sly grin. "He looks more a beaked dandelion, or a pillow with all its feathers stuck on the outside."

"I think he's awesome. And he's really, really friendly. Can we keep him? Please?"

"Don't know why not," Peggy said

"I do," Patrick said with a wink to his sister. "He'll crow too early for this city boy." He pointed a thumb at himself and grinned. "A rooster's worse than an alarm clock. You can't reset him for a different time when you want to sleep in."

Joshua stuck his lip out in a pout.

Patrick pretended to punch him on the shoulder. "I'm joking, Josh. Of course you can keep Fluffy; your mom said so, and you know what she says goes. Besides, he's way cool. But put him outside before he poops on the carpet."

"Ew," Joshua held the chicken at arm's length. "He better not poop on me."

Josh trotted to the front door and let the rooster fly out of his arms. "Stay in the yard," he instructed. "You belong here now." Fluffy crowed and strutted off.

When the boy returned, Patrick said, "Hey, I'm off to town. Want to come along?"

Joshua sat next to his mother and slid his arm around her shoulders. "No. Mom might need me."

"Oh, go on, honey. I can get by on my own for a bit."

Joshua shook his head. "I'm staying here. I'll be outside with Fluffy till Patrick goes."

Patrick stood. "Suit yourself."

As the boy raced out the front door again, Patrick sat in the recliner. "You were saying?"

"Remember the parakeet I had when we were kids?"

"Sure do. Wasn't his name ... Petty ... Pokey ... something like that? "

"Petey. Remember how, when he got old and sick and he kept falling off his perch, you helped me?"

"If you call wringing his scrawny little neck because you couldn't do it help, then yes, I helped you."

"Exactly. And right now, I'm like the bird. I can't stay on my perch and get weaker every day. Can't even hold my cup any more. And I'm holding up your life. So I want you to promise that when I can't talk anymore, you'll suffocate me. Relieve me and everyone else out of this misery."

Patrick felt so shocked he couldn't speak. Then he shook his head. "I can't do that, Peggy. It's wrong."

"It would be more wrong to let me suffer."

"No, suffering is redemptive. It changes us for the better. And it's against my faith to kill someone."

"It's against charity to let me live. For the love of God, please help." Peggy clasped her bony hands together and her gaze dropped to the floor.

"No. You are not a burden to me. I love you and want to be here. Everything and everyone else can just wait."

WHEN PATRICK ARRIVED in town, he threw his letter to Emma Lee into a post box and drove straight to the church where he parked in the lot.

"Can I help you?" the receptionist asked when he entered the office. The sign on the young woman's desk said *Zoe Canter*. Her long blond ponytail bobbed as she spoke. Before he met Emma Lee, before death got in the way of life, Patrick might have been tempted to flirt with this pretty woman. Not today. Maybe he'd never flirt again.

"I'm Patrick Kilkenny and I need to talk to the priest," he said. He ran his fingers through his rust-red hair, noting how long it was getting.

"Fr. Willis is out right now." Zoe opened her appointment book. "He's free tomorrow afternoon between one and four, though. Will any of those times work?"

At that moment, the office door opened and a middle-aged man dressed in black walked in. His head was bald on top, surrounded by short hair on the sides, and his eyes looked tired. Still, his smile looked friendly enough.

"Well, here he is now," Zoe said with a grin. "Hi, Father. You're back early."

"Mrs. Shoemaker wasn't up for visitors today."

"This is Patrick Kilkenny. He was making an appointment to see you."

Fr. Willis took out a handkerchief and wiped his forehead, which was beaded with sweat. "Occupational hazard, wearing black no matter the weather." He wiped his hands on the cloth, too, then shook Patrick's hand. "Glad to meet you. I can see you now, if you like."

At that moment, the phone rang. After answering and listening for a moment, Zoe placed her hand over the phone receiver. "It's the bishop for you. Says it's important."

The priest looked at Patrick and shrugged. "Can you wait?"

"I have a phone call to make, too. I'll do that and come back."

"Great," Fr. Willis said, taking the receiver.

Unsure if he could even talk, let alone be coherent in a phone conversation, Patrick wondered if he should call Emma Lee today. But he had to. This might be his only opportunity for a while. He drove to the grocery store parking lot, entered the phone booth, and dialed the operator. After several seconds, he heard Emma Lee's phone ring: once, twice. He kept counting through ten. Perhaps she was in the bathroom, or in the middle of making dinner. The count grew to fifteen, then twenty with no answer. It was possible that she was delayed at work, missed the bus, or stopped at the park with David on the way home.

He hung up the phone, strolled down the sidewalk to the card store, purchased a few "missing you" cards, then returned to the phone booth and dialed again. This time he let it ring thirty times.

Still, no answer.

On Patrick's way back to the church, he imagined a starving Peggy gasping for breath, unable to move. How could he live with himself if he let her suffer for months that way, against her will? Then he imagined placing a pillow over her face, watching her writhe and struggle and eventually grow limp. He'd hate it more to live with that memory for the rest of his life. Information learned in ethics classes flooded back, reminding him that there was no way he could live with the guilt of killing his sister the rest of his life.

He reentered the church office with the canines of both shame and confusion clamped firmly onto his throat.

This time, the priest led Patrick directly into his office. When they were settled he said, "So what brings you in today?"

Patrick leaned forward in his chair and placed his head in his hands for a few seconds to collect his thoughts, then sat upright and exhaled. "My sister is dying." Patrick covered his face again. Thinking about his sister's request opened a gate in his heart that up to now, he'd been able to keep shut and locked. Behind it, despair snarled with teeth bared, like a big black Doberman. He was quiet for several minutes before he looked up. "Sorry this is taking so long. It's hard."

"Take your time," Fr. Willis said.

"She has cancer."

"Oh, I'm so sorry."

"But that's not ... . She asked me to ..." his words faded to a whisper. "I've loved her my whole life. I hate to see her suffer."

"Of course you do."

He dropped his head. "I don't mind the work. I came to care for her, arrange for my nephew's future, fix up the house. But it's hard to watch her waste away, hear her moans, and see that look in her eyes, the one that challenges me day after day, week after week, to help. But I feel so helpless."

The priest closed his eyes. "Prayer is the best recourse righ now, Patrick. So keep praying, my son. Trust in God."

"Since I arrived, I pray every night.. Huh! Lot of good it does. I pray we'll find a sober, reformed Richard so Joshua can live with his father; I pray that Peggy will be cured; that Carol's boys will treat Joshua like a brother instead of an intruder. But so far, those prayers are unanswered on all counts."

"Have you tried praying for God's will on those issues?"

Patrick shook his head. "Don't know if I'm ready to do that yet."

"People die, Patrick. We can't stop that. What we can do is depend on God to be with us in the pain, to meld our suffering with that of our Savior, Jesus Christ."

"I believe that, but my sister? She doesn't. And she won't listen to me. Would you be able to visit her sometime, give her last rites if she'll let you? She used to believe."

"I'd be happy to." He checked his calendar. "How about tomorrow afternoon?"

As he left the church office this second time, Patrick's leg muscles seemed to soften like candle wax in hot sun, and he wobbled as he climbed into the truck. Sticking the key into the ignition was difficult, driving even more so. Why didn't he tell the priest what Peggy had asked? He felt like such a fake.

12.

The back of my head pulses in pain with each heart beat. I squint from the too-bright light that streams through the bedroom window. I should get dressed, wake David, and get him ready for daycare; I'll have to catch the bus for work soon. At least, I think I do. If it's not Saturday or Sunday. But when I turn to check my alarm clock, I can't find it in the pile of medicine bottles and papers that cover the night stand. I don't understand. I didn't put those bottles there, did I?

I'm reminded of a fall morning, long ago in South Carolina. I was driving to work in dense fog. Cars solidified almost like magic from the mist as they passed, then vaporized seconds later. Everything more than ten feet from me—houses, trees, yards—was invisible. Driving blind, I slowed the car to twenty miles per hour and crept along.

It's as if my life is surrounded by that same fog now, and my ability to see in any direction has compressed to almost nothing.

A tall, grey-haired man enters; he takes my hand. "I'll be leaving soon, my darling." He leads me into the living room. "Rest here on the couch." He places a capsule in my right hand, a glass of water into my left. "Take this now. Before you forget."

I want to ask, *What have you given me? Who are you? What's wrong with me?* Instead, I hear myself say, "Okay," and I swallow the pill.

He squats to tie his shiny wing tips. When he stands again, he props fists on hips and spreads his legs wide. I don't know why, but seeing him stand this way frightens me. My heart picks up speed until its pounding double time. I tremble and collapse onto the couch.

The man stuffs a few papers into his briefcase and peers into the hall mirror. His manicured fingers cinch the knot of his fashionable tie then give his already-smooth, perfectly styled grey hair a once over with a comb. "I'll be at work."

"Does Patrick still work at the plant?" I ask.

As he dons his suit coat the man ignores my question and says, "Carla will drive you to occupational therapy this afternoon and I'll meet you there. I don't expect you to remember, of course. You never do. So I've left a note for her as usual. She should arrive about eight to make you breakfast. Sister Martha wants to see you tomorrow for a session again, though you seem fine to me."

His words float through the air like bubbles; their substance and meaning pop and vanish seconds after he speaks them.

The man continues, "I'll see you later."

"What about David? Should I take him … does he go to…day-care?" When I speak, my voice sounds squeaky and chopped.

"No. You and Carla watch him."

After the man leaves, I sit on the couch and close my eyes. It's as if I've turned on television in my mind. It warms up slowly and I am transported back ten years, when I was eighteen, to Father's funeral. I'm in a line of people filing past the casket. Each stops and bows, then moves on. When I get to the body, the skin looks leather-like; it sags and wrinkles. I touch his cold hand and grow heavy with sorrow, as if I'm carrying a knapsack full of rocks. Who will care for me now? How will I manage to survive? God failed me, left me alone to fend for myself. My faith died when Father did.

I hear the sound of Gordon's voice before I see him. "Why didn't you come with me?" Now his face appears: friendly, farmer-boy strong, pragmatic. If he were here, he'd help me. I know it. But he's in Africa. Helping others, not me. Gone.

Now dark red hair; my breathing quickens. It's Patrick! He was so kind to David, to me. I could have grown to love him. Where is he? Why hasn't he called me? Or written? Or come to visit? Or … has he?

"I'll be back. Please wait. Wait," he says.

"I can't wait. I need you now," I mumble.

New images burst like photographic flashcubes.

Flash! My childhood home in South Carolina, orange as fire in the setting sunlight.

Flash! Long shadows from the canopy of trees, those beautiful old weeping willows and live oaks, swaying in the breeze.

Flash! Pink blossom petals after a frost, covering the walk like tinted snow.

Flash! Mother yelling at Father, suitcase in hand, leaving. Tears. Clinging. Desperation. Gordon packing. Patrick packing. All of them packing. Leaving and not coming back. The pain of all that loss pulses like a huge, infected splinter.

David slips into the room and leaps onto the couch next to me. He wraps both arms around my shoulders, engulfing me in his embrace, and kisses my cheek.

"Hi Mommy. I'm hungry. Need some break-est."

With my lovable, reliable boy next to me, it's easy to forget my sorrow. As a matter of fact, the thoughts that played in my head before he arrived have already sublimed away. I pat his knee. "Hi, David. How's my boy?"

At that moment the doorbell rings. "Who could that be?" I ask.

"It's Carla, Mom. She comes every day when Len-old leaves. Don't you remember?" He hops down and skips to the door.

I rub my hand over my aching head and close my eyes. "No," I whisper. "I don't remember anything."

When Carla enters the living room, she says, "Hi Emma Lee. I'm your nurse, Carla. I'll get breakfast for you and David, then maybe we can go for a walk." She checks a piece of paper the counter. "Oh, I see you have an appointment with your occupational therapist today. We'll make sure you're ready."

"Why am I visiting an occupational therapist? What's wrong with me?"

The nurse pulls a chair up close to me and takes my hand in hers. She speaks slowly, with deliberate simplicity. "You hit your head at work a month ago, and have some memory loss. Your therapist is helping you regain basic skills."

"Oh," I say, overwhelmed. "How do I pay for him? For you?"

"You don't. Dr. Baxter pays my salary. And he pays for everything else, too—your electricity, rent, medical bills. You are *so* lucky. If he hadn't taken over, David would have been sent to the orphanage, and you'd probably be in a nursing home. Yes, you are one lucky woman indeed."

I don't feel lucky. I feel desolate and dejected. Words from an old song come to mind. *You are lost and gone forever, dreadful sorry, Clementine.*

PATRICK CINCHED THE last bracket against the gate frame and threw the socket wrench into his toolbox. The wind, impregnated with fine, brown dust, coated his sweaty bare chest with grit, making him look like he had rolled on a sandy beach. He didn't mind. The dirt here felt friendly compared to the black, industrial flecks that used to settle on his shoulders in Pittsburgh. Still, he should probably take a shower before the priest arrived. He stepped back and pushed the gate open and closed a few times. Satisfied, he snapped his toolbox shut. One more broken thing repaired. The outside of Peggy's house, at least, was beginning to look downright tidy.

At that moment a car came up the driveway. No time for that shower. He pulled on his T-shirt and grabbed his tool box. As he ambled toward the car, the word "*last*" rolled through his brain, over and over, like tumbleweed driven by the wind. It might be the *last* time she talked to a priest. Any day could be her *last* day on earth.

When the priest stepped out, Patrick wiped his hand on his jeans before he extended it. "Father Willis. Thanks for coming."

Inside, Patrick dropped the tools by the front door and introduced Joshua and his sister. Peggy waved a hand over her pajamas and smiled. Her threadbare voice whispered, "Sorry I'm not dressed. Is this a social call?"

"You're fine. Your brother asked me to drop in and talk with you. Perhaps give you last rites if you're up for it."

"Oh, he did, did he? Sneaky devil. He didn't mention it to me."

"Or we can just talk if you'd rather."

She scanned the room. "I haven't got enough energy to tidy up my house or my soul. But I don't mind talking." Motioning with both hands, she said, "You two. Skedaddle. Don't want you eavesdropping on the gory details of my wicked life."

"As if," Patrick said.

Outside, the wind died down, but now thick, dark clouds swirled overhead and the air felt heavy. In Pittsburgh Patrick would have predicted a downpour. But here, though lightning might flash and the wind might blow again, no rain would fall.

Joshua dug his bare toes into the dust and watched two magpies bicker over breakfast scraps meant for the rooster. Shielding his eyes from the sun, the boy scanned the yard for Fluffy. He found his rooster resting in a dusty depression under a bush.

"There you are," Joshua said, jogging across the yard. The boy scooped the rooster into his arms, and stroked its feathers. "Carol will let me take him to her house, won't she?"

Patrick lay in the sparse grass beneath the apricot tree, wove his fingers behind his head, and shut his eyes. A robin twittered from a branch above him. "Don't see why not. They have the space."

Still holding the chicken, Joshua squatted, picked a grass stem with seed head attached, and poked it between his front teeth. The rooster tried to peck at the bobbing stem and Joshua smiled. He set the rooster free and leaned against the tree trunk. "Mom will be in heaven soon." He wrapped his arms around his legs and stuck out his lower lip.

"Yeah, she's lucky."

"Lucky for her and God. Not for me."

"I know what it's like, Josh. My mom died when I was a kid, too."

"But you weren't alone; you had a big sister who took care of you. You had *Mom*."

"And you'll have Bobby and Ricky, and Carol."

"But I don't want to live with *them*." He jammed his fists into his cheeks and scowled.

Patrick sat up and wrapped an arm around Joshua's thin shoulders. "I know. I'm sorry you have to go through this."

The boy leaned his head on Patrick's shoulder. "Can't I live with you? Please?"

"I thought we settled this. Your life is here. My apartment is cramped and has no yard. I work all day so you'd have to go to daycare before and after school. And we certainly couldn't carry Fluffy across the country on an airplane."

"So you could get a job here, and we could live in this house, and I could keep Fluffy, and *not* live with Bobby and Ricky. *Please*."

Many things beckoned Patrick back to Pittsburgh: his good paying job, his friends and life in the city, familiarity, habit. Yes, he was attached to all those. But Emma Lee was most important. Even though he hadn't heard from her, she was somehow streaming hope and energy 3000 miles, all the way from Pittsburgh to Pasco. He was like a ship floundering on rocky shoals, and she was the lighthouse beam guiding him back to safety. Joshua's request to stay in Washington twisted his gut.

Two tears dropped from Joshua's cheeks. "I want Mom to live till I'm 100. Why does she have to die? Why?"

Patrick shook his head. "I don't think anyone can answer that question, kiddo."

The front door opened and the priest waved. "You can come in now," he called. She decided on Last Rites after all."

Joshua wiped away his tears as he and Patrick rose. "Please stay, Patrick. Please."

Talking about Pittsburgh had made Patrick long for the routine of his former life. Now, as he walked to the house with Joshua, it was as if the conversation lit an emotional fuse. Sorrow sparked and snapped from his feet upwards through his body and threatened to explode his anger like dynamite. His feet quit moving.

He wanted to rebel against everything: caring for Joshua, making repairs, even being polite and attentive to Peggy. Right now, he would derive immense satisfaction from taking the sledge hammer and smashing something huge like a wall, a window, or the neighbor's barn. It took every ounce of his will to force his feet to continue walking into the living room.

The priest opened his bag and removed several items including a white cloth, his prayer book, and a thick wooden crucifix. The front of the crucifix slid open to reveal a shallow, cross-shaped wooden box beneath it that held two wax candles and a tiny bottle of holy water. The box also had slots that held the candles and crucifix upright. Patrick fell into the recliner and Joshua sat on the floor.

During the last rites, Patrick couldn't focus. Why did life have to hurt so much? Why did his sister have to die? Why couldn't Joshua be happy with Carol and her family? Why, why, why? He was asking the very same questions that Joshua had, knowing the answers were unobtainable.

When the priest left, Joshua returned to the yard to play, so Patrick and Peggy were alone again.

"That was no random visit. You asked him to talk me out of it, didn't you?"

"Look, Peggy, I'm no saint, but I'm not a killer."

"I know." She hung her head. "It was wrong for me to ask. I had a long talk with Father Willis. He said that my suffering will help me get to heaven if I let it."

"Do you believe that?"

"I want to. And I don't have any other choice, do I?"

Noticing his toolbox near the front door, he wished it contained a tool that could fix this terrible brokenness he felt, but he knew such a thing didn't exist.

"We always have a choice," Patrick replied.

13.

Before waking Joshua for school, Patrick walked down the drive-way, carrying a letter. Although it was mid-October, the air was still short-sleeve warm. He was three feet from the mailbox when Carol's Ford drove up. When his cousin rolled down her window, Patrick stopped jogging. "Hey, Carol, you're here early. Where are the boys?" he asked.

"Zane takes them to school on his Friday off, remember? How's Peggy?"

"Fading. She could barely lift her head yesterday and hasn't eaten a thing in days. It won't be much longer."

Carol shook her head. "I'm so sorry." Perhaps to buoy the conversation, she pointed to the envelope in his hand. "So you're writing to Emma Lee again, I see. Has she ever written back? Even once since you got here?"

He stared at the ground and shrugged; speaking the words would make the truth too real.

A faint smile crossed Carol's lips. "You must have sent, what, like, thirty letters in the past two months?" She slapped the top of the car door with her palm. "Get a clue. She ain't interested in you, Pat, my boy."

"It's not like her to ignore me. All I can think is something happened—she lost her job, moved away—something. I can't quit writing until she tells me to."

Still, he blushed now to think how he had rambled on to Emma Lee about his deepest emotions: the pain of watching Peggy fade away, the struggles he had with Joshua and the adoption thing, and especially, how much he missed her. It was embarrassing to think about now. After a month or so, when Emma Lee still hadn't replied, he had lightened up on his letters' subject matter. In this one, for instance, he had written of last night's sunset crammed with deep purples and gold, how much he enjoyed his runs to the Columbia River on most mornings, and how interesting it was to see some new, large brown bird with a long bill in the yard. He had recounted the story of how the neighbor woman, Betty, stopped by to check on Peggy. When Patrick asked her about the bird, Betty pointed to one in the apple tree, and smiling like she was talking about a special grandchild, she said, "That big boy is a Flicker, our harbinger of Fall." Yes, his letters were almost chatty now, and much less personal.

Carol raised her eyebrows and Patrick knew by the look on her face she was going to give unwanted advice or pontificate, the way she was prone to do. "Ignoring your letters is her way to tell you she's not interested. Most people do that sort of thing. They don't tell it up front; instead they leave you guessing. And it's silly for you to keep hoping she'll respond. Anyone who'd ignore you this long isn't worth the effort." Carol blinked several times. "See you in the house."

She put the Fairlane in gear and continued up the driveway.

As Patrick opened the mailbox, Carol's words haunted him. Perhaps Emma Lee's silence *was* a message. He threw in the envelope with less enthusiasm than usual and reentered the house.

Both Patrick and Carol arrived on the porch as Joshua bolted out the screen door, still in his pajamas. "I checked on Mom. Something's wrong. Come on." He held the door open and beckoned for them to enter. They raced down the hallway together.

In Peggy's bedroom, Carol pulled open the drapes while Patrick checked his sister; school was forgotten. Peggy's slow and mournful moan tore Patrick's heart. As her lungs raked in air, he knew she'd be leaving the world soon. He was reminded of the picture he'd seen of an astronaut floating in space, attached to the space ship with a thin chord. Peggy's connection to the world was like that: thin, tenuous. He knew that astronauts were tethered well, but in Peggy's case the cord would soon break, and she'd drift into eternity.

Joshua dragged a chair closer to his mother and wrapped an arm around her skeletal body. "Is she going to die now, Uncle Patrick?"

His throat clogged by grief, it took effort for Patrick to squeeze out the words. "Yeah. Looks like it, sport. We need to let her."

He wet a washcloth and moistened his sister's lips; he placed a drop of morphine on her tongue. "Peggy," he said, "we know you're suffering. And we give you permission to go when you need to. We'll pray for you." He began the Hail Mary. Near the end of the prayer, his voice lowered and the words came slower. "Holy Mary, Mother of God, pray for us sinners, now … and at the hour … of our death, Amen."

At the word, *death*, Joshua hung his head and let the tears slide silently down his cheeks.

By noon, Peggy's breath changed. Her chest heaved in bursts: six shallow, a long pause, then five or six more short breaths, and a pause. The labored breathing lasted for several more hours until about four-thirty, when, after one arduous inhale, there were no more.

"I love you," Patrick whispered, patting Peggy's hand. "Struggle's over; go with God."

Carol rushed to the bed, dabbing her eyes with a handkerchief. Joshua laid his head on his mother's chest and cried. His grief sounded so sorrowful that Patrick could no longer speak. His own great childhood sadness from his mother's death—sorrow once thought to be gone forever—exploded into every crevice of his being. But this time, he didn't have the luxury of grieving for long. He was the one who had to comfort, arrange, care for others like Peggy had done for him when their mother died.

An hour later, after consoling Joshua and washing his sister's body, Patrick headed to the neighbor's house.

When Betty opened her screen door, Patrick said, "It's Peggy. She …" He wiped the tears from his cheek with the back of his hand. "She's passed on. Can I use your phone to call the funeral home and the priest?"

The woman placed a hand on her chest and her mouth dropped open. "Oh, I'm so sorry, Patrick. Please come in."

IN ALL, PEGGY had suffered six months before the cancer took her. She had grown so thin that there wasn't much of her left for the undertaker to remove. After Patrick answered all the questions and signed the papers, he led his nephew to the couch where they sat together.

Carol joined Patrick and Joshua in the living room. "I stripped the bed and washed the sheets." She cradled her head in her hands. After several more minutes, she said, "I have to talk to you both. I know it's not a good time …."

Patrick sighed. He knew they'd have to talk about Joshua and when he'd go to live with Carol's family. He hated to think he'd give the boy up now, after two months with him. But it had to be done. "You might as well talk. We have to discuss this sometime."

Carol picked at her cuticle. "Um, I have … I've got … well, there's a hitch."

"Spit it out, Carol. What are you saying?"

"Zane. He says we can't take Joshua no more. Says he'll be laid off come December and we don't have but a few hundred dollars saved, and with two kids already, one more would be a hardship."

She grimaced. "I hate to tell you this now. It's a bad day for bad news. But I thought you should know as soon as possible. So you can figure out what to do next and all. I'm so sorry, Patrick, Joshua. I'm so sorry." She pulled a tissue from the box and wiped her eyes. When she looked up, she must have noticed Patrick's wide-eyed expression. She lifted both shoulders and hands, and said, "I feel so bad, but what can I do? Zane made up his mind."

Patrick pressed his palms onto his eyelids. "This messes everything up, Carol."

Joshua sat upright, his face full of hope. "Now you *have* to stay here, Uncle Patrick, and take care of me."

Carol pulled a newspaper from her handbag and shoved it toward Patrick. "I saved yesterday's paper for you. The want-ads have a few chemistry jobs ... out at the Hanford Site mostly."

When Patrick moaned, Carol clicked her tongue. The decibel level of her voice increased and the tone rose, until she was almost screeching. "It wouldn't be the end of the world if you stayed here, you know."

"Really? Sure seems like it to me."

THEY DIDN'T HAVE much money, and few people knew Peggy, so the funeral mass was enough. Then Peggy's body was buried.

Two days later, Patrick drove to town for groceries, stamps, and a newspaper. Perhaps he would find work in town, stay for a while. His funds were drying up, so a paycheck might be helpful. But the headlines reported a layoff at Hanford. Government money was no longer available, the article said, and fifteen hundred people would lose their jobs. He tried several places, sent out resumes, but couldn't find anything.

Patrick didn't want to dwell on the sorrow or his loss; it was too painful. Besides, there was much to accomplish before returning to Pittsburgh. Making lists calmed him, gave him purpose. So he opened his notebook. But instead of recalling tasks he needed to accomplish, the memory of Peggy's death played through his mind for the thousandth time. He recalled how skeletal her hands, face, and body had grown, and how, as Peggy's health declined, he had barely left her side.

He grabbed pen and wrote: buy paint. Rent carpet cleaner. Put ad in paper for furniture. He knew chores would keep him occupied for months, and he was glad. It would keep his mind off the loss of Peggy, off the pain.

Patrick wished October 16th, 1971, could disappear from his memory, but knew it would be emblazoned there forever.

14.

Time warped for Patrick, as if he'd fallen, like Alice, down the Wonderland rabbit hole. Some days he spent what felt like several hours repairing wiring or plumbing, and filling out job applications, only to discover it still wasn't time to start dinner. He now had time to think, to grieve, to waste. And he hated it.

He tried to finish *Hawaii*, the book he started this trip with, but thoughts of his sister and the fragility of life crowded out the story line. Sometimes, he'd plow through several pages without remembering a thing he'd read. Other days he'd contemplate the importance of each moment, only to chastise himself for wasting time thinking about time.

The Monday before Christmas, after watching Joshua board the school bus, Patrick retreated to his room. He hadn't written to Emma Lee since the funeral, but now he felt ready to join the world of the living—at least in relation to her. First he'd write, then after grocery shopping, he'd call. There was so much he wanted to say. He'd tell her he called before, ask her to visit. Then, if she came, maybe he'd take her fishing, or even drive up to Lake Chelan for that boat ride to Stehekin. His spirits lifted.

The room was cold. Howling wind propelled frigid air through his single-paned window, creating a chilly current across his back.

He pulled on a sweater and sat at his desk. To keep himself from spending a fortune on the phone call, Patrick took pen in hand and began a letter.

December 20, 1971

Dear Emma Lee,

I'm planning on calling you this afternoon, but I wanted to explain on paper why I haven't written sooner. My sister died two months ago and it knocked me for a loop. Couldn't function for a while. It's crazy how every day I expect her to come walking in the front door. Like she was on vacation or something. I miss her teasing, her sense of humor. Her death ripped a piece of my heart out. When we didn't eat her famous pecan pie, (we didn't celebrate Thanksgiving this year) it hit me hard that she was gone for good. It's even tougher for Joshua, of course. The boy cries every night. Has for weeks. His grades have tanked but I'm stumped about how to help him.

When I came here, I wanted to grow wise, like King David in the Bible, and help people sort out the truth. I thought God wanted that for me, too. But that must have been my own ego talking, because I seem to be moving further from wisdom instead of toward it.

He stopped writing. As his gaze wandered out the window, he noticed how the ice pellets fell sideways now, littering the ground in white specks. He'd have to leave soon. The treads on Peggy's truck tires were worn so thin they provided very little traction anymore.

The doorbell rang, pulling Patrick from his revere.

Carol was already on the couch when he arrived in the living room. She held her gloves in one hand and a Tupperware container in the other.

"Hi, Patrick. I let myself in; hope you don't mind. The boys and I made some Christmas cookies yesterday and we wanted to share some with you and Josh."

He felt violated, her walking in like that. As he reached for the container, Patrick forced himself to stay polite and calm. Confrontation took too much energy.

"Thanks," he mumbled. To keep himself from complaining, Patrick opened the box and stuffed a green-iced tree cookie into his mouth. Carol wasn't the best of cooks, so he was pleasantly surprised by the buttery flavor. "Hm. They're good. So what are you doing here?"

She wiggled a finger at the cookies. "Of course they're good. My mom's secret recipe, handed down from Grandma Taylor. Oh, could you take them out of there and put them in something else? I'd like the container back."

On his way to the kitchen, she continued to talk, raising her voice so he could hear in the other room. "Hey, did you see Archie Bunker on Saturday? I laughed until I cried, it was so funny. He lost his Christmas bonus." Several seconds of laughter followed.

He poked his head out of the kitchen. "TV's broken, Carol, remember?"

"Oh, yeah, I forgot. Anyhow, I stopped by to invite you and Joshua to Christmas dinner. We'll have our usual white elephant gift exchange. It's so much fun stealing gifts back and forth. You and Josh will love it. You can bring something you already own. And we'll probably watch *All in the Family* or some Christmas special on TV. Last year we saw Bob Hope's Christmas special that was filmed in Vietnam. It will be loads of fun."

Patrick couldn't imagine a worse Christmas if he'd tried. TV shows and stealing gifts? Bobby and Ricky were rowdy and belligerent on good days. Adding a game of greed would dump Yule fuel on already-volatile family dynamics. He and Joshua had planned a quiet celebration that included midnight mass, sleeping in, and special pancakes. Simple. Focused on the birth of Christ. That was it. He'd stick with the plan.

When Patrick didn't respond, she said, "Think about it and talk to Josh. I need to know by Wednesday." She settled back onto the couch, the very spot where Peggy had spent most of her time in the last few weeks of her life. Even that irritated Patrick.

Carol wove her fingers behind her head. "Well, did you find a job yet?"

He shook his head. "Not that it's any of your business, but no."

Like a terrier cornering a rat in its hole, she didn't let the subject go. "Jobs don't find you, ya know. You have to get out there and beat the bushes. I keep seeing positions in the paper that I'm sure you could handle. Like I tell Zane, 'even if you're running the cash register at the grocery store, any job's better than none.' You've got a duty to provide for the boy, so go do it."

Sure, a job here would mean stability for Joshua, but heartache for Patrick. Although he went through the motions, Patrick still hoped he wouldn't be employed here. He had enough money to last until March, if they were thrifty. But he wasn't about to discuss it with his nosy cousin. He stuffed another cookie into his mouth.

"Bet you're living on food stamps. How much money do you have left?"

Patrick rose. "That's none of your business." He strode to the door and opened it wide, letting the cold wind blast in. "You better go now. I've got things to do."

She stood; her gaze scanned the room, as if hoping to find reasons to stay printed on the wall. "Now don't get your dander up. I'm only trying to help." Shoving her fingers into her gloves she said, "You've done so much with this place, Patrick. I know Peggy would be glad you're going to stay."

As he closed the door behind his cousin and headed to the bedroom, Patrick wondered how Carol's husband managed to live with her.

Fifteen minutes later, the letter was ready to mail, and the grocery list had been penned. Patrick bundled into his winter gear and drove Peggy's truck down Road 100 and into Pasco. The heater was broken; he shivered the whole way.

After purchasing groceries, Patrick slid into the phone booth and pressed the folding door shut. Excited about talking with Emma Lee, he took a gulp of air and jammed several quarters into the phone. After he dialed, instead of ringing, the phone gave the familiar three-toned squawk that told him he'd made some type of error.

The operator came said, "The number you called is not in service."

"Oh." If she moved and got a new number, that might explain why he didn't get her the last few times he called, and why she wasn't responding to his letters. "Could you look up Emma Lee Dubois, Pittsburgh, Pennsylvania, please?" He spelled the last name.

After several seconds, the operator said, "There is no one by that name listed. Do you want to try another spelling? Or is there another name you'd like me to find?"

Patrick grimaced and slumped against the phone booth wall. "Where did she go?" he mumbled.

"Excuse me? Please repeat that."

"Um, there's no other name, thanks."

He slid the receiver onto the cradle and closed his eyes. *Where did she go?*

Patrick stumbled back to the truck. On the cold drive back, his fingers clamped the steering wheel so tightly his knuckles whitened. Carol's advice; the phone call; job searches, Joshua. Everything pointed to the same conclusion: he needed to return to Pittsburgh.

The urge to leave Washington grew so strong that Patrick had to stop himself from driving straight to the airport.

Like a spiral, time circled back on itself and suddenly, the three months that had stretched away endlessly that morning felt confining and short now. Was it enough time to accomplish all that needed to be done? He would make it so.

Even in the snow, Patrick sped five miles over the speed limit. On arriving home, he tore up the latest application and threw it in the garbage, then pulled out a clean sheet of paper. He'd write to Three River's Chemical and get his old job back. No matter what, he was going home.

15.

The occupational therapist's office was up one flight in an old brick office building in Belleview. Today, Carla dropped Emma Lee and David off, and Leonard came right from work. As they climbed the stairs, Leonard wished he hadn't opened the mail before he came. The letter from Patrick asking for his old job back irked him big-time.

Inside the office, David bee-lined for the toys as the bleached blond receptionist, Jennifer, greeted them. As Leonard approached her desk, he appreciated how the top of her tight uniform was left unbuttoned, showing cleavage. Some might call her plump, and she was, but pleasingly so. Her eyes seemed to twinkle whenever she spoke to him, as if he and she shared some kind of secret.

There's nothing like a beautiful woman to get a person's attention, Leonard thought.

Emma Lee took on that 'deer in the headlights' look again: eyes wary, searching the room. God, he wished she would quit that. It was embarrassing. When her hands began to shake, he knew she was getting nervous. This place wasn't new; Emma Lee had been here dozens of times over the last four months. Of course she'd have no memory of that. No doubt she was wondering where she was.

He released an audible groan. *Good thing I've taken charge of her life, or she'd forget how to breathe,* Leonard thought. He opened his checkbook. "I'd like to pay the bill from last month."

Jennifer grinned up at him with admiration, showing a sparkling set of straight, white teeth. "We're always willing to take payments, Dr. Baxter,"

Was she flirting? Perhaps he should offer this woman a job. Then he could look at those red, ripe lips and those grapefruit-sized breasts all day long instead of frumpy Rhonda's wrinkled face and tedious, puritan-like attire.

As Leonard signed the check, Emma Lee slipped into a chair near David.

"Don't worry, Mommy. I'll be good while you do ther-pee," the boy said.

Before he could join Emma Lee on the chairs, the occupational therapist, Michael Yamada, came around the corner. "You can come in now, Miss Dubois. Dr. Baxter," he said.

Leonard rolled his eyes. The young man's flashy, checkered bell-bottom pants looked too modern for medical office wear, and his long black hair hung in his eyes, as usual. *Why couldn't Emma Lee have a normal OT?* Leonard thought. *One who wore his clothes and hair like a professional instead of like a shaggy-haired British singer? Why ... he's a Japanese Beatle,* Leonard thought, grunting at his own joke.

In his office, Michael extended a hand. "Hi, Emma Lee. Remember me? I'm your favorite occupational therapist. Call me Michael."

She shook his hand. "Glad to meet you. What ... why am I here?"

He smiled. "After your head injury you lost some skills. So I get to help stuff them back into your brain, if I can. Today I'll do some testing to see if you're getting any better. Have a seat."

"I've been here before?"

"Many times. Most recently, two days ago."

The man smiled too much; another unprofessional sign. Leonard felt surrounded by fakes and frauds.

She rubbed her forehead and squeezed her eyes shut. "I don't remember."

Michael said, "No need. We'll go from here." He handed her a board filled with various connectors: laces, snaps, buckles, zippers, and clips. "We practiced tying bows last time; let's see what stuck."

Leonard smoothed his hair with the palm of his hand. Straightening his pant legs to ensure they wouldn't wrinkle, and cinching his tie knot, he sat near the desk, where, he noticed, Emma Lee's file lay. He didn't have to read it to know the contents. Four months ago, her brain sustained damage near the back and top, in the parietal lobe, causing short term memory loss, problems accomplishing tasks, and inability to make decisions. The memory loss seemed to be her biggest problem right now. She couldn't account for the last hour let alone two days ago. Of course she wouldn't remember Beatle Guy.

He crossed his legs and leaned back in his chair. "You've got to do something, Yamada. She's going to hurt herself big-time if you don't. Like yesterday. Carla and I both reminded her to use a pot holder. Seconds later, she grabbed the oven rack with a bare hand and got those nasty burns on her palm."

Emma Lee turned her hand over and inspected it as if the hand had sprouted there moments ago. "That's how I got these," she mumbled.

"We'll discuss that at the end of the session," Michael said.

Feeling put off, Leonard frowned.

Fifty minutes later, Michael said, "We're done. Good job, Emma Lee. Now, go fetch David while I talk with Dr. Baxter."

When she left, Leonard rose from the chair. "She's regressing, isn't she?"

Michael replaced the therapy board in the closet and pointed to his clipboard. "I'll work up the results and get back to you."

"Don't hide bad news. I saw her fail."

Michael took a seat at the desk and opened the folder. He slid the papers from the clipboard into it. "Progress is subtle and the results take time, so be patient. On first glance, though, I'd say her visual attention and hand-eye coordination have improved."

Leonard smacked the desk with is hand. "What about forgetting yesterday? What about her sticking her hand in the oven? That's not progress."

"It's true, apraxia is a problem, so watch her carefully and keep reminding her. Next time I'll help you form some coping methods you and Carla can use to help her. But such a serious injury takes time to repair." Michael shook his head. "I grant you, some people never improve. But 40% do. I've had one patient regain most of his memory overnight. Like that!" He snapped his fingers. "So don't give up hope."

"Overnight, huh? That must have been a shock."

"A pleasant one. The whole family had a party to celebrate."

As Leonard drove his Cadillac from the parking lot, he felt jostled and unbalanced, as if heading for river rapids on a wooden raft. The letter from Kilkenny asking for his job back, and just now Beatle Boy mentioning overnight recovery, these couldn't be mere coincidences.

Regaining memory overnight would be no celebrating matter, as far as he was concerned. He'd lose Emma Lee for sure. And if she recovered before that sneaky Irishman returned, well, there was no telling what could happen. She might trade the man who saved her life for that gangly, idealistic pipsqueak. He couldn't let that happen.

In the back seat, David started to hum the ABC song and tap on the window. Normally, Leonard would shush the child. But today, he let the boy make noise. It would keep him from overhearing the conversation.

"I'm taking you to town, Emma Lee." When she smiled, he said, "We're buying an engagement ring. I know you've been hoping for one."

She stared at Leonard, eyes wide, lips tight. "I ... have?" She shook her head. "That can't be."

"We've talked about it many times, but you don't remember, that's all." Wishing that he could kiss her right then, he reached across the car and took her hand. "Trust me, my darling; I know what you want, what you need. And after we get the ring, we'll stop at the courthouse to apply for the license and arrange for the wedding. I want to make it soon—next week if possible. David can be the ring bearer. "Won't that be wonderful?"

Emma Lee squeezed her eyes shut and grimaced. He assumed she was trying to recall his proposal, or thinking about what type of ring she'd like. It didn't matter. She would be his.

On Saturday he'd buy some film for his camera and perhaps a new suit for himself. He'd make sure she had a sexy new dress—tight and short. With stilettos. It had to be red and low-cut, and short enough so that her garters would show below the hemline. He'd also visit that new naughty store on Liberty Avenue and purchase some sexy underwear for her. She'd look great for the wedding photos, and even more spectacular afterwards in the bedroom. There would be no reception or party. The quiet ceremony would be enough.

Leonard didn't himself fantasize about sexy lingerie right then. He was on a mission.

"Can we turn on the radio?" David asked.

Emma Lee clicked the button and Al Green's voice crooned about spending life together.

He felt his heart speed up. "You see, Emma Lee? We talk about getting married and the first song we hear is about love. It's our fate to be married."

When Leonard stopped the car at a red light, he cranked the window down and filled his lungs with cold air. He rolled his shoulders to ease the stiffness out of them. Yes, everything was falling into place. They'd be married before any surprise recovery. Before Kilkenny could return and muck things up. While things were perfect.

Now that he thought about it, today's appointment was a sign, a portend telling him to hurry. And he was no fool. He'd listen to the message and marry Emma Lee as soon as possible. As far as he was concerned, a new wife was a great way to start a great new year. 1972 will be "the year of Leonard," he thought.

16.

My favorite Chopin sonata is floating from the record player when I hear the knock. The man says, "I'll get it."

I hear the door open, and a woman's voice say, "What a surprise to see you here, Leonard. I was expecting Carla." I hear the clunk of boots on the floor.

"Let me take your coat."

My gut tightens; who are these people, taking over my apartment and my life?

The strangers talk as they traverse down the hallway. His voice: "She and David are grocery shopping. I took the day off so I could spend it with Emma Lee."

Her voice: "Oh, that's very nice."

I'm standing by the window when they enter. The man says, "Darling, Sister Martha is here for your appointment. I'll be in the kitchen if you need anything."

She hugs me. "Hello, Emma Lee. You look lovely today. Nice music, too."

"Thank-you." I run three fingers through my unruly black curls and stare at the old jeans and sweater I'm wearing; I wonder how this stranger could call me lovely. "Do I know you?"

"Oh, yes. We met at the hospital several months ago. Now we see each other about once a week for therapy and pastoral care."

Pulling the curtain back, I squint as I stare out the window. "I don't need therapy."

"Your doctor thinks otherwise."

"I'm getting better. Today, I drove David to the library." My attention drifts as memory of the trip turns muddy. "At least ... I think that happened today."

Who am I kidding? Thoughts drain through my brain as quickly as water through a colander. And anything left is knotted together like spaghetti noodles.

"Let's sit down, dear, and we can talk about it."

I sink on the couch and prop my head with a fist. This Sister Martha woman slides next to me and takes my other hand in hers. She pats it like I'm sick. "I've seen other people with injuries like yours, and I can only guess how difficult this must be. Tell me about it."

The middle-aged woman doesn't look like a nun to me. Her hair is cut very short but without style. A large crucifix hangs from a chain around her neck and she's wearing a cardigan sweater and long wool skirt. "If you're a nun, why aren't you wearing a habit?" I ask.

"Our order was given the option about three years ago, and we chose to modernize."

"Oh," I say, wondering how many times I've asked that question. My throat tightens.

"Last time we talked about David and your concern about parenting without recall. Do you want to talk more about that?"

I search my memory, but it's like my thoughts have been written on a chalkboard that's always being erased. I sigh so deep it's a groan. "I don't know. I don't know," I whisper.

"When a person loses memory, often great sadness comes with the injury. It's like a part of you has died, and it takes a while to get over that, if you ever do."

I used to be good at checking my emotions like a hat and coat in a restaurant, picking them up later so I could deal with them when I was alone. But now I'm surprised at their boldness. Even though I don't give the tears permission, they burst forth. "I want my memory back," I wail.

"Of course you do. And, God willing, you'll get that."

More tears slip down my cheeks and drip all the way to my sweater. They form beads on the lavender wool that shimmer like liquid pearls before they spread to dark spots. "How long have I been like this?"

"About six months."

I groan. "Then it's hopeless."

The woman wraps her arm over my shoulder. "Right now, it might seem that way, but you're getting better bit by bit. Trust in God, Emma Lee. God is here, in this situation."

"I don't know how, Sister." My tears have no shame; they wet my whole face and spread their influence to the rest of me, until my chin quivers and my shoulders shake.

She hands me a tissue. "There, there. Go ahead, cry it out, dear." Taking my hand again she's silent a few moments, then exclaims, "Oh, my! Are these engagement and wedding rings on your finger?"

Her words shock my tear ducts dry. I stare at the rings. There must be some mistake. "Um ..." I shake my head. "I'm ... not ... sure."

At that moment, a stranger, a fit-looking old man, shuffles into the room. He's wearing dress slacks and buttoned shirt. I don't know him, but he takes my other hand to his lips. "Oh my darling, let me help you remember. We got married yesterday at city hall."

No! I can't be married. I don't even know him. And he's too old for me.

Sister Martha places a hand over her heart. "Such big news! I'm surprised you didn't tell me when I came in, Leonard. No wonder you're home from work. It's your honeymoon. I guess congratulations are in order."

"Thank you. I was hoping Emma Lee would remember and tell you herself."

My eyes dart back and forth, from her face to his. This can't be true. I'd never marry him, would I?

The woman smiles. "The traditionalist in me says I wish you had waited until she regained her memory. But practicality says that might never happen. I have to say that I've been worried about you staying here overnight—a man and a woman together can get into trouble, even when they don't intend to, if you know what I mean. It's better this way." She pats my hand again.

The man crosses his arms, bold and defensive, like a pirate captain forcing someone to walk the plank. "You know I have been respectful of her, I always slept on the couch." I watch him bite down, causing the muscle in his square jaw to tighten as his lips curve upwards into a thin smile. "I love her, and want to care for her for the rest of her life."

Sister Martha shakes her head. "Oh, Leonard, I'm not accusing you. I know you've been patient and above-board, and I appreciate that. But now that you're married, well, that sets my mind at ease. I wish you both the best." She stands. "I'll leave the two of you alone. It's your honeymoon, after all."

As if I'm watching a television show, these people enter and exit my life, act like they know me, even care for me, and I wish I could change the channel, or turn off the set.

The nun pulls me to my feet, then hugs me long and hard, strong arms tight around me. She whispers, "Blessings on you both." When she releases her grasp, she says, "If it's okay, I'll schedule you for next Wednesday, at our usual time."

"I guess so," I mumble. "Whatever you say."

ONCE SHE'S GONE, I slip on my dark glasses, lean against the window frame, and stare out through the glass again. After the snowstorm and freezing rain over the weekend, there was a thaw, but icy piles still line the street. I watch Sister Martha pick her way through the slush to her car, her long coat and skirt nearly touching the ground. I freeze like the ice and wish the world could solidify around me so I'd have time to remember the moment, so her visit would record on my memory. But it's as if my brainwaves dampen like ripples hitting the edge of a pond; images of her visit are already fading.

The sparkle from my ring catches my eye. I'm married! I try to conjure up a memory of the ceremony, but nothing comes—no image of a dress, shoes, flowers—nothing. I can't even remember my husband's name.

A man comes up behind me and slides his hands around my waist. He's tall enough to rest his chin on my head and I feel comforted, secure for a moment. "My darling," he says, kissing the top of my head.

"Have I been married long?" I ask.

"Two days, but we'll be together forever now. I'll take care of you. I already pay your bills, take you to appointments, buy your medicine; I even help you decide what and when you eat. You can't work anymore, so I'll support you forever. We belong together, Emma Lee."

"It must be a lot of work, caring for me. Why do you want to do that?"

"I love helping, doing things for you. You're so beautiful, you deserve it."

The door opens and I hear footsteps. I go to the hallway to see who's coming in this time.

David and a young woman enter. Her long, white-streaked hair surrounds her impish face and she's carrying a grocery sack. "Hi, Emma Lee, Leonard," she says.

David waves a brown Tootsie Roll pop above his head like a trophy. "Mom! Look what Carla gave me. It's chock-lit."

"Yummy. I missed you. How about a hug?"

Before my son reaches my arms, though, the man grabs him by the shoulders. "Wash your hands, boy. You're all sticky." He shoves David to the bathroom.

My disappointment must show, because the woman says, "Don't worry, he'll be back." She points a thumb kitchen-ward. "I've got a few groceries to put away." She leaves and I hear the refrigerator and cupboard doors opening and closing. Another person I don't know who seems to know me well.

"When you finish, you can go, Carla," I hear the man say. "I'll take it from here." He leads me back to the living room as she calls from the kitchen, "Emma Lee, do you want something to drink? Tea, cocoa?"

I frown and stare at the floor. "I … I don't know."

The man places a fist on one hip and points, as if he's commanding army troops. "You know she can't make up her mind, Carla. Give her hot chocolate."

"Sure," she says.

He pulls me to the couch and sidles up next to me. "See? I help you make *all* your decisions—even little ones. That's why we're good together."

David, with a lollypop-filled cheek, races into the room, turns his hands over for inspection, then snuggles on my lap. The man scowls, but continues to talk. "We'll be moving soon."

I cock my head to one side. "Where?"

"To the country. I've wanted to retire to a farm for a while now, and I think I've found the perfect place. Ten acres about four miles from here, on a country road, next to a stream. I think you'll love it. I'm meeting the realtor this evening to take another look, and if all goes well, we'll move by the end of the month."

I feel my heart skip a beat. "But I don't want to move."

"You'll like it there. I'll take care of everything."

My head starts to pound.

A young woman sets a steaming mug on the coffee table. "Here's your hot chocolate, Emma Lee. Well, I'm off for the evening. I'll be back tomorrow to take you to your OT appointment."

"Okay," I say.

A door squeaks closed in my brain, and I feel dazed and shaken. Something important has happened; I can feel it. But I can't remember what.

"Emma Lee, are you with me?" a man says.

I hug David tighter. Who is this man? Why is he here? "I don't know," I say. "I don't know anything."

17.

Over the past two months, the local priest had become Patrick's friend. He'd drop by for coffee after dinner on most Wednesdays, and they'd discuss or even haggle over whatever suited them, from politics to policy to theology. Patrick appreciated his companionship and his counsel.

Today was special, though. It was Ash Wednesday, which meant Lent had officially begun. With ashes rubbed in a smudgy cross on his forehead, Patrick felt ready for the spiritual cleansing Lent might provide—if he let it. But it also meant Fr. Willis would be late for his weekly visit.

"Get busy on your homework," Patrick said to Joshua when they got home from church. "I'll do the dishes."

Ten minutes later Fr. Willis arrived. The man's intelligent face and kind eyes gave the impression that you could trust him. His grin made crinkles at the edge of his eyes and formed dimples on both cheeks.

Patrick escorted him into the house. "Come into the kitchen; I'll make some coffee."

The priest settled at the table and removed his gloves. "So, are you looking forward to going home?"

Patrick glanced down the hallway, ensuring that Joshua's door was closed before he said, "Haven't been thinking much about that. I've got bigger issues right now. Joshua's depression is getting worse. I got his midterm grades today, and they were bad. All he does is mope. Earlier today I signed papers on the house, so it's sold. But that depressed him even more. He accused me of getting rid of everything he loves on purpose. And I guess I am."

"Too bad you can't beam the house and everything in it to Pittsburgh, like people on that Star Trek show. Then you'd move and not move at the same time." Fr. Willis's lips lifted into a sad smile.

After corralling his dark red locks in a rubber band to create a short pony tail at the nape of his neck, Patrick began spooning coffee grounds into the metal basket. "Guess Josh would like that, but I'm sick of trying to keep this place together. It seems like two things fall apart for each one I fix. I'm glad to be done." Patrick cracked his knuckles. "And I'm no good at parenting."

"There is no one else, Patrick. You've got to do it."

When the coffee was on the stove perking, Patrick returned to the dishes as they talked. "What do I know about kids? Nothing, that's what. It's been tough these past two months, and Josh is still in the same school, with his same friends, living in the same house. And I'm here full time. In Pittsburgh all that will change. I'm wondering how it's going to work when I'm gone all day and he's in day-care without any friends."

The priest propped his elbows on the table and placed his chin in his folded hands, but said nothing.

"Got any advice? Any insight? Any words of wisdom? I'm clueless."

"Raising a child from birth doesn't mean a parent knows everything. Sometimes it's guesswork. I've heard from plenty of parents about how hard it is. You're a thoughtful, kind person. Take time to listen to others and to the boy. And pray. Lots. That's my two cents."

Patrick wiped his hands on his thighs and sat at the table. "My prayer is more like ranting these days. But damn it, I'm really mad at God. You'd think he'd cut me some slack after my sister's death, but no. It gets worse every day. Josh is depressed and failing, Carol refused to take the boy after agreeing to do it, the kid's father isn't anywhere to be found, the house sold for $8,025—two-thousand less than it's worth. Back in December I sent a letter to the company in Pittsburgh about getting my job back. I haven't heard, so I don't even know if I have a job! I read somewhere that St. Teresa told God, 'With friends like you, who needs enemies?' Well, I think I agree with her."

"Yeah, you've got hardships, all right. But you can't ignore the positives. The house *did* sell. Your company promised to take you back—eventually. Joshua loves you. I think you'll do much better than you expect with this parenting thing."

"So, I should make lemonade from lemons, right?"

"Well, why not?"

Patrick stood and returned to the dishes. "I don't like the squeeze."

At that, Fr. Willis laughed aloud. "No one does. Hey, got a place in Pittsburgh to move to?"

"My old apartment. Some pals were subletting, so most everything will be there waiting for us. The first thing I'm buying with the house sale money is a headstone for Peggy's grave."

Patrick sucked in a deep breath. His thoughts flew to the cemetery where his sister's body was. His sister's body—turning to dust. *Ashes, to ashes, dust to dust.*

He touched his forehead to feel the grit from the ashes there. It reminded him of something. A few days ago, a huge tree limb fell during a wind storm onto the neighbor's fence. The hole allowed two cows and a horse to escape into his yard. This pain felt like that limb. Something shook it from its rightful place, causing it to fall unexpectedly onto the fence he tended so carefully, the fence he erected to incarcerate his sorrow. Tears threatened to escape, so he sat in silence for a few moments and willed himself not to cry. Finally he said, "After that, I'll buy tickets back to Pittsburgh. Whatever's left I'll use to start a college fund for Josh."

With elbows on the table, the priest tented his fingers and pressed the index fingers to his lips. "Good to see you aren't greedy. That's wisdom breaking through."

Patrick sighed. "I don't know. Maybe I'm desperate, or selfish. A college fund means the kid will grow up and move away, right?"

That comment warranted another dimpled smile from the priest.

The coffee finished perking and Patrick poured two mugs full.

"Thanks," The priest sipped from his mug. "We'll miss you around here."

Patrick wove his fingers together behind his head and leaned into them. "You'll have to put up with me for another four weeks at least, until the house closes. There's so much to arrange. Any chance you could use a fuzzy, white pet chicken?"

ON THE PLANE, Joshua kept complaining. "Why did we have to leave Fluffy with the priest? What if he eats him? I miss my house. I don't want to live in Pittsburgh. Why couldn't we stay in Pasco?"

"Wow, you've got loads to grumble about, and we aren't even there yet." Patrick patted Joshua's knee and tried to remember what the priest said about patience and kindness. "Let's try to see this as a new adventure, shall we?"

Joshua's scowl told him he might feel sorry he ever prayed for patience.

When the taxi dropped them at the apartment building, Patrick unlocked his door for the first time in eight months and led Joshua to the back to his office. "This'll be your room," he said.

Joshua's eyes grew stormy. His lips pouted as he threw his backpack on the floor and slumped into a chair. "Where do I sleep?"

"Don't worry, we'll get you a bed and dresser tomorrow. Tonight, you can camp out on the couch."

The lanky boy swiped the tear with the back of his hand, then dropped his head, letting his red hair fall into his eyes. "I miss my mom," he mumbled.

Patrick squatted and took Joshua's hands in his. "I know you do. Me too."

Joshua turned and placed his chin on the back of his chair. As he stared out the window into the hazy evening, his face reminded Patrick of a mournful hound with sad, wet eyes; his long, stringy hair substituting for the floppy ears. He could almost read the boy's mind. Outside there were no cottonwood trees swaying in the breeze, no clear blue sky reflected in the wide Columbia River. There were no orchards, or quail families, no dogs chasing squirrels, no sage-scented wind.

Instead asphalt and bricks reigned. Fifty feet away, trucks ground through gears, spewing exhaust into the smoky, overcast sky as they sped along the four-lane yellow brick boulevard. Though a mere five hundred feet away, the dark, oily Ohio River was only visible from the top of a steep, weedy hill. Patrick wondered if he would adjust to parenting, and if Joshua could adjust to Pittsburgh.

He pretended to slug Joshua on the shoulder. "Hey, things aren't so bad, kiddo. We have each other. Tomorrow we'll register you for school and day care with Maria. David, my friend's son, went to Maria's. He liked it a lot. You might even get to meet him."

"Don't want to go to school or day care, ever, and I don't want to live here," he shouted, as he wove his arms together in front of his chest.

Losing his temper, Patrick's voice rose several decibels. "Hey, what's with this attitude? Every kid goes to school. And somebody has to take care of you while I'm at work. This is what you asked for, so get over it."

Joshua bolted out of the room and Patrick found him splayed on the couch. "Nobody else has to move all the way across the country like me. Why did Mom have to die? Why?" When he lifted his head, Patrick could see tears dripping from his nose and eyes. They left a huge wet spot on the couch. "I'll never be able to have a pet chicken again."

Patrick sat on the edge of the couch and rubbed Joshua's back. "I know it's hard, Josh, and everything is new, but don't judge it yet. Not while you're feeling so bad. Give it a chance. I predict that soon enough this place will feel like home."

"This will never be home."

That night, as Patrick lay in his bed, he decided he'd start looking for Joshua's father, Richard, in case things didn't work out with the boy here.

Why was it so hard to know what to do, to know what was right? Why did the women he loved die too early? Images of his sister melded with those of his mother. Mom on the couch, coughing, dying. Peggy on the bed, gasping, laboring for air. The hollowed-out space they left extended from gut to chest, and it started to throb. They died too soon, leaving grieving boys behind.

And now it seemed like the whole world was suffering. The news reported heartbreaking stories of death and destruction everywhere. Wars raged, people rioted, airplanes fell from the sky, boats sank. Someone's mother, brother, father, sibling, or child died. Then Patrick recalled how, at the end of Jesus' short career, he himself had been abused and killed. If God couldn't free his own son from suffering and death, who was he to expect it?

Patrick gave his tears permission to flow and he wept with abandon. After several minutes, the emotion subsided, the tears dried up, and his gaze settled on the poster hanging above his dresser, the one he'd purchased after his stuck elevator experience. He read it aloud.

"Wisdom is bright and does not grow dim. By those who love her she is readily seen, and found by those who look for her. Wisdom 6: 12-13."

Perhaps I don't look hard enough, he thought, *but right now, I can't see wisdom anywhere at all. Ashes to ashes, dust to dust.*

18.

My eyes flutter open. The back of my head throbs like usual, but somehow life is different. Recollection of lunch is clear.

I've got memories!

My whole body quivers as I recall: I'm married and pregnant! It hits me hard, as if I've been tackled by Steelers Fullback, John Fuqua. How did I get into this predicament?

My father used to say, "Ignorance is bliss." Yesterday I would have disagreed. Memories are important when you don't have them. But today …? Recall should be like the radio. Then you could turn it off when you need to, when it hurts too much.

I stumble out of bed and into the living room for the second time today, where the man greets me with a kiss and drapes one arm over my shoulders.

"Dinner is almost ready," he says.

As he scans my face, I wonder why he wed me—this wild-haired, frustrated, helpless woman who's lost her mind. I place a hand on my belly. A bigger question is: how could I have married him, and obviously made love to this old man?

He takes one of my hands in his and brings it to his lips. "I'd do anything for you," he says, kissing my fingers. "You're so delicate, like china. I love that about you." His free hand strokes my hair. "Ah, my darling!" He leads me to the couch and settles too close, hip against hip, his arm still cinching us together.

Dropping my shoulders, willing myself to relax, I let this stranger pet me, puppy-like. But his attention scrapes my consciousness, lifting my anxiety like burned beans in a pot of scorched soup.

His gaze drifts out the window and settles there. "I keep remembering our wedding day, you in that sexy dress, standing beside me." He licks his lips; does the memory taste good? I try to shimmy away, put a breath of air between us, but he tightens his grip. My frustration bubbles from deep down and threatens to boil, but I want to turn down the heat, calm my spirit. I think about how, in many countries across the world, women and men who don't know each other until they marry, and most live together fine for the rest of their lives. If I could only see this as an arranged marriage, I might do okay. If only.

Stroking my hair again, he says, "Something changed in you, and I don't like it. Seems to be a set-back more than a breakthrough." He shakes his head. "We'll talk to Yamada about it on Tuesday." Tucking in his lips until they disappear, he flashes a tight smile, making him look tense, not happy. "You rest while I finish dinner. We'll talk later." He frees me from his grasp, plumps the pillow, directs my body to it.

At that moment I hear David whisper, "Uh-oh."

"Now what?" The man strides to the kitchen. "What have you done?" he roars.

"I didn't mean to, Leonard. I wanted to help."

I race to the kitchen, too. David holds an empty metal oregano tin in one hand and its lid in the other. The muscles in the man's jaw pulse and tighten. His face and voice freeze hard. "What the hell were you thinking? You clean that up. Now!"

He shoves the window open. A blast of freezing air swirls green flakes around the room. In the living room and the bedrooms, more windows are yanked open. A cold blast of air whistles down the hallway as the man shoves on his boots and barn coat. Then he hisses, "I'm going to the barn. You get your stupid kid to clean up. When I come back I don't want to see a trace of spice. Maybe I'll make dinner later, maybe not. It would serve him right to go to bed hungry." He stomps out of the house and slams the door behind him.

I'm stunned by the man's instant transformation from kindly caretaker to enraged monster; the shock renders me motionless for a few moments until the cold jars me to action. I slam the kitchen window shut, then race through the house and close the rest. Back in the kitchen, the smell of oregano fills the room. Flakes are everywhere—on the table top, the floor, the counter, and stuck to David's hands and clothing. Tears glisten on his cheeks. His soft brown doe eyes settle on me. Poor boy. He shouldn't have to bear the brunt of the man's anger.

I place my hands on David's shoulders and crouch so we're eye to eye. "It's the spill that made him angry, not you."

The boy swipes his face with his sleeve and flashes a shy, fragile smile. "I know."

"I'll help," I say, not moving. "What … should I do?"

"You sweep. I'll wipe," he says, brushing flakes from his sleeves and pants.

The phone rings. Who could it be? My hand shakes as I pick up the receiver; I whisper, "Hello?"

"Hi, Emma Lee, it's Sister Martha. You missed your appointment yesterday, so I wanted to make sure you were all right."

"What appointment?"

The woman starts talking again, but the meaning of her words swirl and melt before I can grasp them. As she talks, though, I can conjure up an image: tall, kindly woman with salt and pepper hair, flat-heeled shoes, long skirt, white blouse.

"… all right? Emma Lee, are you still there, dear?"

"Um … yes. I'm sorry. What did you say?"

"Would you check your schedule? How does Wednesday afternoon at three work for you?"

My eyes scan the room. Where is that calendar? Oh, yes, next to the stove. "I … guess so."

"You know how to get here, but if you want directions again, I'll give them to you."

I frown with concentration. Getting anywhere on my own seems impossible. "Doesn't he … my husband take me?"

"Not always. Sometimes he has to work. But don't worry, you can drive, and you know the way. Sister Angela can baby-sit David, as usual."

"Why … why am I coming to see you?"

"We're working through your head injury issues—how to live with loss, how God fits into your life, where to go from here. I'm your counselor."

"Oh, thank goodness. I need to talk to someone about what's happened, what's happening. And maybe you can help … I mean, I'm … but I don't remember coming before."

"That's perfectly fine, dear."

"Not for me," I mumble. I locate paper and a pencil on the counter. "Could you give me the directions?"

When I hang up, I wonder if I'll even remember I have an appointment, so I won't take a chance. I write: *See Sister Martha—three p.m. Friday. Directions in coat pocket.* I rip the note from the scratch pad and attach it to the refrigerator door with two magnets. The directions go into my coat pocket.

Thrilled to discover I've remembered my sweeping task after interruption, I pick up the broom again. I have myriad questions. I hope Sister Martha has answers.

19.

Patrick tamed his rust-colored locks into a rubber band and called into the living room, "Get your shoes on, Joshua. We're going to meet Maria." He had calculated the appointment to match the time when Emma Lee might arrive to pick up David, so he didn't want to be late. If he "accidentally" ran into her, he'd give her a good-natured razzing for not writing, but then he'd forgive her. Maybe even ask her to lunch for old times' sake.

Joshua looked up from his comic book and groaned. "Don't wanna; we just got home and I'm tired."

"I know, but she's expecting us." He hoped he was telling the truth when he added, "You'll like her."

Joshua dragged his feet down the hallway to the front door. Ignoring his shoes, he sat cross-legged on the floor, puffed his cheeks with air, and smacked them. A loud gassy vibration escaped his lips. Apparently pleased with the results, he did it several more times before Patrick lost his patience.

"Come on, kiddo. We gotta go." Patrick grunted and pointed to Joshua's shoeless feet.

Half an hour later, Joshua and Patrick stood in front of Maria's house. The door swept open and the dark-haired Italian woman gushed, "Welcome. Thanks for calling me, Patrick." She directed Patrick to the kitchen, and led the boy into the playroom.

In the kitchen, Patrick checked his watch. Five-thirty. Emma Lee might arrive any minute. The room smelled spicy, like cinnamon mixed with oranges. He took a seat at the table and waited. When Maria returned, she poured him a cup of tea and slid some papers toward him. "Here are my rates and hours. When do you want Joshua to start?"

"Tuesday, if that works for you. I have to go to the plant and talk to my boss, find out about getting my job back."

Maria settled into a chair and took a few sips from her mug. Patrick checked his watch again, then picked up the papers and read through them. When he finished, he said, "Okay, no overnights, or holidays. Makes sense. Your rate is fair. Oh, you're finished at six. What if I have to work overtime?" He glanced at the wall clock. It was five-forty-five, now, and still no Emma Lee. Perhaps she hadn't gone to work today.

Curling her feet under her on the chair, Maria took another sip. "I keep children later in emergencies if you let me know. I can't do it every evening. My own family needs some of me, too."

"I get that. And this is exactly what I need, what Josh needs. Glad you had room." Taking the pen in hand, he signed and slid the contract across the table, then checked his watch a third time.

Maria worried the pearls on her necklace as if they were rosary beads. "So how's it been, being back in the big city?"

"We've been too busy. I didn't have bedroom furniture for Joshua, so I bought a mattress this morning. Poor kid will have to sleep on the couch until they deliver it." He pointed to his head and laughed. "And as you can see, we haven't gotten to the barber yet."

She let the smile travel up her face until her eyes sparkled. "I like your hair that way."

"My sister did, too." At the thought of Peggy, tears threatened to break through his genial façade, so he blinked several times. Lifting his pony tail and wiggling it, he said, "But you know how the corporate world is. Women can do anything with their hair, but only male rock stars or hippies can get away with wearing it this way."

They both laughed.

"You keep looking at your watch, Patrick. Do you need to be somewhere else?" she asked, "Or do you have time for another cup?"

He pointed to his mug. As he watched her refill it, Patrick said, "Sorry. I was hoping to see Emma Lee. I sent her several letters while I was away, but never heard from her. When we got back, I stopped at her apartment, but she doesn't live there anymore. I thought maybe I'd run into her here. Do you still watch David?"

Maria replaced the kettle and sat at the table again, she tapped her lips with an index finger. "No. I haven't seen either of them in months. After Emma Lee got hurt, a nun brought the boy here for a few weeks. But then they stopped coming. If she was still going to work, I figured Emma Lee got a better price with someone else."

Patrick leaned forward. "I had no idea she was hurt. What happened?"

"I don't' know much. The nun told me she hit her head at work."

Sucking in a deep breath and exhaling slowly, Patrick shook his head several times. "No wonder she never wrote back."

WHEN PATRICK AND Joshua arrived in the apartment building hallway, Joshua pulled a letter from the mailbox. "Hey, it's from Grandma," he shouted.

Patrick grew excited. "I could sure use some good news." He ripped open the envelope and read aloud.

Dear Patrick,

Thank you for your letter. I was real sorry to hear about Peggy's death. We wanted to come to the funeral, but it cost too much. I'm sure it's hard on you both, though. I wish we could have the boy live with us, but my husband's health won't allow that.

Joshua yanked on his sleeve. "Does she know where Dad is?"

"Don't know yet." He continued reading.

We'd love to see Josh, though, so if you ever make it to Alaska, please visit. So you know, we haven't heard from Richard in a while. He wrote to tell us he got married. Said he's been going to AA and is trying to get sober. The last address I have for him is: 220 Cornflower Road, Austin, TX, but that was more than a year ago. I'm sorry I can't be of more help.

Sincerely, Lana Heister

Patrick started for the stairs and Joshua grabbed his hand to pull him to the elevator. "See? He doesn't care about me."

Eyes still on the letter, Patrick mumbled, "We don't know that."

Joshua raced into the elevator and slammed into the wall with both hands. "If he did, he'd try to find me. I'm hungry; I want some ice cream."

Patrick stuffed the letter into his pocket and hit the button for the second floor. Parenting was harder than he thought. Already he was stomping out emotional fires, arranging day-care, and buying double of everything. No one should have to do it alone, he complained to himself. His appreciation for single parents expanded exponentially.

Back in his apartment, he threw the letter onto the kitchen counter. From the refrigerator he pulled a white paper package of hamburger meat. Then he found the onions, bread crumbs, and eggs for the meatloaf he planned to make, and placed them on the table.

Joshua's father wasn't easy to locate; he might have to give that one up. But he would never drop his search for Emma Lee. Now that he discovered she had been injured, Patrick would ask everyone who knew her, do whatever it took to find out what happened.

20.

Leonard loved the barn, the sheep, and the physical work; he even enjoyed the acrid odors from the urine and manure. All this gave him a reason to leave the house, to be away by himself, and to be completely in charge. Even more, it gave him a feeling of belonging. These animals needed him; they couldn't live without his care.

When Topsy butted his legs for attention, Leonard reached down and scratched the pregnant ewe under her chin. "Oh, yes, you'll be birthing that lamb soon," he crooned. "Another animal to love me." He frowned. "But what was I thinking, letting Emma Lee convince me? I should never have agreed to give your lamb to that stupid boy. I'm too soft."

Turning on the spigot, Leonard filled another bucket with water and poured it into the trough. Then he lifted the pitchfork from the peg and scooped a pile of wet straw and manure into the wheelbarrow. His thoughts drifted to the incident in the kitchen. "David ruined everything, Topsy," he said. "Emma Lee and I would be eating dinner together right now if it weren't for him."

Topsy bleated a response, and he assumed she agreed.

"And something's happened that could mean trouble. But we'll deal with that when it's definite."

After he finished his barn chores, Leonard headed back to the house. On his way down the hill, he hoped Emma Lee would forget about his yelling at David. Then it would all be okay again.

He entered the house and stripped off his coat and boots, then found Emma Lee crouched in the bathroom doorway, brushing David's teeth.

She jumped up when she saw him, and David stared with his big, round, wary eyes.

Leonard said, "The mess cleaned up?"

She nodded.

"Good," he said. That she remembered the incident twisted a lump in his chest. "You know how difficult it is for me to parent at my age. And the boy is incorrigible; it's important for him to know who's in charge."

He took her hand and pulled her toward him, marveling at how tiny she was. Though she fought him, her resistance couldn't conquer his persistence. When her firm breasts met his chest, his whole body tingled with a deep craving. He pulled her head back and bent down, hoping for a kiss, but Emma Lee turned her head and placed a hand over her lips. "Please. No."

Irritation sliced through his hard exterior like an ice fisherman's saw, exposing ego and power that swam beneath the surface. "You owe me; I do everything for you." His demeanor froze again and he released her. "You'll come around."

As he walked away, Leonard turned and spoke over his shoulder. "I'm going to make myself something to eat while you put him to bed. Meet me in the bedroom."

He pulled bread, mayonnaise, and cheese from the refrigerator. Leonard felt energy and anger ebb together, the way black and white paint mixed together turned to muddy grey. His sixty-three-year-old body wasn't what it used to be. Suddenly, he felt gravid with responsibility, having to please and respond to such a young, nubile wife. He poured two fingers of bourbon to buoy his energy and maintain his libido for later, and took a bite of the sandwich. Surely her memory would fade again, and everything would go back to normal. He was looking forward to it.

Grinning like a movie star at a photo shoot, he downed the bourbon and poured another.

As I sit on David's bed reading aloud from *Hop on Pop*, memories of the spice cleanup, the cold wind, and *his* anger all scrub my heart until it's chapped and bleeding. Still, David's requests for another story, a song after, then getting him another drink of water are better than going to bed with that stranger. What if he wants to … well … I can't imagine it. Did we make love last night, or last week? I have no idea, but obviously it happened some time, and the thought disgusts me. I stroke the small bulge below my waist. Can love reach the baby through the father's anger? That's my hope.

Leaving David's room, my bare feet make the wooden floor squeak. I tiptoe down the hallway. Instead of going to the bedroom, I wander the house, letting my fingers touch my surroundings: a lamp, the drapes, the counter top. Nowhere does my brain hold the memory of purchasing this house or moving here, but somehow it feels like home.

Fatigue calls me to the sofa. As drowsiness weighs my eyes, the harsh reality smacks me: with my wounded brain and sketchy memory, work will be impossible. I need this man. My inability to remember locks me into this relationship as surely as a trapped raccoon is stuck in its cage.

An hour later, I wake with a start. Shivering and stiff, I rub my arms to warm them, stretch, and stand. He must be asleep by now. But when I enter the bedroom, he flips on the light. He's lying there on the bed, hands behind his head, stark naked! A screech escapes my mouth; my feet lose their bearing and cause me to fall backwards against the door.

He grins. "Ah, here you are. I've been waiting for you."

Memories of this happening before whack and crack my psyche; I hated it then, as I hate it now. My throat tightens; my guts clench.

The man pats the mattress next to him. "Come to bed, Emma Lee."

That flabby belly, those white legs and scrawny neck; I can't look. My gaze drops as I shuffle to the dresser and pull out flannel pajamas. "Not in the mood."

"Well, I am. I've been waiting all day. You owe me. You promised before our wedding that you'd have sex with me whenever I asked. It's your duty as a wife, remember?"

There's no way to figure out what promises transpired before our wedding. I had no mind or memory of then, and he must know that. Tragically for me, the sum total of my life between injury and now is what he says it is.

When I don't answer he continues, "You're obliged to give me what I want, Emma Lee. It's God's will that a man have sex with his wife. And you *are* my wife."

Letting my knees buckle, my body crumbles to the floor with a thud. Head in hands, I give in to the tears and feel the trap tighten around me. There's no way out.

As he continues to talk, words float and squeeze and sting my brain like jellyfish, making no coherent sense.

He grabs my arm and I hear snippets and scraps: "… injured … trust … wife … God ordained … relax … enjoy." Lifting me to my feet, he forces me to the bed, presses his thin lips against mine, then slides his hand up under my sweater and unhooks my bra. "There. You'll be more comfortable this way. Now, lie on top of me."

Though I'm fatigued to the bone, I push and twist away, tumble off the bed, and head for the door. "Please, leave me alone. I can't do this. Not tonight."

But the naked old man won't stop. He jumps up, too. Pinning me to the door with his weight, he plunges rough cold hands into my sweatpants and clamps on. "Mmm, nice ass," he says. One hand moves upwards, under my sweatshirt, until it surrounds a breast. With the other hand, he yanks my sweatpants and underwear down. He gyrates his hardness against me over and over until I want to vomit.

"You like this; you know you do."

I don't, but I can't to stop it. He's twice my size with his mind made up. I'm so fatigued I can't stand any longer. When my knees give out, he drags me to the bed. There, he yanks my pants and panties off and tosses them across the room. Grunting with pleasure, he spreads my legs and thrusts into me.

Eyes closed, I submit.

Tears stream down my cheeks: rivers of grief. My psyche is squeezed and contorted until its flat, as if pressed between two panes of glass. A mental SOS cuts through the chaos and enters my consciousness, and my heart wails, "Where are you, God? If you're there, help me."

The man slides my sweatshirt over my head and throws it and my bra to the floor. I'm completely naked now, and helpless in every way. I'm his sex slave, his concubine, his play toy. He's strong and healthy enough to use me whenever he wants, and I'm helpless to do anything about it. So that's what this marriage is about—power, sex, and control.

I'm hoping my injury can help me unplug my brain, to forget this event before I can commit it to memory, but I don't know if even that can be counted on.

21.

Monday morning, David trots to the toy corner in the OT waiting room, as if he's done it many times before.

"Don't worry, Mrs. Baxter. I'll keep an eye on your son while you're in therapy as usual," the receptionist says. Her name tag reads Jennifer. She looks familiar.

Leonard and I enter the small office where I notice a poster hanging on the wall near the door, depicting a skull sliced in half. The brain within is sectioned by color. Next to that is a poster of the whole body, showing only nerves. A folder lay open on the otherwise clean desk, but we sit on chairs arranged in a small circle in the center of the room. Neither of us speaks.

I slink into a chair and stare at my feet. He sits ramrod straight, tensing jaw muscles. His fingers form a tight wad.

"Welcome back, Emma Lee. I'm Michael, your occupational therapist, remember?"

Amazingly, I do.

"You look stressed. What's up?"

Leonard cracks his knuckles. "My wife had some kind of setback last week. It's been hell ever since."

Michael sets a laundry basket filled with household items—buttoned dress shirt, laced tennis shoe, hand towels—on the floor in between us. "I'd like to hear about that."

Arms crossed, my husband stretches his legs until his wing tips touch the laundry basket. He frowns, sucks in a deep breath, and exhales a groan. "She didn't recognize me on Friday and since then she's shied away any time I get near her. She says she remembers things, but they are just fabrications of her brain. This must be some kind new symptom. It's a problem. I don't like it, and I want it fixed."

Turning to face me, Michael says, "Want to tell me how it is for you?"

I worry a button on my sweater as I shake my head. There is no way I could tell what happened. He wouldn't believe it.

He shrugs. "Well, then. Let's get to work." He pulls two dish towels from the basket. Handing one to me he says, "We'll begin with something simple—folding towels. You've done it many times. To start, fold it in half," he says, demonstrating, "like this."

Thoughts of bondage, abuse, and rape lasso my reason and tie into knots what little dexterity I might otherwise conjure up. With all that brain traffic and stress, there is too much input; I slide my dark glasses on and shut my eyes.

"Is this too difficult?"

"I'm ... distracted."

"Okay, let's try again. Here, fold it this way first."

After 30 minutes of futile instruction, Michael says, "Dr. Baxter, I think it would be helpful for you to step outside for a few minutes. I'd like to talk to your wife alone."

Leonard's mouth tightens. "Well, she won't remember. I need to be here to help her."

My heart pounds when Michael hustles to the door and opens it. With a slight bow, the black-haired man scoops his hand in a flourish, as if on stage or in a circus ring, and he says, "I know where you'll be. If either of us needs you I'll call." His flashing grin seems to imply, *This will be fine. Trust me.*

The man stands, but his feet stay planted. He assumes that "I'm in charge" stance. An image of him in an office, standing over me with arms crossed, staring, demanding comes to mind. Did we work together? His mouth sets hard. "I think I should stay."

Michael again points out the door and lets his head nod slightly.

Once my husband leaves and the door clicks shut, my shoulders droop. When I lower my head, my unruly curls fall into my eyes.

"So what's going on, Emma Lee?"

With gaze focused on the door, I shudder and grasp my fingers. "I don't know."

Michael takes one of my hands in his and pats it. "Take your time. And don't worry. We're friends, you and I. Even if you don't remember our past meetings, you can trust me. We've been working together almost seven months."

"I woke up a few days ago and didn't know where I was or what happened to me. I miss my work, my old life, all the things I used to be able to do. And I'm living with a stranger. I don't even know his name. How did I end up married to him? Oh, it's so, he… he …" I cover my face with my hands and weep.

When I look up again, I see Michael grinning. As a matter of fact, he looks so happy, I expect him to stand and shout like a fan at a football game. He rubs his hands together then claps. "This is the breakthrough we've been waiting for, hoping for, Emma Lee. Memory's returning." He hands me a tissue. "I'm thrilled for you. You're healing."

"Feels more like I'm falling apart."

"I get that. But now rehabilitation will make sense to you."

I wipe my eyes with a tissue. "So tired. So alone. So … lost. I know I need someone to care for me, but I don't want it to be … him."

Michael is silent a beat, then says, "I'm so sorry."

My voice hushes to a whisper. "I'm being ... he ..."

The office door opens and Jennifer pokes her head in. "Excuse me, Michael, but Dr. Baxter says he's concerned about his wife. Says she's been stressed the past few days and he'd like to take her home to rest."

Michael nods. "All right. Five more minutes." He turns to me. "Go ahead, finish what you were saying."

I twist the tissue in my hands. "Well, my husband uses ..."

The door bursts open. The man rushes into the room, grabs my elbow, and drags me to my feet. "Can't you see my wife is over-tired and confused? This is too much for her."

"Two more minutes. Please," Michael says.

Wrapping his arm around my shoulders, the man shoves me. "I won't have her interrogated like some criminal. If you can't do your job with me in the room, then we're done here. Besides, I have to get back to work. I've got an appointment."

Several seconds elapse before Michael manages to paste a smile on his lips and say, "I ... understand. I'll see you on Thursday as usual, then."

David bounds to his feet when he sees me, and wraps skinny arms around my legs. I hear Jennifer say, "He pays so much attention to her—how nice."

ON THE WAY home from the occupational therapist session, with his left hand on the Cadillac's steering wheel, the man swoops his right hand through the air, punctuating his words, or points at me as he talks.

"You know your brain plays tricks on you, so you can't trust any thought you have. I don't want you spreading lies or exaggerations around town. Yamada and Sister Martha especially shouldn't have to be subjected to your fabrications. So before you say anything to anyone, ask me." He drones on and on, about how I make things up, about how my thoughts can't be trusted, about how crazy and injured and stupid I am. "You think you know what's going on," he continues. "But you're wrong on all counts. You're view of reality is so warped, if it were a board, you'd be good for nothing but firewood."

He repeats himself again; by the third time through, his voice begins to sound like a flock of crows cawing and jabbering.

I wish I were in the back seat with David. He's playing with a Hot Wheels car, running it up his leg and making car noises and ignoring the tirade. Back there, I could plug my ears. But here in the front seat, I'm captive. Leaning my head on the car window, I shut my eyes. Am I mistaken about the episode in the bedroom the other night? Maybe. It's true that my memory can't be trusted.

The man stops the car at the end of the driveway and orders, "You and David get out here. I've got an appointment and have to get back to work."

As my son watches the Cadillac drive away, my gaze drifts up the driveway and my stomach clenches. I wish I could wad that place into a tight ball, like junk mail, and throw it into the garbage. "Let's go for a walk, honey."

David lifts his arms overhead and hops with glee. "Yippee!" he shouts. He races to the creek that parallels the road and hustles down the small bank. When I catch up, my son is squatting at brook's edge, tracing a finger in the chilly water. He picks up a small stone and hurls it. Watching the ripples, he says, "Can I play here?"

"Not now."

David curls his lips in a pretend pout. But he stands and wiggles through the weeds up to the road berm. As we walk away from the house, I notice a clover patch among the other weeds and crouch to investigate. Within moments, I find two four-leafed clovers. Then I remember. Before my injury, I found them everywhere. I smile to realize that another part of my brain is returning. As I stand with clovers in hand, it's like I'm transported back to the lab.

The sounds of the stream, the birds flitting through the trees, the rustle of the branches in the wind barely dent my consciousness and something else takes over. Now, instead of rising from the clover patch near the stream, I'm rising from under my bench at work. I hear what sounds like the air lock opening, wonder why Hiram would leave, check the air lock, can't see it. As I reach across the table to replace a measured plant back under the grow lights, I grab the tray of pots. Then *smack*! Memory of that terrible pain floods back and I swoon.

"Mommy, are you okay?" David says. "You look funny."

I'm back on the road again, holding my son's hand, walking. "Yeah, I'm okay, honey."

Like water behind a dam, determination swells in me; I want to find out what happened to me, and to heal. Mostly, I want to leave the man I married. Yes, I have to get away.

Twenty minutes later David says, "My feet hurt and I'm firsty."

"That's 'thirsty' honey. I don't have anything to drink, but we can sit there and rest a while." We climb the guard rail and settle on a fallen tree trunk that lays a few feet off the road. I watch a squirrel scamper up a leafless maple as a car passes. How free the driver looks. What would it be like, I wonder, if we kept walking and never came back? Or if we hitched a ride to somewhere, anywhere away from here?

David finds a pebble and pitches it into the creek. "Need a drink. Let's go home."

I look right and left. Panic grips me; which way *is* home? Who am I kidding, thinking I could run away? Caring for myself alone would be a challenge, but with two children .... A tear slips from my eye and I say, "I guess I'm stuck."

David stands and pulls on my hand. "I'll help you."

I smile at my son's misunderstanding. Then, squeezing my lids shut to force back the tears, I hold my hand out and say, "Thanks. Hey, let's play follow the leader. You lead us home."

SINCE HE HEARD about Emma Lee's injury, Patrick couldn't stop thinking of her. Where was she? What was she doing? Who was caring for her? Did she return to the South? Now as he drove toward River's Edge Chemical he thought: no wonder she didn't write. Maybe she couldn't.

The first person he met was the receptionist, Katrina Kowalski. When she saw him, she set down her pencil and grinned. Flipping her long hair behind her shoulders she said, "Hey, Patrick, glad to see you. When did you get back?"

"Last week." He checked his watch. "I'm meeting with Baxter about my job in fifteen minutes. Hey, I heard that Emma Lee Dubois got hurt right after I left. Does she still work here?"

Katrina's eyebrows raised and her eyes widened as she sat up straighter. "Didn't you hear? Everybody was talking about it when it happened. She hit her head in the lab and never returned to work. I'm thinking she had some major problems with contamination or something, because apparently, the knock really messed up her mind." Katrina grabbed Patrick's forearm. She glanced down the hallway, then leaned forward and whispered, "And get this. Right around Christmas she actually married Dr. Baxter! It shocked the hell out of everyone."

Patrick's mouth dropped open. "What?" He recalled several conversations he had with Emma Lee about how uncomfortable Dr. Baxter made her feel. He shook his head. "That's nuts."

"You're telling me. She and I both thought he was stalking her. He had a chilling way of showing up wherever she was. One day he even came to the restaurant where we were having lunch and invited himself to our table. Who could have dreamed they'd get married? All my life my mother would say, 'truth is stranger than fiction' and I figured that was her way of saying she didn't like to read novels. But in this case, it's true." She patted the stack of papers on her desk. "Hey, look, I'd like to talk more, but I've got work to do."

Dazed, Patrick continued down the hallway to his boss's office where Baxter's secretary, Rhonda, greeted him with a smile. "Hi, Patrick. Good to see you again. You're early. Dr. B. took his wife to an appointment, but he should be back any minute. Have a seat."

His wife, he thought. Rhonda meant Emma Lee!

Patrick waited several minutes. He took a deep breath and blew it out with force as his mind swirled with thoughts of Joshua, school, Emma Lee, Baxter, his job. Everything seemed to be such a mess.

Finally Dr. Baxter entered the foyer and, opening his office door, motioned for Patrick to follow him. "Kilkenny. Come in."

Patrick couldn't think straight. He plodded after the man and took a chair in silence.

"Heard your sister died. Sorry for your loss," Dr. Baxter mumbled. Then he coughed, as if the politeness poked his throat like a bone. Leonard was quiet for several moments as he shuffled through the folder. Finally he said, "Tried to keep your position open, Kilkenny, but we lost two chemists in the same month. Had to do something. I'm sure you understand. There's a different position open at this plant—mostly paperwork—but it's yours if you want it. Otherwise, you can relocate. We need a laboratory supervisor at the Johnstown plant."

"Johnstown, huh? That's what, a hundred miles away? And the pay?"

Leonard stared out the window. "Same as before if you go to Johnstown. It's cut if you stay. You'll be eligible for promotion if a position comes open, of course." He folded his hands on the desk and pressed his lips together.

Patrick closed his eyes. He didn't want to move again. Running his fingers through his newly-cut hair, he said, "Cut by how much?"

"It's about two-thirds of your prior salary."

Money was important, but not his prime concern right now. Moving would mean finding another school and day-care for Joshua, a new apartment, and most likely, he'd never see Emma Lee again. No, he had to admit, he returned to Pittsburgh because of her. Moving somewhere else was out of the question. "I'll take the position here."

Baxter slid papers across the desk. "This is the contract, and here are the new EPA requirements. You'll be required to adhere to these. Your job would be creating and maintaining the testing schedule according to these rules."

Patrick skimmed the first few paragraphs.

The Environmental Protection Agency (EPA), under the Federal Insecticide, Fungicide and Rodenticide Act (FIFRA) ... New testing is required ... adverse effects to humans ... acute toxic reactions ... poisoning ... memory loss ... birth defects ... brain injury ...

The words "brain injury" and "memory loss" hit him the hardest. Perhaps Emma Lee had been exposed to one of these agents when she got hurt.

"Guess I have my work cut out for me," he said.

Opening the contract to the signature line, he grabbed a pen and signed.

22.

Patrick trudged toward Maria's house that evening, grousing to himself about everything. His first day at work was still five days away and already his job disgusted him. His pay dropped and he got demoted. That was bad. Reams of mind-deadening regulations had to be read and implemented was worse. Then, he was assigned to a windowless basement office, away from everybody. Oh, yes, Baxter must have thought long and hard how to hit him where it hurt most.

On his way home, all he wanted to do was forget—stop at the bar for a beer or put his feet up and watch a Pirates game. Instead, he'd retrieve his nephew from day-care, hustle home, and generate some kind of meal for the boy.

Even dinner caused stress, now. He could no longer wolf down a bowl of cereal or a hunk of chocolate cake for his evening meal. He had to serve real food, like vegetables with milk. This whole working and parenting thing was already getting old.

Maria, dish towel in hand, opened the door and ushered him into the front hallway. As she dried her hands she said, "Hi, Patrick. You're early. Josh did fine, considering."

As he pulled the door closed, Patrick said, "Considering what?"

Maria's eyebrows raised and she combed an errant lock of hair with her fingers. "He and Curtis got into a fight. Come into the living room and sit for a minute."

Following her, Patrick's stomach turned over. He didn't need any more bad news.

"After school the boys were in the playroom together building with blocks. Details are fuzzy, but apparently Joshua got angry about something and kicked the castle over. Curtis confessed to hitting Josh, assuring me that, 'he deserved it.' So Josh threw a handful of blocks—in self-defense, of course. One block smacked Curt, causing his cheek to swell and bruise. The boys had begun wrestling when I showed up. I managed to keep it from escalating to a brawl."

Patrick pressed a palm to his forehead. "Gee, I'm sorry, Maria. Do you kick kids out for bad behavior?"

She laughed as she removed the hair band from her ponytail, tucked in errant strands of hair, and replaced the band. "It'll take more than a scuffle and bruises to get rid of me. I'm tougher than these boys. Sorry, he'll have to stay and work out his issues." She stood. "Let me get Joshua's shoes."

Patrick followed her into the hallway where she handed him two scruffy sneakers. "Look, Patrick, it's obvious Josh has a lot going on. It can't be easy for him, losing his mom so young." She must have noticed the pained look on Patrick's face because she touched his arm and added, "And I'm sure this is tough for you, too, losing your sister. Go easy on yourself."

"I'm tempted to call my cousin in Washington. Maybe if I beg her to take him. That would be easier than this. He could be on a plane tomorrow."

She smiled as they walked down the hallway to the playroom. "I know from experience you should never make a big decision when you're bummed. Besides, Joshua looks up to you. He needs you. This fight? Normal."

"Not sure I believe you, but thanks for the pep talk."

On their walk home, Patrick said, "Why'd you start the fight?"

Joshua scrunched up his face and pursed his lips. "Cause." He was quiet for several seconds. Then he said, "Uncle Patrick, what's a barge?"

"Huh?"

"Curtis told me I had to make a block barge for the moat, but I didn't know what that was. He called me a dummy, said everybody in Pittsburgh knew what a barge was. So I kicked over his stupid castle."

"I see. Well, a barge is a big, flat boat that carries things down the river, stuff like steel or lumber. Did he hurt you?"

Joshua looked sheepish. "No." Then he flashed a shy smile. "But I hurt him. His cheek got black and blue."

"You look proud of that."

"Yeah, well, he stopped calling me names, then."

Patrick felt disappointed. This boy had issues, but there seemed to be so little time to address them. As the grown-up half of this duo, he should probably stop whining about his own problems and focus on Joshua. But how did a person do that? The church and his mother would say pray. He'd try that, but first, he'd start with caring.

Taking the steering wheel in one hand, he wrapped an arm over Joshua's shoulder and pulled him across the seat until the boy was tucked in like a chick under a hen's wing. "It's a tough world, kiddo. Sometimes people make fun of you, treat you badly. But when they do, force usually gets you into more trouble. Better to tell someone in charge. Try that next time. I think Maria would help."

"And what if the person you tell doesn't help? Or there's no one else around?"

He chuckled. "You can always run like crazy." After a few seconds of silence, he said, "And if all else fails, an appropriately thrown block is better than nothing, I guess."

Joshua laughed. "I guess so, too."

Patrick's stomach growled. "Boy, I'm hungry. How about you?"

"Sure am. What's for dinner?"

"I don't feel like cooking. What do you say we go out for burgers and fries?"

"Yeah!" Joshua yelled.

"On our way back from dinner, I want to visit an old friend. We'll stay for a minute or two, to say hi. I think you'll like her and her son. He's about your age."

As HE DID every evening, Leonard dressed in overalls, boots, and coat, and went to feed the sheep. Halfway up the hill to the barn, a rusty orange Datsun heading up his driveway caused him to turn around. Near the house, the car stopped. A scowl crossed Leonard's face when he saw who it was. *Of course. It's pesky Kilkenny—an annoying fly trying to land on my dessert.*

The window rolled down. Patrick placed one arm on the window opening and leaned his head out. The cold March wind caught his now short red hair. "Hey, Doctor Baxter. Thought I'd catch up with Emma Lee, see how she's doing. Is she home?"

Leonard gritted his teeth. His ever-lurking jealousy gnawed his composure like maggots on carrion. Still, he managed to keep his face unexpressive as he spoke. "We're fine. Emma Lee's mending—with my help."

"I was hoping David could meet my nephew, Joshua. My sister's kid. He lives with me now. Thought they might enjoy playing together."

For the first time Leonard noticed the child in the car—a carbon copy of Kilkenny—red hair, deep-set eyes, skinny. "Not possible. We're way too busy."

"Oh, too bad. So maybe we could say hello. Is she home?"

"No."

"Tell her I stopped by, will you? Oh, and thanks for the job. I appreciate it."

Remembering the afternoon's interview turned Leonard's heart cold. He had arranged Patrick's return to River's Edge Chemical with care, ensuring that the Pittsburgh position was uncreative with pay lower than what it should have been. He also beefed up the Johnstown job so only a fool would turn it down. At least, that was his intent. But apparently Kilkenny was as stupid as he was young.

Done with the conversation, Leonard turned on his heel and took a few steps. Then looking over his shoulder he said, "Goodbye, Mr. Kilkenny. She doesn't want to see you. Ever. Don't come back."

As he stomped barnward again, Leonard thought about Emma Lee's recent uncharacteristic behavior. Her rebellion and Patrick's return had both occurred in parallel. That had to be more treachery than synchronicity.

In the barn, as he cleaned stalls and filled the water trough, Leonard chatted with Topsy. "Bet she's been communicating with Patrick all along."

The sheep bleated. He took it as agreement. "And she could have found the letters Patrick sent, too."

Like a spider, dread spun new threads of suspicion in the corner of his mind. He rushed to the feed bin and threw it open. From the limp burlap bag stashed behind a sack of feed, he dragged a parcel wrapped in well-worn brown paper. Unfolding the paper, he counted the envelopes and breathed a sigh of relief. Fifty-two. They were all there, all still sealed.

Leonard ran his fingers through his thinning hair. "You know what these mean, Topsy?"

When the sheep didn't answer, he continued, "I know I shouldn't have kept these, but they prove that I won the prize." Holding a few of the envelopes, Leonard sashayed around the barn floor. When he got near Topsy, he shoved them into the sheep's face and said, "These letters mean Kilkenny wasn't smart enough to get her; I was." Grinning, he rewrapped the paper around the letters. "But I'm not taking chances. She might find them in here." He replaced the letters into the sack and slid them behind the feed bin.

"Now I have to talk to her," he mumbled. "Find out what lies she's telling that would make him so bold, bring him here, out in the open like that."

He rushed through the feeding and watering, then raced back to the house. Yanking the front door open he called, "Emma Lee, where are you?"

She poked her head out from the kitchen and answered in a tiny, nervous voice, "In here."

Off came the overalls, boots and coat. Once they were properly hung on the correct peg and stowed in the right place, straight and neat, he stomped into the kitchen. "Why did that man show up in our driveway looking for you? Did you invite him?"

Emma Lee hung her dish towel and stared at him in confusion, shaking her head from side to side. "Who? I didn't ..."

Her voice had more of a drawl than usual, so Leonard knew she was lying. "You called him, didn't you? What did you tell him? When were you going to tell me about it? Who does he think he is, coming here like that?" With each question his voice grew louder until he was shouting.

David raced to his mother, squeezed between her and Leonard, and pushed on his stepfather's legs. "Leave Mom alone."

Leonard felt his irritation boil. If he had been at work, he would have capped its angry geyser. But this was home; no need to be careful. He yelled, "Who do you think you are, interfering in adult business?"

Emma Lee squeezed between boy and man, squatted, and grabbed David by his shoulders. "This doesn't concern you."

David set his mouth hard and hugged her. "I need to protect you, Mom."

Taking the boy by the shoulders, her voice grew stern. "Listen to me. You must go. Now."

David thrust out his bottom lip. "But …"

"Please go, honey. Please."

Finally the boy stomped away and she stood again.

Leonard sneered. No matter how much you loved them, women took advantage. That was their nature. He liked helping a person who needed it, a person who was sick or bedridden, but not this, not a woman playing him for a fool. She had to be put in her place. They all did. His mother was a prime example. All she did was sit around and smoke cigarettes, demanding that he wait on her. She'd yell, "Bring me a beer!" Or "Make me a sandwich," or "Lenny, change the channel." And she expected him to jump up and do whatever she asked. That would never happen again, not with Emma Lee, not with anyone.

Moving closer so his forehead pressed against hers and pinning her body to the wall with his hands, he said, "I won't have any other man hanging around. If I ever catch one here, I'll shoot him."

Her eyes widened and her mouth dropped open. She looked shocked, like she'd been slapped. "You'd shoot someone? With a gun?"

"Damn straight I'd shoot him. Yes, with a *gun*," he repeated for emphasis. "Got that?"

When she pushed his chest, he decided to free her. He had made his point.

Slumping against the wall, she pressed her fingertips onto her eyelids.

He yanked her arm. "Tomorrow when you see Sister Martha, I don't want you repeating lies about me like you are prone to do, or tell her tales that make me look like an ogre. You hear?"

When she whispered, "You're hurting me," he remembered to release his grip. Oh, he loved her so much—that beautiful face, those round breasts, those curvy hips. Why couldn't she obey? Then everything would be perfect. "You know what I'm saying, don't you?"

He liked how submissive she looked when she nodded her assent.

23.

I help David into the Ford station wagon, then slide behind the wheel. I'm an empty shell, hollowed from last night's fight, and from living with a madman. As I start the car, I rub the back of my head. It hurts more than usual. Is Sister Martha kind and compassionate? Can I trust her enough to share what happened? I don't know, but before I do any of that, first, I have to *find* her. I pull the directions I wrote last Friday from my coat pocket.

The scribbled notes remind me of the treasure maps I drew as a child with my friends, after we learned about the pirates who roamed the coastal waters of Charleston. Mandy, Bubba, or I would bury something—a painted stone, a pencil, a toy—in the dirt, then draw a map from the porch to the treasure. We had one requirement: the burial spot on the map had to be marked with a huge red X. Before each dig, we'd chant together, "X marks the spot."

If Bubba made the map, you might as well kiss the hidden item goodbye. Even he couldn't find it again. On the other hand, Mandy and I were experts. So my sense of direction was good, once. I'm hoping it still is.

I stare at the scrap of paper again. The scribbled notes have no red X, and I'm sure there won't be one painted on Sister Martha's office building, either. So it's up to this paltry brain of mine and a four-year-old boy to ensure we arrive at the right place at the right time.

I read the first instruction. "Turn left at the end of the driveway." Easy enough.

A mile and a half down the country road, still following the directions, I take a right onto Ohio River Boulevard, the yellow brick road I used to see from my apartment window. *I know where I am!* Soon David points to a small brick building on the right. "There it is, Mom. Turn here."

I grin, thrilled with my tiny accomplishment. I park the car and David hops out.

"I'll race you," he yells and tears off.

Giggling at my son's exuberance, I jog after him. When I open the office door, a woman matching my mental image of Sister Martha meets me with a hug. "Hello, my dear. I'm glad you could make it. Please, follow me."

Down the hall a younger woman wearing a white dress and a crucifix opens the door to a playroom and escorts my son in. The mischief in her eyes tells me she enjoys playing with him.

In Sister Martha's office, she says, "How are you, dear? I got worried when I didn't hear from you. I was hoping you weren't ill."

"No, not ill. Getting better. My memory is returning."

"How wonderful!"

"Not all of it, of course. I can remember some of what happened before the accident, but not the accident itself or what happened since. One day I woke up and boom! I discovered I'm wounded, married, pregnant, lost my job, and completely dependent. My occupational therapist called it a breakthrough, good news; he said I'll start remembering more, now."

Sister Martha raises both arms heavenward. "Oh, praise be to God." Her eyes turn soft and she purses her lips. "But you don't look like you're celebrating, dear. Of course, this can't be easy, losing eight months of your life, waking to so many changes." She circles her index finger in front of her heart. "I'd like to hear what's been happening inside. Want to talk about that?"

"Well … ." I place my hand on my belly. "Feels like I'm drowning in memories. Sometimes they come so fast, I can't catch my breath. And I don't even know if what I'm recalling is true. I can't seem to depend on anything anymore, and that scares me."

Sister Martha tents her fingers and rests her chin on them. I'm glad she doesn't tell me what to do, or that I should stop feeling what I'm feeling.

I'm tempted to spill my guts, tell her all that's happening at home, cry about the man who is apparently my husband, explain how hard it is, but I'm nervous. I fiddle with my ring and say, "How long have you known me?"

The nun's lips curve into a serene smile. She settles back into her chair as if ready to tell a story, one she apparently has told often.

"Since you got hurt. I'm the hospital chaplain. I came into your room when the human relations woman from your work was there. She asked me to help with David. There was an element of desperation in her plea. She said you didn't have any family nearby, and no one could take David. So Sister Angela and took him in for a few weeks until you were released.

"Once you left the hospital, there was no one to care for you, either. As you might recall, Leonard was your boss at the time. He took a personal interest in your well-being, stepped right up to the challenge and tended to your every need while you were recuperating. It was his money that paid for your medicines, doctors, round-the-clock nursing care; his determination and clout got you therapy and specialist appointments you needed. What a godsend he was, I tell you. And still is, the way he continues to care for you.

"Social services checked up on you, of course. But I'd wager that without Dr. Baxter taking care of the details, David would be in foster care or the orphanage by now. And who knows what would have become of you? It could have been bad."

She shakes her head and gazes through me, growing silent for a few moments. Returning to the present, she pats my knee and says, "I look forward to accompanying you through this journey."

It hits me that Sister Martha likes my husband: the man who raped me, the man who abused me. She *likes* him. I stare at the floor and then out the window. "I don't remember anything about my accident, our wedding, or moving to the farm."

"But memories are returning?"

"Certain incidents pop into my brain. Like this morning, I remembered all the details about the day David's father, Gordon, left for the Peace Corps. How I cried, wondered how I'd get along without him. That reminded me of the day my friend, Patrick, left for Washington State, and the sadness I had that day, too. Remembering him reminded me of the people I had come to know at the lab when I worked there. All that seems like yesterday, but my near past is shaky. I still can't remember my husband's name most of the time."

I don't say that I *do* recall his warning: "*I'll shoot Patrick if he ever comes around again.*" And "*Don't talk about what happens here, or else.*" Am I allowed to talk about sex with a nun? What if she tells him what I've said and he takes it out on me, or shoots someone?

My voice lowers, as if he can overhear me. "I don't remember marrying him. He doesn't love David."

Her face takes on a look of compassion and she nods slightly. "Many people find it difficult to parent a step-child. I can talk to him for you, suggest that he join our step-parent support group if you like. I think it could help."

I bolt to my feet so quickly that I knock my chair over. "No! Don't do that."

Sister Martha raises her eyebrows and re-rights the chair. "Oh, my. What's wrong?"

I wilt back onto the chair and my whole body shakes. "The man … he's … scary. I keep … I don't know." I cover my face with my hands. "Please don't mention this to him. He'd be angry that I told you."

She leans forward in her chair. "Oh, my dear, how difficult this must be for you. Certainly, I will keep what you say confidential, but I can assure you that Leonard cares for you. I saw how he treated you before you were married. There's deep tenderness there, but it's often hidden by his shy nature." Sister Martha takes my hands in hers. "He saved your life."

"I know." I smile, trying to convince myself that I'm glad about that.

"Don't forget to look for God in this. You need help, and Leonard is willing to give that. Could seeing this as an arranged marriage make a difference?"

"I thought of that." I cover my face with my hands and weep.

Sister Martha speaks in hushed tones, like we're in a funeral parlor.

As I weep, the words run through my mind like a hamster on a wheel, round and round. *"What happens in the family stays in the family. I'll shoot Patrick if he ever comes around again."*

I squeeze my eyes shut and wrap my arms around my waist. "An arranged marriage. I'll try that again."

Still shaky, I stand and slide my arms into my coat sleeves. "Time to go home."

24.

Early Friday morning, Sister Martha wasn't even dressed yet when the phone rang. But habit forced her to pick up the receiver. "Sister Martha speaking," she said, trying to sound awake and cheerful.

A woman's voice whispered, "This is Emma Lee."

"Oh my dear, hello. How are you? I've been worried about you since our last session."

"Um, I … I won't be seeing you anymore." Her voice sounded flat, almost mechanical.

Martha felt crestfallen. "But Emma Lee, you made a huge breakthrough. We should see each other more often, not less. Won't you please reconsider?"

"I want to, but … he said … well, he said … I can't." Click! The call was ended.

When she replaced the phone onto its cradle, Sr. Martha dialed Emma Lee's number and let the phone ring eight times, but there was no answer. Her gut twisted. Something wasn't right, she could feel it. She sat for several minutes wondering what to do next. Eventually she grabbed her coat, headed outside, and strode down the street to think.

Did Leonard force Emma Lee to quit seeing her? It didn't make any sense. Perhaps Emma Lee was confused; perhaps she misinterpreted. "I must have failed her," she mumbled.

Coat and hat on, Sr. Martha paced down Church Street. The wind whipped through the thin wool and she shivered. At the end of the block she turned around and raced back to her office, needing answers. She jumped in her car and drove as fast as she dared down the boulevard, across the bridge, and to the parking lot of River's Edge Chemical. When she entered the building, a tall, beautiful woman behind the reception desk greeted her. Her name tag said "Katrina."

"Good morning," the woman said. "May I help you?"

"I need to speak with Dr. Leonard Baxter right away, please."

"Do you have an appointment? He is usually booked."

"Tell him Sister Martha Lenzner is here about his wife." When she saw the alarm on Katrina's face she said, "No emergency, but it's urgent."

After a ten-minute wait, Sister Martha was escorted into Dr. Baxter's office. As usual, his expression held no emotion. "Martha. What can I do for you?"

She inhaled deeply. "Emma Lee called to tell me she'll no longer be coming to see me. She seemed to indicate you told her she couldn't. I don't understand, Leonard. You know she was making progress with me, and she must continue. Please tell me what's going on. Is there a problem I should know about?"

There was a long pause. Finally Leonard said, "Emma Lee had some issues with her last session. I don't know why she said *I* want to stop her coming. We both thought it best that she take some time off from seeing you. It's nothing personal about you. It's her. She needs some time to process. You understand."

Sister Martha pressed her forehead into her hand and closed her eyes for a moment. Determined to make her point, she said, "This seems premature. I'd like her to come at least one more time, to wrap things up, decide where we go from here."

"Look, Sister, she can't come see you right now. Practicing her occupational therapy takes a lot of time, and even that seems to overwhelm her. She's fragile. And I don't think she should be pushed too hard. I'm sure we both want what's best for her."

Sister Martha felt stuck. "I understand. I want you to know, though, she's welcome to return at any time."

THE ACRID ODOR of pesticide stung his lungs as Patrick trotted up the steps to Three River's Chemical and yanked open the huge wooden front door. He wondered why he even wanted this job. It wasn't the pay, or the atmosphere, for sure. He'd start looking for something else right away, but this job would fill Joshua's belly and keep a roof over their heads.

Inside the building, Katrina sat behind the tall reception desk like a judge in a courtroom, and donned her parade float smile. "Hello, Patrick," she said. "What brings you back here so soon?"

"Paperwork."

In the H.R. office, Patrick found Nancy biting a hangnail as she pushed closed a file drawer with her hip. She said, "Hey, Patrick, good to see you again. Come with me."

She directed him to a chair at a small, round table in the corner. Plopping a pile of paperwork down in front of him, she said, "You'll need to fill out all of these. Once you're done, we can go over them, if you like."

Patrick spent over an hour replicating his name, address, social security number, along with other information on each form, grumbling to himself about the repetitions. But his mind was on the meeting with Katrina.

All the forms were complete at noon; he handed the pile to Nancy.

"See you on Monday, then," she said.

As he neared the reception desk, a middle-aged woman wearing a long wool coat over a denim jumper and flat-healed leather shoes burst from Baxter's office. Her face was flushed and her lips pursed. The short hair and crucifix told Patrick she was a nun, but what would a nun be doing here, in the chemical factory?

Patrick said to her, "Are you all right, Sister?"

"I got bad news. Doctor Baxter's wife won't be coming for counseling any longer."

"Emma Lee? She's all right?"

The surprise registered on Sister Martha's face when she said, "Do you know her?"

"Yes, we were friends before I took a leave of absence."

"Small world. This morning she fired me as her counselor. I was hoping to convince Dr. Baxter to help her change her mind."

Patrick felt sure it wasn't Emma Lee's decision to relieve this nun from her duties. He glanced at the clock on the wall. "How about lunch, Sister? Gino's is right down the street. My treat."

"Why thank you, young man. I'd love that. I missed breakfast."

When they reached the restaurant, Sister Martha said, "What's good?"

"Soup of the day. Homemade."

The heavyset waitress waddled over, dropped two glasses of water on the table. She tapped her pen on the pad a few times and asked, "What'll it be?"

Patrick ordered the French dip; Sister Martha chose chicken noodle soup and sandwich, and the waitress sauntered off.

"I have to admit I have an ulterior motive for bringing you here, Sister. I knew Emma Lee before she got hurt, and I liked her enough to write to her while I was away. Now I see why she never answered those letters."

He traced a scar in the tabletop with his index finger. "I'm surprised she's married, and shocked that she married Dr. Baxter. I visited the farm, hoping to talk with her, but got intercepted by Baxter who forbade me to see Emma Lee ever. Then he threw me off the property."

The waitress dropped the plates of food and the bowl of soup onto the table. Once she was gone, Sister Martha took a bite and swallowed before she said, "Oh, dear. Do you think he was jealous? You are a good looking young man."

"Possible. But what do you know about it, Sister? What is going on with her, with him?"

Sister Martha smiled. "It's simple. She was completely helpless after the injury. Leonard was there for her, and he likes helping."

"I know that man. He's controlling and manipulative. Bet he's keeping her captive."

She took a sip of water, then shaking her head slowly, she said, "You sure have an active imagination. But I'll tell you what. If she comes back to see me, I'll ask her. Okay?"

"I guess it has to be okay. I can't do anything else about it."

Friday evening Katrina stood outside the Cathedral of Learning, gym bag over her shoulder. She had showered and reapplied her makeup after the class. Looking up, she caught a glimpse of someone jogging across the university lawn. It wasn't Michael. The stride wasn't fluid enough, the legs too short, the body too uncoordinated.

Shortly after, he arrived. "Hi," he said, sliding his arm around her waist. "Are you ready for dinner?"

Katrina arched a brushed eyebrow. "Nothing like dancing to improve the appetite. I'm starving."

He slid his hand behind her back. "Okay. Let me dance up an appetite, too."

Moving to nonexistent music, he led her through a series of steps and swirls. As the dance ended he dipped her head down until her hair brushed the ground. When she was upright again, he bowed.

She flushed. "That was wonderful. You're the first guy I've dated who knew how to dance."

"Thank you. My mother thought it important that every man know the basics, and made sure I had lessons. Turns out she was right; those lessons paid off. I got you." Taking her chin in his hand, he brought his lips to meet hers: a delicate, sensual touch.

Warmth shot from her belly up to her cheeks and she let herself melt. Her body ached for more. But reason butted in, urging caution. She wouldn't allow herself to fall for him too quickly, like she had done with Sloan and all the others. This time she'd move with caution. When she pushed him away she purred, "Whoa, that was quite a kiss."

He grinned. "And there are plenty more where that came from. Want another sample?"

She laughed and put both hands on his chest. "Down, boy. Dinner's calling."

He pointed down the alley. "My car's right there."

Picking up her gym bag, Michael let Katrina hook her arm through his; together they strolled to the MGB and drove off.

"So how's work?" Katrina asked.

"It's like a dance, some slow parts, some fast. Some dips and twirls. One case really intrigues me right now."

Katrina said, "I'd love to hear about it."

"I've been seeing this woman with a head injury for about seven months now. On Tuesday she had a major breakthrough; she regained some short-term memory and I thought I'd see immediate progress from then on. But yesterday she slipped backwards and she hardly said a word."

Katrina felt intrigued. "Is that normal?"

He shook his head. "No. Someone or something is mucking up her progress. But that's the great thing about this work. I get to figure it out. In her case, I think it has something to do with the husband. She tried to tell me about it, but he interrupted. He does seem to care for her. I mean, he brings her to appointments, makes sure she practices her therapy. But he's an odd character, much older than her, stern, and rather controlling."

She faced Michael, hands splayed in surprise. "Is this Emma Lee Baxter you're talking about?" When his jaw dropped, Katrina continued, "I used to work with her. I was there the day she was injured."

He pulled the car into the lot behind the restaurant and parked. Keeping his hands on the steering wheel, he said, "Small world, huh?"

An uneasy feeling tunneled through Katrina. "I know Dr. Baxter, too. He's my boss. Let me tell you, he's very stuck on himself, and way, way creepy. I'd call him lecherous. Back when Emma Lee started to work, she was sure he was stalking her."

"Hm. It's starting to make sense." Then he grinned, took a tendril of her hair between his fingers, and twirled it. "But let's not ruin our evening talking business. You're beautiful, do you know that? I could sit here and look at your face all night." He winked.

She shook off her uneasiness and giggled. "I'm sure you could. But I was promised dinner, and I'm starving."

He slipped out of the car, opened her door with a bow, and said, "Your wish is my command. Dinner it is."

25.

"I'm going grocery shopping. Make sure you hang the laundry when it's done, feed the sheep, and gather the eggs," Leonard barked. "I made a furnace repair appointment for next Saturday, so you won't have to worry about that."

I know my brain is still injured; I accept that I need to be told almost everything, but his bossy attitude stinks. I pull my hands from the dishwater, dry them on my apron, and gaze at the graying geezer who now controls my life. Yes, I'm his slave. He owns me, and I am afraid of him. I have to do *what* the man wants, *when* he wants it. But I've learned how to turn my mind off during those times. It's not that hard, really; my injured brain is easily distracted.

I am grateful for some things. Supervision. Shelter. Sustenance. But mostly, I'm thankful that David can live with me, not in the orphanage. Not with strangers.

Sliding my ever-present notebook from my pocket, I enter the furnace appointment and other chores into it.

After Leonard drives away, David places his bowl in the sink. "I'll go feed the chickens and check on Topsy. You come when you're done, Mom."

I agree, feeling the ache in my heart. The boy must parent his parent. No child should have to do that.

Shoving on his boots, he yells, "See ya later," and dashes out the door.

I slide my hands back into the dishwater. Life has become more bearable since I've understood the "rules" and I've found little ways around them. Like last night. I whispered my desire to see Sister Martha again in his ear after he'd fulfilled himself sexually, and he said he'd think about it. Not complete success, but at least not a no.

I scrub the rest of the dishes, and then check my notebook for my next task. Can I live the rest of my life this way? Shrugging, I decide that's too heavy a question for a chilly Saturday morning.

I hear the washing machine sloshing. I can't hang out the laundry yet, so I head to the barn.

I step over the muddy puddle that formed in the rain last evening and open the dark, unpainted barn door. The barn air smells heavy with the thick odor of wet wool and dust. Somehow it comforts me.

"Look, Mom," David says, pointing to the rays of sun sneaking through the cracks between the wall boards. Long strips of sunlight stream across the barn. They sparkle with silver dust mote flecks. "The dust is dancing in the sunlight." He swipes his hand through the rays, wiggling his fingers.

"That's cool," I say.

"After we do our chores, can I look for the kittens? I saw the mother cat squeezing behind the feed bin. I'll bet her babies are back there."

"Sure." I pick up a bucket to fill the water trough as David scratches the other sheep under their chins. He hums a few bars of *Mary Had a Little Lamb*.

Topsy doesn't come for her usual petting. Instead she stands on the far side of the stall, stamping her feet and bleating. David points to her swollen udder. "Look, Mom. It's gi-gunda."

"The lamb should be here soon," I say. "What will you call it?"

If it's a boy, I'm going to call it Jojo. If it's a girl, then …" he props a finger on his chin and looks upwards. Grinning, says, "I'll call a girl Jojo, too. Can't wait to hold it."

When I open the old wooden bin, the odor of oats fills my nostrils and I gag. Repressing my urge to throw up, I scoop a can full of feed.

David peers in. "I could fit in there."

I rest the heavy wooden lid on the wall behind the bin and pour the mash into the tray. "I guess you could, all right." Then I laugh. "My adventurer, always looking for new places to explore, aren't you?"

"Will you help me get in?" he asks.

I lift my son and let him slide into the near-empty deep wooden box.

He pumps his arms with excitement. "This is so cool." Then he hunches down. "Close the lid." When I do, he giggles. "See? I'm disappeared."

As I open the lid again I hold my breath against the smell. Helping him out and closing the bin again, I exhale and say, "Yep. That's cool."

David giggles again. Sliding sideways, he slips behind the bin. "See? I fit in here, too."

I peer into the dark space. "Come out of there, you little scamp. We've got work to do."

"It's my new secret place. And I found something," he says.

"Kittens?" I ask.

He drags a brown paper package out from within a burlap feed sack and hands it to me. "Look-it."

I turn over the package. "Maybe it's a map to buried treasure," I say. "Or a bunch of money."

Setting the bundle on the feed bin lid, I unwrap it. Several white envelopes flutter into the straw.

David wiggles out from behind the bin, picks up the envelopes, and hand them to me. "What are they, Mommy?"

The envelopes are addressed to me. As I fan through the stack, I notice that all of them were postmarked Pasco, Washington. I count them. Fifty-two letters—all in the same handwriting, all addressed to my apartment, all from Patrick.

I slide to the floor and cradle my head in my hands, trying to think. I never knew Patrick sent me letters. They aren't open, so I obviously haven't read them.

My hands shake as I pick up a letter, rip it open, and read.

October 10, 1971

Dear Emma Lee,

I miss you. I think about you every day and wonder why I haven't heard from you. I tried to call again yesterday, but your phone was disconnected. I guess that means you've moved on. Yet, for some reason I can't stop writing to you.

I'm glad I'm here, though. My sister is fading fast and it won't be long now before she dies. On one hand, I'll miss her dearly. On the other, I'm glad she'll be out of pain. It's so hard on her and Joshua.

When I'm not tending to Peggy, I've been busy. Today I repaired the fence. When I get home, if you haven't moved back to South Carolina, I hope we can get together and be friends again.

The letter went on about the weather and other repairs, and it was signed: *Love, Patrick.*

I clasp the paper to my breast, close my eyes, and sigh, too stunned to move. I think again about the man I've married and my stomach twists. Things could be different. Patrick cared once. Could he still, now that I am so injured?

We hear tires crunching on rocks in the driveway, so David races to the barn door and looks out. "It's him, Mommy. Daddy Leonard is home."

I stare at the stack of letters in my lap. How did they get behind the feed bin? The thought strikes me like a wrecking ball. Leonard must have hidden them. I don't want him to know I found the letters, not until I figure out what to do about them. "Help me get these back in the paper wrapper, honey. Hurry."

We fold the brown paper around the letters again and slide the package into the burlap sack. Then I shove it back behind the bin. Trying to ignore the sickening pain that now knots my gut, I fill a bucket with water and pour it into the trough.

A plaintive bleat catches our attention. Topsy kneels on her front knees, then folds her body onto the ground. After a few moments, she jumps up again. When she bleats, she sounds as if she's in pain. Then suddenly a big blob appears under her tail.

"Look!" David yells and points to Topsy. "Jojo's coming. My lamb is coming!"

We race to the stall. Now the lamb's head and front feet slide out of the mother sheep. It's wrapped in a clear, wet, slimy skin.

"We'll wait and watch to see if she needs any help." I sit in the straw nearby and David squats next to me.

Topsy stands throughout the birth and David keeps encouraging her. "This is so cool," he says. "Kind of messy and gross, too, though."

The lamb, wet and slimy, smelling of blood and musk, drops head first to the straw. When it's completely out, Topsy starts licking the slime from her baby.

David scrunches his nose. "Ew, why does she do that?"

"It helps dry the baby so it stays warm, and it's good for her, too."

The lamb stands on wobbly legs while its mother keeps licking it.

David jumps and yells, and throws his arms around in excitement. "This is the best thing that ever happened to me," he says. "I have a pet!"

"Emma Lee?" I hear my name called. "Are you in here?"

"Over here by the sheep," I reply. "The lamb. It's here!"

David is trying to corral the lamb in his arms when the baby lurches and begins suckling a teat on its mother's udder. David giggles and says, "Look, Jojo can walk. An' he's only new-born."

"Of course he can walk," the man grumbles. "Lambs are smarter than little boys."

"So can lambs learn tricks?" David asks. "I want to teach him some."

"Never mind about that. You have chores to do, young man."

David's forehead wrinkles. "I already fed the sheep and collected the eggs like you said."

"Good, because this lamb comes with conditions. He's yours as long as you're obedient. That means you do your chores and you take care of him, and you can keep him. If not, he comes back to me. You understand?"

David looks solemn now, with brows knitted and lips pursed, he nods his head.

"You can't take him back. You gave him to David," I protest.

The man points at me and scowls again. "This is none of your business. It's between me and the boy. Besides, he has to learn responsibility somehow. This is good for him."

When he stares at the open feed bin, I shake, praying he won't think about the letters.

"And close the bin after you use it," he scolds, slamming it down. "The mice will get into it."

26.

Katrina peeled an orange and popped a slice into her mouth. She stood in front of her full-length mirror, assessing the damage of yesterday's late night with Michael. Three hours was all she had to turn this hung-over, worn-looking body into a beauty queen. She had to get busy.

The phone rang. "Hey, girl, Tanisha here. I found your leg warmers in the locker room after class. I'll bring them Monday."

"Oh, thanks."

Katrina and Tanisha had been in classes together for the past four years, and if all went well, both women would be graduating from the University of Pittsburgh in June with a degree in dance. Tall and willowy, Tanisha had close-shaved hair and flashing dark eyes. They both loved modern dance. Tanisha often boasted that she was a true by-product of the American melting pot: a conglomeration of black, Hispanic, Russian, and Samoan. Still, she embraced the Black culture in Pittsburgh, married a black man, and lived on the North Side.

"How's Michael?" she asked.

"He's good. No, great. He can dance, even without music."

"So. It's getting serious, then?"

Katrina laughed and fell into her recliner. "Not yet. I keep wondering if I could stand being married."

"That sounds *real* serious."

"No, thinking about marriage actually helps me avoid it. Like, what if he expected home-cooked meals? Or wanted me to mend his holey socks? Or have a kid right away, buy a house, or do any of that suburban junk? I wouldn't be able to handle it."

"I know he's gorgeous, so you probably forget that there's more to him than his beautiful body." Tanisha said. "But you should be talkin' about that stuff with him."

"That might give him the wrong impression. I have no desire to take up where my mother left off. No, I'm avoiding domesticity—forever if possible."

"Not everyone who gets married ends up in suburbia, honey. I didn't. Take it from me, there are many ways to make marriage work."

"Maybe." She heard the wail of a child through the phone.

"Well, the baby woke up. Gotta go. See you on Monday."

When she hung up, Katrina headed to the bathroom. It dawned on her that having sex with a man before she knew him thrust the relationship into unanticipated (and unwanted) directions and unspoken expectations. On his part, a sense of ownership and entitlement. On hers, feeling used, piled with a boatload of guilt. "Not worth it," she said aloud.

Her stomach growled. If she hadn't been preparing for a date, she would have driven across the bridge to *Perfect Pierogi* and eaten three of the fried potato dumplings fresh from the skillet. Thinking of the Polish pierogi restaurant reminded her of the lunch she had with Emma Lee several months ago, when Dr. Baxter just showed up and invited himself to their table. Everyone noticed how Baxter had watched Emma Lee with more leer than smile. Katrina had forgotten about that. Living with Baxter had to be harsh if not horrendous.

Three hours later, Katrina's face wore foundation, blush, lipstick, eye shadow and liner, brow pencil, and mascara, transforming her from dull to delicious.

When Michael arrived, he scanned her up and down and grinned. "You're gorgeous."

He wasn't much taller than her five-feet ten, but he was built like a swimmer with wide shoulders and narrow waist. And oh, he looked delicious in his black tuxedo. This wasn't a special occasion, nothing more than an ordinary Saturday date. But she felt special. When he swept into her living room like he owned it, she couldn't resist smiling.

Cupping her chin in his hands, he brought his lips to meet hers. A lovely heat traveled from her belly to her ears. It softened her bones until her insides felt like lava lamp liquid. "You've got one potent set of lips there," she said, weaving her fingers behind his neck.

He hooked an arm around her waist and eased her closer, letting his straight, black hair fall into his eyes. "You know what the song says." He began singing. "If you wanna know if he loves you so, it's in his kiss."

The corners of her mouth rose to a pouty smile. "And of course, songs are never wrong."

"Never," he said, shaking his head with fake solemnity. "Hey, I'm a bit early. We could sit and talk for a bit. What do you say?"

If he was like the others, he'd quickly switch from words to actions. This would be the test. She grabbed two bottles of Iron City from the refrigerator and slid onto the couch next to him. Clinking her beer bottle against his, she said, "Okay, you start."

He slid an arm around her shoulders.

Here it comes, she thought.

He settled back and said, "So tell me, what are your plans after graduation? What drives you?"

In the past, (even twenty minutes prior) she wouldn't have given him an opportunity to know her deeper thoughts. But something shifted. So she expounded on her passion for fashion and dance, her desire to open a studio, and her aversion to living in the suburbs. Ten minutes stretched to thirty. Still, his gaze stayed on her face.

When she finished, he said, "I gotta tell you, I'm falling for you, Katrina. Head over heels. I love you." When he leaned forward to kiss her again, she stood.

"I'll be right back."

She stumbled down the hallway, feeling out of balance. She closed the bathroom door behind her and stared at her reflection in the mirror. "Buck up, girl," she scolded herself. "If you can handle the drunk ones, you can certainly handle the one who says he loves you."

When she returned to the living room, amusement danced in Michael's eyes. He took her hand. "Judging from your reaction, I must have overstepped my bounds. But I can wait for as long as it takes." He lifted her coat. "Time to go."

Sliding arms into coat sleeves, Katrina realized how different he was. Somehow being with him was more secure; nicer. Yeah, he was really nice. Now, she'd be extra careful.

27.

I yawn and take a sip of orange juice. Last night was difficult and I'm sleep deprived. First, David woke twice with nightmares. Then, before Leonard left for work, he roused me for sex. In the few days since regaining my memory, I've managed to train myself to be docile. I numb my emotions and try to forget. This morning, after he finished with me, he insisted we eat breakfast together. He made eggs and toast and coffee, which I could barely eat.

Now, the man is gone, and David is up, so I can smile.

He squeezes the juice from his grapefruit. Much of it misses the spoon and lands on his plate. He scowls, lifts the plate, and pours the juice into his mouth. Wagging his head he says, "Mom, today I'm going to teach Jojo to roll over."

"That's nice," I say, taking another sip of juice.

After breakfast, David and I tromp to the barn. I carry water to the troughs; David collects the eggs and reminds me to feed the sheep. When all my chores are complete, I sit in the straw next to the sheep stall, pull my ever-present notebook from my pocket, and cross the chores off the list.

"You can play now, David," I say, rubbing my forehead. "My head hurts some, so I'll just sit and watch."

He climbs through the boards to the sheep; I settle onto the straw next to the feed bin and take a deep breath. Odors of dust, feed, hay, and manure pepper the air, creating a farmer's perfume. Back when I lived in Aiken, I was a city girl through and through, a Southern Belle, a young woman destined for finer things. But here in the barn, I have begun to appreciate the basics such as sheep and hay and water. My jewels are now fresh dewdrops sparkling in the morning sun. To me, fancy clothes are jeans without mud on them. And my dress-up boots are those made of leather instead of rubber.

As I watch David romp with his new pet, I'm so glad I have this boy; he's my joy. Watching him reminds me of the baby in my womb, and my smile widens. I lean back on the wooden bin and close my eyes, and the letters come to mind. Why had Patrick written so many? I have to find out.

I crawl to the side of the bin and yank the burlap sack out from behind it. I unwrap them, and then try to put them into order by date. Soon I'm so confused that I give up and start reading.

The first letter I open today is dated September 12, 1971. Patrick tells of the harsh heat, golden sunsets, clear blue water in the Columbia River, coyotes and quail, meadow larks and maddening monotony. "It's beautiful here, in a stark kind of way," the letter says.

I slide to the floor and cradle my head in my hands, trying to think. I can't remember when to eat or how to add numbers anymore, but I can vividly recall Patrick.

I hear a giggle and look up. David stands with his arms around Jojo's neck, and the lamb is licking his cheek. It's so cute I smile.

"Look, Mom. He's my friend."

"Jojo loves you, for sure. So do I," I say.

I watch them play a few minutes, then I return to reading. The next envelope is from October. His sister is unable to eat anymore, and his words are gloomy and sad. My head throbs, but I continue to read. In the next letter, Patrick tells how he cared for Peggy, giving sponge baths and morphine, and how he helped Joshua with his homework. I set down the letter and stare at the dust floating in the air and wish that Patrick had taken me with him, or that I had not hurt my head, and especially, that I hadn't been tricked into marriage.

A few minutes after ten, I hear tires crunching rock that signals a vehicle is entering the driveway. Has Leonard returned from work so soon? In panic, I jam the letter back into its envelope and shove it into my coat pocket. I race to the barn door and peer out.

It isn't him. *Thank God,* I think. "Someone's here, David," I say. "We need to find out who."

I force myself to return to the letters; I straighten, stack, then rewrap them in the paper, and replace the whole package into the sack behind the feed bin. *But what if he moves them,* I think. *I won't be able to read them.* I grab the sack again and stash it in the far corner of the barn, under a pile of hay.

One minute later I'm jogging down the hill. I meet the man near his truck.

"Here you are. I thought no one was home." He shoves a clipboard toward me. "Name's Tuck. Got a work order to fix your furnace. Was scheduled for Saturday, but got a cancellation. I had to drive right by here, so thought I'd see if anyone was home."

My hands start to shake, and I stutter, "Did … did my husband tell you what's wrong? He was supposed to show you."

The man pokes the paper several times. "I've got it all here."

Two hours later he ascends the basement stairs. "No wonder you didn't get enough heat from the system. One of the elements was burned out." He hands me a blackened part. "I cleaned out some dust and re-placed this. You can see here where it charred? The aluminum wires overheated and started to smolder. Lucky it didn't start a fire. I replaced those wires with copper ones. It should work fine now."

I frown, unsure of what he's telling me. "Thank you, sir."

"Not sir, Tuck, remember?"

"All right, Tuck," I say.

He shoves a clipboard at me. "Here's the total; want to pay now or send a check?"

I stare at the number. I have no money, no checks, no way to pay him. "We'll mail you the payment, if that's okay."

He points to a line near the bottom. "Okay, sign here."

After I do, he tears the yellow copy away from the others, scribbles his number at the bottom, and says, "Call if you have any problems."

I sigh with relief when he leaves. It takes so much energy to act normal.

When Leonard arrives home, he finds me in the kitchen, trying to wash dishes, a task I'm not very efficient at. I keep forgetting what to do next.

When he slides his arms around my waist, I pull away and dry my hands. I locate the yellow invoice and hand it to him. "This guy, Tuck, came to fix the furnace today. Here's the bill. Said we can mail them a check. Oh, and he forgot his hat. I'll call him tomorrow so he can pick it up."

He stares at the hat, then takes the paper and spends several seconds perusing it. His scowl gives a hint that there is some problem. When he pinches his lower lip between two fingers, I'm sure.

"What's wrong?" I ask. "Did he make a mistake?"

"The man left his number here. Why did he do that?"

I feel my hands begin to shudder. "I don't remember."

"You came on to him, didn't you?"

"I told you everything I know."

"But you remembered his name—Tuck, wasn't it? Why did you let him in the house when I wasn't here? What did you do with him?"

Perhaps this is a test, to see if I reported well enough, mentioned the correct detail. I don't know what though, other than the furnace was broken, but shaking more, I still try. I shut my eyes in concentration. "I told him it wasn't working right, that it was cold in here, and I showed him the furnace ..."

"You let a stranger into the house while you were here alone."

Confused, I stumble over my words, "Well … yes. I had to. How else could he …"

"He came when I wasn't here. You know his name and can't remember mine. He left his phone number, and you expect me to believe all he did was fix the furnace? You probably had sex with him in the basement, didn't you?"

With raised eyebrows and open mouth, I wilt onto the couch, incredulous that he should even suggest such a thing. "David, go to your room." I wait until he's gone before I sputter, "I … I don't know what you're talking about."

"I know what you are. You're a little slut. You throw yourself at any man who comes along. This repair man—was he good looking, strong, virile?" He leans in close, so his mouth is at my ear. "Did he whisper sweet nothings in your ear, convince you he's better than me?"

"He repaired the furnace, that's all," I wail.

"And you took advantage of him being here. Oh, don't look so shocked. You know how you are. You say you can't remember, but you can't fool me. You remember, all right, but you do whatever you damn well please."

The letters come to mind, letters hidden from me for months—fifty-two opportunities for me to remember Patrick, to know he cared. Fifty-two lies from this man when he didn't say a word.

With nothing to lose, I stand, prop my hands on my hips, and say, "Don't you dare accuse me of hiding things from you. What about all those letters from Patrick. You hid those from me for months."

Leonard's face grows red and his eyes bulge large. He jumps to his feet. Grabbing both of my shoulders in his hands, he shakes me until my head wobbles, and shouts, "How dare you! I kept those letters from you for your own good. You weren't able to read them. Hearing from that jerk, Patrick, would have twisted your mind. I should have burned them." He rants for several more minutes. "Kilkenny doesn't care for you, never will care the way I do. But now I know you can't be trusted."

I hiss through clenched teeth, "I would never have an affair with a stranger. I did nothing wrong."

Leonard makes a fist and shakes it at me. "You don't remember anything." Pointing out the window, he says, "You could have slept with every man living along this creek. For all I know, you've slept with every guy in town! But that will stop. It will all stop."

He falls into a chair and leans his head far back so he's staring at the ceiling. After several seconds he says, "I've made up my mind. You'll have to cancel your occupational therapy session tomorrow because I can't go with you. I've got something to do at work. Something very important. Something that will benefit the both of us and solve our problems once and for all."

28.

David and I enter the office to an odor of lilac with an undertone of soap filling the air, as if the cleaning crew is still working somewhere. Jennifer looks up from her desk. "Hi David, Mrs. Baxter. I'm surprised to see you, today. I got a call from Doctor Baxter earlier cancelling your appointment."

"It's okay, isn't it?" I ask.

"Of course." Jennifer tucks a stray lock of hair behind her ear and gives me a toothy smile. "I'm sorry to say we gave your time away to someone on the waiting list, but the next patient isn't here yet, so you can see Mr. Yamada until then. I'll tell him you're here."

A woman with a child of about twelve wait on the upholstered chairs, but I can't sit; I'm too nervous. I stretch and stare out the window where I go over what I've decided to say, and how I'm going to say it.

A few moments later, David is constructing a tower from Bristle Blocks in the kids' corner and I'm watching the rain pelt the cold earth beyond the glass when my occupational therapist strides to the waiting room. I know him; I remember. The realization brings a smile to my face.

"Emma Lee. This is a pleasant surprise," Michael says.

"My … husband couldn't make it, and thought I couldn't come on my own."

He smiles. "Well, obviously, you can, and I'm glad. We have about ten minutes so come on back."

In the office, Michael directs me to a chair at the small, round table in the corner. It's got several papers on it, a few sharp pencils, a box of tissues, and a folder. He points to one of the papers and says, "I had some math planned for you, so we could do a bit if you like. But I recall from the last session, you wanted to tell me something and we got interrupted." He folds his hands together and settles back in his chair. "Which will it be?"

"I think … well …" I pull a tissue from the box and twist one corner of it into a point. Then I shred it. One tear wets my eyelashes, and leaks down my cheek. Once it escapes, the rest take liberties, too. Though I try, I can't stop hundreds from leaking out. "I had this all planned, what I'd say, how I'd say it. But already my plan isn't working."

"Take your time."

"He told me to keep it secret."

"By 'he' you mean Leonard?"

I nod. I'd have thought that by now I'd remember the name of this man who controls me—my owner. I stare at my hands and remember taping plastic gloves to the protective overall sleeves as Leonard Baxter arrives in the changing room. Dr. Leonard Baxter, PhD, my boss, then and now.

"I'm here to observe you," he announces.

The only thing he's wearing is paper underwear, and his very naked gut and waxy legs show too much white for me to bear. But there's no shame or embarrassment on his face; he seems to flaunt the skin, enjoying the naked display. I drop my gaze to the floor and hoist the air tank onto my back. All these precautions and I'm not protected. Not from him. Not from his anger, his control. Not from his naked body.

My before-injury past fuses with my after-injury past until confusion clobbers clarity and I can't evoke one coherent thought. I rub my forehead. "I don't know why I'm here."

Jennifer enters the office and says, "Sorry to interrupt, but your next patient is here. And you have a lunch appointment after, so you can't delay."

"Two minutes," Michael says. When the door closes, he says, "You came for therapy, Emma Lee. Occupational therapy. You're learning how to function in the world again after your head injury."

I weave my fingers together and press my lips to my knuckles. "I know that part. But right now I need ... I need ... it shouldn't be a crime to know the repairman's name, should it?"

He looks confused, but answers, "No, it should not. It isn't."

"He's trying to control me. In the lab, at home, everywhere; I found the letters, though. That proves I'm not crazy. At least, I think it does. Right?"

"You aren't crazy. What letters?"

Two minutes! This is my chance to talk; who knows when I'll be here again on my own? I must use the time to the best of my ability. But when I open my mouth, words that I don't recognize—muddled, messy, topsy-turvy, words—tumble out. "The control. This .... The wedding wasn't .... "

The tears come in earnest now, and no matter how hard I try to explain, my thoughts wiggle and squirm and slide away. I drop my head, blow my nose. I press on, a mad rush toward muddle, as if I'm at the edge of a cliff. "I'm his puppet. Blamed for everything: accidents, negative emotions, suspicions, confusion, even the weather. I'm forced into it. David's nightmares tell it all .... "

Michael swipes his straight black hair from his eyes and raises a hand. "Hold it; hold it. I'm not getting any of this." He pulls his chair closer and leans forward. "Can you start at the beginning?"

"I don't know the beginning. It keeps changing."

"Okay. Pick any subject and start with that."

"He's always there, following me, hovering. Watching. Trying to control me."

The air lock door opens. I wind my way through the cluttered lab, around pipes that twist like huge snakes with valves; Dr. Baxter is at my heels. We both know where to squeeze, duck, or turn in this cramped room to avoid injury. When I reach my work station at the far end of the room, he hovers behind me, clipboard in hand, writing, checking, inspecting, pressing too close. I unlock the controlled substance cabinet and remove a container holding 2, 4-D. Toxic, deadly 2, 4-D. It will kill me if I'm not careful. So I'm *very* careful. Securing the jar on the work table, I open it, and extract one millimeter with an automatic pipette. I follow the procedure exactly, but my hands shake. That feeling of being judged, never good enough, comes on me so strong, I'm almost paralyzed by it. It causes more claustrophobia than the mask and hood. He steps forward until I feel his body against my air tank and I want to scream.

I'm ten again, in the living room with my mother, the one person I wanted to love me most. She stands with hands on full-skirted hips, a frown on her lovely face, patting her perfect hair, watching me curtsy. It's not deep or long enough, not *submissive* enough.

"Look at the floor, not at me, child. Can't you do anything right?" She shimmies behind me, presses me into the correct position like a puppet, swats me when I move the wrong way. Do it again. Make it perfect.

Back then, I embraced perfection as my friend; compliance made me lovable. Now I recognize perfection as a sham: me morphing into another for his pleasure, ease, gain, and control. Like him.

"He controls everything. I'm his slave. He even tells me my thoughts are wrong. Sometimes I feel like I'm going crazy. Am I Mr. Yamada? Am I?"

Michael touches my hand, like I do with David when I'm trying to calm him. "No. You've had a major injury and it takes time to heal. Reality can shift during this time; it takes a while to understand, to sort it all out, to make sense of what's real, what isn't. Things get scrambled."

"You think I'm exaggerating."

"No, not at all." Michael stands and paces the room. "Look, Emma Lee. I've seen this many times. You've had a terrible loss. You're unable to do almost anything that you used to do. It makes sense that you feel controlled. A good counselor will help you through this."

I sigh, deep and long. "So you can't help me?"

"Yes I can, but not in this area. I specialize in improving your life skills, not emotions. The fact that you remember any of this, your past, is wonderful, considering where you were last week. It's miraculous, in fact."

"Some miracle," I mumble. No wonder I've given up God.

Jennifer opens the door again and peers at us.

Michael holds up a finger. "One more minute."

When she leaves again, he says, "Would it help for me to talk to your husband for you?"

The fear is so strong I nearly shout, "No." Then my voice dims to a whisper. "No, please don't talk to him. Please. He'll punish me for telling you this."

Michael takes both of my hands in his. "I'll contact your counselor, see what can be done from her side. We'll talk again."

I'm still shaking as I plod out of the office. "Time to go, David," I say.

"Can I finish my castle?" David asks.

I let my body crumple into a chair. "Sure. Take your time."

While David builds a tower taller than he is with the sticky plastic blocks, I close my eyes and take a deep breath. Can Mr. Yamada help me? My husband is a noted scientist, a Good Samaritan who took in a helpless cripple. I'm a pathetic, delusional, wounded woman who can't speak in coherent sentences.

Twenty minutes later, I push open the front door to the building as another woman enters. Her mouth drops open.

"Oh, I don't believe it. Emma Lee," she gushes. "How are you?"

She looks and sounds familiar, but no name comes to mind. My face must register my confusion because she points to herself and says, "I'm Katrina. We used to work together, remember? Before you got hurt." She tussles David's hair and says, "And you sure have grown since I saw you last."

David pushes her hand away. I smile and grasp Katrina's outstretched, beautifully-manicured fingers. "Oh, yes, Katrina. How are you? Do you have an appointment with Mr. Yamada, too?"

She laughs. "In a way. We're going to lunch. How are you?"

"Getting better."

"Patrick told me he stopped by your house but Dr. B. wouldn't let him see you."

"Patrick? Really?" A million thoughts cram my mind, but I can't verbalize any of them. Of course, Leonard wouldn't want me to see Patrick. But I need to; want to. "So he's back in town then?"

Katrina's long auburn hair blows into her face. "Let's step into the hallway," she says, picking away strands of hair that stick to her lipstick.

The door closes. "I'd like to see him," I say. "Do you know how to get in touch with him?"

Katrina purses her lips. "Yeah, well … I do see him at work."

I pull out my notebook, look up my phone number and scribble it on a blank page. I rip out the page and shove it into Katrina's hand. "Tell him to call in the daytime when my husband is at work."

Katrina folds the paper and slips it into her wallet. "Will do." She touches my hand. "Look, I'd love to talk longer, but I'm on my lunch break." She takes a few steps down the hall. "Nice seeing you both," she calls over her shoulder.

I stumble to my car, my mind reeling. I have no doubts about Leonard discovering my visit to Michael. I wonder what type of punishment, what extra sexual favors I'll have to endure for this transgression.

29.

First thing when he arrived at work, Leonard had called the Three River's Chemical president, Walter Slazenger.

"I was going to wait until I turned sixty-five to retire, but I changed my mind. I'd like to do it now."

"My office at ten," Walter had replied.

Leonard brokered a deal where he'd receive 85% of his expected retirement income in monthly installments for the rest of his life. In return, he promised to spend one day a week for the next six months at work, training his successor and consulting. They had settled on the 30th of April as his last day. It was exactly what Leonard had hoped for.

He strode to his office with a rare grin on his face and closed his door. Scanning the room, he wondered if he'd miss this place. The heavy drapes that his first wife, Janice, had purchased still hid the chemical tanks, smoke, and contaminated pools beyond the dirty glass. He'd leave them for the next vice-president. But he liked the 19th century antique wing back chair that sat in the corner. He'd had that for over forty years. Again, Janice bought it for him at an estate sale—a rich home in Shadyside being remodeled, she had said. He had reserved the chair for important visitors, ones he wanted to impress. Once he even invited Emma Lee sit in it. So that would go home with him.

Feeling cocky, Leonard pulled the Queen Ann chair close to his mahogany desk. He rarely sat in it himself, but today was different. Today, everything changed. It no longer mattered that he might scuff the finish, or that someone might find him here wasting time with his feet up. It no longer mattered that he got his work done, or that his employees did what they were told. He no longer cared about any of it. His goal now was to be home.

He grabbed his book, *Sheep Management and Production - A Practical Guide for Farmers and Students*, and placed his feet, shoes and all, on the desk. Opening his book to the chapter on sheep diseases and cures, Leonard read how Scabies had been eradicated from the US the previous year because of advances in the fight against pests, and his company was a forerunner in that war. True, Three River's Chemical got bad press when some do-gooder decided to report about how it polluted the earth, the air, or river with toxic emissions. But wasn't life about trade-offs? This one accomplishment—eliminating Scabies—saved millions of dollars for the sheep herders. A little bit of pollution for a major breakthrough in sheep health was surely worth it. The way he saw it, he and other chemists were heroes!

Returning to his book, Leonard read about the life cycle and symptoms of sheep bot next. The flies deposit eggs on sheep muzzles, which hatch into larvae that crawl into sheep sinuses. If left unchecked, sheep bot could kill an animal, even a whole flock. A snotty nose was the first symptom, the book told him. Leonard stopped to think. Hadn't he noticed something like that in the new lamb? He made a mental note to check when he got home.

His book recommended drenching. "Hmph," he mumbled. "No way I'd use ivermectin. The competition sells that. Maybe an arsenate. I can get that here."

The phone rang and he reluctantly put down his book to answer. "Yes?" he barked.

"Hiram Eisenbaum on the phone for you, sir," his secretary, Rhonda, said.

Leonard rolled his eyes. Eisenbaum: a useless, helpless man who couldn't think for himself. A man who called every day, sometimes several times, for direction. Leonard thought he was an idiot, but seniority ruled, and with Emma Lee and Patrick unavailable, there was no one else to run the botanical testing lab. He dropped his feet to the ground and grabbed the receiver.

"Yes, what is it this time?" he shouted.

"Uh, sorry to bother you, sir, but we received that shipment of permethrin—the synthetic derivative of chrysanthemums? I need some help with setting up my testing schedule."

Eisenbaum certainly had chutzpah, calling about this. He and Leonard had gone over the requirements for the testing procedures several times in the last two weeks. "I know what permethrin is, you fool. What do you want?"

"Um ..."

Leonard gritted his teeth and tapped his pen on the desk. "Spit it out, man. I'm busy."

"Can you remind me again what plants we should begin testing with and what dosage? I want to be sure I've got it right."

Leonard threw the pen across the room. Never mind that permethrin could cause nerve damage and, in larger doses, tremors or even death. If he were in the lab with Eisenbaum right now, he'd dump that new shipment of the neurotoxin right down the man's throat. "Don't you write anything down?"

"Well, we weren't in my office ..."

Leonard swore beneath his breath, blaming Hiram for his anger. Then he blamed Emma Lee. If she were still working here, outlining the testing schedule would have been her job, and she would have done it without a hitch. Lastly, and most important, he blamed

Kilkenny. If Patrick wasn't obsessed with Emma Lee, he would be in charge of the department right now and it would be running smoothly. A thought struck him. He smiled and said, "Talk to Kilkenny. Tell him I said he should set up this project for you."

"Thank you, sir," Hiram mumbled as Leonard slammed down the phone.

His face relaxed as he leaned back in the chair and opened his book again. Another irritating task delegated away.

On the chart of cures and treatments, several pesticides had been listed as either manufactured or tested here in this plant. Of course, permethrin wasn't on the list yet. It wasn't scheduled for commercial distribution for approximately five more years. *Well*, he thought, *perhaps I could do a few experiments on my own, at home.* He'd make sure he got everything he needed.

At eleven-thirty, instead of eating lunch at work, Leonard decided to go home. He buzzed his secretary. "Rhonda, if anyone calls, tell them I'm in a meeting and won't be available for the rest of the afternoon."

"Yes, sir."

He grabbed his coat, his briefcase, and a cardboard box from his closet, and left.

As he entered the hallway, he ignored the workers rushing past him. Emma Lee, his beautiful, petite, sexy wife and the sheep that loved him came to mind; they were at home, waiting for him. And they were all he really cared about now.

Plodding down the dingy, gray and black linoleum-tiled hallway, Leonard imagined how it would be soon. Emma Lee and he would be together all day, every day, lounging late in bed after morning sex. He could touch or kiss her whenever he wanted. His libido was aroused, and he quickened his pace. The sooner he was home the better.

At the end of the corridor Leonard unlocked a storeroom that held samples of every substance that River's Edge Chemical had ever tested. When he pulled open the heavy door, a cloud of chemical odors accosted his senses, making his eyes water. Near the door, as he passed the arsenates, he grabbed a bottle and stuck it into his box. Then he shuffled down the aisle of shelves and scanned the names on jars of chemicals as he went. Several had been stored so long the tops were covered in dust. When he got to the shelf with substances starting with P, he grabbed a pint of permethrin and slid it into the box. He locked the storeroom door and walked directly to his Cadillac, slid the box of toxic substances into the trunk, and drove away.

When he arrived home, Emma Lee's car wasn't in the driveway and he grumbled, "Where is she now? I can't trust her with anything." His thoughts of a quick romp in bed before lunch fizzled.

After he wolfed down his sandwich, Leonard changed his clothes, grabbed the box of pesticides and a jar, and hiked to the barn. Topsy's bleat cheered him. "I'm glad you still love me," he said, scratching her under her chin. "No one else seems to."

He inspected her nose. No infection; no sores or flies that he could see. He checked the other sheep. All seemed fine until he got to the lamb. Holding the animal between his legs, he lifted its head upward. Was that a maggot he saw on its nose? Maybe. His eyesight wasn't what it used to be. Still, with his bifocals …. He leaned close and at that moment the lamb raised his head. The bridge of its nose smacked his face. He reeled backwards and fell onto the barn floor, bruising his tailbone as the lamb scampered away.

A stream of blood ran from Leonard's nose, over his lips and down his chin. "Damn stupid lamb," he said. As he wiped his face with his handkerchief, he recalled how affectionate Jojo was with David. Too affectionate. David seemed to have an inordinate power over that lamb. *The boy makes that lamb hate me,* he thought.

If Jojo had an infection, there was no way David could treat this problem himself. Leonard would have to do it for him. Otherwise, all the sheep would get infected and that would be the end of his flock.

He grasped the lamb again. On closer inspection, Leonard was fairly sure that Jojo was infected with Bot larvae. Of course. That had to be why the lamb was so touchy.

Into the jar he poured a tablespoon of permethrin, then filled the jar with water. He sucked up the diluted water into the fly spryer. One by one, he sprayed his sheep, wetting their coats and especially their heads. When he finished, he stared at the trouble-making lamb. He poured another three tablespoons of insecticide into the sprayer for good measure, and screwed the lid back on. He shoved the lamb outside the barn and tied it to a post. There he sprayed the lamb until it was dripping wet.

Leonard left Jojo outside for several minutes while he cleaned the stalls and gave the sheep water. It was a warm day, so he herded his small flock outside. Then he went back to let the lamb loose.

He was surprised to see it lying on the ground; its chest was heaving. Its legs were shaking and its mouth hung open. The strong odor of pesticide permeated the air and Leonard felt his chest tighten. He must be allergic to permethrin! Laboring to expel the air in his lungs, he pointed at the lamb and yelled, "Damn you. This is your fault. You'll stay there until the smell is gone."

Back in the barn, Leonard felt his breath return as each exhale got easier. Thank goodness he wasn't allergic to the hay.

He emptied out the sprayer and hung it on its nail, placed the pesticide in the cabinet with the other chemicals, and returned to the house. There he dumped his barn clothes in the laundry. After his shower, he wrapped a towel around his hips. He grabbed a magazine, and settled onto the bed. As he waited for Emma Lee, he imagined how wonderful life was going to be when he was home all day, every day.

30.

"I'm sorry to bother you at work, Patrick, but Joshua wants to talk with you," Maria said over the phone. Her tone sounded apologetic.

Patrick stared at the grey concrete walls of his office as he pressed a palm into his forehead. He had almost finished a complex calculation when the phone rang, and it took a lot of effort for him not to impart the irritation he felt. "No, it's fine, really. Call whenever you need to." He hoped that she'd say no when he asked, "Do I need to come get him?"

"Any infecting of the other kids is already done. If everyone else gets the chicken pox from him now, they'll all get sick at the same time, and make my life easier."

"I don't know if the kids would agree, but that works for me. Can you put him on?"

When Joshua came on the phone, his voice sounded weak. "I want to go home, Uncle Patrick. I don't feel good."

"I know, Sport. But I can't get away from work right now. Maria said you can stay."

Josh started to cry. "It's not fair. I used to stay home with Mom when I got sick. You have to come get me."

"Look, I have to work. I'll be there as soon as I can." Hearing his tone's hard edge, he forced himself to try again. Dropping his voice a few decibels, he continued, "I know it's hard. Maria says you can lie on the couch until I get there, and she'll give you some medicine so you won't be so itchy."

Perhaps resigned or too tired to continue, the boy said, "Okay. But get here as soon as you can."

After a few moments of silence, Maria was back on the line. "Thanks, Patrick. We'll see you this evening."

When he hung up the receiver, Patrick's mood turned dark. He shouldn't have yelled at the boy. At this rate he'd be old and gray and still no wiser. He stood and paced into the dark, concrete hallway. As he passed the door to the animal testing lab, he wondered what horrors lay behind it. Were there new cancers developing in the rats, or new ulcers? Were some stunted in growth, twitching nervously, or wasting away? It was enough to make a person want to go back to Washington.

Thinking of Washington reminded him of last evening's phone call from Carol. She found Joshua's father, Richard, in Walla Walla. "Call information, Patrick," she instructed.

Good old ever-directive Cousin Carol, still trying to run his life, even from 3000 miles away.

As Patrick rounded a corner near his office, he almost collided with Hiram Eisenbaum.

"Oh," the man squeaked. "I was coming to see you."

Patrick leaned against the wall and folded his arms. "I can only guess why. More work? Another assignment?"

"Baxter said you should create the critical path of the permethrin feasibility."

Patrick stared down into Hiram's bald spot. "You're the laboratory head now. Isn't that *your* job?"

"Um, well … but Baxter … assigned you."

"I get a supervisor's work load and responsibility without the pay or clout? It figures."

Turning on his heel, Patrick strode back to his cubbyhole. He was outside his door when he heard the phone ring again. "Kilkenny," he shouted, picking up the receiver.

"Patrick, it's Katrina. I got back from lunch and you'll never guess what happened."

"I don't have time for guesses; why don't you tell me?"

As if telling a juicy secret, she giggled. "I was on my way to meet my boyfriend and I ran right into Emma Lee—literally. There she was, coming out of the building that I was going into. Can you imagine?"

Patrick's irritation evaporated. He pointed to a chair for Hiram to wait and spun his chair around. Forgetting Hiram, he propped his elbows on his desk. "So what did she say? Did she remember me? How can I get in touch with her?"

"Whoa, slow down, big boy. She gave me her phone number, said you should call her—but only when Dr. B. is at work. I was in a hurry; so was she; that's all, really. Got a pencil handy?" She dictated the number.

"Thanks, Katrina. I owe you."

"Bet your bottom dollar. Don't forget it. I'll collect, too."

As he hung up the receiver, Patrick stared at the number and his head spun with ideas. He wanted to call Emma Lee immediately, but he had to be cautious. He checked his watch. 1:15. Dr. B. had been strolling down the hallway around eleven. He remembered because it was the only time Patrick had ever seen Baxter smiling. Now, Patrick surmised, Dr. B. would most likely be in his office, or in some meeting, or perhaps still at lunch. Right now was probably the perfect time to call.

"Hiram, come back in an hour. I have something important to do."

The man rose and, looking confused, stumbled off.

Patrick he had to be sure about Dr. Baxter. He picked up the phone and dialed.

"Dr. Baxter's office," Rhonda said.

"This is Patrick Kilkenny. I need to speak with the boss. Tell him it's about the permethrin project."

"He's in a meeting all afternoon. I can have him call you tomorrow."

"Great. You do that."

Smiling, he pressed the button to sever the call, then he dialed the number Katrina had given him.

31.

When I drive the boulevard, I often savor the soft yellow color of the paving bricks that have served as the roadway surface since the boulevard was built more than thirty years ago. I love the comforting rumble that the tires make on them. It reminds me of how I'll never be: a little bumpy and noisy, but solid, and dependable, too. Right now, I'm feeling sorry for myself, conflicted. My botched meeting with Michael and the chance encounter with Katrina feel like ice and fire.

I let one hand direct the steering wheel while I rub my neck with the other. Michael must think I'm crazy as well as brainless. Maybe I am. The time with him was a major waste, one I'll certainly pay for later. And will Katrina remember to give Patrick my number? My sigh comes from deep down, unable to express all the frustration, anger, and sorrow I feel. Things could have been so different.

I have to leave my husband, I decide. Well, at least … I want to leave him. Perhaps I should keep driving, return to Aiken, or head north to Canada. I could disappear into Ohio, or New York, maybe.

Okay, I know I can't do that *right* now; I'd be lost before I got out of town. And I'd never find a job. Feeling stuck, I squeeze my eyes shut to stop the tears.

"Watch out!" David yells as the car heads for the curb.

I wipe my tears and refocus. Right after the Avalon Bridge, traffic slows to a crawl. I flip on the radio and hear the words of a song, "Rainy days and Mondays always get me down."

"I like rainy days," David says. "I get to stomp in the puddles and use the umbrella. What are Mondays? Are they bad?" he asks.

"No, honey, a Monday is the first day of the week." Thinking of Leonard I add, "It's the day people go back to work after being off for two days. I actually love Mondays; they make me happy." '

David says, "I'm hungry, Mom." He rubs his tummy and frowns.

"We'll be home soon. Then you can have lunch."

But I'm wrong. Traffic is stop-and-go for fifteen more minutes, and I wish I knew an alternate route. Unfortunately, my sick little brain is programed with only one way home, the way I'm going. So we stay stuck in traffic.

Finally we pass the actual work zone. A huge dump truck pours steaming black asphalt onto the yellow bricks. Of course this renovation will speed travel and make the boulevard quieter, but covering these bricks with asphalt seems like a sacrilege and I shake my head in dismay.

Ten minutes later I pull into our driveway and notice the Cadillac! My hands shake as I pull on the brake. When I open the car door and step out, my legs wobble like my bones have liquefied. I was hoping to eat lunch and slip into my room for a nap, but with him home, the nap looks unlikely. As I approach the house, I hear the phone, so I run. The door is unlocked; I manage to answer on the fifth ring.

"Hello?" I say, nervous and breathless.

David taps my arm. "I'm gonna make lunch." He skips into the kitchen.

I close my eyes to concentrate. A familiar voice says, "Emma Lee, I'm so glad I caught you. It's Patrick—Patrick Kilkenny. Remember me? Katrina told me she saw you, gave me your number. I've been worried about you."

Patrick! Any other time it would have been heavenly to hear from him. But now that I know my husband is somewhere nearby, my anxiety clogs clear thinking as sure as a stopcock. I stare down the hallway. Is *he* in the house? I cup my hand over the mouthpiece and whisper. "Thank you for calling. I ..."

At that moment I hear the bedroom door open and bare feet on the wooden hallway floor. "Can't talk. Gotta go."

I slam down the receiver and turn. My breath shortens to a pant. The man I live with, the man I fear pads into the room wearing only a towel, revealing his skinny white legs and waxy bare chest. "Here you are. Where have you been?" he says.

Blushing, I turn my head away. "Please, don't come in here like that. What about David?"

Still frowning, he scans me up and down. "David understands. Who was that on the phone?"

My head feels squeezed, as if it's clamped in a vise, causing my temples to pound. Before the injury I had difficulty lying. Now, it's impossible. I know he'll find out everything; he'll read my face. Maybe he can read my thoughts.

"Um ... just ... ." I try to change the subject. "Why are you home so early?"

He shuffles closer and corrals me with both arms, pinning me to the wall. "I told you I was going to retire. I did that today. And two weeks from now, I'll be home full time. After the details were arranged, I didn't feel like working the rest of the day, so I left to spend time with you. But you weren't here!"

His bitter smile sends chills to my core. He presses closer and I can feel his hardness against me. He whispers in my ear, trying to make his voice soft and alluring, but to me it sounds scary. "Good thing you're here now. I'm excited. Can you tell?"

At that moment, my son races in from the kitchen and grabs my hand, trying to save me. "Lunch is ready, Mom. Come now."

The man kisses my neck; I push the man away. "Please, don't. Not in front of David."

His arms drop, releasing me from his trap. "We'll discuss where you've been and the phone call later. Enjoy your lunch. I expect you to join me in the bedroom when you finish, so you'll need your energy." He winks and I want to gag.

Once my husband is gone, I let David lead me into the kitchen where I take a few nibbles of the sandwich and grin like a mannequin. "This is yummy, honey. Thanks."

They boy shrugs; he's not fooled by my phony enthusiasm.

"Hey, listen, when we're finished, you can go outside and play. I have to do something in the bedroom."

He leans until our noses nearly touch. He whispers, "Don't, Mommy. Don't go in there. Come outside with me instead. We can run away."

My gaze settles on the dish. "I wish we could, honey. I wish we could."

As he grabbed his jacket, David felt heavy, as if a large stone hung from his neck. He knew what would happen. It was always the same. After Mom disappeared with Leonard into the bedroom, she'd stay there with him a long time. David would have to entertain himself. If he played in the house, he'd have to find a way to drown out the weird noises that he heard. Leonard sometimes grunted or even yelled. Sometimes David had to poke his fingers in his ears so he wouldn't have to listen. Or he'd turn the television up real loud. Today, he was glad it was warm so he could play in the yard.

Outside, bees buzzed and the soft breeze blew fresh air for his nose. He kicked a ball around the yard for several minutes. When his legs felt tired and he was out of breath, he sprawled on his back in the grass.

Looking at the sky, David squinted and tried to imagine the shapes there, the way his mother had done with him many times before. Oh, there was an elephant with a long trunk. It moved and morphed into a car. Above the house roof he could see a teddy bear. Then, bored with clouds, he rolled to his stomach.

A robin flitted to the yard, chirped a few times, then cocked its head, as if it were listening to the ground. David watched in wonder as the bird hopped and listened, hopped and listened. A few moments later, it poked the grass with its beak and tugged the end of a huge worm out of the ground. David almost yelped in amazement.

That's when he heard it—a sheep bleating. It sounded sad or hungry. He stood and shielded his eyes from the sun with a hand. He could see the sheep in the pasture, but couldn't tell which one was calling. There it was again. Baaah. Baaaah.

David stood and trotted up the path. Perhaps he could play with Jojo for a while. That was the funnest thing, scampering with the lamb, hugging its neck. He would have preferred to have a boy as a best friend, or a big brother. Maybe a lamb was better because it never fought with him like a boy would. On his way to the barn he noticed violets in the grass. He squatted and picked a handful of them. He'd give them to Mom later. She'd like that.

He reached the barn and climbed under the fence, then galloped toward the sheep. Topsy raised her head and bleated.

"So you're the one calling me. Where's your baby, Topsy? Where's Jojo? I want to play with him."

When she bleated, David thought she sounded like she was crying. He scratched her under her chin and stroked her back. Then he noticed her udder. It seemed extra big and hard, like it was before she had the baby. Maybe she was sick. And where was Jojo?

David raced around the pasture now, searching for his lamb. He looked behind the shed and in the tall grass. He checked the shady spot under the pump house roof where the lamb liked to rest. But there was no sign of Jojo.

Then he saw, over by the door to the stall, in the other pasture, something white lying next to a post. David dropped his violets and dashed toward it.

He wiggled under the fence. When he got closer, he saw that the white blob was Jojo, his precious lamb! But it didn't look friendly today. Its open, staring eyes had flies crawling over them. Its mouth was slightly ajar, and slimy stuff was dripping out of it. The boy squatted next to his pet and stroked its coat. It was wet and smelled yucky.

David knew that animals had to breathe. And Jojo wasn't breathing. What was wrong with him? Why didn't he get up? He lifted Jojo's head; it felt heavy. Now David's hands were stinky and he got worried. No matter what Mom and Leonard were doing, he had to tell them right now about the lamb.

The boy raced back to the fence, crawled under it, and ran the whole way to the house. Out of breath, he crashed through the front door.

Leonard was on the couch, dressed in old jeans and a sweat shirt now, reading the newspaper. He peered at David over the top of his paper and cleared his throat. "What's so important, young man, that you have to bolt in here like that? Walk in the house."

David knew that he'd probably get in trouble, but he didn't have time to think about it. He had to save his lamb. "I need Mommy." He raced to the bedroom door and pounded on it. "Mom, come quick. Something's wrong with Jojo."

He heard his mother say, "Be there in a minute, honey."

As Emma Lee emerged from the bedroom, she squinted and scrubbed her curls with her fingers. "What's wrong?"

He grabbed her hand and tugged. "He can't get up. You have to come with me to the barn right now."

Emma Lee dragged on her boots and raced after David to the pasture.

When they arrived at the bundle of white fleece, she gasped. "Oh, no."

"I found him this way, Mommy. Is he dead?"

She squatted down and touched the lamb's head. A tear leaked down her cheek as she untied the rope from the lamb's neck. "Yes, honey, he's dead. He must have gotten into something bad. It smells terrible."

David started to cry. "But he's my best friend, Mommy. I don't want him to die."

Emma Lee wrapped her arm around his shoulders. "I'm so sorry. I know you loved him."

David crumpled to the ground, buried his face on his mother's chest, and sobbed.

32.

When David and I enter the house, we're both dirt streaked and reek of permethrin. He's still sobbing, "My Jojo! I want my lamby." He crumples to the floor.

My husband is in the living room reading the newspaper with a basket of folded clothes at his feet. When he sees us, he wrinkles his nose. "You two stink." He turns his wrist over to check his watch. "And you've been gone over an hour. What took you so long?"

I perch on the chair arm and press a hand into my forehead. "The lamb's dead. We buried him."

Leonard folds his paper and places it on the coffee table, precisely squaring off the edges before he speaks. He points at David as if his finger is a revolver. "Life's hard, boy. Get over it. Back when I was a kid, I got beat up all the time by the local hoods. Once they even broke my arm. Did I complain? Hell no. If I did, my father beat me more. Crying is for sissies; buck up and be a man. You learn to survive by blocking out pain."

My words escape before I can stop them. "He's not a man; he's a little boy. He needs to grieve and cry for the lamb. It was special to him—his friend."

"Well, I won't have him whining about it around me." He flutters his hand. "Go cry somewhere else."

David looks at me through wet lashes. I tilt my head in the direction of the bathroom. "How about getting cleaned up? Call me when the water's ready and I'll help you scrub," I say.

David stomps off and I sink back. Before my arms touch the upholstery, Leonard yanks me to my feet. He grabs a towel from the basket and drapes it over the chair. "Now you can sit." Once I do, he returns to the couch and says, "I want to know where you were this morning. Did you visit Yamada without my permission?"

"What happened to Jojo? David found him tied to a post, all wet, smelling like insecticide. You sprayed him, didn't you?"

His hand smacks the coffee table and his voice intensifies. "How dare you interrogate me like *I've* done something wrong? Damn right, I sprayed him. The lamb had bot flies. Didn't want him infecting the rest. Don't change the subject. I want to know what you told Yamada. You can't hide the truth from me; I can tell when you're lying."

"That wasn't treatment; he was soaking wet with that stuff. You killed him on purpose, didn't you?"

Shaking a finger at me, he says, "Oh, no, you aren't getting away with this, twisting the facts, making it look like I'm at fault, like you always do." He stomps to my chair and stands over me, blocking the light, an obelisk of irascibility. His voice, instead of growing louder, though, has taken on a slow, metered cadence, and suddenly, he and I are in an office—an extravagant one.

He's at the tall window where long, gold- and black-striped velvet drapes hang. The cherry desk stands between us. With his back to me, he says something about payoff and dumping. Surprise registers on his face when he sees me, and he slams down the receiver.

I'm invited to sit in his red and gold brocade wing back chair and his voice takes on that slow, metered, *you're really an imbecile but I'll humor you* tone. His teeth show, as if he's trying to smile, but it doesn't work. Perhaps the smile muscles have atrophied. He clears his throat.

"I don't *need* to explain, but I will. What you heard was the end of a series of long negotiations with State regulators. The company driver misread the map. Dumped his load in the wrong place. We've admitted guilt, paid the fine."

My concerns—that the dump was on purpose and officials were paid off—were combed away like tangles from my wild black hair. But the angst, fear, and helplessness I felt then now flood me.

He moves his face close to mine so I feel his breath when he talks. "You're the one who's confused. You're the one who is injured and irrational, not right in the head. Yes, you've tied this whole thing into a huge knot based on your own little twisted, crazy view of the world. So get this straight. I tried to *heal* that lamb. I was doing a good thing. The flies obviously got to it before I could. So the lamb's death is really your fault. If you weren't so soft, David wouldn't have had the animal in the first place. The boy's too young to care for a pet. But did you think about that? Oh, no, you insisted. And I want to give you everything, so I gave in. But if the lamb had been in my care from the beginning, I would have noticed the infection sooner and wouldn't have had to give him such a big dose. I was too late. Yes, this is your fault."

"You blame me for this?"

He turns and saunters to the window. Staring out to the barn, he says, "You're confused and disobedient, and you'll need to be punished. I'll decide how, once I know what kind of damage you've done." He turns and stares at me. "Why did you visit Yamada? What sort of lies did you tell him?"

"I don't lie."

"Yes you do. You tell people that I don't care about you, that I'm cruel, that I mistreat you. Do you know what you are? You're a dog who bites its master, that's what. You see how you are? Heartless.

And mindless, too! There's no way you can live on your own. You're handicapped, dirt under society's nails, a misfit."

Back at my chair, he takes my hand and kisses it. And suddenly we're in his car together with David in the back seat. I can see naked trees and snow flurries out the window as we drive.

"Ah, my darling," he's saying. "We'll get our license today, then make an appointment at the court house. I want to buy you everything: beautiful jewelry, designer clothes—whatever you like. But I'll start with a ring and an outfit for the ceremony. Red would be nice, don't you think? I know you'll love that."

I shake my head to remove the memories as anxiety snaps my heart like a mousetrap. I pull my hand away, disgusted with his lewd smile, those cold eyes, with myself for getting into this situation.

He pokes an index finger at me. "You should be thanking me. I dragged you from near death and nursed you to health again, you thankless, selfish bitch."

Smacking his chest with his palm, he yells, You're alive because if me! Don't forget, I pay for everything: your fancy underwear, good food, this house. I even cook and do laundry. Most women would kill for this setup, for a guy like me. But you? You moan and complain, and make people think your life is *so hard*. Oh, poor Emma Lee."

He goes on for several more minutes. The more he talks, the smaller I shrink. I try to blot out his tirade, focus my attention on the variations of color in the wood grain of the floor, but his words dissect my subconscious like a scalpel.

"Look at me when I talk to you, damn it," he yells.

Lifting my gaze, I focus through him, hoping my fear doesn't show, but knowing it does.

He grips my jaw and moves so close we're nose to nose. I push him away and bolt to my feet, then race to the window. He comes up behind me and drapes an arm over my shoulder. When I try to wiggle away, he clamps me closer. His voice grows conciliatory, soft, and gentle again. "You're hurt, you need me. Now, tell me the truth about Yamada. You went to see him, didn't you?"

I stay silent.

His arm wrenches me closer and he whispers, "It's not so hard to tell the truth. Say it. You went to see Yamada, then you twisted the truth; lied to him. I can handle it."

I shake my head. "No, I didn't."

He grabs my shoulders and shakes them. "Are you having an affair with the man? That's why you went to see him behind my back, isn't it?" He waits for several seconds before he says, "No need to confess. Your silence is a sure sign of guilt."

The only thing I'm guilty of is losing my mind.

"Mom, can you come help me?" David calls from the bathroom.

Saved by the child. "One minute, honey," I reply, and swipe a tear from my cheek.

"You'll have to be punished, of course. I hate doing it, but it's the only way to keep you from lying again," he says.

I turn back to the window. "I didn't lie."

"I could keep your car keys so the only way you can go anywhere is with me, or with my permission. But I'm not heartless. In an emergency, you might need to drive David to a doctor or something. So I'll look for another occupational therapist—a woman this time—who won't try to steal you away. Meanwhile, I expect you to tell me everywhere you go and why you go there. Got that?"

When I don't respond, he lowers his voice and hisses, "You—got—that?" He enunciates each word like a gunshot.

I was sure of myself and the facts before I entered the house. But now I'm dumping sense and sensibility like coal down a chute. Soon it will all be gone and I'll return to being a blithering idiot. What is real? Was he trying to save the lamb or kill it? Is he good to me or cruel? I don't know anymore, and I can't locate my voice, so to stop his tirade, I nod.

"Speak up."

"I got it," I whisper, feeling my prison cell shrink.

"Good. And one last thing. Who was on the phone?"

If I say Sister Martha, he'll know I'm lying. I haven't spoken with her in weeks. I blurt out the only name I can think of. "Katrina. I met her outside Mr. Yamada's office and she said she'd call me."

His eyebrows rise like my answer surprises him. "Don't lie to me. Who was it, really? The furnace repair man? Kilkenny? Your newest fling, Yamada?"

Again, I'm silent.

He raises both hands and speaks to the ceiling when he says, "You have so many men; you're like Helen of Troy. It's maddening, trying to protect you from all of them." Dropping his hands, he weaves his fingers behind his back and paces the room again. The corners of his thin lips rise into a slight smile. "You're mine and I plan to protect what is my property from all interlopers. You can count on that."

"Mom!" David calls. "I need you."

"Now go stop that kid from yelling, then clean yourself up while you're at it. I'm going out."

I can't leave the room fast enough.

33.

The MGB lurched into second gear and screamed through a curve. Michael's thoughts turned from torque and acceleration to Katrina, the beautiful, tall, shapely, love-of-his-life. Ah, Katrina. He knew he wanted her in his life forever.

It was his habit to masticate decisions like a cow chewing cud. For example, he had taken six years to graduate from college because he couldn't settle on a major. He never painted his apartment because many colors were his favorite. Before he purchased his car, he walked or took the bus for five years. Each model had its good points. Sometimes he didn't even go to bed because he couldn't decide to turn off the television. But once he did make up his mind, it was set. And he had decided on Katrina. He'd propose marriage soon. She might say no, but she'd soften. He could wait as long as it took. Then he'd happily embrace lawn mowers and swing sets and long commutes for life with her.

His wide bell bottomed pants swished together as he walked into his office. Jennifer greeted him with a smile and a stack of mail.

"Hey, traveler. Welcome back. How was Atlantic City?"

"Didn't see much of it. Spent most of my time inside the conference center."

"You were there five days and you didn't take any time off to sit on the beach? What were you thinking?"

Michael sorted through the stack of envelopes as he spoke. "It was rainy, so there was no point." He looked at her and asked, "Who's my first appointment?"

"Emma Lee. Should be here in ten minutes."

Michael smiled. "Good. She's my success story. And I think she finally trusts me."

"Cool." Reaching for the ringing phone, Jennifer said, "I'll let you know when she gets here."

Michael entered the therapy room and began to set up for the session.

Ten minutes later, Jennifer buzzed him. "Your patient's here."

When Emma Lee and Leonard entered, Michael had to stop himself from staring. Leonard's arm was draped over his wife's shoulder and he hustled her along, as if she couldn't walk on her own. The skin stretched tight over her face and her eyes stared out of hollow cheeks, giving her a skeletal look.

What happened to you? Michael thought as he shook her hand. "Emma Lee, Dr. Baxter, welcome. Please come in."

Emma Lee fell into a chair. Dr. Baxter stood behind her, hands on her shoulders, and as usual, he spoke for her. "She's going backwards. Nothing is sticking." Leonard frowned and his jaw tensed. "I need answers."

Michael picked up his clipboard and pen and sat next to Emma Lee. "Please, have a seat, Dr. Baxter and we'll begin. Emma Lee, can you recall when the problems started?"

She opened her mouth to speak, but Leonard's words plowed over hers. "Five days ago. At first I thought she was faking. Then I figured it was morning sickness. But people don't lose memory from pregnancy."

Trying to hear from Emma Lee, Michael directed his question to her again. "Have you seen your doctor?"

Leonard said, "Saw that quack yesterday. He says she's caught something, but couldn't say what, so he didn't prescribe anything. Just to be safe with the baby. The idiot."

Michael went to his desk and checked his appointment book. "Perhaps we should reschedule for a time when you feel better. How about Thursday?"

Leonard slapped the desk with his hand and Emma Lee jumped at the noise. "No. No delays. You need to fix this now. Besides, Thursday I'm at work all day. Got to train my replacement."

Emma Lee rubbed her forehead and said, "I'm feeling better than yesterday; I think I could drive myself."

Leonard's eyes narrowed. "Don't even try."

"It shouldn't be a problem," Michael said. "She's done it before."

"I said no. She'll get lost."

Feeling exasperated, Michael said, "Even when she had no short term memory, she could drive, Dr. Baxter. You've got to give her some space."

Dr. Baxter pointed one finger at Michael and spoke through clenched teeth, "You're causing more harm than good, Yamada. I know what's best for her, you don't. So don't tell me about what she can and can't do. You're as useless as that crappy doctor."

Michael stared at Emma Lee's file, trying to control the anger that scorched his neck and cheeks like sunburn. When he was sure he could speak without rancor, he said, "Look, Dr. Baxter, this new illness and memory loss that Emma Lee's experiencing has nothing to do with what happens in this office."

Baxter moved to within inches from Michael, arms crossed, mouth set. "I think it does. If her memory doesn't improve by next week, you're out. You got that?"

The words hovered over the room like a storm cloud.

"Loud and clear. Now, shall we get to work?"

Several seconds passed before Dr. Baxter sat.

When Michael began therapy, Dr. Baxter acted like a disgruntled sports fan, fuming on the sidelines. Michael did his best to go through the scheduled activities, and Emma Lee tried to cooperate, but she was unable to learn anything.

An hour later, when the Baxters left his office, Michael felt exhausted. Still, he liked her and didn't want to lose her as a patient. He'd stay after work to research the connection between head injuries and illness.

Michael was so distracted by thoughts of regression, difficult husbands, referrals, and what he could do to help his patient, that for the rest of the day, he didn't give one more thought to Katrina, engagement, or a house in the suburbs.

SISTER MARTHA OPENED the car door, threw in her purse, then climbed in herself. When she became a nun thirty years prior, voluminous folds in her habit skirt concealed great pockets that held anything from keys to a bible, and her rosary always hung from a rope around her waist, causing the beads to rustle when she walked.

But after the Second Vatican Council, her religious order changed from a veil and long black uniform to simple conservative clothing. So now, she wore long skirts and white blouses. And she carried a purse. She didn't miss the veil, but she did miss the beads' rustle, and those deep pockets.

Six feet tall and solidly built, Sister Martha towered over most people. Even now, at age fifty, her energy still surpassed that of the third graders she used to teach. But that didn't make her domineering. She used her energy to help others. It was her push that started support groups in her parish for single parents, the first in the diocese to include the divorced. It was at her insistence that the priest at the local parish created a drug prevention program for youth. And even though she wasn't paid for it, she added visits to Dixmont Mental

Hospital to her chaplain rounds. People told her what a great impact she had on the community. They commended her on her dynamism, said she made a difference, but she attributed her energy to prayer and to God.

Today, as the nun drove up the newly-paved section of the boulevard to Belleview, her prior patient, Emma Lee, came to mind and she wondered how the young mother was faring. *That poor woman lost her whole life when she lost her memory*, she thought. *Help her, Lord,* she prayed.

Arriving at Woolworths Five and Dime Store, she found the shoe care section near the front counter. Placing a container of black polish into her basket, she noticed Dr. Baxter in the check-out line. Her spirits lifted as she slid in behind him and tapped his shoulder. "Hello, Dr. Baxter, I'm so glad to see you. How is your lovely wife, Emma Lee? I've been praying for her."

When Leonard turned, his eyes looked tired. His mouth stayed tight and his brows rose, as if questioning who she was.

She held out a hand.

After several seconds, he shook her hand and mumbled, "Sorry. I'm distracted. Emma Lee hasn't been well. I just dropped her home after an occupational therapy session that didn't go well. The OT we have is useless so I'll be looking for another."

Sister Martha touched his arm. "Really? I thought she was making progress with him."

"Yes, before. But now there are some scary personality changes and emotional stuff with Emma Lee that he can't handle. And she's losing memory again."

"Oh, I'm so sorry to hear that."

He dropped his voice. "And she's grown sneaky. Last week she went to see Yamada on her own without telling me, then tried to hide it. When I questioned her, she avoided me. She's irrational, too. Blames me for everything, even the lamb's death."

"I don't understand. What happened to the lamb?"

It was Leonard's turn at the cash register. He set a bottle of cod liver oil and a small box of empty gel capsules on the counter and fumbled through his pocket for cash. After his items were bagged, he said, "The lamb got a bot fly infection. When I found out, I treated it right away to try and save it, but it was too late. The lamb died. That seemed to put Emma Lee over the edge. She got angry. With me! As if I killed the lamb."

Sister Martha placed one hand on her heart and said, "Oh, dear, how hard that must be for you." She paid for her polish, slid her purchase into her purse, and they left the store together.

Outside, he looked in both directions and dropped his voice to a whisper before he continued. "I don't want to shock you, Sister, but I'm certain she's having an affair with her occupational therapist. And not just him. She flirts with everyone, even the furnace repairman! I tell you, she's turned into a whole new person—not in a good way." He clenched his mouth shut again as he shook his head slowly.

There were times when Sister Martha had doubts about this man, especially after her talk with Patrick. But right now, her heart broke for Leonard. She wished she could embrace him, but knew he didn't like hugs. "I'm so sorry."

The man walked down the street with her in silence, as if it hurt too much for him to say more. When they reached her car, she pulled out her keys. Before she unlocked the old station wagon, she said, "Would it be all right if I stopped by and visited her? Perhaps if she talked with me, woman to woman? Not a counseling session or anything."

"No. She's sick and confused. You'll make it worse. We'll work it out ourselves. Besides, I'm sure she won't see you; she's closed herself off from everyone—except those men." He glanced at his watch. "Uh-oh. It's late. I've got to get back to work."

As Leonard hustled away, she noticed how stiff he seemed, like he was made of wood. His body told his tale of woe, and she knew that Emma Lee and Leonard both needed extra grace right now.

On instinct, Sister Martha reached down for her rosary. It wasn't attached to her belt any longer, of course. She smiled at her little memory lapse, then taking her rosary from her purse, she began to pray.

34.

Smoke fills the kitchen from what used to be cheese sandwiches. "Ew, is that lunch?" David asks, pointing to the blackened mess in the skillet.

"Well, it was, but I'm starting over. Want to help?"

He nods and grabs a butter knife.

As charcoaled cheese and blackened bread get scraped into the garbage, my stomach churns. This is worse than morning sickness—more like food poisoning. I know because when I was ten, I ate a huge helping of sunbaked potato salad at a picnic. Around midnight, I threw up, and every hour after that, threw up again. The next day, I felt shriveled and sick, like the Ancient Mariner. My current pain is like that, but has lasted six days instead of six hours.

I reach for a capsule, prescribed to stop the nausea. They look scary: green and big. I'm surprised they fit down my esophagus. But Leonard says they're doctor's orders, so down it goes.

Once the black mess is disposed of, I scrub the pan while David spreads butter smooth and easy. Guess there are some perks to having a brainless mother. He carries the buttered bread with two hands to the newly-cleaned pan, plops it in, butter side down, and returns to the table to begin another. As he spreads, he says, "Are you still feeling sick?"

"I didn't throw up in the car. That means I'm getting better, right?" I smile, trying to look healthier than I feel.

David stops his buttering, as if some terrible thought struck him; his jaw drops and his eyes snap wide. "Do you think you caught what Jojo had? You won't die like the lamb, will you, Mom?"

Jojo's death seven days prior seems so long ago; I'd almost forgotten. "I have an achy belly and joints, but not what the lamb had," I say. "People don't catch the same sicknesses as sheep, honey. And I'm not going to die."

"Good," he says, nodding. "Good."

After shoving open a window to let the spring air in and the smoke out, I pull cheese from the refrigerator. I'm ready to add slices to the buttered bread when the phone rings. Jumping at the sound, I remind myself to turn off the gas (to keep from burning the bread again) and answer. A familiar voice says, "Hi, Emma Lee; it's Patrick."

The room begins to swirl; I fall into a chair. Suddenly, I feel exposed, as if the very walls are listening. I whisper, "Patrick. It's so good to hear your voice."

"I've missed you," he says.

My heart races. Talking to him scares me to death. "Please, you shouldn't call me. He was here last time and I got into trouble. If he found out that it was you ..."

"I'm sorry about that, Emma Lee. I didn't know. Today, Baxter is talking to someone outside the animal testing lab, right down the hallway from my office, so don't worry. Please, talk to me. I miss you so much."

Despite the medicine, my stomach's still rebelling against the little breakfast it contains. "So you're back for good, then," I whisper.

"Yes, and I have to see you. Can you meet me for lunch?

"Oh, no. That's not possible."

"Baxter will never know. I heard directly from his secretary that there's a lunch meeting with the directors today that he can't get out of."

"I ... I've been sick. I can't possibly ..."

"Please. I've got to see you."

My hands shake and I stammer, "What if ..."

"Emma Lee, I've thought about you every day I was away; mailed you dozens of letters. I feel so badly I wasn't here for you. Please, for old times' sake, please meet me. With Baxter retiring soon, we might not get another chance."

"Maybe. Where?"

"There's a little place along the boulevard called Family Buffet. No one from work ever goes there. Say, one o'clock?"

I want to say yes, but if I'm found out, who knows what the man is capable of? Several seconds tick by. "I'll ... try."

"I'll be there waiting. Please come."

When I hear a knock at my door I don't even say goodbye. I slam down the receiver. With shaking hands I peek out.

Sister Martha's smile is broad and genuine. She hugs me like a mother greeting a lost child, and gushes, "Emma Lee, my dear. So good to see you!"

I let her arms engulf me and I burst into tears. "Oh, Sister Martha."

After letting me cry for several minutes, she releases me and says to David, "Oh, my, you're as tall as a tree! Sister Angela wishes you'd come by and play with her sometime." She grabs both of my hands together in one of hers and pats them.

"I'm on my way to Dixmont to see some patients, so I don't have much time, but I had to stop by to see you."

"I ... I'm not allowed, I mean, I think it's ... well ..." I'm already accused of terrible things by my husband. I said yes to meeting Patrick for lunch. How much more trouble could I get in for talking to Sister Martha? I hold open the door. "Please come in."

The woman enters the living room but doesn't sit. She glances at her watch again. "They only let me into the mental hospital at lunch time, between noon and one. But the inmates there so desperately need God, it's worth it. How have you been, dear? You look so pale."

"Not well. I've got stomach trouble, headache. All my joints hurt. I forgot how to make the bed yesterday, burned lunch today. I'm afraid I'm going backwards."

"Leonard told me."

Hearing his name, my hands begin a small tremor. "Leonard? You've seen him?"

"This morning, in Woolworths. I wish you'd return for counseling. I think it would help." Sister Martha glances at her watch again, hugs me, and says, "I have to go, but I'll call tomorrow. Think about it." Then she's out the door.

She waves furiously over her head, and I yell goodbye. Always goodbye. Suddenly I don't want to say goodbye any longer. I want to say hello: to Patrick, Sister Martha, to the whole world. I'm sick of being sick, stuck here on the farm, alone, sick of being controlled and manipulated. I remember Patrick's kindness, his playful manner, his beautiful blue eyes, and realize I'll regret it forever if I don't meet him today.

"David, let's skip the sandwiches and go to lunch today with someone we used to know. Patrick."

"Who's that?"

It was only eight months ago that Patrick left, but I suppose that's an eternity to a child. "You played Legos and ball with him while we helped him pack, remember? Before I got hurt."

He closes his eyes and scrunches his mouth, squeezing memory from tightened muscles like cider from apples. Finally he smiles. "Yeah. I liked him, didn't I?"

"Yes, and he liked you. You were buddies."

I head to the bathroom where, with shaky hands, I spread foundation over my face and run a comb through my scraggly black hair. It has grown long in the past few months, but I can't figure out how to get a haircut. In my room, I scan my wardrobe. I have nothing to wear that will fit over my four-month-pregnant belly except sweats. So that's what I wear.

As I drive along the boulevard, I scan the traffic coming at me, worrying the whole time that I'll see the Cadillac. I don't. Ten minutes later I pull into the small parking lot of the fading blue one-story building. Cars fill six of the seven parking spots in the front. I drive around back where a short stone wall is the only protection from the steep cliff and Ohio River below. I park next to the building, hiding my car from view.

I squeeze David's hand for courage, open the restaurant's side door, and step in. Patrick stands and walks toward us; his strong, lean build takes my breath away. I had forgotten how handsome he is. Taking my hands in his, he escorts me to the booth. "Emma Lee, I've missed you so very much." He tussles David's dark hair. "And look at you! You're so tall already."

David smile looks shy, but he lets Patrick climb into the booth beside him. "That's what Sister Martha said."

"Well, she's right."

We read our menus for several moments, but I know I won't be able to decide. After my head injury, choosing is difficult; quick decisions, such as menu picks, are near impossible. So when the young smiling waitress arrives, my head starts pounding and the room begins to spin.

She asks in a giggly-high voice, "So, what will it be?"

David asks for grilled cheese and chocolate milk.

"What about you?" Patrick asks me.

I bury my face in my hands. "I don't know. I can't choose."

"No pressure here. What do you like? Salad?"

"I can't choose," I wail. "Order for me." I cover my eyes with my hands.

Patrick asks the waitress, "What salads do you have?"

"Caesar, cob, noodle, chicken, or green salad, with blue cheese, thousand island, Italian, oil and vinegar, or Caesar dressing."

"The lady will have a cob salad with Italian dressing on the side. Will that be okay for you?" he asks me.

I nod.

"Okay, and I'll take a hamburger and fries."

When the waitress goes, he says to David, "Did you bring me a toy?"

Grinning, David drags a small Matchbox car from his pocket. "You can play with this," he says.

Patrick races the miniature Corvette across the table, bumping it into the water glass, the napkin, my hand. Hearing David's giggles impales me with grief. This nice, handsome, attractive, *kind*, young man who sits across from me, playing with my son, should be the man in David's life, not the crazy man I live with now. That other man doesn't even like David, let alone play with the boy. I want to beg Patrick to take me away, care for me, hide me. Instead, I say, "I'm so glad you called."

Patrick returns the car to David and reaches across the table to take my hands in his again. "How terrible this must be for you, Emma Lee. I wish I could have been here for you. Are you happy? Do you like living with Leonard?"

"I'm dealing. He helps me practice my therapy. He pays the bills."

The waitress plunks three plates on the table. David splits apart his toasted bread pieces, stretching the cheese in long strands. He pokes one corner of the sandwich into a pile of ketchup, licks the ketchup off, and pokes it again. Today, I don't care how he eats. If he's content, that's all I need.

My fork separates slivers of ham and hardboiled egg pieces from the lettuce as if I plan to eat them. But I don't get more than a mouthful down before my stomach rebels. Nausea and dizziness squeeze my stomach and scramble my thoughts. I lay my fork down.

"Of course he's taking care of your physical needs, but what does your heart say about this marriage?"

I shake my head and stare at the table as the tears start.

"Oh, Emma Lee, how did you get in this fix? How did you ever end up married to this guy?"

I shut my eyes, drawing courage from the darkness. "The injury knocked out my short-term memory. When it came back, I was married.

Didn't even know my husband's name." I sniff, and wipe my nose on my napkin. "I still forget it most of the time." I put my hand on my belly. "And I'm pregnant." I brush away more tears.

"Oh, Emma Lee. I'm so sorry."

"No. It's okay. I love the baby. But I'm scared of him, Patrick. My husband ..." Pressing my fist to my mouth to stop the words, I look over at David and shake my head several times and I whisper, "He ... he's mean."

"Can I have your hardboiled egg, Mom?" David asks.

"Sure." I open my eyes again and scan Patrick's face. I want to make sure I suck up my full allotment of his handsome kindness while we're together. I might not ever see him again.

Patrick's eyes bore into mine and he frowns. "Look, Emma Lee. I didn't know about your accident until I got back, so I couldn't help you before. But I want to help now. I care for you. Have since the day I met you there in the hallway outside your apartment."

When he mentions my apartment, I'm reminded of our first meeting. I had been stuck outside, unable to make the key work, when he strode into the building. "Hi," he said. "Name's Patrick Kilkenny. I live upstairs in 302." He set his grocery sack on the floor. "Can I help?"

At the time, I wondered if it was a good idea, letting a stranger open my door. But I had no other choice. It was that or sleep in the hallway. I handed over the key. He instructed me on how to jiggle it, and magically, the door swung open.

Those same long, manly fingers connected to the same strong hands and lean, muscular arms are now wrapped around a coffee cup. How I wish they were wrapped around me right now.

I glance at the restaurant door, then at my son, who has finished his sandwich and is now emptying his glass of milk.

Leaning forward, I whisper, "You can't imagine how badly I want to leave him."

"Then we'll make that happen."

I sigh. "How, Patrick? I can't work. You know that. I think I have disability payments, but they're not much. With two kids and no job, I can't live on that. I'm a parasite."

"Don't say that. We can work it out. I can help you get a divorce."

I shake my head. "He'd fight that to the end, maybe *my* end. Besides, it takes someone with brains and money to go to court. That's not me, for sure. I'm poor, dependent, and wounded. I can't even choose what to eat for lunch! I won't burden you with that, with me."

"You let me worry about that."

Up to now, I'd known I had lost my past. But now, I realize, I've lost my present and future, too. I'm hit by sorrow so strong, it's like I've been smacked with a stick. I'll never be able to escape from the man I'm with. And even if I do, it's not only me, but also my son and the baby growing within me, who will need support. I'm a burden. The pain of the realization is too much to bear.

"I shouldn't have come, Patrick. It's not fair to either of us." I slide out of the booth and struggle with my jacket. "Forget about me and move on with your life. Please."

Patrick stands and hugs me. "I won't give up," he says.

David slides out of the booth, shifting his focus from one adult to the other, perhaps confused about his role in this.

"We have to go, David. Show Mr. Kilkenny your good manners."

David reaches out his hand. "Goodbye Patrick. Thanks for lunch."

"You're welcome. Bring your mother back to see me again soon," Patrick says.

Blinded by my tears, I let David lead me as if he's my seeing-eye son. And right now, he is.

35.

Patrick slid into the driver's seat and slammed the door. As he backed out of the restaurant lot, he admitted to himself that he had loved Emma Lee since the day he met her. If she hadn't gotten married, he would be courting her, injury and all. As he drove across the bridge, he thought about what to do next. How should he proceed? His thoughts carried him through the afternoon. He called an attorney and the state disabilities office. And although he had a huge report to write, he accomplished little work the rest of the afternoon.

At day-care, Maria escorted Patrick into the playroom. As he waited for Joshua to clear the floor of blocks, inspiration hit him. "Hey, Maria, know of any places for rent in the neighborhood?"

"You looking to move?"

Unzipping his Steelers jacket, Patrick shook his head. "No, it's for a friend. You remember Emma Lee? It has to be low cost, with two bedrooms. She hasn't got much money."

Maria propped one hand on her hip and twisted her pearl necklace with the other. Knitting her brows she said, "Didn't you tell me she was married, living on a farm someplace?"

"Yeah, but that isn't working out."

"What a shame. It hasn't been that long."

"Guess that's relative," he mumbled.

"What?"

When he shook his head, she continued, "Gloria rents out her top floor sometimes. Has to like the person, mind you, but its empty right now. And reasonably priced. She likes kids, too."

"It sounds perfect. Would you ask if we can look at it during the week sometime?"

"Sure."

Patrick walked with Maria and Joshua to the front door. The sitter handed the boy his coat and they stepped out onto the porch. Joshua bolted into the yard like a colt released from his stall. Maria leaned against the open door frame. Lifting her chin, she said, "So how's your quest to find his dad going? He tells me you might have a lead. Will you send him back to Washington?"

"Don't know if Richard is even sober, let alone wanting the boy. My guess is I won't find him. But I promised Joshua I'd try. He misses home."

Maria smiled. Placing a hand on his arm, she said, "Good luck with that. And with the apartment thing."

After dinner, Joshua was watching Sonny and Cher on television when Patrick picked up the phone. "I'd like the phone number for Richard Heister in Walla Walla, Washington," he said.

After giving him the number, the operator said, "Would you like me to dial it for you?"

Patrick stammered, "Ah, no thank you."

As he hung up the receiver, a woman on television caressed her face, cooing that Dove soap included "one-quarter cleansing cream." Joshua turned, but let the sound blare. "So?"

"Turn it down." Patrick sat on the couch, elbows on knees, chin on fists.

Joshua flipped off the TV and lay flat on the floor. "Did you get it?"

"I got his phone number all right—just like that." Patrick snapped his fingers. "Didn't think it would be that easy."

Wrapping his arms over his head, Joshua said, "Don't call. Don't tell him I'm here."

Patrick scratched his head. "What? You've been bothering me every blasted day about going back to Washington, about how I had to hurry and get the number and get you back there. Now I shouldn't call? You better explain yourself, kiddo."

Joshua moved his arms so they covered his face. "I made a friend at school, and day-care isn't so bad. Besides, I want to stay with you."

"What about your dad?"

Turning onto his stomach, Joshua said, "I don't want to live with him. He hates me. Please, don't make me."

Patrick rolled his eyes. "Living with your father won't be a jail sentence. Nobody's going to make you go if you don't want to. But your dad might not know your mother died. Telling him is the right thing to do. I have to do that, at least."

Joshua squeezed his eyes tight and smashed his cheeks with his hands until his lips puckered. "Then you talk. I'm not going to."

"Okay."

Patrick picked up the receiver again. It would be about four o'clock in Washington, and if Richard was working, he probably wouldn't be home yet. But Patrick had courage now. He might not later. He let the phone ring seven times with no answer.

Joshua stuck out his lower lip. "See? He doesn't care."

"Hey, he's not home, that's all. In the meantime, go brush your teeth and get pajamas on for bed."

As he herded Joshua to the bathroom, Patrick thought again about Emma Lee. He'd wait until he saw Baxter in the hallway, then call about the apartment. He'd get her out of that house and out of that marriage, one way or another.

Ring!

David wasn't usually allowed to answer the phone, but today, five days after his very first lunch at a real restaurant, was different. Today, when she couldn't get out of bed, his mom had told him he was the man of the house, and he'd have to do everything including feed the chickens and collect the eggs—and answer the phone.

He picked up the receiver, trying to remember her instructions and whispered, "Hello?"

"Hey, kiddo. This is Patrick. Can I talk to your mom?"

He shook his head. "Uh-uh. She's sick. Can you fix her?"

"Wish I could. Has she seen the doctor?"

"No. Leonard says she has flu and it will go away all by itself."

"Can you bring the phone to her?"

David was very worried. When Mom's eyes were open—which wasn't very often now—they rolled around like marbles on concrete, and her head seemed too heavy for her to lift. It really scared him. David wished he could drive. He'd take her to the doctor himself.

"I'll try."

He hoisted the phone off the table and carried it down the hallway. He dropped the receiver twice, and wasn't sure if the cord would reach, but it did. He pushed her bedroom door open and peeked in. "Mom, Patrick wants to talk to you."

Her squinting eyes, barely open, seemed puffy and red around the edges. "Who?"

"Patrick." He spoke into the receiver now. "Okay, here she is." David had to leave the phone in the hallway. He stretched the receiver cord to its full length and laid the receiver on the pillow next to his mother's ear and said, "Talk, Mom."

"Hello?" David thought her voice sounded scratchy and weird, all air and hardly any sound. He moved closer so he could hear what Patrick said.

"Emma Lee, I'm worried about you. What's wrong?"

"Who ... is this?"

David felt a stab of fear. How could his mother forget Patrick?

"It's Patrick. We met a few days ago for lunch. You must remember."

"My head aches. Dizzy. Don't know what … can't …"

"Look, I'm working on finding you a place to stay and I've been talking to a lawyer about an annulment. I won't leave you there with him."

When she shifted, her arm hit the receiver. It slid off the bed and crashed to the floor, making a loud clunk.

David picked it up and said, "Mom needs help. You have to come, Patrick. She takes the medicine, but she gets worse. Please help."

"I'll get there as soon as I can, David."

But when he hung up the phone, David shuddered. What if Mom was wrong? What if people did catch sickness from sheep, and what if she got sicker and sicker and died? Then he'd be all alone with Leonard. If that happened, he'd run away. He couldn't live here without her. He returned the phone to the living room, fell onto the couch, and cried.

36.

Because mimeograph ink could stain, Katrina wore out-of-date bell bottoms and a plain blue cotton cardigan that made her feel grumpier than the work did. Normally, Rhonda would be doing this job, but she was on vacation all week.

Just my luck, Katrina thought. Baxter wanted three copies filed, and one for each board member. That made unlucky thirteen. There was no way carbon paper would do the job. It would have to be mimeographed.

She disabled her typewriter ribbon to make the keys sharper, and typed each page as a stencil. It took her all week; her nails were nearly ruined with the effort. Now that she finished typing, she replaced the ribbon, but this project wasn't finished.

Katrina hugged the box filled with the 242 stencils and sauntered down the hallway to the break room. That's where the ancient mimeograph machine lived. Installed there before World War II to muffle the loud ka-chink, ka-chink, ka-chink it made when running, the mimeograph was an anachronism, a relic that belonged in the dump—like Baxter himself, she thought.

She had asked her boss many times to spring for one of those new Xerox copy machines. All you had to do, the salesman told her, was place the original under the cover, and press the button. Nice, crisp, black copies on shiny paper spit out the other side in moments. The machine even counted for you, and stopped when the number was met. There was no stencil to type, and no mess to deal with. She sighed, knowing that most likely hell would have to freeze over before this company spent any money on modernizing.

When she looked up, Patrick was hustling toward her. He pulled her to the wall. "Katrina. Just the person I wanted to see."

"Hey, watch the stencils."

"I need your help."

Katrina rolled her eyes and set the box on the floor. "I'm busy."

"But this is your specialty."

"Why are you whispering?" She held up a hand. "No, wait, let me guess. It's about Emma Lee."

"Yes, and something's really wrong. Can you meet me after work?"

She frowned. "Um, why don't you tell me now?"

"I can't discuss it here. Never know who's listening."

On one hand she didn't want to get involved. On the other, she did feel a thimbleful of curiosity. Her shoulders raised and lowered, a slow shrug. "You're paranoid, you know that? But hey, it's been a hard day and I could use a good laugh." She turned her wrist over and tapped her watch. "So, how about Gino's at five-fifteen?"

"I'll be there." Patrick headed for the stairs.

She picked up her box and continued down the hallway. In the break room, Katrina separated the waxed stencil from its backing, attached it to the roller, then turned on the machine. As she counted each page, Katrina's thoughts drifted to Michael. He had his faults. He could be bull-headed and slow to decide. But she loved his physique, his good manners, how he kissed her. And there was something about his generosity that made her heart sing.

She turned off the machine, changed the stencil, and flipped it on again. After thirteen revolutions, she replaced the stencil yet again. Three hours later, Katrina left ten collated, stapled copies in Baxter's office, and filed the other three.

Back at her desk, Katrina wondered about her meeting with Patrick. Would he ask her to deliver love notes? Convince Emma Lee to leave the old goat? Smuggle Emma Lee away for secret trysts at his apartment? She'd know soon.

At five o'clock, Katrina grabbed her leather fringed shoulder bag and coat and picked her way to Gino's, careful to protect her shoes and stockings from the weeds and mud. As usual, the place was filled with workers of every type. She noticed Patrick near the window; she slid onto a chair, placed her purse onto the table, and leaned toward Patrick. "Now what's so secret we can't talk about it at work?"

"Emma Lee's been sick off and on for days. When I called her this morning, she could barely talk. It's got to be Baxter's doing."

She laughed. "That's it? That's your big secret? Get real, Patrick. I know he's a creep, but Baxter doesn't control germs. People get sick all by themselves."

The waitress plodded over, her flat feet flapping the floor, slap, slap. She pulled out her tablet, and grabbed the pencil that was tucked over her ear. "What'll it be?"

"Just coffee," Patrick said.

Katrina nodded. "Me too."

When the woman left, Patrick continued. "Yes, but this is different. I met her for lunch last week. She said she had been sick the week before, but was on the mend. Then today, almost a week later, she can't even talk. He's doing this."

"Okay, that could be. I wouldn't put it past the old goat. But maybe it's just a relapse. It happens. You think you're better. Then you overexert, and whoosh, you get worse."

Patrick shook his head several times. "I'm telling you, it's more than that. She doesn't even remember we met."

"Does that shatter your ego?"

"That's not the point. From what David says, she's going downhill fast, but Dr. B. hasn't taken her to the doctor. I've got to go over there, see what I can do. But here's the rub. When I stopped at their house a while back, Baxter threw me off his place. Warned me to never come back. I won't get very far if I go when he's around. He even accused me of having an affair with her."

"So are you?" She gave him a sly grin.

"Last week was the first time I'd seen her since I got back. There's something wrong, I'm telling you. I can feel it. But I can't do this alone."

The waitress came with two cups. She slid them onto the table and filled each with steaming coffee. Katrina took a sip and waited a beat. Finally she said, "I might be willing to help. It could be amusing to thwart Baxter. So what's your plan?"

"Tomorrow's his retirement party. I want to leave work and drive out to Emma Lee's place, take her to the doctor. Your job would be to distract Baxter until the party starts or until I get back, whichever comes first."

"And you've thought of how that could be accomplished?"

"Yeah. Wear something sexy. He's a sucker for that. Go to his office around eleven and pretend you need help with, oh, I don't know. Make it up. Be sure he doesn't leave the building, is all. Can you do that?"

Her lips rose in a slight smile. "I'm up for the challenge—sounds fun."

"I've seen that red miniskirt you own. It always gets a second look from him."

"Okay. That and my tight white sweater should do it. Glad that mimeograph job is done."

"Add your reddest lipstick."

"Are you challenging my ability to entice a man?" She rubbed her palms together, as if kneading clay. "He's putty in my hands."

"I'll trust you on that." His shoulders relaxed and he leaned back against the wall. "Okay, so once you're in his office, I'll head to the Baxter farm. I'll be back by one o'clock."

"You got it." Katrina was grinning now. The game was on. "Baxter isn't easily distracted, you know. It's going to be tough. And I don't think he's ever talked that long with me before. So tell me, oh great white defender of damsels in distress, what's in it for me?"

He smacked his forehead. "A feeling of good will, doing a good deed. Will that be enough?"

"The way I see it, I'm doing your dirty work. I have to spend an hour with that sleazy man while you gallivant off with your new love."

Patrick stared at the ceiling. He took another swig of coffee and then breathed in and exhaled slowly. Finally he spoke with slow, deliberate words, hands flat on the table. "Look, I'm worried about her, that's all. Why does this have to be so hard?"

"I want you to understand that I'm doing you a big favor here."

"Okay, I'm forever indebted to you for this." He pulled out his check book and a pen. "So how much do you want to do this job? Will $50 be enough?"

She stared at him. "I can see you're touchy about this subject, Patrick. I don't want your money. I want gratitude. I'll distract Baxter, and you owe me a favor of my choice."

He reached his hand across the table and shook hers. "It's a deal."

37.

At eleven a.m., Katrina headed into Baxter's office, reviewing the plan she and Patrick made the evening before. First she'd feign helplessness, then switch to being teary and incoherent. Could she prattle on for thirty minutes? Of course she could.

Baxter was at his door, coat in hand when she and Patrick arrived. Patrick continued on out the door as Katrina stopped Baxter. "Oh, sir. I'm so glad I caught you before you left. I need to talk with you."

Her boss scanned her up and down. "It will have to wait, Miss Kowalski. I'm on my way out."

She placed the box of used stencils and one copy of the full report on the floor and hoped her countenance gave the impression she was distressed.

"But it's important." She sighed as if what she was about to say weighed her down.

He propped both fists on his hips. "See me later. I have to run home for something and get back before that damned retirement party." He checked his watch. "That leaves me fifty minutes. Come back Monday. Better yet, skip me all together. Brackenridge can take care of it. He'll be taking over when I'm gone, anyhow."

She discarded her 'damsel in distress' act and switched to plan B. Dropping her head, she fluttered her eyelashes and donned a demure smile. "I wouldn't ask you this, but … it's important. Please. I need five minutes of your time."

He sighed. "All right. But make it quick."

She picked up the box and placed it on his desk. "I must confess. I came in here on pretense," she said. "I brought the stencils and the report, yes, but honestly, sir … ." She took out her handkerchief and, not smearing her mascara, dabbed her cheeks below her eyes. "I have a *personal* problem—very personal. Can I trust you to be discreet?"

He looked at his watch again, scanned her up and down, then took a seat behind his desk. "Uh, of course. What exactly can I do for you, Katrina?"

She placed both palms on the desk and leaned forward. In this position, she knew his gaze fell directly on the smooth, firm tops of her breasts peeking from the top of her tight, scoop-necked white sweater. Taking full advantage, she pressed her arms inward to deepen her cleavage.

He twisted his mouth into a thin grin and ran his hands through his sparse hair. She likened his expression to that of a plantation overseer examining a slave woman standing naked on the auction block. The blatant ogling might have wilted another woman, but Katrina counted on it. She slid into his brocade wing chair, letting her miniskirt hike up her thigh a few inches. When she gave her skirt hem an obligatory, yet useless tug, he looked so caught up in the motion that she expected saliva to begin running down his chin.

A surge of adrenalin shot through her. He was caught! Like the handler for the circus bear, she was in her element now, at the same time arousing yet controlling the testosterone-driven beast she called 'boss.' She pulled the elastic band from her hair, releasing the long, chestnut locks. Then, giving her head a little shake, which caused her curls to cascade over her shoulders, she purred, "Oh, thank you. I don't know who else to turn to."

He sat immobile for several moments, hands clasped, mouth puckered: stunned by her beauty, her raw sexuality, her chutzpa (at least that's what she hoped) while he waited for her to speak. Apparently, he'd forgotten completely that he was in a hurry.

"At the all-hands meeting, someone said that if any of us had a problem ... with, you know ..." She dropped her voice to a whisper, "sex ... and such ... we should report that to your office. And, well ... I don't think it would be right." She crumpled her handkerchief to a ball. "If I talked to someone, who might not ... or who could .... It's private, you know, and yet ... ." Dabbing her cheek again, she sniffed. "Here I am, having to talk about it. I don't know if I can, really ... ." She blew her nose and closed her eyes, hoping he'd attribute her silence to reticence rather than evasion.

He looked confused, which pleased her. "Take your time, Ms. Kowalski."

Drawing this out, saying nothing while saying a lot, required great skill and thought. Like the pirouettes she performed in ballet, it was all about balance.

"Thank you."

Katrina closed her eyes. She conjured up a memory, one that would give her the right frame of mind and emotion.

"I have a hard time talking about it. I need to tell you this up front. It's not every day that someone does this, you know. Or that I have to endure it. But it's so hard when it happens. It's like ... back when I was in high school one evening after a basketball game? A boy from my American History class, Harry Langlois, cornered me in a dark hallway. He shoved me against the wall and tried to ... ."

Baxter seemed to come alive. He leaned forward and propped his elbows on the desk, chin on his fists.

"Thank goodness they came. You know, before anything happened. Guys from the other team. They got lost trying to find their way out of the school."

Katrina talked about the dark hallway, how tall the guys were who found her, how long it took to leave the school after that. She highlighted her report to the principal about Harry, and how he got into trouble.

After ten minutes, Baxter stood. "I don't have time for this."

She dabbed her cheeks again, and stood too. Placing a hand on his arm she said, "But we haven't even gotten to my work issue."

"And what would that be?"

"Please, don't rush me. It was traumatic." Katrina fell back into the chair and covered her face with her hands. "I don't know if I should tell," she said. Tears welled in her eyes until her vision grew blurry. She sat for several minutes, letting the tears flow, trying to feel the pain, the humiliation that hadn't happened.

Glancing at her watch again, Katrina noticed that there were twenty more minutes until the retirement party. Even if she finished now, it would be good enough. He didn't have enough time to go home and return.

She stood and scooped up her box of stencils. Sniffing, she said, "I changed my mind, Dr. Baxter. I can't talk about this yet. I'm sure you understand. I'll see you at the party."

Pretending to stifle a sob, she turned so he couldn't see her smirk, and ran from the room.

PATRICK WANTED TO purchase flowers for her, but knew he shouldn't. Too incriminating. As he sped along the narrow valley, a peregrine falcon swooped from a tree and impaled a squirrel on the roadway. Any other day he would have stopped to watch, but not today. Nothing mattered except Emma Lee's welfare.

A few miles down the road he turned left onto a driveway that led up a hill to the farmhouse. Seeing it, he grew excited. He'd spring Emma Lee from this prison and she'd be free forever. Sometimes he let his mind imagine what it would be like to be married to her. Yes, she'd take some care, but he was used to that. It would be a pleasure to take her to therapy, or to the doctor, or to the grocery store because he'd be with her.

Fifteen minutes had elapsed from the time he left to now as he parked and sprinted through the grassy yard to the house. It took several minutes after his knock before the door cracked open. David poked his head out the door.

"Hi, David. I came to visit your mommy."

The boy said, "She's really sick. You gotta help her."

Patrick followed David to the bedroom. When he entered, Emma Lee turned. Her sunken cheeks, cracked lips, deep dark circles under shut eyes caused his breath to catch.

"I came to get you," he stammered.

Emma Lee opened her eyes mere slits; one hand shook as she reached for him; the other pointed to her throat. "Thank you. Hard to talk; caught something. Head's pounding, too."

Patrick pulled a chair up to the bed and stroked her forehead. "After I talked with you yesterday, all I could think about was how to help. I've been so worried."

"Thought I was getting better, but … ." Emma Lee wrinkled her forehead; her words faded.

Patrick felt his gut tighten. This wasn't the flu.

When he heard tires crunching on rock, his heart pounded. Was Baxter here? Racing to the window, he peered through the curtains. An old station wagon was pulling up next to his car. Not Leonard. He whispered a prayer of thanks.

"Are you expecting someone, Emma Lee?" he asked.

"Don't know," she mumbled.

He stood. "I'll get the door."

When he opened it, Sister Martha stood on the porch. "Good to see you again, Patrick," she said. "I didn't expect to see you here."

Patrick shook her hand. "Likewise. Please, come in."

They walked into the bedroom together.

"Hello, dear," she said. "I promised I'd return, and from the looks of you, it was none too soon."

Emma Lee's eyes rolled into her lids. She leaned over and threw up into the basin on the night stand.

Pulling Patrick aside, Martha whispered, "She's dehydrated. You can tell by how her skin wrinkles on her arms and face, and the peeling lips, glassy eyes. She needs to be in the hospital, immediately."

"I'm with you, Sister," he said. "I'll start packing and we'll get her out of here." He asked David, "Where's the luggage?"

David climbed into the closet and pulled out a duffle bag. He opened Emma Lee's drawer and pulled out a pair of pajamas. "She'll need these, won't she?"

"Thanks, kiddo," Patrick said. He threw the pajamas into the bag along with underwear, socks, a sweat shirt and pants.

Sister Martha returned, carrying the clean basin and wet washcloth; she wiped Emma Lee's face and put her shoes on. "I'll call Dr. Baxter later, so he knows where Emma Lee and David are."

Patrick zipped up the bag. "Let's get her in the car."

Sister Martha said, "Okay. David, you'll stay with Sister Angela while we take your mom to the hospital."

"No. Please don't take her away."

"It's okay, honey. She'll get better."

"Then let me go with her."

"I'm sorry. Little boys aren't allowed in the hospital. When she gets better she'll come back for you."

David began to cry. "But she's going to die like Jojo did. Please don't take her."

Patrick squatted. He hoped he was telling the truth when he said, "Don't worry. She won't die."

Patrick slid Emma Lee's arm over his shoulder and lifted her. Sister Martha tucked the bowl and towels under one arm, and slid her shoulder under Emma Lee's other arm. The three of them limped to the door with David hugging his mother's legs.

They escorted Emma Lee to the back seat of Patrick's car, where she lay on the seat.

David tried to climb in with her, but Sister Martha took his hand. "No, honey, you have to come with me."

Sobbing, David let the nun lead him to her car and he climbed into the front seat.

Patrick started Katrina's car and drove as fast as he dared, and for the hundredth time today, prayed for the welfare of a woman he loved.

38.

Michael sat in his usual booth near the window of the Oak Street Diner and ordered his usual lunch—tuna salad sandwich on rye with potato salad and coffee. But this was no usual Friday. He was taking Katrina to Swan Lake, performed by the Pittsburgh Ballet Theater, then to dinner. Of course, sharing the ballet and a meal with her would be fun, but neither of those caused his assessment of the day's importance. No, what happened after dinner would make the whole day sparkle.

The waitress shuffled over. Her name tag read Dolly, but she didn't look like a doll. Her gray hair was pulled back in a bun and covered with a net. Her skin was wrinkled and pale from years of waitress service and she had a slight hunch to her back. She set a plate of food in front of him and said, "Here you go, Mikey. Your usual." She flashed him a quick smile. "You're late. Hard day at work?"

He shrugged and grinned. "Nope. I had an errand to run. Bought a ring."

"An *engagement* ring?"

He winked. "Yep. Want to see it?"

Dolly placed the coffee carafe on the table. "Sure do."

When he pulled the box from his pocket and opened it, she gasped. "Don't that beat all. That'n's a beauty, all right! Them's emeralds on the side?"

"The jeweler called it his 'masterpiece'," Michael said. "It's unique and lovely, like Katrina."

"Gorgeous, honey. I never sawr a triangle diamond before. Hey, I 'member the picture you showed me of your girl. She's quite a looker, that one. What's she do again?"

"She's studying ballet." He imagined her in her leotard, tights, and toe shoes, one leg over the bar, stretching her hamstrings, reaching, folding, glowing. The image brought a smile to his lips.

"Before I met her, I'd never been to any dance performance. Now, I know all about every type: modern dance, ballet, and jazz—more than most people learn in a lifetime, I bet. I like it. And I love her."

"Man, you look positively love-sick. She's one lucky girl," Dolly said. "So how will you do it? Propose, I mean."

"I have it all planned. After the ballet, I'll park at the bottom of Mt. Washington and together we'll ride the incline to the top. Then, we'll stroll to Carlyle's Restaurant."

"Wow. I heard that's the best steak house in the city."

"Yep. With a spectacular view to match. I'll order her favorite: steak and lobster. And when the coffee and cheesecake arrives, I'll drop down on one knee and present her with the ring."

Dolly grinned wide, showing a hole where a missing bottom tooth should be. "Very romantic, honey. Got a date in mind?"

He laughed and leaned back in his chair. "It could be a while. She's so independent, I don't even know if she'll say yes right away. But she'll soften, and I'm a patient guy. Once we're married, I'm going to help her set up a dance studio."

The waitress propped one hand on her hip. "Well, she'd be a dang fool to turn you down. I'd do anything for a ring like that." Her grin widened. "Oh, and you're nice, too." She winked and grabbed the coffee carafe handle. "Anytime you want, bring her in. I'll tell her jist how special you are."

Dolly shuffled to the next table as Michael slid the ring back into his pocket. He closed his eyes and lifted his cup to inhale the deep, rich aroma. He wished he could propose right now. He mouthed the words. "Katrina, lovely, wonderful woman of my life, will you marry me?"

He took a bite of his sandwich and stared out the window. He could almost see the city lights sparkling in her eyes like the emeralds on the ring. No matter what she said—yes or no—he knew she would be his soon enough. Yes, it was going to be a great evening.

After finishing lunch, Michael threw three quarters on the table for a tip and left.

As he entered his office, he heard the phone ringing. Jennifer was nowhere in sight so he grabbed the receiver and barked, "Oak Street Occupational Therapy."

A man's voice said, "I'm looking for Michael Yamada."

"Speaking."

"This is Broderick Domini from Suburban General Hospital admissions department. A woman named Emma Lee Baxter was admitted an hour ago. Records show you're her occupational therapist, and that she's still under your care for her prior head injury. Is that right?"

Michael frowned. What was Emma Lee doing in the hospital? "Yes."

"Her doctor would like to consult with you about her this afternoon at 5:30."

Michael planned to be in his bathroom shaving and showering at 5:30, to ensure he'd be odor free and smooth-faced for the passionate kiss after his proposal. He cared about Emma Lee, and wanted to help her as much as possible, but not at the expense of his big night. There wasn't enough time to fit in a visit to the hospital.

"That's too late. How about 4:00?"

"I'm afraid not, sir. The doctor's in surgery all afternoon."

"Tomorrow morning then?"

"The patient is drifting in and out of consciousness. Dr. Rudnick believes your input is vital to his understanding what's happening."

He took a deep breath and convinced himself that everything would work out. "Okay. I can give him ten minutes. What room is she in?"

Michael tucked the receiver under his chin and peeled off his jacket. He fell into his office chair, picked up a pen, and grabbed a tablet of paper. As he wrote the room number and the doctor's name, he considered sending Jennifer instead, or backing out altogether. But as he wrote, the last meeting he had with Emma Lee came to mind. She had looked so ill and her brain had been playing tricks on her again. Something was happening to her that he didn't understand, something unusual. Perhaps the doctor could shed light on things for him.

So, although he was tempted, he wouldn't skip consulting with Emma Lee's doctor. Instead, he'd leave work early to shower and shave beforehand. Ten minutes with the doctor wouldn't kill him. He'd still be able to pick up Katrina by six and they'd still get to their seats by seven, no sweat. So why were his armpits wet?

PATRICK SAT IN the waiting area on an orange plastic chair while the odors of canned corn, meatloaf, and alcohol wafted through the air. His stomach growled and he realized he had missed lunch. The elevator door opened and Sister Martha exited, her shoulder bag smacking her with each stride. She slid onto a sagging, over-stuffed chair next to him. "Thanks for staying, Patrick. How's Emma Lee?"

A distracted, busy-looking nurse hustled past them and entered Emma Lee's room. "Glad you're here. I've got to get back to work." He stood. "They put her on IVs in the emergency room, then brought her up here. An intern is with her now. Doctor's in surgery and won't see her until later. That's all I know." Patrick leaned closer to Sister Martha and whispered, "I think Leonard's poisoning her."

Sister Martha's eyes shot open and she placed a hand near her throat. "That's a very strong allegation, Patrick."

"But it's true. I'm a chemist in a pesticide plant, so I know. Her symptoms are classic."

"Maybe it's accidental. Leonard loves her."

"Nausea and dehydration aren't caused by love, Martha. Those glazed-over eyes aren't either. And you know as well as I do, it's not the flu." Patrick clenched his fists, and worked the muscles of his jaw. "Baxter has full access to a whole array of chemicals. For instance, if an organic arsenate was his poison of choice, symptoms would start with mild headaches and hoarseness. It would cause her to have difficulty talking, and a dry, tight throat. She has those symptoms. Then things would progress to violent abdominal pain and pressure, greenish or yellowish vomit, and convulsions. Sound familiar? Baxter knows all about what dosage to use, how to administer it, and how to keep from contaminating himself."

"Okay," Sister Martha said. "Let's say you're right. Why would Leonard do that? What's there to gain? He wants her to get better."

"Better, maybe, but not completely well. If she develops her own mind about things, he'd lose control. And I know for a fact he'll give anything to keep control."

Sister Martha tilted her head. "You sure have a lot of emotion about this. Are you … involved with her?"

Patrick shook his head vehemently. "No. I'm concerned. As a friend."

The nun raised her eyebrows.

He ran the fingers of both hands through his red hair. "I won't lie; I do love her. Have since the day we met. But we aren't involved, at least not that way."

Sister Martha clasped her hands together as if in prayer and shook her head. "Patrick, don't blame Dr. Baxter without evidence.

Let's wait for the doctors to tell us what's wrong before we form erroneous conclusions."

Patrick jumped to his feet and pointed to Emma Lee's room. "But what if I'm right, Sister? What if she is being poisoned? We can't err on the side of caution at the expense of her life."

"Of course we can't. And we should tell the medical staff to test for poisons." Sister Martha stared down the hallway. Pressing her clasped hands to her lips she sat in silence for a moment before she continued. "But until we find out otherwise, we need to support her without accusing anyone. That's the best thing we can do. I'm going to call Dr. Baxter now, tell him she's here."

"Then I'm leaving. But think about this, Sister. If we're too cautious, give him too big of benefit of the doubt, she could be dead before we figure it out."

39.

Separating himself from the hospital lobby noise, Patrick closed himself into to the phone booth like an astronaut in a space capsule. He grabbed the phone book and leaning back against the glass, searched through the government pages for the police. No matter what Sister Martha thought, there was no way he'd let Emma Lee's suffering to come to the same end as Peggy's.

He slipped a dime in the slot. Seconds after he dialed, he heard, "Precinct Ten, Venezia speaking."

"I'd like to report a crime. Dr. Leonard Baxter has been poisoning his wife, Emma Lee. She was admitted to Suburban General Hospital, Room 314 about an hour ago. She'd been having headaches and confusion, and now there's diarrhea and drowsiness. Probably an arsenate overdose. I have a master's degree in chemistry, so I recognize the symptoms. She might have died if we hadn't brought her in. I told the nurse to run the tests."

"And you are …?"

"A concerned citizen."

"We need a name."

"Yeah, well … can't give that yet. Don't want Baxter to discover who turned him in, at least not yet. But Sister Martha Lenzner was with me. She's a chaplain at the hospital. You can talk to her."

"I see. Got evidence?"

"I'll get back to you on that."

"You aren't giving us much to go on, here."

"But it's still true. Do your job. Investigate."

Patrick hung up. Gray skies and a light rain greeted him as he trudged to the car.

Driving back to work, Patrick kept thinking about the two people he cared about most: Emma Lee and Joshua. Today, he had visited Emma Lee in time. That had to be grace.

"Thanks for your help today, God," he mumbled as he drove. "Make sure she lives."

His thoughts turned to Joshua, then. The kid could certainly use a break, too. So to round things out, he added, "And Lord, help me find Joshua's father so the boy can return to Washington. If he wants to."

When he drove into the plant parking lot, Patrick checked his watch. The retirement celebration would be wrapping up. It would be at least an hour before anyone noticed he wasn't at work. So instead of entering the building, he went to Gino's Diner. There, at the pay phone, he pulled a slip of paper from his wallet with Richard Heister's phone number, then he slipped several quarters into the slot and dialed. Having given up after the tenth ring, he was hanging up the receiver when he heard a groggy, "Hello?"

"I'm looking for Richard Heister."

"This is. You ain't from the collection agency, are you?" the man grumbled.

"No. I'm Patrick Kilkenny, Your first wife Peggy's brother."

Richard yawned and growled, "What d'ya want?"

"I'm calling to tell you that Peggy died."

The man seemed to wake up then. "No! What happened?"

"Cancer. She was sick for a while."

"Man, that sucks."

"Yes, it does. And your son, Joshua, needs you."

"No, he don't. I failed him."

"You still have time; he's only seven."

There was a long pause, then, "Look, man, I got a new woman, baby … .You want money? I ain't got much, but I'll try and send some."

Patrick's gut twisted. "I don't want your stupid money. I want you to care about Joshua."

"The kid don't even know me."

"You can change that."

"No, I can't."

The dial tone buzzed.

Patrick slammed down the receiver and stomped off.

He entered the plant, raced down the hallway, took the stairs two at a time, slammed his office door closed, and fell into a chair. Eyes squeezed shut and teeth gritted, Patrick couldn't stop his anger from mounting. Richard was so irresponsible it made him want to scream.

There was no escaping the truth: Joshua was here to stay. Patrick would be full time parent-teacher conference attendee, mood-swing arbitrator, homework policeman, and of course, breadwinner for the rest of the boy's life. He was a *father*.

Knitting his fingers behind his head, Patrick leaned back in his chair and stared at the ceiling. *Father*. The word carried a huge burden.

The funny thing was, the more he thought about all that responsibility and commitment, all that extra work and stress, the broader his smile grew.

THE WINDOWLESS BASEMENT room was built in the 1930s, and wasn't turned into the cafeteria until ten years later when the company added several long tables and wooden folding chairs. A few years after that, they constructed a small stage on one end, and bumped out a tiny kitchen on the other where one lone cook made sandwiches for lunch each day. Outside of that, the space was used for breaks, larger meetings, and in a pinch, as an auditorium for events such as this.

Some people took seats at the tables. On stage, the vice president stepped up to the microphone. He tapped it twice and said, "Testing, testing."

The conversation in the room diminished.

He continued, "Dr. Baxter, on behalf of the company, I invite you to the podium so we can present you with your retirement watch."

When he heard the thin applause, all color drained from Dr. Baxter's face. He stood and cleared his throat. Tugging at his collar with a finger, Leonard waited until the microphone quit screeching before he spoke. His ten minute speech rambled through his years at the plant and the changes he saw during that time. It ended with thanks for the watch and one sentence about his farm and future.

Again, the applause was thin; conversation promptly resumed.

Offstage, Baxter stared at the drab olive-green concrete walls, and wished he was home with Emma Lee. As he approached the serving table, a secretary from the animal testing division served him a piece of cake. He likened her stature to a fire hydrant, or perhaps a hippopotamus walking upright, on its hind legs.

"Would you like ice cream with this?" she asked. "We have Isley's butter pecan or vanilla."

"No ice cream," he grumbled.

"How about some coffee?"

Baxter shook his head and picked up the plastic fork. As he poked the cake, Leonard scanned the room. Employees greeted, joked, smiled, and ate, oblivious to his presence.

He sucked air into his lungs and expelled it with a groan. This place provoked bipolar emotions in him. On one level, he felt connected to it as if it were home. Sometimes it caused him to feel powerful and young, like earlier when Katrina came into his office. Mostly, though, when the polluted air choked him, or when regulations strangled his creativity, or like now when he was forced to eat dry cake with all these people who didn't really care about him, he couldn't wait to leave.

When Leonard looked up again, he noticed Hiram Eisenbaum coming down the hallway. Hiram extended his right hand. "Congratulations on your retirement, sir. What are you going to grow on your farm?"

"Sheep and strawberries. And spend time with my wife and new baby. She's pregnant, you know."

"I heard. Congratulations, sir. And speaking of Emma Lee, will she be joining us today? I was hoping to talk with her, see how she's doing."

"No, she has the flu."

Hiram shook his head. "Oh, too bad. She probably doesn't remember, but the day she hit her head is branded in my brain forever. I think about it every day. Sometimes I even dream about dragging her out of there. I was so scared; I thought she was going to die. Thank goodness she didn't, huh? Could you tell her from me that I hope she's well soon? Tell her I missed seeing her again."

Baxter didn't like men asking about his wife. Was Hiram involved with her, too? Not wanting to give the man any more energy or affirmation than necessary, he nodded and looked away.

Hiram shifted his weight from one foot to the other and back again. He shoved a bite of ice cream into his mouth and waited. After several moments, when Dr. Baxter still didn't respond, he said, "Well … g-good knowing you."

Leonard focused on his cake so intently one might think he was picking out ants.

Hiram shrugged, dropped his plate in the garbage, and strode out of the room.

A few others came to wish Leonard well. Most asked about Emma Lee.

When he finished eating, Leonard was shunted to the doorway by the same secretary who had given him the cake. There, like a groom in a receiving line, he was instructed to greet the employees as they passed. On their way by, some people did shake his hand. Others nodded. A few smiled. Leonard reveled in their uncomfortable gazes and fake expressions. They were jealous, of course. After all, he was leaving this stinking hole and they were stuck here.

Katrina and Nancy were two of the last to leave. He winked at Katrina, but she didn't seem to notice.

With plastic spoon poised ready to slurp the last bite of melted ice cream, Nancy said, "So where's Emma Lee this afternoon, sir? I sent her the invitation. Lots of people wanted to see her." She downed the ice cream like an oyster.

He was sick of explaining. Emma Lee seemed to be more popular than he was. "Like I told Hiram and the others, she's ill and couldn't come."

"Too bad."

At that moment, Rhonda raced into the room; she looked flustered, like an agitated chicken.

"Phone call, Dr. Baxter. A woman named Sister Martha Lenzner."

"Tell her I'll call her back."

"I tried. She said it was about your wife and it was very important. Said she'd hold until you got to the phone."

Leonard didn't rush. He knew Sister Martha. She always seemed to need something "important." Perhaps she wanted permission to visit Emma Lee again, or she wanted to tell him about some new program at church that his wife would like. No matter what that woman wanted, he wasn't about to oblige her too quickly.

He shook the hands of two more people before he strolled back to his office and picked up the receiver.

"Baxter here. Are you still there, Sister?" he said, hoping she had hung up.

"Yes, thanks for answering, Leonard."

"So what's so important that you had to call me at work?"

"I stopped in to see Emma Lee at home this morning and found her dehydrated and quite sick. I was very concerned for her—alarmed really, at her condition. We brought her right to the hospital and they admitted her."

He sucked in his breath. "You should have called me first."

"There wasn't time. She could have died."

"Where's David?"

"He's with Sister Angela."

"And how is Emma Lee doing, now that she's in the clutches of the medical establishment?"

"Oh, much better—she's on an IV and medication for the nausea, and a sedative. That's why I called. You need to be here with her. There are papers to sign, and I'm sure she'd like to see you when she wakes up."

He cursed under his breath.

"What did you say?"

"I'll be there as soon as I can."

40.

She looked up when Leonard entered the room. She had expected him to be glad that his wife was being cared for. But the deep furrows that chiseled his forehead told her it stressed him big-time.

Running his fingers through his thinning hair he said, "How is she." A demand rather than a question.

Some people would probably interpret his tone as abrupt or even anti-social. But Sister Martha prided herself in being able to see behind his tough-guy façade. Back when she was helping care for Emma Lee, Leonard told her how his first wife, Janice, died here, and how fearful he was of hospitals.

She extended her hand to him. "I'm glad you could come so soon, Leonard. She's doing much better. Give her a few days; she'll be fine."

"It's a hospital, damn it. It's the worst place for her. I don't want her here." He stood, eyes closed, rocking back and forth, silent for several moments.

She waited, strumming her fingers on her knees.

Finally he said, "Hospitals kill people."

Sister Martha clasped her hands as if in prayer, covering the large crucifix she always wore. "Not this time. They saved Emma Lee's life. And the baby. Both of them might have died otherwise." Interpreting his scowl as anxiety, she said, "Don't worry. She'll be fine."

He breathed in and loudly exhaled, his shoulders sagging with the effort. But when he lifted his head and stared at her, his face seemed to harden. "I love her so. I can't stand to see her here. I'll get her out as soon as possible. And I'll pick David up from your place on my way home."

"We can keep him overnight if you like."

"No. I don't want you to be burdened with him. Besides, he has chores to do."

She nodded. "Sure. That's fine. If you need someone to watch him tomorrow, let me know."

Leonard stared at Emma Lee again. He seemed to be struggling with something, but his outward control was impressive. His face lost all trace of emotion. He stared out the window for a few moments and then ran a hand across his face, then nodded. "Sure. When I visit Emma Lee again."

The loudspeaker in the hallway came to life. "Sister Martha Lenzner please report to the second floor."

She wished she could stay longer. She might be able to draw Leonard out and help him process all of this. "I've got to get back to work now, but I'll stop by later. If you're still here, we can talk. Otherwise, give me a call, even this weekend would be okay, and we'll set something up."

Leonard fell into a chair. "Thank you, but I've done it before and I can do it again. I think this is what God put me on the earth for—to care for invalid women."

The nun nodded. On her way to the next patient, she wondered about Leonard. He had his faults, but he seemed sincere. Was Patrick right? She hoped not.

LEONARD SAT NEXT to Emma Lee's bed and watched her chest rise and fall in a steady rhythm. Her face, often full of stress and pain in the past few months, looked so serene. Smooth, taut skin stretched over her high cheek bones, giving her an other-worldly look that took his breath away. *Like Sleeping Beauty*, he thought. He smiled to himself and took her hand in his. He had managed to ensure that his beautiful wife, the woman of his dreams, would be with him forever. Everything was for her own good, of course. She needed him. He had almost managed that once before, but Janice had the audacity to die on him. This was his second chance.

"My darling," he whispered. "I want you to know how much I love you. There's no life for me without you." He folded the sheet down so he could see the swell of Emma Lee's breasts under her hospital gown. He still couldn't get over his luck, marrying this sweet young thing. He felt comfortable with Emma Lee like this. He could talk to her, make amends for what he had to do to keep her from leaving. And in this state, she was the best listener. "At first I hated it when Janice died." His voice caught and his throat grew pinched and he whispered, "I felt so alone."

Leonard squeezed his eyes shut and thought back four years. At the time, few people knew how deadly smoking was. But then all of a sudden, it seemed like everyone he knew had lung cancer, or emphysema, or some other breathing problem. His wife was no exception. Janice had smoked for almost forty years and her cancer was discovered late. There was nothing the medical community could do.

He continued whispering, "She suffered so much that at the end, I had to do something. It was my duty as a loving husband, wasn't it? Take away the pain? But I didn't think she'd die."

Leonard scanned Emma Lee's body again, then tucked the sheet back up over her and stroked her hair. "But now I'm glad Janice is gone. I wouldn't have found you otherwise. And you're so much more beautiful, especially like this."

At that moment Emma Lee's eyelids shot open. She didn't speak, but she glared with a look that ricocheted through his soul like a scream smacking canyon walls.

He dropped her hand as if it were on fire. His heart pounded, his mouth went dry, and he shuddered.

Those eyes!

The elation he felt moments before crumbled to dust and he felt skittish now. He flashed a nervous glance over his shoulder, but no one was there.

When his gaze returned to Emma Lee, her eyes were shut; her breathing and the beep-beep of the heart monitor were both steady. He took a deep breath.

It was nothing, he assured himself. A dream. He could manage, monitor, and manipulate this moment, this woman. He could. She wouldn't die; no, she'd survive. And she'd love him; let him care for her. She would. All it took was a bit of foresight and planning and he was good at those. He stretched overhead and took a deep breath. *Relax,* he told himself.

Still nervous, Leonard took Emma Lee's hand in his again, but now he didn't speak. It was too dangerous. He'd stay until dinner time, watching her lovely face, reminding himself of his great fortune to have her in his life. Then he'd pick up that damned boy and feed him something.

Five minutes after four o'clock a policeman stumbled into Emma Lee's room. The middle-aged man's round beer belly caused his tight uniform jacket to gap between buttons. He slipped his hat off, tucked it under his arm, and ran a hand over his balding scalp. Huffing with exertion from his short walk down the hallway from the elevator, he pulled out his badge and flashed it for Leonard. "You Dr. Baxter?"

Leonard looked the policeman up and down. Irritated by the interruption, he said, "I am. Who are you?"

"Officer Venezia. I need to ask you and your wife some questions."

When Leonard stood, his six-foot frame towered over the policeman's head. He noted with disdain the man's bald spot. He sucked in his breath and propped both fists on his hips and hissed, "She's asleep. Please go away."

"Sorry. This will take a few minutes. What brought your wife to the hospital?"

Leonard motioned the policeman to move back from the bed, and waited until the man obliged before he spoke. "She's been sick. Had the flu or something. Dehydration, the doctor said."

Officer Venezia pulled a small tablet of paper and a pen from his pocket. "Has she had any exposure to toxic substances like pesticides, rat poison, or the like?"

Leonard felt so irritated he wanted to scream, but he was used to this kind of harassment. He knew how to deflect and deflate those who overstepped their authority. His face took on the impassive façade he wore when he felt threatened, and he sneered, "She's pregnant, officer. We're very careful about that stuff. What's this about?"

"Can't say, sir. Just answer the question."

"This is ridiculous. I'm busy. Come back another time."

Officer Venezia scribbled something on his pad of paper. "When did you first notice her illness?"

"She's been ill a long time. Had a head injury last year and has not been well since."

Venezia sighed. "Uh-huh. What about her most recent nausea and memory loss?"

Leonard waved his hand. "After she hit her head, most of her short term memory was gone and she was often nauseous. We got married; she got pregnant. Morning sickness came every day, then. It's hard to say exactly when it got worse. Why are you harassing me with all these questions?"

"Where were you when she was brought in?"

"What right do you have to question me as if I were some common criminal? I was at work, like I am every day." He spat the words. "I came as soon as I was called. Now if you don't mind, I'm going back to my wife's bedside."

The officer closed his book and slid it into his pocket. "I'll be in the hall waiting to talk with her doctor. If you think of anything else, let me know. And call me if she wakes up."

41.

At five-fifteen, Michael grabbed the phone at work and dialed Katrina. She answered after the second ring.

He sighed with relief. "Hey, sweet one. Glad I got you."

"Oh-oh. You don't have to work late, do you? Not tonight. Please say you'll be on time."

"Don't worry your pretty little head. I have to make a minor detour to give a doctor some info on Emma Lee at the hospital. It shouldn't take more than half an hour, though. So I'll be at your door by six-ten as planned; I promise."

He heard Katrina sigh and he could imagine that cute pout of hers turning to a frown. "Oh, Michael. You know they won't let us into our seats if the lights have gone down. I've been looking forward to this performance for weeks."

"No worries, love. I'll be there."

As he hung up the phone, Michael doubted his own words. It could all work ... if the doctor was prompt and wasn't verbose. If the boulevard wasn't being worked on causing traffic tie-up, if, if, if ... .

He raced out of the office, hopped into his MGB, and tore down the street to the hospital parking lot. Inside Suburban General, he banged the elevator button several times. Impatient, he abandoned the elevator and took the stairs two at a time. At five twenty-nine, Michael exited the stairwell and raced down the hallway.

Irritated about the timing of this meeting, Michael was still glad that Emma Lee had been admitted. Hopefully the staff could figure out why she had the relapse. But why did it have to be tonight?

To his surprise, a policeman and not the doctor stood outside Emma Lee's hospital room door.

"You Mrs. Baxter's doctor?" the policeman asked.

"No, occupational therapist." He turned his wrist over to check his watch. "Supposed to meet the doc here five thirty. Where is he?"

"Guess we're both waiting for him." The officer pulled out his pen and booklet again. "Mind if I ask you a few questions?"

"Okay. What's going on?"

"Following up on an anonymous tip. Ta tell ya the truth, it was prob'ly a crank call. But we have to investigate anyhow. Waste of taxpayer's dollars, if ya ask me." As he opened his notebook he mumbled, "Nobody ever does, though." He motioned with his head at Emma Lee's room. "What do you know about Mrs. Baxter?"

"Not much. I see her and Dr. Baxter twice a week, sometimes more often, for occupational therapy. Up to about a week ago, her memory showed steady improvement. But then something changed and it was worse each time she came in."

"Is that normal for head-injury patients?"

"No." Michael rubbed his chin and nodded slowly. "Now that I think about it, the memory loss and her illness seemed to appear together. That's really all I know."

The policeman scribbled some notes. "Thanks. Your name? For the record."

"Michael Yamada."

When Michael entered Emma Lee's room, Leonard was sitting by her bedside, holding his wife's hand. "Hi Dr. Baxter. How is she?"

Leonard didn't take his eyes from Emma Lee's face. "She seems peaceful now. Not throwing up anymore, at least." He scowled and pointed a thumb toward hallway. "I can't believe the police are here. It's ridiculous. What could they possibly be investigating?"

Michael shrugged. "Who knows?" He picked up the phone and dialed 0. "This is Michael Yamada. Could you page Doctor Rudnick to Emma Lee Baxter's room? Thanks." A moment later he heard the intercom call the doctor's name. "I'll be outside if you need me," he said.

In the hallway, Michael leaned against the wall. He watched the nurses fill out charts. Aides, orderlies, doctors and nurses hustled by carrying little cups of pills, or bedpans, or charts, or towels, and he imagined the moments evaporating like puddled water on a hot day. Soon, like the bottom of such a puddle, his name would be mud.

The policeman dragged a plastic chair from the room, shoved his hulking form into it, and stared at the elevator doors. His body oozed over the chair seat like a giant water balloon as the walkie-talkie he carried screeched to life. "There's an accident on the boulevard, block 300. Officer respond."

Venezia clicked the button and said, "I'm on my way."

Michael thought the policeman looked relieved as he shoved his notebook and pen into his back pocket and settled his hat on his head. "Tell the doc I'll be back in the morning, will ya?"

"Okay," Michael said. But he wasn't sure he'd wait long enough to see the doctor. He poked his head into the room again. "I've got to get going, Dr. Baxter. Tell the doctor I'll catch up with him later."

As Michael pressed the elevator button, the doors opened and a doctor stepped out. "Mr. Yamada?" the man asked. "I'm Dr. Rudnick."

"Nice to meet you, but I'm late for an appointment."

"I'm leaving for a conference early tomorrow morning. Can you give me about twenty minutes?"

Michael stared at his watch. 5:45. He wasn't dressed for the ballet yet, but other than that he was ready. Duty to work and concern for

Emma Lee took hold. "You can have ten minutes, tops. Then, I'm gone."

KATRINA CHECKED HER hair for the fifth time and fumed. Michael was late. She had spent weeks calling, writing, and schmoozing friends in high places (otherwise known as season ticket holders) to get these great seats, and she didn't want to miss one moment of Swan Lake. It was her favorite ballet. Besides the performance, there were people to watch, outfits to ogle, music to appreciate. Almost everyone from her ballet class would be attending, along with anybody who was somebody. Missing that would be criminal!

Standing in front of her full-length mirror, Katrina took inventory. She was wearing her floor-length silver chiffon evening gown and matching Gucci stilettos that she purchased on clearance last summer. In this dress she could meet the queen. Lifting the skirt, she smoothed her slip and grumbled, "Where is that man?"

At six-thirty-two Michael stood at her door in his tux, bow tie askew, roses in hand. His long, Beatles-like, black hair needed combing and from his sheepish grin, she could tell he felt badly about his late arrival. Still, it would take more than flowers and that beguiling smile to make up for this.

He handed her the deep red buds. "For you, my darling. Beautiful flowers for a beautiful woman. You look gorgeous."

Katrina grabbed her purse and shawl from the couch where she had them ready. She donned her most determined pout and shook a finger at him. "Don't try to placate me with compliments, Mr. Michael Yamada. You're late. Very, very late, and you know how important this is to me. We should be there by now."

Michael lowered his eyes, staring at the floor, hair falling into his eyes. "I'm really sorry, Kat. Forgive me?" When he raised his eyes, she couldn't bear seeing that delicious, handsome face. It was too sweet, too repentant. She wanted to stay angry for a long, long time, so she refused to look at him again. "We'll see how late we are. Then ask me again."

He draped the soft wool pashmina over her shoulders and they walked to the car in silence, her anger lingering beneath the surface like frigid water beneath thin ice.

When they were both in the car, he turned on the ignition and said, "I'll drive fast."

With wide eyes and set mouth she grumbled, "Don't end up with a ticket on top of everything else."

42.

Clamping onto David's hand, I yell, "Run!"
Together we race out of the barn. When we reach the woods, my son finds the trail and leads the way; brambles scratch our arms and legs, and one of my feet catches on a rotting log. I topple onto the ground, jamming my shoulder and scraping the back of my hand. Both throb as I struggle to stand again. I brush off the rotting leaves and mud that cling to my cheeks and clothes, then I lift David onto my hip. I try to run, but he weighs me down. My heart pounds loud and shrill: beep, beep, beep. My feet sink into the muddy leaves. When I turn, I see the wolf drawing closer, tongue out, teeth bared. He's in no hurry.

Out of breath, I set David down. I reach for a dead branch to use as a club, but the rotting wood crumbles to bits. The wolf seems to know; his mouth draws back in a fang-filled grin. Those blood-red eyes never stop staring at me.

The scratches on my legs and arms throb and I can feel my pulse in my temples. No matter about me; I'll fight to the death to protect my son. I shove David behind me and yell, "Get away!"

Now close, the wolf circles us. I turn to keep David behind me.

"Leave us alone!" I yell, kicking out. My foot strikes its snout. The wolf yelps and backs away.

The kick disturbs the thin membrane that separates dream from reality. Soon, that membrane solidifies into a wall of consciousness. The forest and wolf (but not the terror), sink into the pool of my subconscious. I grow aware of brightness and squint open my eyes to pink sunrise light that filters through blind slats. I lay in a bed that's not my own. From the looks of it, I'm in a hospital. A piece of tape secures a needle in a small vein on the back of my hand. The needle is connected to a clear plastic tube that winds from my vein back to a bag of liquid, which hangs on a stand behind my head. I lift my head and check under the covers. I'm dressed in a hospital gown and nothing else.

The steady blip-blip broadcasts the rhythm of my heart as someone rolls a cart in down the hallway outside my door. The air is laced with the odor of antiseptic soap with a touch of bacon and coffee. Sucking in several deep breaths, I whisper: *It was a dream. A dream.* But my hands are shaking and I'm gasping for breath.

Hunger squeezes my stomach and I smile. The terrible pain I'd experienced daily for the last week or so is gone.

I stare at my hand again. It throbs like it did in the dream. Letting my eyes fall shut, I drop my head back onto the pillow and try to relax. After several deep breaths, I'm almost asleep again when I hear someone enter the room.

A thin, tired-looking young man wearing a white lab coat and carrying a chart sidles up to the bed. "I'm Doctor Theodore Stephanopoulos, standing in for Dr. Rudnick. My name's a mouthful, so you can call me Dr. Tad. Everyone else does." He flips over the first page and reads for a few minutes.

"Where am I? How'd I get here?"

"Suburban General. You were admitted yesterday through the ER."

"What's wrong with me?"

The doctor reads from his clipboard. "Says here you were dehydrated, incoherent, and in and out of consciousness. We're running some tests to figure out why." He leafs through the chart. "I see you had a head injury, so we'll be evaluating your memory, too. Looks like your occupational therapist reported you were getting better until recently." He hangs the chart on the end of the bed. "Lie back and relax while I check your vitals." He peers into my throat and pupils. He measures my pulse, my lungs, and palpates my spleen, then checks the uterus. "Four months pregnant?"

"I guess. How long do I have to stay here?"

"If all goes well, you should be back in your own bed by Tuesday or Wednesday." The doctor turns to leave. "Anything else?"

I want to ask him about how to get free, how to fight the wolf, how to protect my son and the baby in the womb. But I know he has no answers for those questions. I shake my head.

"I'll check on you this afternoon."

A few minutes later I hear a light knock. I turn to see Patrick peering around the curtain.

"Up for company?" he asks.

"Patrick! Oh, I'm so glad to see you. How did you know I was here?"

"I brought you in, remember?"

My smile feels tired and drawn, a wisp of its former self. "No. I don't, but thank you."

He sits next to the bed and takes my hand in his. "I'm glad to see you're awake. And lucid."

I pull my hand away. "Please ..."

Patrick returns to the door and closes it. He sits again. "I've been going over your symptoms. It looks to me like Leonard's been poisoning you. He could have gotten almost anything from the lab—arsenates, cyanide, or any of several other poisonous substances that could make you feel this way. I reported it to the police. Anonymously, of course."

"Poison! That can't be. Why would he do that?"

"To keep you under his control. To keep you with him."

"It doesn't make sense."

"Of course not. Leonard's a maniac, and crazy people don't make sense."

I shake my head. "What if he finds out? He might hurt you. Or David."

"Or you. I can take care of myself, but you and David are in danger. When you get out of here, don't go back. You can't. I won't let you."

I fall silent for several minutes. Then I say, "I'll have to think about it."

"What's to think about? We'll rescue David and you can leave forever."

"I can't work. How will I live?"

"I'll take care of you."

I feel the mantle of dependency slip over me like a soft, cashmere robe; the temptation to let it happen teases and grabs. I've been cared for most of my life by various men. First by my father, then by David's father, then by Leonard. Now Patrick seems to be vying for the job.

I stare at the IV in my arm, then at the man who promises freedom—or a different captivity. My gaze shifts to the window where I see dirty smoke billowing up from the chemical plants across the river where I used to work. The sound of the traffic from the boulevard below and footsteps of nurses in the hallway filter into my room. I'm quiet for several minutes before I shake my head again.

"It would be wrong to live together, Patrick. We aren't married. Besides, I moved to Pittsburgh to be independent. If I let you support me, I'd be trading one person's care-taking for another." I draw in a huge breath. Several seconds tick by. "But what choice do I have?"

He takes my hand again and smiles. "No, I want you to be free. I'd set up an apartment for you and David. I might have found one already. You've got to leave to save your life. It's the only way."

Closing my eyes, I nod slightly and sigh. "I agree. But I don't like it."

MICHAEL WOKE EARLY for a Saturday—six fifty-two a.m. He rolled over and frowned at the small velvet box that sat on his night stand. He popped it open and stared at the beautiful triangular diamond. It caught the morning light and sent a thousand sparkles around the room. Remembering the night before, he punched his pillow and yelled, "Aaaa! Why did it all fall apart?"

They had arrived late for the ballet—a terrible sin, according to Katrina. Because they had those great seats, the ones she had worked so hard to get way down in front, he and she had to remain in the foyer until the second act. Another terrible sin. As strains of music wafted out into the hallway, Katrina had leaned against the wall for a while, then finally sat on the bench there and cried.

Michael had felt helpless at first, but grew more frustrated and irritated with the whole mess as the night wore on.

After the ballet, Katrina had said, "Take me home. I've got a terrible headache."

He remembered her soft, bare shoulders, and how they looked when she removed her Pashmina, and how beautiful her figure had looked draped in that silver silk. Her gorgeous legs in those spectacular stilettos tapped a song of longing and desire that teased him as they went into the performance hall, and perforated his heart on the way out.

At her front door, he had wanted to run his fingers through that lustrous hair, kiss those supple lips, and beg her to reconsider. Instead, he mumbled his apology, sounding pathetic even to himself. "I'll call you tomorrow," he had said. "I want to make this up to you."

He shuddered now as he recalled her cold reply. "You know what? I think we should take a break from each other for a while."

He fingered the ring and gritted his teeth. He had been ready to propose; she was breaking up. Yes, there'd be a break, all right. A heart break, to be exact. Who was this woman he wanted to marry? Was she so self-centered that the ballet was more important than someone's health? Why hadn't he thought more about all this? Was he wrong to go to the hospital when they called? Perhaps he should have skipped yesterday and gone this morning. He felt so confused.

He closed the ring box lid and stomped into the bathroom. Turning on the shower, he stepped in and let the hot water flow over him. In spite of her faults and selfishness, he did love Katrina, and *wanted* to marry her. But she was so hot headed. Was she the woman he *should* marry? If so, he'd have to work hard to open her eyes to the truth that they belonged together. Given that she didn't even want to talk to him, that might take a lot of time and effort. Was the relationship worth it? At that moment, he wasn't at all sure.

43.

Saturday morning, David woke with a headache. He stared at the ceiling and grasped the corner of the blanket in his fist, remembering how much he wanted to stay with Sister Angela last night. Why had Leonard forced him to come home? Dinner was terrible, cereal and milk, and now he was hungry. And scared. He didn't like being here without his mom. He couldn't remember a time when she hadn't been with him, except for when she hit her head. His thumb moved toward his mouth. He stared at it for a moment, and slid his hand back under the covers. Only babies sucked their thumbs.

David remembered very little of his life before Pittsburgh. Right after his fourth birthday his mother said they had to move. Some of the kids in that old neighborhood teased him for not having a daddy, and they called his mother names. So he had been glad to leave.

At first he liked Pittsburgh. His baby-sitter was nice, and the kids didn't know anything about him or his mom. But then Mommy got hurt and they came to live with Leonard, and life was much worse than it had been, even down south.

Even though he didn't have a daddy before, David knew daddies weren't supposed to be mean. None of the kids in day-care had mean daddies. And the dads on television never yelled or made fun of their kids the way Leonard did. He never saw the Brady Bunch dad push his kids away when they wanted to hug their mom, for instance. A tear slipped down David's cheek.

Oh, Mom!

She was the one who made everything good. She was the one who helped him live with all the meanness and hurt from Leonard. Although she couldn't stop bad things from happening—Jojo still died—at least she was there to help him through it. Without her, David felt small and very, very alone.

He slipped out of bed and tiptoed into the kitchen. He pulled a bowl out from the cupboard, filled it with cereal, and was heaving the milk jug from the refrigerator when Leonard entered the front door, carrying the newspaper.

David poured his milk and took a huge bite of cereal, trying to fill what felt like a hole in his stomach. With mouth still full he asked, "When's Mom coming back from the hospital?"

Leonard fell onto the living room couch and propped the paper in front of his face. "Don't talk with your mouth full. I don't know."

"But I need her to be home. I miss her."

"Don't whine. She'll come home when the doctor decides. After you eat, we're going to the barn to do chores."

David didn't want to go to the barn with Leonard. The man would probably yell and direct and scold, as usual, and he didn't like even thinking about it. So even though he was still hungry, the frequency of spoons full entering his mouth slowed way down until the crispy rice kernels became soggy maggot-like slime floating in his milk.

When he heard the paper fall onto the coffee table, though, he held his breath. There would be no more delay.

Leonard, wearing an old checkered shirt, his overalls, and socks, plodded into the kitchen. "You've dallied long enough, young man. You have five minutes to be ready, breakfast or not. Now get moving."

David recognized that look. He knew it meant angry words and perhaps even physical punishment if he didn't comply. After shoving two more bites of cereal into his mouth, David raced to his room. Yesterday's clothes were resurrected from his bedroom floor. At the front door, he yanked on his boots. Then, plodding behind Leonard like a mule, David tromped to the barn.

There, Leonard handed the boy a can and lifted the bin lid. "You feed the sheep. I'll clean stalls."

David scooped grain and poured it into the trough. It took several trips to feed all six sheep. When he finished, he said, "I'm all done. Can I go play now?"

Leonard grumbled, "You think all there is to do all day is chase butterflies and throw rocks, don't you? Your mother dotes on you, gives you everything you want; she spoils you. Well, that won't happen when I'm around. Here," he said, shoving a bottle into the boy's hands. "I'm going to show you how to treat worms in sheep. You'll need to know this when you grow up."

David looked at him quizzically.

Leonard kept talking. "This is what I've been working on at the plant these last ten years. Chemicals are changing everything for the livestock industry. We've discovered cures for parasites and other diseases. There have been productivity gains everywhere, saving millions of dollars. These chemicals are changing the world, boy." He poked David on the chest several times as he talked. "Now let's get busy."

David didn't understand what para-sipes were, or any of the other things Leonard said about chemi-cools or pro-duck-somethings. But he knew he didn't like being poked. He swatted Leonard's hand. "Don't!" he yelled.

"I'm not going to take your insolence today, kid. You'll obey me or else."

David kicked Leonard on the shin.

"You asked for it, you little beast." Leonard grabbed David's arm and twisted.

"Ow, ow, stop!" David cried.

Leonard opened the empty feed bin and grabbed David around the waist. The boy squirmed and struggled and kicked. But Leonard was stronger. David felt himself being lifted off his feet. A moment later he fell into the empty bin and the heavy lid came slamming down; he was locked in the musty, dark and cramped wooden box.

He heard a muffled chuckle and Leonard's voice. "That'll teach you."

"Let me out. I'm scared! Leonard, let me out!" David yelled.

I'll come back after you've gotten that smart-aleck attitude scared out of you."

David squirmed around until he lay on his back with his feet upwards. He kicked the lid several times. *Bang! Bang! Bang!* But the heavy wooden lid barely moved. He tried shoving it with his shoulder. He willed himself to be stronger, to be Superman. He could do it. He could lift this lid. When he pushed very hard, the lid rose a few inches. He slid his hand out the small gap he created, feeling success. But soon the lid pressed and squeezed and then smashed his arm muscles. Finally unable to stand the pain any longer, and unable to open the lid higher, he pulled his arm back into the bin and let the lid drop again.

As the realization that he couldn't escape settled in, the tears began. David screamed, "Get me out! I want out!"

The minutes ticked by but nothing happened; David grew tired. His legs hurt from being bent. His throat felt scratchy and sore from all the yelling. His eyes itched and stung from the dust and all that crying, and he felt so thirsty he thought he would die. He curled into a ball and wrapped his arms around his knees. He cried for several more minutes, then in deep despair and fatigue, fell asleep.

He woke to a thin stream of light filtering through the crack between bin and lid. At first, David didn't remember where he was and he tried to stretch. His feet and elbows hit the walls, and he heard the faint bleat of a sheep. Then he remembered: he was in feed-bin prison. He started to cry again.

A while later, what seemed to David to be many hours, the lid opened. Someone, a black silhouette against the blinding light, hovered above him.

"You've been in here two hours. Have you learned your lesson? Answer me," Leonard said.

David had to pee and he felt hungry and thirsty. He couldn't look at the mean man, but he nodded so he'd be let out.

Leonard propped the bin lid on the back wall. "Then you can come out now. But if you don't behave ... ."

As David climbed out, he didn't feel repentant. He wanted to hit and scream. And he didn't want to stay here at the farm any longer. It wasn't that far to the boulevard. He took the trip often in the car. Certainly he could walk there himself. And once he reached town, maybe he could walk to the convent where he could find Sister Martha and Sister Angela. One of them would surely drive him to the hospital to see Mom. Yes, that's what he'd do. If Mom didn't come back by tomorrow, he'd go and find her.

SISTER MARTHA FINISHED lunch and took out her appointment book. She scanned her day's events. She'd finish her monthly report, zip off to the hospital and make her rounds, and be back in time to make dinner.

When she thought of the hospital, she remembered yesterday, and how sick Emma Lee had been, and how helpless the poor woman looked. Emma Lee had so many problems, it didn't seem fair. She stopped writing and closed her eyes. "Protect her and heal her," she prayed.

Turning back to her appointment book, Sister Martha shook her head. The Baxters were such an odd couple. Emma Lee, the beautiful yet damaged young woman, depended on her husband for almost everything. Then there was Leonard, the kind but obsessive and insecure old man who seemed to depend on that caring for his happiness and purpose in life. She wondered what Leonard would do if Emma Lee should die. Or vice versa.

Ring! She picked up the receiver.

"Martha, it's Leonard. Can you watch David? I'd like to visit Emma Lee."

"I think Sister Angela is available. Let me check."

A half hour later Leonard's Cadillac pulled into the parking lot. When Sister Martha opened the convent door, David hopped out of the car and ran to her. She thought his face looked red and his eyes swollen, as if he had been crying. "I want to see Mom. Can you take me, please?" he begged, wrapping his arms around her legs.

Her heart broke for him, he looked so sad. She squatted. "I'm sorry, David, but they don't allow children into the hospital. You might make her sicker. Wait a few more days and she'll be home with you."

The boy shoved his hands into his pockets, thrust out his lower lip, and kicked a rock. Then another. His shoulders slumped.

Noticing that Leonard had put his car into reverse and was backing away, Sister Martha motioned for him to open his window. He scowled, but the window did go down. Staring at his watch, he said, "What is it? I've got to get going."

"Please. I need to speak with you for a moment."

He put the car into park. "Five minutes."

Sister Martha squatted so that she could look at Leonard as she spoke. "I'm sure that all this must weigh on you now that Emma Lee's in the hospital. It can't be easy."

"What's your point, Martha?"

"I'd like to invite you to join our new support group. It's for men, talking about men's issues. We've got a few members who are stepparents, some divorced. And a psychologist from the church runs it. A man, of course. I think you'd like it."

Leonard waved his hand and started the car. "I'm fine." He put the car into reverse again. "Gotta go."

Sister Martha stood and shielded her eyes from the sun. "But what if she never regains her memory, Leonard?"What if she were to die?"

"She wouldn't dare," he said, then rolled up his window and backed the Cadillac away.

Sister Martha watched Leonard's car until it turned from Church Street onto the boulevard; she wished she had managed to convince him. Everyone needed someone. She'd keep asking.

44.

"Grace should be in to remove your IV later. One more step toward going home, right?" the nurses' aide, Barbara, gives me a wide toothy grin, as if a horse she bet on won the Preakness. As she works, she chats on about last night's Pirates' game and Roberto Clemente. "He's the best hitter in the league, don't you think? It's so exciting." She plumps my pillow and refills the water pitcher. "I'll bet the Pirates are on their way to a fifth world title this year."

I'm not into the Pirates. At all. I can barely remember my own name, let alone baseball scores or rules. But I'm happy to have anyone talk with me, so I try to follow the conversation.

She pulls the curtain and helps me change my gown. When I lean back, a sharp pain stabs my abdomen. I grimace.

"What's up?"

"My belly and head hurt. Think I'll try to nap for a while."

"Great idea, honey. I'll try to keep all those blood sucking phlebotomists and pesky doctors away for a while."

As the aide leaves, a uniformed policeman enters the room. He flashes his badge. "Mrs. Baxter? I'm officer Venezia. I was here yesterday, but you were asleep. I'd like to ask you a few questions, if you don't mind."

"Ah, okay."

"Can you tell me when your nausea started?"

"Patrick called you, didn't he?"

"Can't say, Ma'am. Please answer the question."

Feeling exposed, I pull the sheet up to my neck and rest my head on the pillow. I let my eyes fall shut. All I can think of, though, is Jojo dying, of David alone with Leonard, of Patrick's warning, of the wolf.

"Mrs. Baxter? Are you still awake?"

I open my eyes. "I think better with my eyes closed. I caught the flu a week ago? No, maybe two weeks." I press a palm to my forehead, but can't extract more facts. "Oh, I don't know. I started to get better. Then I got worse again."

"Were you exposed to any chemicals that you know of—rat poisoning, herbal sprays, anything like that?"

I shake my head and shrug. "It's possible, but I can't say." His pained expression tells me he's wishing he was anywhere but here. "You know I hit my head, don't you?"

He writes on his pad of paper. "Yep. I'd like permission to look at your medical records."

I prop myself on my elbows and point to the chart hanging from the foot of my bed. "Go ahead."

He grabs the clipboard, plunks his hefty body onto the chair, and begins to flip through the papers. I lie back on my pillow with gritted teeth; the pain in my abdomen bites deep, as if a live crocodile is trying to eat its way out.

"You don't look so good, ma'am."

"Stomach problems." I push the buzzer. When Barbara arrives, I say, "Can you help me to the bathroom?"

The aide says to the officer, "Give us a few minutes, will you?"

"I'll be in the hallway, Mrs. Baxter. For some reason you're one of the hardest people to contact," he grumbles. "And you can't even leave the hospital room." As the man heads for the door he says, "Call me when you're done, would ya? I've got a few more questions."

With the aide's help, I stumble to the bathroom and she waits outside the door. When I stand to flush, I notice that the water in the bowl is bright red and my heart nearly stops. I open the door a crack and yell, "I'm bleeding!"

Barbara takes my hand and helps me stumble back to bed. My knees are shaky and my head spins. The aide slips a pad under me and pulls up the sheet. "I'll send in the doctor. And get rid of the policeman."

About ten minutes later the young resident, Dr. Stephanopoulos, arrives at my bedside. "You sure keep me hopping, Emma Lee."

"Wouldn't want you to feel unneeded. Am I losing the baby?"

The doctor presses on my abdomen. "It's possible. You'll have to stay prone for a few days to prevent that."

I rub my belly and remember when I was pregnant with David. Before he was born, I had gotten strong pressure from many others to abort. Lydia Rae, a friend from work, assured me, "You'll be marked for life if you have the baby. No one will ever want to marry you."

Abortion was illegal, but no matter. She gave me the name of a nurse who could remove the baby "safely." (Safe for me, not the baby, of course.)

I couldn't do it. My "face" wasn't as important as a child's life.

Once David was born, I suffered ridicule, sure. But David became the love of my life. He still is. There is no way I'll let anything happen to this baby if I can help it. Suddenly, the way seems clear. To save the lives of my children and myself, I must leave Leonard. No other choice makes sense.

LEONARD FINALLY ESCAPED Sister Martha's meddling and drove to the hospital. He was insulted that she would suggest therapy, even if it was only a men's group. He'd be crazy to spend time with all those losers.

When he arrived at the hospital, Leonard parked at the far end of the lot as was his habit, (away from any other vehicle to prevent anyone from hitting his beautiful, white driving machine with their door or bumper). As he entered the elevator, he felt slightly off balance. He wondered if the policeman would be in the room, and if so, what he'd say, and how long it would be before Emma Lee could come home.

Leonard hoped he *wouldn't* see that look in her eyes again—the one he saw last night; that scary, other-worldly look that scared him. No, he wanted to see that adoring, timid, dependent face of hers, the one he had seen hundreds of times when he had control, the look that proved she needed him. That vulnerability made her so lovely. It made him want to care for her. It was what made her so enticing.

On the third floor he saw no policeman. Instead, workers in white scurried in and out of rooms collecting lunch trays. He breathed in deeply and entered Emma Lee's room. It was empty except for her. Good. He'd have her undivided attention.

He sat next to the bed and took her hand in his. "Oh, my darling. I'm so glad you're doing better. I've missed you. I need you to come home."

This afternoon the skin beneath her eyes was dark and puffy, making her look older. She opened her beautiful lavender eyes for a moment, then shut them again.

"How's David?" she asked.

Remembering David's internment in the feed bin, he said, "The boy's fine. He disobeyed me this morning, but I think he learned his lesson." Losing interest in the subject he said, "I'm glad you're awake. I have some important things to talk about."

"So tired."

He sat and pulled the chair closer to the bed. "I know, my love. But I want to reiterate that this sickness comes from disobedience. All you have to do is comply and you'll stay healthy. I love you so much, Emma Lee. You know I can't live without you."

How pale she was. Something was definitely amiss. "What's the matter, darling?"

No answer.

He sat in silence for several minutes, looking at her face, watching her breathe.

When he stood to stretch, she spoke so quietly he could barely hear, but it sounded like, "You poisoned me, didn't you?"

He returned to the bed, scowling; his lips drew in tight. "What did you say?"

At that moment, Nurse Grace entered. "I expected to be taking out your IV, Emma Lee, not adding another bag. Guess you're staying for a few more days." She attached a plastic bag full of liquid to the metal stand behind the bed. "I'll need to take her vitals and check her pelvis, now, Dr. Baxter. Please step out of the room."

"What's going on? I demand to know."

"Your wife is bleeding. She could lose the baby; it's touch and go for now. We have to keep her in bed and calm, so she's been sedated. Hopefully the child will stay put, but you never know."

He placed a hand over his eyes as fear and anger mounted. If Emma Lee had been obedient he wouldn't have had to intervene. And the baby wouldn't be in jeopardy. Why didn't she listen?

Leonard stood in the hallway for several minutes, thinking. She dare not take herself or the child from him. He had counted on this baby to be his legacy to the world, and she was spoiling everything.

Fear sunk its teeth deep into his heart, then. It was the big brother of the fear that frayed his thoughts at night when he was alone, the father of fear that suffocated him when he thought about death, and it spawned the fear that promised to swallow him into the earth like a coffin if he didn't keep fighting against it.

When the nurse left again, he tiptoed back into Emma Lee's room. He grabbed her hand, lifted it to his lips, and kissed her fingers. "Oh, my darling, I'm not going to let anything harm you. Or the baby. We'll be together forever."

When she didn't respond he snarled, "You did this on purpose, didn't you?"

No answer.

"As long as you stay with me, I'll protect you." A sinister look stole over his face. "But beware. I will never let you ..."

There was a knock and Sister Martha entered the room.

"Hi, Emma Lee. Leonard. I stopped by to let you know that David misses you. He wanted me to bring him here to see you, but I told him I couldn't. Poor little guy. His eyes were all red and puffy, probably from crying for you."

The muscle on Leonard's jaw twitched as rage swelled and throbbed like a finger smashed in a door. He was tempted to order Sister Martha out. With her here, how could he ensure Emma Lee knew her place: at home, on the farm, with him? How could he tell Emma Lee that if she left, no matter where she went, no matter the cost, he'd hunt her down, drag her back, and punish her?

When Sister Martha sat and opened her Bible, he realized there was no getting rid of her.

"It's not easy to find God in suffering. But rest assured, God is here with you, my dear," she said. "I'd like to read you a scripture."

Emma Lee would be stuck here for a few more days. There would be time enough to discuss all this later, he assured himself. Unwilling to be subjected to another one of Sister Martha's little moral teachings, he stood. "I've got chores to do. I'll be back tomorrow."

45.

Sister Martha notices the chart at the bottom of my bed. "Oh, I didn't know your middle name was Roxanne. Very pretty."

"You think so? I never liked it."

She tents her fingers under her chin. "Really?"

"Before I was born, my dad loved the 1942 Ginger Rogers film, *Roxie Hart*. When Mother woke from the anesthetic, she discovered that my father had put 'Emma Lee Roxanne' on the birth certificate. He laughed when she got angry about it. Could you pour me some water?"

Sister Martha fills my cup and hands it to me. "People are funny."

After taking a sip, I say, "But *Roxie Hart* was a remake of a silent film, *Chicago*. In it, a jazz-loving, boozing, two-timing woman kills her boyfriend in cold blood to get rid of him. When I saw that film in college, murder seemed like such a terrible way to get someone. But now, well, given the right circumstances ..."

"There but for the grace of God go I?"

I try to laugh. "I guess. So how's my boy?"

Sister Martha pats my hand. "We take care of him when Leonard asks. He's a bit sad without you, of course. He misses you, for sure. Don't forget, though. God is here for you. Turn to Jesus when you need help. He's trustworthy."

"I can't imagine Jesus caring about me and my little problems. Doesn't he have bigger things to worry about?"

She pats my hand. "Everything about you is important to God. I'd like to pray with you. Would that be all right?"

I have little evidence that prayers do anything, but I lack energy to resist. "Um … sure."

She takes my hands in hers so I close my eyes. After a few moments of silence, she whispers, "Dear Lord, please bless this woman and the child growing within her. Show her how to trust you, and how to listen to your voice. And please heal her, if it's your will."

"And save my baby's life," I add.

Calm settles over me, as if I've been covered by one of those heated blankets the nurses pass out, and I let myself rest in it. Oh, if only I could feel this all the time.

Then moments later, I imagine the wolf from my dream. It bares long fangs and glares at my belly as if ready to rip me open and devour my child. He seems so real, I yell, "No!" My eyes snap open.

"What happened?" Sister Martha asks.

"A wolf, growling like it was right here in the room. We prayed! Why would God do that?"

She wraps an arm around my shoulder. "Don't be afraid. God is with you, even in your fear, even when you have to confront scary things. You can trust God with anything."

"I don't trust anyone, not even myself."

She sits next to me on the bed, presses my head to her shoulder, and strokes my hair. "So let me ask you, how's that working for you?"

All of a sudden, I'm so tired I can hardly talk. I lean into her and let my eyes close. "Not so great."

"God will carry your burdens if you let Him. Let go, dear."

I'm silent for several moments, trying to make sense of it all. "If you don't mind, I'd like to sleep now."

"Of course." She releases me from her gentle hold and stands. "Thank you for letting me pray with you."

"Uh-huh."

In the silence of the setting sun, the prayer comes to mind again. During it, I heard no bells, saw no lights, and got no great revelation. Simply sweet, warm comfort. Was it God? I'm too inexperienced with prayer to know the answer to that question, so I bow my head and whisper, "Okay, God, if you really exist, help me. I am mindless, sick, and pregnant. Completely powerless. I'm controlled by a crazy old man. The lives of my children are in danger. Maybe mine too. And I know I'm doomed to fail on my own. So I'll hand this fight over to you. Let's see what you can do."

I don't feel different, but the world feels a tiny bit more hopeful. In a moment, I'm asleep.

46.

Patrick couldn't stop the grin spreading across his face. Minutes from now, Emma Lee would be leaving the hospital with him instead of Leonard. The plans they made together were coming to fruition and he was elated. She would be, too. Carrying a small bouquet of multi-colored carnations and a key, he entered the hospital and took the stairs two at a time.

When he strode into Emma Lee's room, she was dressed, standing next to the bed, adding items to a duffle bag. The buttons of her blouse were done wrong and her hair was uncombed. She looked up and said, "Oh, hello."

He slid the key into her palm and presented her with the flowers. "I've got it all arranged. There's an apartment over a garage you can use for a few weeks until we find you a nicer place. We'll apply for food stamps, Social Security, and Medicaid. I've got an attorney all lined up to sue the company for disability. This will all work out."

She swiped a lock of her springy black curls from her eyes and said, "Excuse me, but you must have the wrong person."

He reminded himself that her memory wasn't great. He tried again. "It's me, Patrick. I'm taking you away to save your life. We made plans, remember?"

She dropped her chin. "You know, the other day I was reading Don Quixote. Very interesting how a man could think that windmills were dragons, don't you think?"

He grabbed both of her arms and stared into her lavender eyes. "Please remember, Emma Lee, I'm Patrick. I'm taking you away from here."

"Whoever you are, please go. My husband will be here any moment to take me home."

Patrick felt desperate. "You got here because he was poisoning you. If you go back, nothing will keep him from continuing." He pressed a hand to his forehead. "We'll call the police, get a restraining order."

"You're scaring me."

"What about the apartment? The arrangements? You can't do this!"

"I don't know what you're talking about."

Patrick paced the room. Renting the apartment for her would have been a drain on his income, but he could almost taste her freedom. And he had to admit, he was looking forward to seeing her every day. Had she gone daft? Was she hypnotized? Was this relapse permanent? "Emma Lee, you're being poisoned, and you've got to get away. With me. Now!"

She turned and let her gaze focus on his face. "Why do you keep saying that? I don't even know who you are. Please go away."

AT THAT MOMENT, Leonard Baxter stormed into the room. "What the hell are you doing here, Kilkenny? I told you to stay out of our lives."

"It's a free country."

"Not when you're visiting *my wife*. Now get out or I'm calling the police." He shoved Patrick.

Patrick stumbled backward, regained his footing, and walloped Leonard on the jaw with a fist. Leonard reeled backward; his cheek swelled to a deep red welt.

"You'll pay for this, Kilkenny," he said, grabbing the water pitcher.

Nurse Grace, in a crisp white polyester pantsuit, raced into the room. Looking stern, she inserted herself between the men and stomped a foot. "You two are acting like children. Stop fighting this instant."

With Emma Lee's water pitcher in one hand and rubbing his cheek with the other, Leonard eyed the nurse up and down. She was taller than Emma Lee. Her fitted white pantsuit revealed a well-toned body. Another time he would stop to appreciate her form, but now, Kilkenny messed up even that.

With hands outstretched, Grace said, "Put down the pitcher, Dr. Baxter." To Patrick she said, "You should go."

"Yes, and I'm taking Emma Lee with me."

The nurse said, "No, you and I are leaving. Now." To Leonard she said, "You stay here and help your wife pack."

Leonard set down the pitcher and yelled after Patrick, "Don't dare come near her again or else … ."

As Patrick and Grace entered the hallway, two muscular orderlies arrived. Each grabbed one of Patrick's arms from behind.

Grace said, "Thanks, guys. Escort him from the building."

Struggling as he was dragged away, Patrick yelled, "Don't let her go with him. He'll kill her."

Grace returned to Emma Lee's room. "That was tense. Who is he?"

"A crazy trouble maker from work. Delusional," Leonard said.

Grace took in a deep breath and shut her eyes for a moment. "Okay, back to business," she said. "We'll miss you around here, Emma Lee." She handed her patient a clipboard with papers and pointed to a line near the bottom of the sheet. "Please, sign here. It states that you were given exit instructions and you know the doctor has released you."

Emma Lee shrugged. "I didn't get any instructions."

"Sure you did, honey. About ten minutes ago."

Leonard hadn't expected any memory lapse, but her confusion made his heart soar. They were back to the basics now, where they should be: her depending on him for everything. He wasn't sure how he got so lucky, how she had gotten better and worse at the same time. But he was glad it had happened. He would sign the paperwork. "You should know her memory can't be counted on. Let me see those instructions, and I'll sign the release."

"I'll get you a copy."

"I want to talk to the doctor, get it from him exactly what needs to be done."

Grace said, "I'll have him paged. It may take a while so have a seat."

Emma Lee stared out the window. Leonard fell into the chair with hunched shoulders and crossed arms.

"The sheep are doing well. I've got a shearer coming next week. We'll have fleece to sell at the farmer's market and fair, or maybe you can learn to spin. David and I pulled all the weeds in the strawberry patch yesterday. It took about four hours, but now the field is perfect. If the weather holds out, we should have plenty of strawberries to sell." When she nodded, he felt validated. Something was definitely different with this woman. He saw no fear in her face, just blankness. Finally, she was obedient. He could hardly contain his glee.

When the doctor appeared, he grabbed the chart and sat on the bed facing Leonard. "So I hear you need exit instructions again?"

"She forgets everything, doctor. You'll have to inform me."

The doctor nodded as if he understood, but Leonard knew. There was no way anyone else could ever understand.

"She'll need to drink plenty of fluids, and continue with her prenatal vitamins. No sexual intercourse for the next two weeks at least, until she can return for an internal exam. She must rest. Otherwise she could lose the baby, and we want that child to stay put for a few more months. Emma Lee, you're to stay off your feet. In bed as much as possible. Make sure she takes her antibiotics." He scanned the chart again, then looked up. When he spoke again he seemed to be staring right through Leonard. "Hopefully it won't happen, but if she starts bleeding again, bring her in immediately. Don't wait. Got that? Immediately."

Leonard now wished he hadn't heard the instructions. He had spent last evening and all morning imagining homecoming sex with Emma Lee. Now, to keep his child, he would have to postpone that pleasure.

"Oh, the things I have to give up appeasing everyone else. Damn!" he grumbled.

47.

"Mom, oh Mom, you're here!" David yelped when he saw his mother through the window. He jumped up and down, clapping. This was the best day of his life: his mom came back. After she left, most nights he had laid in bed, crying, sure she had died in that stinky old hospital. Other times he would be playing outside and the fear would hit him—what if he had to live with Leonard for the rest of his life without her? And something would nibble his stomach, and make his insides feel all tight and queasy. He had not eaten well while she was gone, so his arms and legs looked extra skinny now. But he could still run.

He raced out of the convent and over to the Cadillac. By the time he reached it, Emma Lee had opened the car door. She engulfed him in her arms and he felt as if the air had grown warmer. She was alive and smiling at him. It was the most wonderful sight in the whole wide world.

"Oh, honey, I'm so glad to see you."

He let his body melt as he encircled her neck with his arms. All would be well now. Burying his nose in her cheek, he inhaled deeply, loving her sweet, soft scent; like violets mixed with bubble bath, he thought. He smiled when her hair tickled his eyes. Then a giggle effervesced deep within him like bubbles in soda pop and burst forth before he could stop it. "I'm so glad you're here. Oh, I missed you."

Sister Martha arrived at the car. She squatted down and spoke to Emma Lee. "How are you feeling, dear? You look pale."

"I'm fine, thank you. Have we met before?" she asked. "You look … familiar."

The nun patted her hand. "Of course, dear. I'm your friend, Sister Martha. And your counselor. I'll be checking in on you from time to time. Maybe tomorrow, after you've had the opportunity to settle in. Would that work for you?"

"David, get in the car," Leonard scolded.

David didn't move. Leonard didn't worry him anymore. He wasn't going to let go of his mother that quickly. He stood with his arms around her shoulders and waited as she spoke with Sister Martha.

While his mother was away, he hadn't had a lot of time to himself, but he made sure he drew a picture for her every day. He couldn't wait to show them to her. Every day he had begged Leonard to take his pictures to the hospital, but of course the man never did. When David wasn't pulling weeds, he was conjuring up potions and soup and special paints using mud and squashed berries and weeds and flowers. He would show all that to her when they got home. Mom would love to see what he'd made, and play with him. He couldn't wait.

When they arrived home, David hoped to spend some time with his mother, it didn't matter where. Even if she had to be in bed, maybe she'd read him a story. Or they could build with Legos.

When they arrived home, though, Leonard parked the car and pointed out the window.

"David, that bucket is still there on the lawn. I told you to put that away this morning. I can't believe how absent minded you are. Run that to the barn this instant."

David scowled. Why did he have to do it? It was Leonard who had carried the bucket down to the house in the first place and left it there. But David knew obedience took less time than rebellion. And today he didn't want anything to come between him and his mother. So when the automobile stopped, he jumped out. He dragged the bucket up to the barn as fast as his legs could carry him. All the while, he felt nervous that Mom and Leonard would disappear into the bedroom like they often did, and he wouldn't get to sit with her.

When he returned from the barn, though, she was waiting on the front porch, rocking on the glider. "Look. This appeared in the grass. It's for you." She handed him a four-leaf clover and patted the seat next to her. "Come sit with me, David. I've missed you so much."

He took the clover and smiled. Then he snuggled close to his mother. "Me too, Mom. I thought you were died."

"That's *dead*, Honey, you thought I was *dead*. But I'm not. I'm right here with you."

Emma Lee wrapped an arm around David. "And I love you very, very much." He laid his head on her lap. "Now I want to hear all about how you've been and what you've been doing while I was away."

THURSDAY EVENING, AFTER her dance class and shower, Katrina plodded through the University of Pittsburgh's Cathedral of Learning with her friend, Tanisha. She felt relieved, disappointed, and confused all at the same time. It wasn't fair. In the past, every time she broke up with a guy she had felt grateful. Why did this one have to be different—and so difficult?

In the grand hall she couldn't stop herself from staring at the table where she and Michael had met several times after class. Her gaze drifted upwards to the soaring arched ceiling, and she recalled his awe when she had first brought him here. It had been so genuine, so real. She smiled in spite of herself.

Tanisha bumped her shoulder and said, "Well, for a girl who broke up with her guy, you sure ain't sulking."

Katrina shook her head in defiance. "Nope. I'm glad. Don't have to deal with that heavy load of love and attention anymore." She freed her hair from the elastic band and raked her fingers through it.

"Uh-huh. Having someone love you so hard is surely somethin' *awful*." Tanisha clicked her tongue. "Wouldn't wish that on my worst enemy."

"Okay, I admit. He was good to me." She walked in silence for several seconds before she said, "Everything reminds me of him. Even this room."

"No wonder. That guy's a prince. Gave you flowers for no reason, opened doors, took you to dinner. My man don't do that stuff. As far as I'm concerned, you're plumb crazy for letting him go."

She was quiet for several seconds before she added, "But to tell you the truth, mostly I miss his opinions and ideas. I miss *him*. Michael does have a way of turning ordinary to extra-ordinary."

"You know your problem? You're so used to things being bad, you can't handle good."

Katrina glanced at her watch. 8:32 P.M. Sighing, she threw her gym bag over her shoulder. "Hm. I've got to go, Tanisha. Don't want to miss the bus. See you next week."

When she pushed open the huge wooden door, cold rain pelted her. "Bad luck," she mumbled to herself. "No umbrella."

Wishing she had chosen her hooded jacket regardless of its poor fashion statement, she turned up her collar and fastened the top button of her red London Fog trench coat. As she hustled down the steps, she was drenched in the downpour, and shivered. She dropped her head and picked up the pace.

The weather reminded her of the day she left home five years ago. When she returned from work one afternoon, her mother and father were immersed in one of their daily battles about picky, stupid things. Something had clicked inside of her. There was no way she could listen to one more crash, one more shout. She threw some clothes in a suitcase and left. That day was the worst storm in twenty years—residual weather from a coastal hurricane. Katrina vowed then to find a kind man who'd amuse and enthuse rather than abuse her, someone who'd focus on conversation and comfort instead of conflict. And she had found that man in Michael. She scrunched up her face.

Tanisha was right. I broke up with him for being too nice, she thought. *And for being kind to someone else, and doing his job.* It didn't make any sense, now that she thought about it.

At that moment, a car pulled up to the curb. Michael stuck his head out of the window. "Couldn't let you stand here in the rain getting soaked. Hop in and I'll take you home."

Only seconds prior she had felt remorseful and repentant, but seeing Michael now flipped the switch back to anger. He was too accommodating. Not feisty enough. Should she waylay her pride to take the ride?

Lightning flashed, thunder crashed, and the rain fell in huge, cold drops that chilled her to the bone. Her long hair streamed with water now, and her skirt and slip clung to her soaking wet stockings. She shrugged.

He hopped out, umbrella in hand. "No commitments, Katrina. Get out of the rain," he yelled through the din of the downpour. "Here, let me take that." He grabbed her bag.

Katrina hesitated one moment only before she hustled into the warm, dry vehicle. Okay, no commitments; it was a ride. That's all. And perhaps they could talk. Her heart ached to talk.

As she squeezed water from her dripping hair, her emotions jumped from ire to penitence and back so fast they felt like sparks from one of those static electricity generators she had seen at the science center. Being near him forced her to address her emotions: gratitude, fear of commitment, loss of independence.

Deep down, she was angry with herself for breaking up with him. But mostly, she was livid that she'd have to admit she was wrong.

Wallowing in humiliation sounded too hard. She wouldn't do it. Not now.

At least his car was dry.

48.

It was 5 A.M. when Patrick climbed onto the bus. Only the cleaning staff and night watchman would be at work, so he probably wouldn't get caught. But if he was, well, that might mean his job. Hers too. He had wanted to do this by himself, but she wouldn't lend the keys. Kind of ironic, really. The person with the least amount of training and knowledge of the chemicals had the most access. Patrick closed his eyes. Might as well get a few winks before committing his crime.

The sky wore hints of pink when the bus stopped abruptly and startled him awake. Under the bridge far below him on the Ohio River, a barge filled with crates and rolls of steel was being nudged downstream by a tugboat.

Seeing them reminded Patrick of when he was twelve. After school one muggy afternoon, he and his friend Joey Ozworski ended up at the river skinny dipping. He smiled when he remembered the freedom he felt, swimming in that chilly, dirty water without the encumbrance of clothing. The further out he swam, the stronger the current grew; the swells from a passing barge and tugboat left him gasping for air. If he had been less strong, that could have been his last day on earth. Good thing it wasn't. Who else would help Emma Lee out of her predicament?

The swells that threatened to drown her now must be very strong, indeed. He still couldn't get over her refusal to leave Leonard. Had Baxter slipped her poison even in the hospital? Now that he thought about it, based on the way she changed throughout the week, that was likely. On Monday she was healing and ready to go with him. On Tuesday, she spaced out for minutes at a time and forgot he was in the room. By Wednesday, the day he had tried to secret her away, she appeared to be more zombie than woman. It made him crazy that he couldn't do anything about her situation.

As the bus slowed near the plant, Patrick grabbed a chrome pole and stood. After exiting through the side door, his long legs strode toward River's Edge Chemical. He was arriving at work two hours before starting time. Hopefully, it was early enough to get the job done before others showed up.

Only three cars were in the plant parking lot. One belonged to the night watchman, one to the cleaning lady. The front door of the third vehicle opened and Katrina stepped out. Placing her hands on the hood behind her, she leaned against the front bumper and said, "I'm putting my head on the chopping block here, you know."

Patrick waved a hand. "And I appreciate it. But nothing's going to happen. No one cares about this old stuff but us." He hoped he sounded more confident than he felt.

"There is no 'us.' You care about it. I'm doing this for Emma Lee."

He frowned. "And the tickets of course."

She held out a hand and grinned. "Glad you mentioned them. Give."

He reached into his back pocket, retrieved two tickets from his wallet, but didn't hand them over. Not yet.

It had taken him a week to convince Katrina to let him into work and the store room early. First he offered her tickets to the Pirates game, seats behind the batter's box.

"Not something I'm interested in," she had said.

He couldn't understand how anyone could refuse great Pirates tickets.

The next day, when he met her in the hallway on the way to lunch, he tried again. "So what do you want, then? Money?"

She had flipped her chestnut hair behind her shoulders, the way she often did, and said, "Look, I feel for Emma Lee, but I don't think your plan will work. And something like this could get both of us canned. I'm supposed to be trustworthy, ya' know." She placed a hand on her chest. "I took an oath about those keys. Besides, you have nothing I want badly enough."

She was wrong. That afternoon he had asked Rhonda what Katrina might like.

"That's easy," she said. "She'd go gaga over tickets to the Martha Graham Dance Company show. But it's been sold out for months. Hey, you aren't sweet on her, are you?"

He had smiled and said, "Early birthday present."

"Well since you're in such a generous mood, mine's June tenth."

That evening, Patrick called a ticket scalper he'd talked to about the Pirates tickets. When he heard the price, he shouted, "Fifty dollars for two tickets! They were ten dollars at the box office."

The man acted nonchalant. "That's fifty *each*."

Patrick's mouth dropped open. "Um," he stammered. "Give me a minute to think." Should he spend two days' wages on tickets with the hope that Katrina would want them? What if Rhonda was wrong, or Katrina was busy that evening?

"Look, I got two more buyers waitin' if ya don't take 'em. Make up your mind."

Patrick thought of Emma Lee, living with that bastard, Leonard. There was no alternative. He sucked in his breath and tried to figure out how he and Joshua could live on macaroni and cheese for the next month. "I'll take them."

When Patrick brought the tickets to work the next day and showed them to Katrina, she cooed. "Oooo, I love Martha Graham. Spectacular choreography; and her dancers are out of this world." She looked at Patrick with a reverence he had never seen on her face before, and her voice rose an octave. "This show has been sold out like forever. How did you get them?"

Before she could touch the tickets, he pulled them away. "Not so fast. What do you say? Will you do it?"

She tapped two lacquered nails on her chin. He could almost see her mind churning. "I've done worse for a lot less." She sighed. "This might get me fired, but it's a deal."

He slid the tickets into his pocket. "They're yours as soon as it's over."

And now, here they were, skulking toward the building like thieves, on their way to truth and freedom. He made a mental note to thank Rhonda for the tip. Maybe he'd even get her a gift for her birthday like she asked.

Katrina unlocked the front door and they snuck down the hallway on tiptoe. The building creaked; he jumped. She covered her mouth to squelch the giggle that rose in her throat, so it came out in snorts.

Patrick jabbed her with his elbow and whispered, "Cut it out. You sound like a sick duck. Someone will hear us."

"Yeah, sorry," she said, smiling. "But you look so nervous."

When Katrina unlocked the storeroom door, they stepped back in time. The shelves were lined with glass bottles and cans from every year the plant was in operation. They were of many different hues: grey, green, blue, clear, rusty. Some were filled with liquids, others powder. The substances, too, came in many colors—mustard, red, orange, white, black. Everything was covered in a layer of dust, and the strong chemical odor permeated the room.

Katrina fanned the air as if she could waft away the odor. "Oh, it stinks in here, Patrick. I'm leaving."

He grabbed her arm. "Not so fast. We have to get evidence and get out, and I need your help to scan the room. You take that aisle, I'll take this one."

"What are we looking for?"

"I don't know. Anything that doesn't seem right."

Two minutes later, Patrick whispered, "Katrina, I found something. An empty space where a jar used to be."

He wrote down the number on the shelf: A-22-1944.

"Oh. I found one missing over here," Katrina said.

"Okay, at least two jars are gone. With these numbers, I'll know in ten minutes what they were and, hopefully, how long they've been gone. Let's get out of here."

As they exited the room, Patrick was the giddy one. He was on the way to finding what pesticides had poisoned Emma Lee, and proving that Baxter was the one who had done it. He raced to his office with new purpose.

LEONARD SCOURED THE kitchen for his keys. They weren't on the hook by the front door where he usually kept them. Not in his pockets, nor in the living room. Did that brat take them? He searched the gadget drawer and his jacket. Not there.

Emma Lee had a doctor's appointment they had to get to, and they'd stop by the occupational therapist's office after. Without keys he'd have to take her car, which he was loath to do. Finally, he stomped to the bathroom to use the toilet and comb his hair. And there, on the counter, were the keys. He hadn't left them there, that was for sure.

Now that Emma Lee was home from the hospital minus her short term memory again, life should have been perfect. But it wasn't. Weird things started happening almost immediately, like the keys being misplaced, for instance. And she was different—docile and agreeable, yes, but odd and dense too. He noticed it right off when he parked in the driveway on their return from the hospital. David had jumped out to take care of the bucket, but she had sat immobile. When she still didn't move after he had gotten out, he reopened his car door and said, "You can get out now. You're home."

"Oh, home. Sure," she said. But she didn't budge. "How do I get out?"

He couldn't believe she had forgotten how to exit the car. She opened it fine at Sister Martha's. "Grab and pull the handle, push the door open, then step out," he had barked. But when she knit her brow in concentration, staring at him, he had walked around the car, opened the door for her, taken her hand, and helped her out. After that, his opening her car door had become the norm.

Besides getting out of cars, she also didn't remember to close doors, or answer the phone, or eat. He had to instruct her on how to brush her teeth, what shoe to put on which foot, even how to turn on the television. Not once, but every time. She couldn't fold clothes anymore, forgot what she was saying, and lost things. And each day she seemed worse, not better.

Leonard finished combing his hair. He threw the keys into his pants pocket and herded Emma Lee and David to the car. Fifty minutes later, after dropping David with the sisters and sitting through Emma Lee's doctor visit, they pulled up in front of Michael Yamada's office.

"Where are we?" she asked, as she stepped out of the car door he had opened. "I'm tired and need to go home."

"Of course you are, but this will take just five minutes. Don't you remember? I told you this morning at breakfast. After the doctor, you have a short consultation with your occupational therapist."

She shuffled to the doorway as if in pain. "Do I know him?"

"Of course you do."

Emma Lee tilted her head and shrugged her shoulders. She looked so repentant; he could almost read it as an apology. But forgiving wasn't on his agenda. Fixing this new twist was.

In the therapy room, Michael Yamada directed them to chairs, but Leonard didn't want to sit. He wanted to complain and demand, and that was best done standing. "Emma Lee's memory is weird now, Yamada," he said. "What's going on?" He began pacing the room.

The dark-haired occupational therapist shook his head and said, "The human mind is complex. But it is flexible and resilient. We have to wait for her mind to work this out for itself."

Leonard wanted to wrap his fingers around Yamada's throat until those Oriental eyes bulged. Maybe that would "work things out." Instead, he clenched his fists and shoved them into his pockets. He felt as if he were falling from a plane without a parachute. "She's not right."

Michael shrugged. "It's been what, a week since Emma Lee got out of the hospital? Whatever illness put her there may have affected the undamaged parts of her brain. Or changed how her brain is remembering. You'll have to give it more time."

"We don't have more time," he shouted. "Last evening, even though I helped her put water in the pot and gave her explicit instructions, she burned peas into carbon ball bearings. It stunk up the house something awful."

She dropped her head, "You had every right to be angry. I'm so sorry for doing that."

"When she's well and able to come for therapy again, we can reevaluate and I'll have more answers for you then," Yamada said.

"Damn straight, you will," Leonard answered.

Leonard left the office feeling more frustrated than when he arrived. As he walked down the hallway with Emma Lee, she turned to him and said, "Thank you for helping me. You're very kind."

Leonard stopped dead. You're welcome," he mumbled. He looked into her eyes, hoping to see love reflected there. But instead her face looked troubled.

"Do I know you?" she asked.

Irritation kicked him again and he almost barked, "Of course you know me. I'm Leonard, your husband."

She pursed her lips and slid her hand over her forehead, then raked her fingers through her hair. "Husband? I didn't know I was married. Where is …?"

He waited. When she didn't continue, he shook his hands in the air and yelled, "What? Where is what?"

Emma Lee turned her lovely lavender emotionless eyes in his direction. "I didn't say anything."

"You did. You said …" He sighed. "Oh, never mind."

Leonard drove homeward, picked up David, and continued to the farm. As the car came around a bend near the driveway, all three passengers gasped. Five sheep stood in the middle of the road and a sixth lay near the center line. A young man wearing blue jeans, ball cap, and leather jacket squatted near it, his car stashed in the brush on the road berm.

"The sheep!" Leonard yelled. "How'd they get out?" He parked in the driveway and jumped out. As he raced to his sheep, something off-balance and disturbing rose in his chest. Who was to blame for this? David could have left the gate open. But more likely, this was Emma Lee's doing.

When he reached the road he yelled, "Topsy! You've hit Topsy!" Leonard couldn't stop his anger and he didn't want to. It exploded in word bursts like a cap gun. "Idiot! Careless fool. Murderer!"

The young man shoved both hands into pockets. "Look. I came around the bend and there they were. Couldn't see them 'till I was on them, with the sun and all. Damn near killed myself trying to avoid the lot. Must have a hole in your fence somewhere."

"I walk the fence every single week." He poked the man's chest. "You let them out, didn't you?"

"Look, I'm sorry about the sheep, but I had nothing to do with them being here." He pulled out his wallet. "Let me pay you for the one I hit."

Leonard squatted and stroked Topsy's coat. "You've done enough damage. Go."

"Suit yourself," he said. The man shoved his wallet into his back pocket, jumped into his car, and drove off.

Once the car was gone, Leonard led his other sheep homeward To David, he said, "Boy, get out here and herd them home."

Again Leonard hunched over Topsy. Her eyes were closed, her breathing shallow. Her right front leg was twisted; a foot stuck out at an odd angle. Blood trickled from her mouth.

"Help me get her off the road," he barked to Emma Lee.

When she placed both hands on the window, prisoner-like, and stared at him, he gritted his teeth and opened the door. At the sheep, he instructed Emma Lee where to lift and how to move the animal to limit any more damage.

Once Topsy was off the road, Leonard crouched over her and touched her neck. The faint pulse he had felt before was gone; the sheep was dead. He covered his face with his hands and squeezed his eyes tight. Why did everything he ever loved have to die?

Before, Emma Lee had been the perfect wife and he could live with her memory lapse. But that woman had disappeared and in her place, he got a brand new problem. A strange new Emma Lee.

Maybe she could fool everyone else into believing she was helpless, but not him. No, he was wise to her tricks. He'd catch her and expose her intentions. He'd force her to confess her evil ways. And then, he'd make her pay. He stared at his lovable Topsy. Yes, she'd have to pay.

49.

When she left the storage room, Katrina stomped directly to the ladies room where she scrubbed her hands and arms, and splashed water on her face. All those chemicals and all that guilt stuck like charged particles on a TV screen.

How did I let him talk me into that? she scolded herself. She wished she could quit her job now—simply walk away. She imagined what an ad for her replacement should (but wouldn't) say: "Wanted: woman willing to spend countless hours performing mindless mimeographing, greeting, and schmoozing while breathing toxic and/or deadly chemicals all day and helping others commit crimes. Pay commensurate with stupidity." Her lips rose into a rueful smile.

Katrina opened her purse to find her lipstick and saw the tickets again. It was like discovering a lucky rabbit's foot or a special talisman. Okay, the job was dirty and stressful. She had taken several risks letting Patrick into the storeroom, but it turned out okay. They hadn't been discovered, and he got what he wanted, with a possible bonus of helping Emma Lee. And she now had tickets to the most important event of the Pittsburgh dance season. All she needed now was someone to go with her.

When Katrina finally got to her desk, instead of starting work, she called Tanisha.

"Hey, you are going to die when you hear this. I got two tickets to Saturday's Martha Graham performance. I'm inviting you to join me."

Tanisha squealed. "Martha Graham! Thought those tickets were sold out for months." Then she exhaled a deep, loud moan. "It hurts me to say this, but I can't. Rocky and I are going to Columbus for the weekend to celebrate Mom's sixtieth. Big family barbecue with all my brothers and sisters; can't get out of it." She was quiet a beat, then said, "So ask Michael. This is your chance to make up."

Katrina picked up a pencil and doodled several swirls on a file folder before she spoke again, trying to sound light and nonchalant. "Don't know if I'm ready for that."

Tanisha clicked her tongue. Usually her North Side Pittsburgh accent was subtle, but now she turned it on. "Girl, we already discussed this. You are cra-zy if you don't get back together. The way I see it, ain't nothin' more you could want in a man."

"He has issues."

"Honey, every man has issues." Tanisha laughed aloud. Her rare, earthy honesty shone when she said, "But his good manners, good looks, and good job go a long way to cancel those out."

Katrina started laughing too, reminded again of why she liked Tanisha so much. "Maybe you're right about that."

Katrina could imagine Tanisha's grin that flashed big, straight white teeth. "Damn straight, I am. I'd go after him myself if I wasn't already married."

"Well, I'll think about it. But humble pie wasn't on my diet this week."

At this, Tanisha roared with laughter again. "Honey, take it from me. There ain't nothing better than a little humiliation for wrapping a man around your finger. They love it when they think they're top dog. Hey, by the way, thanks for the invite. I want you to tell me all about the performance after class next Tuesday."

"Okay. See you then."

Having been reminded of his good qualities again, Katrina missed Michael something fierce. Now that she thought about it, she had enjoyed every minute of their time together. Even the disagreements. She couldn't conjure up one good reason why she broke up with the most wonderful man she had ever known. Katrina picked up the receiver to call Michael now. Before she lost her nerve.

At that moment, Patrick dashed to her desk.

"Wait till you hear this." He scanned the hallway then glanced over his shoulder. Seeing no one, he leaned over her desk and dropped his voice. "Last month there was an audit of that store room. Since then, one container of permethrin and one of arsenate have been removed. But get this. There's no record of who took them, and they haven't shown up in any of the labs. Gotta tell the police; I need your car."

Katrina replaced the phone receiver. "Why don't you just call? Or drive your own car."

"Mine's in the shop getting new brake shoes. And there's no time to waste. Emma Lee is home with Baxter now. He's bound to try to poison her again."

She slid back and exhaled loudly. "You think he'd do that?"

Nodding furiously, he said, "Absolutely. Please. The keys." He reached out his hand.

Her stomach twisted. She recalled the promise she made to herself in the women's room and was tempted to say no. Instead, she retrieved the keys from her purse. "If anything happens to this car, I'll kill you. And I need it back before quitting time."

He smiled. "Thanks, Katrina. I'll drive it like it was my own."

"That's what I'm afraid of," she grumbled.

Katrina plunked her elbows on the desktop and jammed her cheeks onto her fists. She tapped out a galloping rhythm on the desk with her lacquered nails, building up her nerve. A few minutes later, she grabbed the receiver and dialed Michael's office number.

"Orchard Occupational Therapy. Michael Yamada here."

She squeezed the tickets and forged on. "Hi, Michael. It's me."

"Katrina. What a surprise."

She waited a beat, unsure of how to approach the apology. He solved her dilemma when he said, "I can't talk right now; my patient arrived."

"Wait," she almost shouted. Realizing she was too loud, she willed her voice to soften. "This will only take a minute. I wanted to thank you for the ride the other night. And to ask you—as one who appreciates dance—if you'd like to go with me to the Martha Graham production on Saturday. I thought you might enjoy it."

"Oh, I see. Because I appreciate dance, huh?" he was silent a beat. "Thanks for the invite."

"Um, does that mean you'll go?"

"I'll have to cancel my plans, but sure, I'm game."

Plans? What plans? "Great. I'll pick you up at six."

When she hung up, Katrina fell back in her chair and stared at the ceiling. Good. He would go. But she had no time to apologize, so unless she called him again (which she hoped to avoid) along with a spectacular dance performance, Saturday's agenda would include a large serving of face-to-face humiliation.

"Darn, how I hate humble pie," she grumbled.

At the farmhouse, Sister Martha rang the bell.

David answered the door. "Mom's resting."

"Okay. Then I'll talk with Leonard first. Is he here?"

The boy pointed to the garden. "He's pulling weeds. Said I have to stay in the house and match socks."

"Is that fun?"

"Better than pulling weeds."

"I'll be back," Sister Martha said. She lifted her skirt and tromped through the field, which was still damp from last night's storm. Her soles collected clay clods as she walked, changing her shoes from leather to lead. "Hey, there, Leonard," she said when she reached the garden. "Nice day, isn't it?"

"Gonna rain," he said, not looking up from his weed pulling. "What do you want?"

"Next meeting for the men's sharing group is Monday evening. I'm inviting you again."

"You drove here for that? I'm busy. Won't make it." He yanked a weed with exaggerated energy.

"It must be hard for you," she said.

Leonard stood, propped a fist on his hip, and let his gaze settle on the storm clouds rolling in from the west. He threw his rake, shovel, and hoe into the wheelbarrow and began pushing it to the house. She thought the conversation was over but he surprised her by saying, "It's not me that needs help; it's her. She's faking it. This new memory loss stuff is a bunch of crap."

Sister Martha shook her head. "How can you say that?"

As he pushed the wheelbarrow over the uneven ground, the tools rattled and clanked and the sky rumbled. "I can tell."

"That makes no sense. People don't pretend to lose memory."

As the two reached the front porch, rain drops the size of marbles pelted them. He shielded his face with a hand. "She wants to leave me for that slimy Kilkenny. But she won't get away with it."

Sister Martha stood immobile as rain soaked through her denim jumper. The idea of a brain-injured woman conjuring up such a plan seemed ludicrous. "Listen to yourself, Leonard. That makes no sense. She needs you. You care for her." She gazed up at the dark thunderhead clouds overhead. "If you won't come to the sharing group, perhaps you and Emma Lee could come for therapy again. I think I could help."

Leonard dropped the wheelbarrow's handles and waved a fist in the air. His eyes seemed to bore through her. "I don't need stupid counseling or some namby-pamby men's group to tell me what's wrong with Emma Lee. She's a lying, deceptive manipulator. She's evil."

Sister Martha stood in shock, unable to speak. A flash of lightning streaked the sky and thunder rumbled through the valley as the rain turned to a deluge. Leonard stood still; she bounded up the stairs and stood under the porch roof. "The only way you can fight evil is with Christ, Leonard," she yelled over the din. Placing her hand on her heart, she said, "For the sake of your soul, you have to love and forgive. Learn to be other-centered, not vindictive. I thought you knew that, and believed it, by the way you sacrificed for her."

Leonard grabbed the wheelbarrow handles again. His clothes and hair were drenched now and he shouted, "You shouldn't worry about my soul, Sister. You should worry about hers. It's been taken over by a manipulative, selfish devil that's destroying me and our marriage. If you want to help, do something about that!"

As he tromped off, pushing the wheelbarrow along the slick, muddy path to the barn, the man Sister Martha thought she knew melted in the rain. She stood on the porch until she regained her composure, then rang the bell for a second time.

Emma Lee answered.

Sister Martha stood and hugged her. "I'm sorry to bother you, dear."

Emma Lee let her into the living room and fell into the chair on top of the socks. "I don't know what to do with these." She pulled several sealed envelopes from her apron pocket and flicked them onto the coffee table.

David climbed into his mother's lap and pressed his face into her neck, as if her odor assured him that this was his mother. Emma Lee glanced at Sister Martha and her eyes shot open. "Who are you?"

The nun stepped out of her muddy shoes and spread a towel over the couch to protect it from her wet skirt. "I'm Sister Martha, your counselor." She read the envelopes. Each was addressed to Emma Lee Dubois at her old apartment.

Pointing to the letters, Sister Martha said, "Tell me about these."

Emma Lee shrugged. "David found them in the barn behind the feed bin. In a burlap sack."

She picked up an envelope. "May I read one?"

"Sure."

David slipped off Emma Lee's lap, grabbed a Matchbox car, and rolled it across the room; his mother stood and stared out the window.

Sister Martha ripped open an envelope. The letter inside was dated October of the prior year.

Dear Emma Lee,

It's still hot and dry here, the way I feel from not hearing from you. I wish you'd write. I miss you. My sister saw the doctor today. He says there's not much time left ..."

She skimmed to the bottom of the page. It was signed, "Love, Patrick"

Sister Martha sucked in her breath. "I don't understand. You never received any letters from Patrick at the apartment. Of course, if you did, I probably wouldn't have seen them. Leonard ... ."

She wanted to believe Leonard had saved the letters for Emma Lee, to give her when her memory returned. But she knew that was wishful thinking.

Emma Lee pulled the curtain aside and gazed out. "Who's Leonard?"

"Your husband, dear."

Emma Lee turned and stared at her. "I have a husband?"

"Bless your heart. Is it okay with you if I take a few of these with me?" she asked.

Emma Lee nodded. "Sure. Take them all."

"Thank you." Sister Martha rose. "I have to get going but thanks for talking with me. And sharing the letters. I'll stop by again soon."

Martha shoved five envelopes into her purse, slid her feet back into the muddy shoes, and left.

On her drive home, the nun's shoulders tightened as she gripped the steering wheel with one hand and smacked it with the other. The Code of Ethics for Christian Counselors demanded she report deadly threats, but she had never cause to do so before. She wasn't sure if this threat was deadly, but she wouldn't take any chances. The agency office would hear from her today. Smacking the steering wheel again, she yelled, "How could I have been so blind?"

50.

Patrick avoided the conference room where his boss and fifteen others bickered over Love Canal Project details. Two benefits to his demotion: he wasn't expected to attend such meetings, and the boss was preoccupied so he had more freedom.

Once inside his office, he slammed the door and grabbed the phone book. Wily old Baxter might be able to outsmart an injured, confused woman, but the man would have to get up mighty early to outsmart Patrick. He found the number, grabbed the phone, and dialed.

"Suburban Police. How may I assist you?"

"I need to talk with Officer Venezia. I've got evidence for one of his cases."

After Patrick ticked off relevant information, he was put on hold for several minutes. He finally heard the officer's raspy voice. "Venezia here."

"I've discovered important evidence in Emma Lee Baxter's case. I'd like to bring it in. Say, fifteen minutes?"

"You the guy who reported this in the first place?"

"I am. I've got proof that two different chemicals disappeared from a locked, controlled storeroom at River's Edge Chemical sometime during the last three months. Baxter was one of the four people with access. He could have walked off with the stuff easy. If Emma Lee's tests show positive for either substance, that could clinch the case, right?"

"It's a start. You got a name this time, buddy? Who am I talking to?"

"Patrick Kilkenny. See you in fifteen."

Everyone at the plant had greeted Baxter's retirement with enthusiasm, expecting positive change. Unfortunately, his replacement was worse. The man made up in arrogance what he lacked in stature. He dressed in tailor-made suits and flung orders like an army general. Behind his back, employees called him Napoleon. In compliance with new, stricter employee regulations, Rhonda reported everything to her new boss, including people leaving work for any reason. So Patrick decided to use the truth to his advantage; even the boss would respect a visit to the police.

With case and keys in hand, Patrick arrived at the front office wearing the appropriate nervous-concern on his face. "Afternoon, Rhonda."

She glanced at him a moment and then back into the file drawer. "Hey, Patrick. What can I do for you?"

"The police want to see me about something pertaining to Dr. Baxter. I gotta go."

Rhonda raised her brows as her eyes widened. "Oh, I thought they had that all sorted out. What do they want from you?"

He gave his head a somber shake. "I'm not quite sure, but I'll keep you posted. Tell the boss, will you? I'll be back as soon as I can."

When the phone rang, Rhonda sang, "Good morning," into the receiver, and held up one finger, his signal to wait.

Patrick ignored her. In moments he was in Katrina's car, driving out of the parking lot. Thunder rolled as he crossed the bridge; at the police station, rain fell from the sky in buckets. Throwing his jacket over his head, Patrick raced to the building. When he entered, the smell of coffee and popcorn mixed with mold assaulted his nostrils. He was directed to wait in the hallway where he chose the second orange plastic chair. As he sat, steam rose from his wet pants legs.

Seven minutes later, the portly officer waddled down the hallway with the swagger of a pregnant woman, toes pointing outward, baggy pants swaying. Out of breath, he leaned one hand against the dirty tan wall and said simply, "Kilkenny. Follow me."

In his office, the policeman wedged himself between the chair and the desk like a meatball between two slices of bread. He collected general information then finally asked, "Let's see what you got."

Still standing, Patrick flicked open his briefcase and dragged out the folder. "This is the list of chemicals from our annual audit. It was done last month." He placed the open folder on the desk and pointed to a line on page three. "Twelve containers of arsenates were placed in storage back in 1944, and in section P we had three containers of permethrin. But this morning when I checked, one of each is missing."

Officer Venezia ignored his stomach rubbing the desk. Generating low, rumbling noises in his throat, and uttering an occasional "humph" he scanned the file and scribbled notes. Finally after a swig of muddy brown coffee, he said, "Interesting. But no proof Baxter took the stuff."

"Yeah, I know. But it's got to be good for something."

"Sit, Kilkenny. We need to talk."

Patrick scooped three books and a magazine from the chair before he could sit.

Venezia leaned in, conspiratorial-like. He held a hand next to his mouth and dropped his voice. "You seem like a nice kid; I like you. But I'm in a bind here. My supervisor is pushing for us to close this case; Baxter has clout—knows the judge and has a good lawyer. *You and I* might think he's guilty as sin, but our opinions ain't worth squat without serious proof. I'll try and get a warrant with what you brought, but no guarantees."

When Patrick groaned the officer held up a hand. "Get hold of yourself, son. It ain't the end of the world. I'll send a car out to that farm this afternoon to check on Mizz Baxter, make sure she's okay and all. Who knows? The officers might see something."

When the phone rang, Venezia grabbed the receiver. "Yeah, what?" he barked. After listening a few moments he said, "Okay, put her through." He placed his hand over the receiver. "Wait in the hall for a sec; I gotta take this."

Patrick shrugged and left the room. From his orange chair vantage point in the hallway, he could hear some of Venezia's conversation.

"Mail fraud … a felony. …bring them in. Yeah. Till five."

Patrick was returning to the office when the receptionist whisked past him and handed Officer Venezia a manila envelope. "This came from the hospital," she said.

Patrick's feet felt cemented to the floor. This could be Emma Lee's toxicology report. He wasn't going to leave until he heard the results.

Officer Venezia pulled out the pages, scanned them, and threw them onto the desk. "We're in luck. Looks like more evidence."

Patrick read the words upside down. "Urinary arsenate level: 235 micrograms per day. Indicates chronic exposure (unless seafood was ingested). Patient's repeat twenty-four-hour urinary test confirmed the results. Chelating therapy is warranted."

Venezia grabbed the receiver from its cradle and barked, "Get me Judge Blackstone. I need a search warrant. Yeah, yeah." He placed his hand over the mouthpiece again, waved his hand backward at Patrick, as if shooing a fly, and said, "Go back to work, Kilkenny. We'll take it from here."

As Patrick left the office, he couldn't bring himself to return to the plant. He was so close. While he had the car, he'd take a side trip to the farm, to make sure Emma Lee was all right.

WHY IS EVERYONE against me? Leonard replaced the hoe, shovel, and rake to their places in the barn, straightening the handles so that each tool hung exactly vertical. The boy, Yamada, Emma Lee, and now even the nun! Though he didn't want to, he'd have to punish Emma Lee again. Yes, she'd pay for twisting everyone's mind.

He waited until Sister Martha drove away before he went back outside. As lightning crashed, he leaned the ladder against the barn. Setting his face to the rain, he climbed up and snipped the telephone line. The wire fell to the ground.

Back inside the barn, Leonard opened the empty feed bin and pulled out a jar wrapped in a burlap sack. As he stared at the thick green liquid, he wondered how much he'd need to give her this time. He hated to think that his offspring could die; he had wanted a namesake. But it couldn't be helped; he had to ensure the devil was exorcised from her. She was young. She'd have another.

He folded his handkerchief into a triangle and tied two ends behind his head so the bulk of it covered his nose like a bandit's mask. After propping the bottle of arsenate in the corner, he threw a ball of twine and a pair of scissors into the stall next to it, then tromped up the stairs where he shoved two bales of straw down the chute. Back downstairs again, Leonard dragged the bales into the stall.

As he worked, he organized the session in his head. He'd tell her how important it was that she admit her mistakes, and change her story so everyone heard from her how good he was to her. He'd make her understand that she couldn't continue her evil ways. If she didn't cooperate he wasn't above torture.

When finished, Leonard scanned his handiwork with satisfaction. The straw bales, the rope, the arsenate—everything was ready. And so was he.

He stomped back to the house. Rivulets trickled down his face, off his sleeves, and from his nose. In a rare, bold defiance of routine, he left on his boots and coat as he barged through the front door.

Emma Lee was playing with David on the floor in the living room. Yanking her arm, he ordered, "Come with me, now!"

She shook her head and pulled away from him. David jumped up "Leave her alone!"

Leonard shoved David. "This is none of your business. I need your mother in the barn."

The boy tumbled onto the wooden floor and began to cry.

Emma Lee stared at Leonard with those deep violet eyes. Once they could have drawn him in, entranced him. Now, they seemed almost spooky in their intensity and he shuddered. Her voice, calm and steely, said, "Don't hurt the boy. I'll go with you; let me get my coat."

He spoke through clenched teeth. "No. No coat, no boots. Just you. Now."

Holding tight to Emma Lee's arm, Leonard dragged her barefoot out the door.

David followed after them. He held Emma Lee's jacket out. "Take it."

"Get back to the house, you brat!" Leonard yelled, pushing David away. The boy burst into tears again. "Don't hurt my Mom."

When Leonard gripped the boy's wrist, David bit his arm. "You little brat! How dare you!" Before Leonard could hit the boy, Emma Lee slid between them. "No! Don't hurt him. It's not his fight. David, go back to the house. Now."

Rain mixed with tears as he wailed, "No, I want to help …"

"You can't, honey. Now go."

With a huge sob, David turned, and ran back to the house.

51.

After Leonard dragged Mom to the barn, David knew he had to do something. In the house he grabbed the phone. He didn't know how to call the police, but maybe whoever he talked to could get help. When he picked up the receiver, though, he heard nothing. The phone didn't work!

His heart pumped so hard he thought blood might come through his nose. He peered through the window at the barn. Leonard and Mom must have gone in. He put on his boots and coat and slipped out the side door. Running into the woods that skirted the yard, David raced the rest of the way in the cover of the trees until he arrived at the barn. There, he climbed the hill so he could enter the barn on the upper floor. He opened the door a crack and peeked in, praying that Mommy and Leonard were downstairs. When he didn't see or hear them, he tiptoed in.

David lay down on his belly and peered through the hay chute. It took several minutes for his eyes to adjust to the darkness, so he couldn't see anything at first. But eventually he saw the feed bin and the stalls way below him. There, Leonard was yelling at Mommy.

I SLIPPED SEVERAL times on the slick clay path as I stumbled to the barn, so now I'm drenched, exhausted, and caked with wet red clay. The man shoves me into a stall where shivering, I huddle on the bale of straw. "I'm c-cold," I stutter.

He wraps my wrists and ankles together with twine. "Oh, how I loved you, and yet you find so many ways to deceive me, to lie about me. You're disgusting!" he screams.

I continue to shiver; soon my whole body trembles.

"Repent and confess now. If you don't, I'm going to expel the demon that I know lives in you."

"Who ... are you?"

He grabs a handful of my wet, black curls and yanks my head back. "There you go again, tormenting me with that pretend loss of memory. Your faking drives me crazy. You know very well who I am, who everyone is. Admit it, you liar."

"Which of us is the liar?"

He smacks my face; I lose my balance and I fall off the bale. I lay there for a few minutes, wondering if I'll ever see David again, if I'll survive this.

I think back to the day in the hospital when I decided on my plan, the day Sister Martha prayed with me. I was sure God was directing this. But now, well, even if I 'confess' it won't make any difference. This crazy man will probably kill me no matter what I say.

I struggle back to sitting and whisper, "I don't remember much, but I'm fairly sure you can't beat memory back into the brain."

"You think you're so sm ...." He stops mid-sentence.

We both hear wheels crunching gravel in the drive. He races to door and peers out. After a few minutes he yells, "I can't believe it. That creep, Kilkenny, is coming up here. Why don't people mind their own business?"

He shoves a rag into my mouth, lifts me like a sack of oats, and throws me head-first into the empty feed bin. The lid closes with a bang and I'm left in cold, hard darkness.

WHEN HE HEARD gravel crunch in the driveway, David tiptoed to the front of the barn and peered through a crack between the wall boards. A car pulled up and parked and he was tempted to run down and tell whoever it was how Leonard had treated his mom. But instead he eased back to the hay chute and peered down again. When Leonard dragged his mom to the feed bin and threw her in, David had to force himself not to run downstairs. But he knew he couldn't overpower Leonard, and he wasn't about to be locked in that bin again, himself.

Leonard picked up a piece of two-by-four and hid behind a pile of hay bales right inside the doorway. David grew very worried.

About five minutes later, the barn door opened and a tall man stood silhouetted against the bright sky outside. The man took a few steps into the dimly lit barn, stopped and called, "Emma Lee? David? Leonard? Is anyone here?"

It was Patrick! Now Mom would be saved.

Instead, David watched as Leonard crept out from his hiding place and stood between Patrick and the doorway. Whack! The sound of the board hitting Patrick's forehead sickened David, who let out an involuntary squeak and hid his face in his arms.

"Ah!" Patrick yelled. He grabbed his head, swayed, stumbled backwards, and tumbled onto the hay-covered barn floor.

Leonard drew closer and lifted a foot to kick, but before he could, Patrick grabbed his leg and yanked it. Leonard fell into the hay and the men began to wrestle. David could see a dark line of blood drip down Patrick's face as the men kicked and grabbed and punched each other. He could hear their grunts and yells and heavy breathing all the way upstairs. Finally, Leonard managed to grab the stick again. He stood and swung with all his might, hitting Patrick on the back of the head this time. When Patrick crumpled into the hay unmoving, David's heart sank. He watched in anguish as Leonard collected the twine and scissors from the stall and tied Patrick's hands together behind his back. David couldn't believe an old man like Leonard could beat Patrick in a fight.

Leonard left Patrick in the hay and stumbled to the feed bin. As he opened the lid and leaned in, feet burst out and smacked him in his face. "Argh," he cried. "You ungrateful bitch. I gave you everything—a house, a child, a bed for that brat of yours. I took you to doctors and did everything I could for you to help you get better. But do you show any gratitude? Oh, no. You treat me like dirt. I know you've been having an affair with that man," he said, pointing at Patrick. "But you won't get away with it anymore."

He smacked Mommy right on the cheek and pulled her from the bin. David couldn't stand seeing Leonard hurt Mom. He had to do something. He opened the door at the top of the stairs and took one step down. Just then, he heard another car in the driveway.

"Why won't everyone leave me alone?" Leonard yelled. He shoved Mom back into the feed bin, slammed the lid down again, and this time placed a sack of oats on top of it.

David backed up the step he had come down. But his foot caught on the stair and he fell with a bang. He landed on his bottom and slid feet first down the whole flight of coarse wooden stairs.

When he heard the noise, Leonard turned. "Hey! What are you doing here, brat?"

David was stunned by the fall and lay in the hay for a moment. But when Leonard grabbed for his collar, the boy rolled away and scrambled to his feet. He raced to the feed bin and slid behind it, out of Leonard's reach.

Leonard peered into the hole, reaching as far as he could. "Come out of there." Then his face took on that too-nice, fake smile that David had come to hate. "I won't hurt you. You can help me get your mother out of the feed bin."

David hunkered further back and shook his head.

For several more minutes Leonard continued to urge him, then the man's face disappeared. David heard him walking in the hay, and then he heard a voice say, "Well, Dr. Baxter. I thought I'd find you up here."

He heard hay shifting, and then, "Hey, That's Mr. Kilkenny. He's out cold. What happened?"

Leonard said, "He barreled into the barn, demanding that I let my wife leave with him. They were having an affair. He pushed me, smacked me in the jaw with that two by four. I've got this bruise to prove it. In the fight I managed to get the stick from him. Didn't think I'd knock him out, though. Went to call you guys and an ambulance, but my phone is dead."

David couldn't believe that Leonard would lie to a policeman. He didn't think anyone was supposed to do that. Then he heard the policeman say, "I'll radio the station, get them to send an ambulance. Be right back."

After that, David didn't hear much but some shuffling and rummaging. And a few minutes later Leonard yelled, "You can all go to hell."

Everything was quiet for a few minutes until he heard the crackling, and smelled—smoke!

The boy crawled out from behind the bin and peered around the corner. A flame flickered in the hay, then raced along the barn floor. It crackled and smoked as it spread. And he couldn't see Leonard anywhere.

David had to do something *now*. He found the scissors, cut the twine from Patrick's wrists, and shook him. "Get up. Get up! I need help and there's a fire."

A groggy Patrick opened his eyes, rubbed his temples, and moaned. "Ah, my head. What?"

David shook Patrick's shoulders again. "Hurry. The barn's on fire." The boy handed the scissors to Patrick. "You have to help! Mom's tied up. In the feed bin."

When Patrick finally looked awake and stood, David raced to the faucet and shoved a bucket under it.

Patrick staggered to the big wooden bin. Giving a huge grunt, he shoved the sack of oats off the lid and opened it. He cut the twine from Emma Lee's hands and feet. "Here, put your arms over my shoulders and I'll get you out of there," he said.

Once on the ground, Emma Lee hauled the bucket of water toward the fire. Patrick grabbed an empty gunny sack and beat the flames.

When the fire was out, Emma Lee pulled David to her and engulfed him in a hug. "You saved us, honey. Thank you."

David wrapped his arms around his mother's neck and held on tight. "I'm so glad you didn't die. I love you."

When he pulled away from his mother, though, David noticed blood running down each of her legs, staining both feet red. "You're bleeding, Mom. Did you get hurt?"

She shook her head slowly and then she slumped to the ground on the hay. "The baby," she whispered.

A few minutes later Officer Venezia waddled back into the barn and scratched his head. "Hey, I could smell the smoke clear down at the house. What happened? And where'd you come from?"

"Mom was in the feed bin where Leonard locked her up. She's bleeding and needs a doctor."

Venezia ordered his partner to call for another ambulance. Patrick draped his arm around Emma Lee's shoulders.

The policeman asked David, "And how about you, son?"

"I was hiding behind the feed bin where he couldn't reach me."

Patrick pointed a thumb toward the door. "There's more. Baxter set the barn on fire, smacked me with a two-by-four, and tried to kill Emma Lee. Where is the bastard?"

Officer Venezia shook his head several times. "He drove off; almost ran into my car. Guess you were right, Kilkenny. I'll call in an APB on him. He won't get far."

David tapped the officer on the arm. "You have to find him and make sure he can't hurt my mommy anymore."

Venezia placed a hand on David's shoulder. "Don't worry, son. First, we'll take your mom to the doctor, and we'll protect both of you. And Mr. Kilkenny, too. Okay?"

The boy pressed his lips together. Leonard was crafty and mean. David recalled how strong the man seemed when he lifted Mom into the feed bin, and smacked Patrick with the stick. He could do things that David didn't believe were possible for an old man. But the police had guns, and they said they'd stay. So he said, "I guess … that will be okay."

52.

As she waited for the new coat of red lacquer on her nails to dry, Katrina read the Pittsburgh Post-Gazette article Patrick gave her. It described the fight, the fire, and the chemicals, and how the police stopped Dr. Baxter right across the Sewickley Bridge. It went on to say that he was being held on charges of assault and attempted murder. She laughed when she read his statement. "I'm the victim here. My wife caused all the problems. She's a pathological liar."

Katrina could easily believe that Baxter had stolen chemicals, or that he poisoned Emma Lee. But it was difficult for her to imagine the staid, controlled Dr. Baxter hitting Patrick over the head with a hunk of wood. She shook her head. Sometimes you couldn't tell what a person was capable of.

She blew on her nails and shrugged. The paper called David and Patrick heroes. Apparently, Patrick was right about Baxter poisoning Emma Lee. That brought her some satisfaction for helping him. But nothing could squelch her inner turmoil about the evening to come. How would Michael react? Would he be vindictive, whiny, aloof, or needy? She wouldn't blame him for any of those. But for some reason she couldn't stop herself from imagining kissing his lips, or staring into his wonderful, dark eyes.

The more she thought about Michael, the more she realized Tanisha was right. She loved him. And now she had a problem. Rekindling a relationship that she dissolved was foreign territory for her.

"Now what?" she grumbled as she slid her panty hose up. "Now what?"

Stop it! she scolded herself. Most of the time, all she had to do was dress up and accessorize to feel in control. But she was out of her element with the humility thing.

Katrina hopped into her car and drove to Michael's apartment. As she strode into the building she gave herself a little pep talk. "Be cool. This is friends, going out, having fun. Nothing more."

When Michael answered the door though, she couldn't stop herself from sucking in sharply. He looked amazing: black tuxedo with tails, white bow tie that accentuated his straight black hair.

He put a top hat on and reached for her hand. "Katrina, you look lovely. I'm almost ready. Please come in."

Still in shock, she stammered, "You look great, too."

Michael presented her with a corsage of three small deep red roses with baby's breath. "This is for you." He slipped the elastic band over her wrist.

"Oh, you shouldn't have."

"Why not? It's a special performance. You should look special to match."

Feeling tongue-tied now, Katrina gave him the keys to her car and let him drive.

They arrived at their destination thirty minutes early. Michael found a parking space on the street. He opened her door and bowed. "Let me assist you."

She loved how serious and gentlemanly he was. She wanted to enjoy herself for one night. So she let him take her hand and wind it through his arm.

"What lovely weather we're having, huh?" he said, pointing to the gray, cloudy sky.

First she felt confused, then she giggled.

They strolled together the half block to the theater, laughing and joking. Katrina felt shivery and excited to be walking with him again; it felt normal, right. She said, "Look, Michael. I need to, well, I wanted to say that ..."

"Yes?" he said, smiling.

She decided it was best to plunge in, say what she wanted to say before she lost her nerve. "I've been thinking about this since I broke up with you. I feel so stupid. I acted badly; made a huge mistake."

"So you're saying you were an ass and you'd like me to take you back?"

Anger stole into her now, and it was harder to say what she wanted. "Well, I wasn't going to say it quite that way. Look, I'm really sorry I hurt you and I'd like us to date again."

His teeth showed now. "Apology accepted." He took both of her hands in his, and looked straight into Katrina's eyes. "My love, I can only date you under one condition."

She sighed. It seemed as if the men in her life were always putting conditions on her—requiring things she didn't want to give. "Oh? What would that be?" she asked, allowing her skepticism to creep into her voice.

"That you're honest with me."

Katrina was silent for several seconds. "That's it?" It sounded too simple.

They entered the theater. When they found their seats, Katrina let Michael remove her coat and she settled into her chair before she answered. "I've been hiding since like, forever." She grimaced. "I realized this afternoon, though, that I don't want to do that anymore. At least ... not with you. So I'm willing to give this thing between us another go. With honesty."

The lights dimmed and the orchestra began the overture. He took her hands in his, leaned over, and whispered in her ear, "Well, then, Katrina, it's settled. We're officially dating again."

He took her chin in his hand, turned her head, and kissed her as the curtain rose. No matter how good or bad the dancers are, this would without a doubt be the most exciting dance performance she had ever attended.

I STROLL OUT of the attorney's office with Patrick and Sister Martha.

"It's my goal to make sure you get a fair shake on this divorce and settlement," Patrick says. "And it's almost done. All the paperwork is in order for power of attorney. One more signature and you'll have complete control over all his money and property."

It had been a long, hard month. Before this, no one but David and I knew how diabolical and obsessive Leonard Baxter really is. He even admitted that he had hit me on the head to make sure I didn't talk to the EPA about illegal dumping.

"Saul is a good attorney," Sister Martha says. "I've known him for years. You can trust he'll be honest. Prompt, too, so this won't drag on for months while you struggle to pay the bills."

Patrick says, "Finally, you're free. How does it feel?"

I scan the paperwork and smile. "Numb so far. I'll let you know."

Sister Martha pats my hand as she often does, like I'm her child. "And that will happen next week. We'll bring these papers to Dixmont for the director to sign, and once he does, the money will flow. Oh, Emma Lee, I'm so happy for you."

My stomach squeezes. "You're sure he's locked up? In the insane asylum?"

Patrick says, "For sure."

I shake my head and grunt. "Amazing. He still blames me, you know." I walk a few steps in silence, then say, "What if I forget to pay a bill? What if I run out? I forgot what Mr. Applebee said. How much money do I have access to again?"

Sister Martha smiles. "Mr. Applebee will make sure everything is paid, including your taxes. There's over $100,000 in the bank account, and about a half of a million in investments, so you won't run out for a very long time. Maybe never."

I pull Patrick closer and walk three abreast, as if I'm Dorothy in Oz, with the lion and the scarecrow beside me, on the yellow brick road. I grin and say, "You two are priceless. I couldn't make it without you."

Patrick laughs. "Yep, and don't you forget it."

My son's whole body seems different; he moves with the ease of a child instead of a wary cat. And there was a new exuberance that cheers me. I hear him singing, "They're heeeere." Even his voice sounds different—older, bigger, freer, more resonant somehow.

I open the door. "Welcome, Sister Martha, Sister Angela. Give me a minute to get my things."

I return to the kitchen and check my ever-present appointment calendar. "Here are the papers and that extra clothing they asked for. Guess that's it." At the front door I grab my purse. "I'm ready."

Today, Sister Angela will stay with David while I'm gone.

Sister Martha and I climb into the car and she turns onto the country road that takes us to the Ohio River Boulevard. A few minutes later we're traveling on yellow bricks, heading down river, to the west. I hear the steady rumble of tires on bricks. This section still hasn't been covered by asphalt yet, and I'm glad. The bricks give a certain class to the road.

She glances at me, then back to the street. "I hope you're sleeping better now, dear."

As I stare out over the Ohio River I say, "Every so often something stirs up my brain and I have flashbacks or nightmares, but most nights I do." I smooth my skirt. The late spring air whips tendrils of my dark curls so I crank the window closed. "You'll be glad to know that I credit God for this. It was His idea for me to fake a new memory loss, and I'm sure God helped everyone save me."

She smiles. "Glad you noticed."

Sister Martha's car enters the driveway that winds up the hill toward Dixmont, and we park in the lot in front of the new, four-story, yellow-brick building. Several more buildings surround us. The huge one on the edge of the hill has two wings that sweep forward in a V-shape. The point affords an expansive view of the river valley below. "It's lovely up here," I say.

"Are you angry with him for all he's done to you?" Sister Martha asks.

I shrug. "He's crazy, Martha. I'd waste my time being angry about it all. Besides, good has come from it."

She parks and places a hand on mine. "That day—when he flipped—he tried to convince me that you were trying to frame him. Were you?"

I sigh and lean my head back on the car seat. Out the window I see rolling hills and the river below. "I knew he'd never stop on his own. The way I saw it, before anyone else besides Patrick recognized what he was doing, I'd either lose my mind all the way or die. So I had to do something. I used an exaggeration of the facts to reveal the truth, that's all."

Sister Martha's eyes widen. "That was risky. Thank God you survived."

"Yes, I do thank God, because it was only after you prayed with me that I thought of it. And I'm pretty sure God gave me the strength to carry it out. Otherwise, David and I would probably be dead, like the baby." I swipe a tear with the back of her hand. "I really wanted that child. David wanted a sibling. I'm so sorry I lost him."

"Me, too, dear." Martha rubs her forehead. "The child was the innocent victim in this." She reaches for my hand again and squeezes it. "I'm so sorry I didn't help sooner. Honestly, I don't know how I could have been so blind. I should have recognized Leonard's personality disorder right off. I've committed one of the worst sins for a therapist: not recognizing a life-threatening problem. Please, forgive me."

I shake my head. "That man was a master at duping others. I don't blame you for being sucked in." I open the car door and grab my stuff. "Might as well get this over with."

We enter the mental facility and stop at the front desk. "Who are you here to see?" the receptionist asks.

"Leonard Baxter," Martha says.

I open the sack. "I brought some underwear and socks, as requested. And I have legal papers for his doctor to sign."

The woman behind the desk takes the forms. "Let me find out where Dr. Trenton is, and check on Mr. Baxter."

She spends several minutes on the phone. When she hangs up, the woman says, "They're sending an orderly down from the men's ward for you. He'll take you to up there." She picks up the paperwork and unlocks the door to the hallway. "Wait here. I'll be back in a few minutes with the signature."

What will it be like, seeing him again? I shudder to consider it. But everyone—Mr. Yamada, Sister Martha, Patrick, my attorney, the doctor, the policeman—they all told me it's a good idea. This way, I'll know for sure that he's locked up, unable to hurt me again. But I fidget as we wait on the hard wooden chairs, feeling like a cat on a leash.

A few minutes later the short, round-faced receptionist returns with the papers. "Here you go. All signed."

The signature is better than gold bullion, and my next breath is so deep, it's as if my lungs finally remember their job. Now I'll have enough money forever. I feel so free that I want to dance.

As I slip the paperwork back into the manila envelope, a rail-thin young man dressed in blue cotton scrubs enters the office. Pimples cover his face and his short blond hair sticks straight up. He extends his hand and squeaks, "I'm Andrew. I'll escort you to the men's ward." The youth's Adam's apple bobs when he speaks. "Sorry to tell you that Mr. Baxter had electroshock therapy this morning, so he's still a bit out of it. He won't be able to talk to you."

I see this as a good sign.

As Andrew leads us across the lawn to the V-shaped building, he seems excited to show the place off. He explains which building holds the cafeteria, which holds the dance hall, the general store, and the water treatment plant. "It's like a whole city of its own," he says. "We have great barbers, and even the workers can use them," he gloats, but his hair doesn't look like he's used the services in a long time. When we reach the doorway, he unlocks it and escorts us in.

We climb the stairs to the second floor men's ward, which is constructed like a wheel. The nurses' station is the hub. It includes a central, expansive area with a desk and file cabinets. Curtained windows surround the desk. Behind each window a wedge-shaped room holds one inmate. At any time, a nurse can open the curtain and watch a patient from behind the glass. A hallway runs around the outside of the rooms, allowing access through doors there.

As we enter the nurses' station, I shudder and grab Sister Martha's arm. "I don't think this is such a good idea. It scares me to even think about seeing him again."

Sister Martha pats my hand. "Don't worry. He's probably not even conscious."

When the nurse opens the curtain to Leonard's room, Sister Martha and I peer in like voyeurs. The old man lies there with squinted eyes, his mouth moving in soundless words. His eyes settle on mine and they take on a fierceness that could pierce armor. I draw a deep breath and a burst of gratitude swells my heart. He's imprisoned, unable to hurt us any longer. I'm safe. We are all safe. And I'm free to focus on the future.

I'm quiet on the return home. There had been so many changes in the past month, I can hardly take them all in—the fight, the fire, the trial, the sentencing, the fortune, the man in prison. And there will be more to come in the next several weeks. David's birthday is next week. He will be five.

But I'm alive, and away from that man. I'm saved.

53.

Michael leafed through his notes from the past three sessions with Emma Lee. Ever since Leonard's internment, she had changed. She now remembered to enter most tasks into her planner, and consulted it every day. Perhaps her fear had limited her improvement before, or maybe this was her normal healing process. Whatever the cause, Emma Lee's brain seemed to be making up for lost time.

"You look great," he said. "Please, have a seat. You've come so far, we need to identify new therapy goals. What would you *like* to learn?"

"Teach me how to use the stove without adding to my scars." She pulled up her sleeve to reveal a new blister across her forearm. "I'm sick of these."

"Good idea. And I hear you have trouble with decisions. Perhaps we can practice techniques for menu selection."

She shut her eyes. "I had hoped we'd be working on baby care and how to change diapers. I'm so sad I lost the baby." She took out a tissue and wiped her eyes. She was quiet for several moments.

Michael wished he could say something to make the pain go away, but time would have to do that. Meanwhile, he'd meet her where she was, let her grieve the loss of the child, and help her move on.

He took her hand in his. "I'm so sorry."

"Thank you for your kindness." Emma Lee wiped her eyes with the back of her hand. "Thanks for everything."

"You are welcome," he said, nodding, "My pleasure."

DAVID SKIPPED INTO the house and dropped a pile of envelopes onto the coffee table. "Hey, Mom, mail's here," he yelled.

Emma Lee slid onto the couch to sort through the envelopes. She lifted up the thin one and said, "Hm, airmail. Wonder who it's from."

"What's airmail?" David asked.

"It's a letter from a different country. You can tell because the paper is really thin and it has this blue and red line design around the edges like this, see?" As she grabbed the letter opener she turned the envelope over.

Curious, David leaned on her shoulder as she slit open the envelope. When she pulled out the sheet of folded velum, a small photograph fell onto the table. David examined the face staring back at him. The man in the picture wore a simple white buttoned shirt, khaki pants, and a broad-brimmed hat. His face was darkly tanned. It looked as if he might be standing on a beach, because there were palm trees behind him. "Who's this?" David asked.

"Let me see," Emma Lee said, taking the picture. Several seconds went by before she said, "I'm ... not sure."

She unfolded the letter and gasped.

David hoped this letter wasn't bad news. He moved closer.

Mom wrapped an arm around David's shoulder and squeezed. Although she had a smile on her face, David thought she still looked upset. "What's it say?" he asked.

"Remember a long time ago we wrote to your daddy, Gordon? This is from him. And he sent money for us," she said, holding up a piece of paper for him to see.

David inserted himself between Emma Lee's arms. He grabbed her face and squeezed her cheeks together. "My daddy! Oh, read the letter now," he insisted.

She grinned the way she did when she told a joke and her eyes sparkled in that teasing way of hers. "Well, now, I don't know. Maybe we should wait until after dinner, make it a special treat."

David thought his heart would burst if he had to wait even one second longer. He shoved his nose and forehead against hers, squeezed her cheeks harder, and said, "Please, oh, pretty please with sugar on top. Read the letter."

She chuckled. "Okay, since you're so insistent—and you asked so nicely." She unfolded the letter and read:

Dear Emma Lee and David,

Sorry it took so long for me to write. I finished my stint in the Peace Corps last summer and found a job with a humanitarian aid group called World Vision. They sent me to Java where I'm teaching people new farming methods. My mother forwarded your letter to me, but it had to chase me around the globe. I was surprised but glad to hear from you. I won't deny that finding out I'm a father was a shock. But I'm thrilled. Tell David I hope to visit when I get back to the States in about six months, if that's okay with you. The picture of me is for him. The money is for both of you. Thanks again for writing.

Sincerely, Gordon."

She handed the picture to David. "You can keep this in your room, if you like."

"Yippee!" David whooped. "Thanks," he said, cupping the small photograph in two hands. He stared at the picture intently.

A new feeling welled up in him, one he didn't quite understand. It was big and warm and cozy, like snuggling in a down comforter next to a fireplace on a cold day. It felt so big he was almost afraid of it. He grinned, showing the space where his first lost tooth used to be.

David wiggled out from Emma Lee's arms, raised both arms in the air and fell backward onto the couch. "I got a daddy!" he cried. "A real daddy. And I can't wait to meet him."

Mom's smile wasn't as big as his was, but she was smiling, too.

PATRICK'S 1968 DATSUN bounced up the driveway to Emma Lee's farm. He parked next to Baxter's white Cadillac. The boys had met a week ago, and Patrick had promised Joshua that he could return to play.

He grabbed the bouquet of yellow roses from his back seat. As he opened his car door, he noticed David leading a black lamb down from the barn.

David, with lamb in tow, waved an arm and yelled, " Patrick, Joshua. Lookit! I got a new lamb. Mom got her for me so I'd have somebody to play with again."

Patrick hopped out of the car and wrapped David in a hug. "Way cool. What's his name?"

"Koko. She's not a him, she's a girl." He scrunched his nose. "But she's okay."

"Goes to show. Sometimes girls can be fun."

"Guess so," David said.

Patrick scanned the property, as if he didn't see David. "Do you know any spare boys hanging around who might like to play with Joshua?"

David giggled and stared at his bare feet. "Me. I want to play with him, and even you can, too, Patrick."

"You go ahead. I'll be out later. First I have to give these flowers to your mother."

"Let's play tag with the lamb. You're it!" David tapped Joshua on the shoulder, and raced away with the lamb in tow. Over his shoulder he yelled, "The barn is base. Bet you can't catch me."

"Bet I can," Joshua yelled back and bounded off.

On the porch, Patrick hid the roses behind his back and knocked.

WHEN I OPEN the door Patrick pulls roses from behind him like a magician and says, "These are for you. Their beauty pales next to yours. You're the most gorgeous woman in Allegheny County."

I lift one eyebrow and drawl, "Only the county? Honestly, I thought you might be at least state-wide in your praise."

His lips form a mischievous grin. "Well, I heard there's a Miss Pennsylvania contest in Philadelphia this week, so I didn't want to be too grandiose. But you're the most beautiful woman in the world to me."

I giggle. "I'm a pushover for compliments. Come in. David was thrilled when I told him he would be able to play with Joshua."

"I'm glad the boys like each other."

"So what's the scoop? Can he stay?"

"Matter of fact, I got a letter from Richard two days ago, giving me guardian status. Has a new family and not much money. And I'm glad. Things are getting better at school. I'm getting used to parenting. I even like him around—most days."

I usher him into the house. Once the door closes behind us, Patrick scoops me into his arms and pulls me close. "Two things. First, since Leonard is locked safely away, I must ask. Madam, would you please go out to dinner with me Saturday evening? I've got a sitter lined up for the boys at my place. I'll pick you both up, and David can sleep over."

My smile wrinkles her nose. "It sounds wonderful. And number two?"

"Come to church with us on Sunday and lunch after at my apartment. Josh and I are moving to a house with a yard next month, so this might be your last chance to see your old stomping grounds. Remember the light at the end of the hallway?" he grins. "It's still burned out."

I say, "I accept your invitations. So give me a moment to write them down." I turn to escape his arms, but he tightens his grip.

"Look at me," he says.

When I do, I feel my heart pound. I want him to caress me and confess his love for me. His lips move toward mine, and we kiss. I let the passion of that connection express my longing.

I'm still in his arms when he says, "I love you madly. Please marry me."

Tears well and it takes effort for me to keep them contained. "I love you too, Patrick. And that kiss was heavenly, so perhaps you've forgotten one tiny but important detail. I'm not yet divorced. And unfortunately, the man I am attached to was a bit overwhelmin'." I place both hands on his chest and look up into his sparkling eyes. "I'm too nervous about commitment to consider marriage right now. Can you be patient with me?"

Patrick shrugs and grins, showing his dimple and straight, white teeth. He takes my hands in his and stares deeply into my eyes again. "Patience is my middle name. When you're ready, I'll be here."

"I love you, Patrick."

I leave his arms with reticence to enter the dates into my calendar. When I look up, through the window I see David and Joshua romping with the lamb. The cat sits in the sun licking itself and the breeze rustles the tree leaves. A cardinal flits from a tree branch to the fence. It's a joy to appreciate all this beauty without the fear. How thankful I am for Patrick.

I'm silent for so long, Patrick says, "Are you okay?"

"Oh, sorry. I drifted off. I was remembering how good you've been to me. You're so wise. You were the only one who could see what Leonard was doing. Without your persistence with the police and everyone else, I'd be dead. Thank you so much."

He drops onto the couch next to me. "You're welcome. Just goes to show. Prayer does work."

"I'll say."

"How can you stay here?" he asks, "considering what almost happened to you in the barn."

I lay my head against his shoulder and he wraps an arm around me, gathering me in like a shawl.

"David and I are happy here. He loves the animals, the yard. This is his home. Mine too. Besides, I don't have the energy to move."

He props his chin on his fist. "Everything could have been different. If I hadn't left when I did ... maybe none of this would have happened."

I shrug. "We can't undo the past, Patrick. Besides, I learned a lot from this."

He knits his brow, looking very serious. "You're the rare person who could find any good in what Baxter did to you."

I shrug. "I don't find good in his actions; only what came from them. It's what Sister Martha called 'finding God in all things.' And you know what? I like it. I'm happier when I look for the good."

"Yeah?"

I laugh and point out the window. "From all that suffering, I ended up with several things I always wanted: a place of my own and enough money to stay home from work to raise my son. Most important, I've learned about Jesus, and count on him to help me every day. That's the best gift of all"

"There. That openness, that honesty? I love it. Actually, I love everything about you. With you in my life, I'm a better person." Patrick kisses my cheek. He stands, weaves his thumbs into his belt loops. "I could use a cup of coffee. Want some? Then after, we can go out and play with the boys."

I cover my mouth with a hand and yawn. "Tell you what. I have no idea how to make coffee, so help yourself. Then feel free to play while I grab a short nap."

He throws the afghan over my legs, then kisses my forehead. "I'll be back," he says.

"I'm counting on it," I say.

Ellen Tomaszewski started writing late, after her four children used up most of her brain and body. Still, she keeps at it. She was born and raised in Pittsburgh, PA and moved to Washington State after marriage where she and her husband still live on the shrub steppes of the Columbia Valley. In *Toxic*, the author tried to unpack the damage done by our attachments, to explore what would happen if a man pursued control of a woman above everything else.

Ms. Tomaszewski's memoir, *Rose Colored Glasses* (previously titled *My Blindy Girl)* focuses on her experience as mother to a visually impaired child. Her next project will be a series for children.

Ellen owns a small publishing business, Etcetera Press, LLC. In snippets of time between business and writing, she can't stop herself from volunteering. Shes board chair for the Arts Foundation of the Mid-Columbia and created a writers' workshop, Rivers of Ink.

www.ingramcontent.com/pod-product-compliance
Lightning Source LLC
Chambersburg PA
CBHW030557180626
46816CB00005B/1587